Jackie Kabler was born in Coventry but spent much of her childhood in Ireland. She worked as a newspaper reporter and then a television news correspondent for twenty years, spending nearly a decade on GMTV followed by stints with ITN and BBC News. During that time, she covered major stories around the world including the Kosovo crisis, the impeachment of President Clinton, the Asian tsunami, famine in Ethiopia, the Soham murders and the disappearance of Madeleine McCann. Jackie now divides her time between crime writing and her job as a presenter on shopping channel QVC. She has a degree in zoology, runs long distances for fun and lives in Gloucestershire with her husband.

www.jackiekabler.com
🐦 @jackiekabler
📷 @officialjackiekabler

Also by Jackie Kabler

Am I Guilty?

The Perfect Couple

Jackie Kabler

OneMoreChapter
an imprint of HarperCollins*Publishers* Ltd
1 London Bridge Street
London SE1 9GF

www.harpercollins.co.uk

This paperback edition 2020
21 22 23 24 LSC 10 9 8 7 6 5 4 3 2 1

First published in Great Britain in ebook format by
HarperCollins*Publishers* 2020

A catalogue record for this book
is available from the British Library

ISBN: 978-0-00-844462-4

Set in Birka by Palimpsest Book Production Ltd, Falkirk
Stirlingshire

Printed and bound in the United States of America by
LSC Communications

Chapter 1

It was the silence I noticed first. When Danny was around there was always noise, singing or humming, the tap-tapping of a laptop keyboard, the prolonged clatter of spoon against ceramic mug as he stirred his black coffee vigorously for far too long, in my view, for a man who didn't even take sugar in it – what was he stirring? But I loved it, his noisiness, despite my regular protestations to the contrary. I'd lived alone for far too long before Danny, and the constant clamour made me feel connected, alive. Happy. So that evening, as I pushed the front door open and slid the key out of the lock, expecting a welcoming yell from the living room or to see, within seconds, his grinning face peering around the kitchen door, disappointment hit me like an icy wave.

'Danny? Danny, I'm home. Where are you?'

I could tell even as I spoke that he wasn't in but, flicking the lights on and dumping my overnight bag on the table by the door, I began a quick tour of the house anyway, my foot-steps echoing on the polished parquet of the hall floor. My frown deepened as I pushed each door open, the rooms dark and empty. Where was he? He'd promised, the previous evening when he'd emailed to say goodnight, that he'd be here when I got back, that he'd cook dinner. Even promised, I remembered as I headed for the kitchen, to have a bottle of my favourite cava chilling; a welcome home, Friday night treat. *If he'd forgotten …*

'Dammit, Danny. Seriously?'

I glared at the contents of the fridge. It looked exactly as I'd left it on Thursday morning – a half-full milk container, a block of cheese with one corner hacked off, a pack of sausages with four missing, the four we'd eaten for breakfast before I'd headed off on my latest press trip. No cava. No sign of any fresh food. He hadn't even gone *shopping*? What was going on? Had something happened at work, delaying him? He'd told me he'd be finishing at lunchtime that day, for once, that he'd have plenty of time to do the supermarket run for a change, save me doing it on Saturday morning as I usually did, while he stayed at home to run the vacuum round and flick a duster over the shelves. A break from the little routine we'd quickly fallen into, *happily* fallen into, since we'd moved to Bristol, and into the beautiful house in up-market Clifton. It hadn't always been like that, but when we moved he'd said he wanted to help around the house more, do more of the chores I hated, and I hadn't argued. We'd only been in our new home for three weeks, but the words 'domestic bliss' pretty much summed things up, cringeworthy as it sounded even to me.

'You can have a lie-in on Saturday, Gem. You'll be knackered after all that debauchery at your fancy spa hotel,' he'd said over our full English, reaching across the breakfast table to wipe a splodge of ketchup from my bottom lip, his finger soft against my skin.

'It's *work*,' I'd retorted, waggling my fork at him, then smiling as I speared another piece of black pudding. 'Well ... maybe a teeny bit of debauchery too though.'

'I don't doubt it. You journalists, and your hard-livin', hard-drinkin' ways.'

His accent, normally soft west of Ireland, was suddenly full-on Moore Street Market, Dublin, and I swallowed quickly and laughed.

'Yeah, right. We'll have a few drinks, but we'll all be in bed by eleven, I guarantee it. Too many exhausted mummies in the group now. A night away without the kids means they can finally get a decent night's sleep for once.'

He raised his thick, dark eyebrows – once a monobrow, until I'd finally pinned him to the bed one day, brandishing my tweezers – and I laughed again at his comically exaggerated expression of disbelief.

'Oh, shut up.'

'I didn't say a word!'

He'd leapt from his chair then, dragging me from my seat and into a hug, whispering into my hair.

'I'll miss you. But have a great time. You deserve it.'

So where are you now, Danny? I slammed the fridge door and reached into the pocket of my zebra print coat for my mobile, then remembered. Bugger. There'd been some sort of delay with Danny's new workplace providing him with a company mobile phone – it would, they'd promised, finally be ready for Monday – and as he'd handed in his old one when he'd left his previous job, he was temporarily phone-less. For a moment, I considered ringing his office, asking them if he'd been made to work late, then sighed and decided against it. A bit much, probably, when he'd only been in the job for such a short time, to have his wife calling, wondering where he was. Email, then? He still had his tablet, and emailing had worked reasonably well over the past few weeks when we'd needed to get hold of each other. We both had Skype too, for emergencies, although we hadn't needed to use it so far, and just like calling his office, I thought Skyping him might be a bit intrusive. Yes, email.

I perched on the edge of one of the dining chairs and tapped out a message.

I'm home. Where are you? And, more to the point, where's my dinner? And my FIZZ!? G xx

I hit send, checked the time, and stood up with a sigh. Just after seven. I'd go and unpack, have a nice hot shower, change. We could get some food delivered instead of cooking, and maybe Danny could call in at the off-licence on his way home to pick up some bubbly, I thought. I glanced around the kitchen, noticing that at least he'd washed up, wiped down the surfaces, replaced the chopping knives neatly in their wooden block. Everything was spotless in fact, a faint smell of bleach in the air, even the stainless-steel cooker hood gleaming. I felt my mild irritation subsiding. It would be work, that was all. It wasn't his fault he'd been delayed. He'd be home soon. Slipping my coat from my shoulders, I headed back down the hall to retrieve my bags.

Chapter 2

'Holy cow. It's like looking at brothers. Coincidence, or not? What do you make of that, guv?'

Detective Sergeant Devon Clarke glanced over his shoulder. Behind him, Detective Chief Inspector Helena Dickens nodded slowly, indigo eyes fixed on the two photos on the board.

'I dunno. Not yet, anyway. But yes, they do look spookily similar. Weird, eh?'

She looked at her watch. Just after seven. She sighed and turned to the room, wincing slightly as she felt a twinge in her lower back. Last night's run had been too long and too fast, she thought.

'OK, gather round everyone. I'm sorry to do this to you all on a Friday evening, but with a second murder on our hands now I'm going to have to ask you to work right through the weekend, as I'm sure you've already guessed. Let's just go through what we've got so far, so it's all clear in everyone's minds, and then I'll distribute jobs.'

She waited, turning back to scan the board as chairs scraped and feet shuffled; then the room fell silent, the rain which had started to fall an hour ago beating an urgent tattoo against the windows, the air thick with the smell of stale coffee.

'Thanks. Right, well I know some of you have just been brought into Bristol today to swell our numbers, so thank you for that. I'm DCI Helena Dickens, senior investigating officer. This is DS Devon Clarke.'

She waved a hand towards Devon, who dipped his head.

'It's been a while since Avon Police has had two murders on its hands in such a short time frame, so we're about to get very busy. There's nothing at the moment to suggest that the two killings are linked, although we're still waiting on the forensics report on the latest. But ...' she paused and exchanged glances with Devon, 'well, let's start at the beginning. Devon, can you take us through what we know about Mervin Elliott?'

'Sure.'

Devon nodded, and cleared his throat.

'OK. This is Mervin Elliott.'

He pointed to the photograph on the top left corner of the board.

'Thirty-two years old, men's clothing shop manager – one of those trendy places in Cabot Circus. Single, heterosexual, no children, lived alone in an apartment down at the harbourside. His body was found on Clifton Down by a dog walker just over two weeks ago, early on the morning of Wednesday, the thirteenth of February. Here, just off Ladies Mile, near Stoke Road.' He pointed at a map of The Downs, the vast public open space to the north of the affluent suburb of Clifton. 'His body was half hidden by shrubs, a bush, something like that. Time of death estimated to be about ten or eleven hours earlier, so between seven and eight the night before, Tuesday, the twelfth. Cause of death, blow to the head. No other significant injuries. No murder weapon found.'

He paused, rubbed his nose and continued.

'According to everyone we've spoken to so far, he was a nice, normal guy. Worked hard, single as I said; his mates said he'd been on the odd date recently, usually women he met online, but hadn't found anyone he wanted to get serious with. Sociable bloke though, liked a night out by all accounts, but wasn't a drug user or even a particularly big drinker. He was big into fitness, member of a gym – that big 24-hour one at the harbour, near his flat. Looked after himself. No criminal record. No obvious motive at all for his murder. Looked like he'd been out running the night he was killed – he was wearing trainers and exercise gear when his body was found. But he had a pretty nice sports watch on, and a decent phone in his pocket, and they weren't touched. Parts of The Downs get their share of doggers and so on at night, people cruising for action, but there was no sign of recent sexual activity on the body, no evidence he was there for anything like that. And so far, we've not found any witnesses to the attack. It would have been dark at that time of course. But so far, we have very little to go on. No forensics of any use. Nada.'

A phone suddenly trilled on a desk at the back of the room, and Devon waited while one of the young detective constables sprinted to grab it, answering it in hushed tones then grimacing at Devon.

'Nothing major,' she mouthed.

Devon nodded and turned back to the board.

'OK, so that's Mervin Elliott. This ...' he gestured at the photograph to the right of the first, 'is Ryan Jones. His body was found yesterday morning, Thursday, the twenty-eighth of February, in a lane between two houses on Berkeley Rise. That's here, just off Saville Road.'

He ran his finger across the map.

'Saville Road borders Durdham Down to the east. And, for those unfamiliar with The Downs, Durdham Down is the northern part, north of Stoke Road. Clifton Down is the southern bit. About four hundred acres in total.'

'So ... the two bodies were found, what? Less than a mile apart?'

The question came from somewhere at the back of the assembled group of officers. Devon nodded.

'About that, yes. Again, cause of death was probably head injuries but we're waiting for the results of the post mortem – should be with us any minute; they've had a bit of a backlog down there, couple of nasty car accidents got in ahead of us. He also had a couple of minor injuries elsewhere but nothing significant. His head injury was again consistent with being attacked with a heavy weapon of some sort. Again though no sign of that murder weapon. Early days on this one though, as he was only found yesterday. At the scene time of death was again estimated to have been about ten hours earlier, so sometime on Wednesday evening. He was found by a local resident who was out for an early morning cycle and took a shortcut down the lane. We got an ID from the victim's wallet, which was still in his pocket with about fifty quid in it. Ryan was thirty-one and also single, no kids, dated a bit but again

8

no serious girlfriend as far as we know at this early stage. Worked as an accountant for a firm in Queen Square. Again, early days but so far he sounds a bit like our first victim – nice, normal guy, no record.'

He paused and turned to look at Helena.

'No CCTV in the area he was found, I assume?' she asked.

Devon shook his head.

'No cameras in that area at all. It's a lot more built up than where Mervin was found though, obviously, so we started doing house to house yesterday afternoon, but so far nobody seems to have seen or heard anything.'

Helena sighed.

'Remind us what he was wearing? Ryan, I mean.'

Devon turned back to the board.

'Normal clothes. As in, not running gear or anything. Jeans, trainers, a navy jumper, big black puffa coat. It was cold on Wednesday night. And no, we haven't worked out yet what he was doing in the area. He lived at an address in ...' he frowned, eyes searching the board, 'in Redcliffe. So two, three miles away from where he was found.'

'Thanks, Devon.'

Helena cleared her throat and turned to the room.

'OK, so that's the basics. Two dead men, both with head injuries, both murdered in The Downs area within a couple of weeks of each other. Both successful and hardworking, both in their early thirties. Two men whom, as far as we know at the moment, had no involvement in any sort of criminal activity. And, two men who look ...' she turned back to the board again, tapping first the photo of Mervin and then Ryan's image, 'who look, quite frankly, like bloody twins. The same dark curly hair, dark eyes, thick eyebrows. Similar height and build. Might mean nothing but ...' she shrugged and turned back to face the assembled officers, 'kind of weird, eh? OK, listen. Let's not get too hung up on their appearances for now. And of course, there may be no connection between these two murders whatsoever. But we can't rule it out, not at this stage, considering the similarities between the two cases. Let's keep an open mind and let the facts guide us.

'Forensics on Ryan might help when we get them, if we're lucky. But in the meantime, let's talk to as many of their friends and family members as possible, and see if there are any common factors – Redcliffe and the harbour aren't that far apart, so did these two hang out in the same bars, did they know each other, did they have any mutual friends or common interests? And why were they both on – or, in Ryan's case, very close to – The Downs, on the nights they died? OK, so Mervin was there running, and it's a nice place to run, I run there myself now and again. But he's a member of a gym and, even if he preferred running outdoors, there are plenty of routes to choose from around Bristol. So why there, specifically? Was it something he did regularly? And why was Ryan in the area? Was he visiting a friend, a relative? We need to know everything about these two, and fast.'

She stopped talking, watching as her colleagues scribbled notes on their pads, many of them exchanging glances. She knew instantly what they were thinking. It was something she'd thought herself, immediately and with a sudden sick, sinking feeling in her stomach, when Ryan Jones's photograph had been stuck on the board yesterday next to Mervin Elliott's. If these two murders *were* connected, if they'd been carried out by the same person, well ...

She swallowed hard. It needed to be three, though, officially. *Three* murders, to fit the most widely used UK definition. And so far it was only two. *Please God*, she thought, *let it stay that way*.

Two was bad enough.

But three ...

Three, and she might just have a serial killer on her hands.

Chapter 3

'Where the *hell* are you, Danny? This is getting *ridiculous*.'
I stopped pacing up and down the kitchen for a moment to stand and stare out of the rain-streaked window into the elegant courtyard at the back of the house, willing him to suddenly appear, my fists clenched, nails digging into my palms. It was late Saturday afternoon and, despite my best efforts all day to track my husband down, I'd come up with precisely nothing. I needed to make some more phone calls, but I'd have to calm myself down first. I took a deep breath, trying to slow my racing heartbeat, and rested my forehead against the cold glass, eyes flitting across the yard. On two levels separated by a row of pleached hornbeam trees, the beautifully designed limestone-paved space had enthralled me from the moment Danny and I had first come to view the place. In the centre of the top level nearest the house, water bubbled gently from a polished metal sphere perched on top of a stone plinth, next to which sat a huge glass-topped table, six wrought iron chairs tucked underneath it. The outdoor dining area had been given an exotic, tropical feel more reminiscent of Bali than Bristol thanks to artfully planted

bamboo, phormiums and tree ferns, the space illuminated at night by hundreds of tiny lights dotted among the foliage. At the front of the top terrace, steps led down to the lower level, where on either side of the back gate bay trees swayed gently in the wind in tall graphite pots, and raised herb beds lined the walls; our very own kitchen garden in the heart of the city. Even on a wet Saturday in March, and even when I was feeling so utterly miserable, a tiny shiver of pleasure ran through me.

'A fountain! There's a *fountain*, Danny!' I'd squeaked when we'd first walked in through the back gate, and he'd laughed and squeezed my hand. We'd wondered why the letting agent had suggested meeting at the back of the house instead of at the front door, but it suddenly made perfect sense. It was stunning.

'It's more of a water feature, but OK. You and your fancy courtyard fetish,' Danny had whispered as we were led indoors, both of us knowing instantly that no matter what the interior was like, this place already had me hooked. He was right; I'd always yearned for a courtyard garden. A peaceful place to entertain friends, to sit in the sun with a glass of wine on a summer evening, to lounge with a book on a Sunday afternoon, and no lawn to mow? Pretty damn perfect in my book.

We'd had a lovely home in London, but as so often in the capital, a place in a central location with any sort of decent outside space was hard to find. We'd made the small roof terrace of our apartment as beautiful as we could, but the Bristol courtyard had seemed huge in comparison.

'There's even a proper bicycle shed, look, down there in the corner of that lower level. I can finally stop having to chain my gorgeous bike to the front railings and you can finally quit moaning about how it lowers the tone,' Danny had said, and I'd clapped my hands and done a little happy dance, making him laugh.

That Saturday though, as I stared out of the window, I could see that, just as it had been since I came back from my trip, the smart wooden lean-to where his beloved bike usually stood was empty. I looked at the blank space for a few more seconds, my vision blurring, then jumped as a cold, damp nose nuzzled my hand.

'Hey, Albert. Where's Danny then, eh?' I whispered, and he cocked his head, eyes fixed on mine, and whimpered. I didn't blame him; I felt like whimpering myself. My stomach churning, my eyes dry and scratchy from crying and lack of sleep, I glanced at the empty courtyard one more time then turned from the window and started pacing again. Albert stood watching me for a moment, then whined softly and trotted off to his bed in the corner of the kitchen.

On Friday night I'd finally ordered pizzas, picking at mine as I constantly refreshed my emails, expecting an apologetic message from Danny to pop into my inbox at any moment. When nothing came, I'd finally, grumpily, assumed he was pulling an all-nighter, and had gone to bed, noticing as I crawled under the duvet that he'd even changed the bedding while I was away, the pillow case fresh and crisp against my cheek. *His bloody job*, I thought. He loved it, but I wasn't always so keen. Danny was an IT security specialist, analysing and fixing systems breaches, defending companies against online hacking.

'I fight cybercrime. I'm basically a security superhero,' he'd announced with a theatrical wave of his arms on our first date, and I'd rolled my eyes, grinning and, if I was honest, not quite understanding what he did at all, while still being secretly impressed.

What the job meant in reality though was long hours and frequent emergency call-outs, and although this would be the first such occasion in this new job, it wasn't that unusual for him to have to work through the night if something had gone wrong with an important client's computer system. When we first met he'd been working for a company in Chiswick, in west London, earning a healthy six-figure salary. When we'd talked about leaving the capital, I'd assumed it would mean Danny accepting a lower wage, but that hadn't been the case, something that had surprised me until I realized that his new firm, ACR Security, had itself relocated from central London a couple of years back, taking advantage of the lower rents in the UK's eleventh biggest city.

'Makes sense,' Danny had said, when he'd first floated the idea of us moving out of London. 'There's a great job up for grabs in Bristol, and the internet's the internet, my job's going to be the same anywhere, same pay too. And think how much further our money will go without London prices, you know? And you can do your job from anywhere too, can't you, Gem? You'd love it, I know you would, the quality of life would be so much better. Bristol's a lovely city, and you've got Devon and Cornwall just a few hours down the road, and the

Cotswolds not far in the other direction, and it's a uni city so there are plenty of good bars and restaurants, and the architecture's gorgeous ...'

'OK, OK, you've sold it to me, let's do it!'

In truth, he hadn't really had to work very hard to convince me. He was right that as a freelance journalist, I could pretty much work from wherever I wanted to, and London didn't have any great hold on me anymore. It was too busy, too stressful, and in recent years I'd often craved a gentler life, more greenery, less noise. And so he took the job he'd been offered, and we'd packed up our modern apartment just off Chiswick High Road and moved into this lovely, high-ceilinged Victorian semi with the wonderful courtyard in the leafy Bristol suburb of Clifton. We'd only been married a year, and had still been renting in London, not wanting to commit to a huge mortgage until we'd decided where we wanted to settle. Even though Bristol felt right to both of us, we didn't want to jump into buying there too soon either, wanting to give ourselves time to make sure we were both still happy with our jobs and the Bristol lifestyle and to find the perfect forever home.

'We'll rent, just for a year or so. Somewhere nice though. Best part of town,' Danny had said as we'd scrolled excitedly through the property listings online, amazed at how low the rents seemed compared with what we'd been paying in Chiswick. And so it all came together perfectly, and after just a few days, I knew I was home. Danny appeared to feel the same, even if his working hours were just as long as they'd been in London, something I hated but had grown to accept.

Even so, I'd been so looking forward to seeing him on Friday night that I'd felt miserable, sleeping badly, waking every hour to see if the empty space in the bed next to me had been filled by his warm, weary body.

When he still hadn't called by nine o'clock on Saturday morning I'd started to really worry. This wasn't right. Pushing aside my reluctance to appear the nagging wife, I'd looked up the switchboard number for his company and dialled it. It had gone straight to voicemail, informing me that ACR Security was now closed and would reopen at 9 a.m. on Monday, and advising that clients with an urgent issue should call the emergency number on their contract.

'What about *wives* with an urgent issue?' I'd shouted down the phone, then ended the call, my heart beginning to pound. If his office was closed, where the hell was Danny? Had he had an accident on his way home? That flipping bike. I'd always thought it odd that he didn't drive, but he'd shrugged cheerily when I'd asked him about it.

'Never needed to. Plenty of good public transport in Dublin when I was a student. And then London ... I mean, who drives in London? Congestion charge, parking is ridiculous ... ah, bike's the way to go, Gem. And we've got your car, haven't we, when we need it? No point wasting money on two.'

He had a point. But I still worried about him commuting on that thing. And so when I couldn't track him down at his office, and after I'd tried to Skype him half a dozen times only to find he was offline every time, I started to ring the hospitals. There seemed to be only a few in Bristol with accident and emergency departments, and after I'd ruled out the children's and eye hospitals there were only two left, Southmead and Bristol Royal Infirmary. My hands shaking, I called both, but neither had any record of a male with Danny's date of birth or fitting his description being admitted in the past twenty-four hours. For a minute, a wave of relief washed over me, before fear gripped me again. If he wasn't at work, or hurt, where else could he be? If he'd decided on a last-minute trip to see a friend, he'd have called me, wouldn't he? But that was just *so* unlikely, when he'd promised to be there when I got home, cooking dinner for me. So maybe he *was* at work, after all, and the office switchboard had just been left in weekend mode. But why hadn't he answered my email, or contacted me to let me know where he was? Surely, however busy he was, he'd have had time to do that? He'd know how worried I'd be.

Breathing deeply, trying to keep on top of the anxiety which was threatening to overwhelm me, I tapped out another email.

Danny, where are you? I'm seriously worried now. I've tried your office but it's just going to voicemail. PLEASE let me know you're OK? Gxx

I pressed send and checked the time. Midday, on Saturday. I hadn't heard from him since the goodnight email he'd sent me at about eleven on Thursday night, the one I'd read in my hotel room. Just over thirty-six hours. It just wasn't right, wasn't *normal*, not for us. Should I call the police? But what if he really *was* just frantically busy at work, trying to fix some sort of online disaster for a major client, totally losing track of time? Imagine his mortification if the police suddenly turned up at his office, the sniggers of his new work mates, the mutterings about neurotic wives. No, I couldn't call the police; it was too soon. I was being silly. He'd reply to this latest email any minute now, and everything would be fine, I told myself. *By this evening we'll be snuggled on the sofa drinking wine and laughing at me and my stupid over-reaction.*

I'd gone out briefly to collect Albert from the nearby kennels – I'd dropped him off on Wednesday night before I left on Thursday morning – Danny's long and unpredictable working hours not compatible with dog care – desperately hoping that by the time we arrived home, my husband would be back, wearily brewing coffee in the kitchen or sprawled, exhausted, on the sofa after a long night in the office. But he wasn't, and so at lunchtime, and uncharacteristically for me, because doing it too often made me feel fearful and anxious, I turned on the BBC Radio Bristol news. I'd worked in newsrooms for years before going freelance, covering so many stories that had shocked and sickened me, and although I'd become harder and tougher as time had gone on, more able to handle the horror of reporting on yet another stabbing, yet another sense-less murder, there had come a point when the life I'd led back then had all become too much for me, and I'd simply walked out and left it all behind. I'd stopped watching the news completely for months after I quit, stopped reading the papers, finding solace in my ignorance about the true state of the world, switching to lifestyle journalism when I returned to work, leaving crime and politics behind me. But now my husband had vanished, and so I turned the radio on, feeling shaky as I listened for stories about accidents, car crashes, unidentified bodies.

There weren't any, but in the afternoon, and feeling a little foolish, I slipped Albert's lead on and went out to walk Danny's route to and from work, some vague idea in my head that maybe he'd been knocked off his bike by a car and had been tossed, unconscious, into a hedge or alleyway. Ridiculous, even I knew that, in a big city where he'd surely have been spotted within minutes, but I did it anyway. I'd realized before we set out that I didn't even *know* his exact route to work, or even if he took the same route every day – as a cyclist, there were so many options, so many shortcuts you could take. So I studied a map, picked what looked like the two most likely routes, the most logical roads to take to travel between our house in Monville Road and Danny's office in Royal York Crescent, and did both, one one way, the other on the return. His office was clearly closed when I got there, but I rang the doorbell anyway, and peered in through the windows at unlit rooms empty of people, before turning round and heading home again, my sense of desperation growing. I found nothing on either route, of course. No bike, no helmet, no Danny.

I spent the rest of the afternoon pacing around the house, staring out of the windows, yelling pointlessly at my absent spouse and intermittently bursting into tears. Finally, I checked the time – almost six o'clock – and made myself sit down and start making some more calls. It had been too long, and I needed help; I couldn't handle this on my own, not any longer. I'd met a few people in the short time we'd been in Bristol, a couple of whom I already felt could potentially become good friends, but the relationships were too new, I thought, to burden with something like this. In terms of old friends, most of the couples we hung out with had originally been friends of *mine*, and I didn't think that any of them would be able to help, not at that stage; if Danny *had* gone away to visit someone without telling me, unlikely though that seemed, it would probably have been one of his own mates. I didn't have contact details for any of his Irish friends, but I found numbers for two of the colleagues he'd been palliest with in his old job in London, and for his former boss. They all sounded a little bemused – no, they hadn't heard from him since he'd left, but ... *you know what this job's like, he probably has no idea what time it is or how long he's been head down at his desk, he'll probably turn up in a couple of hours, don't worry, Gemma. Keep us posted though, OK?*

I wished I had an out-of-hours number for Danny's new boss, just in case, but I didn't, and I couldn't even remember his name. So – family, then? Danny had a cousin in London, but the rest of his family lived in the west of Ireland, and after some consideration I decided against calling them, for a while at least. I'd never felt that comfortable around his cousin Quinn, and his mum, Bridget, was tricky at the best of times. His dad, Donal, had died not long before we got married, and Danny had never been close to either of his parents; there was no point in sending Bridget into a panic if, in the end, there was nothing at all to worry about. I didn't call *my* parents either – they were nervy types, both of them, and I couldn't handle their distress, not on my own, not while I was feeling so horribly anxious myself. And so

I kept dialling other numbers, and when Danny's friends couldn't help, I decided to phone a few of my own after all, not so much to ask if they'd heard from my missing husband but for advice, for comfort, although I found little of the latter.

'Shit, Gemma, that's worrying. I'd be calling the police, if I were you.'

'Oh Gem, darling, how awful! Do you want me to come down? Just say the word. But I'm sure he'll turn up soon, it probably is just a work thing ...'

'Bloody men. But Danny's usually so reliable, isn't he? I don't know what to think, Gem. Maybe give it until tomorrow and then report him missing? You don't ... well, I hate to ask, but you don't think he's got another woman, do you?'

It was something that hadn't crossed my mind until then, and when I'd put the phone down after speaking to Eva, one of my closest friends, I swallowed hard, trying to consider the possibility. No, it just couldn't be true. Since we'd moved to Bristol we hadn't had a night apart until Thursday when I'd gone on my press trip, and we'd spent every second of every weekend together too, sorting out our new home. When would he have had *time*? We'd been pretty much inseparable most of the time before we moved too ... we were still virtually newlyweds, after all. Well, not entirely inseparable; we'd obviously had the odd night apart, work trips and 'girls' and 'boys' nights out, and Danny was the type of guy who sometimes just wanted his own space, but ... I shook my head. If he'd been having an affair, I'd have known, wouldn't I? Whatever was going on, it wasn't that. Could he have left me for some other reason though? I stood up, pulling my cashmere cardigan – the baby blue one Danny had bought me for Christmas – more tightly around me, and walked slowly from the lounge and down the corridor to the kitchen to peer out into the dark, empty yard again. Albert jumped up too and followed closely behind me, his nose butting my shins. He was almost as anxious as I was, I could see that, his doggy senses always keenly attuned to mine, and I crouched down beside him, stroking his soft head, looking into his dark brown, intelligent eyes, muttering soothing nonsense as my mind continued to race.

If Danny *had* left me, what possible reason could he have? And he hadn't taken anything with him, had he? I realized with a shiver that I didn't know. I hadn't looked, hadn't even thought to check. Suddenly light-headed with fear, I rushed upstairs to the bedroom, pulling open drawers, clawing at the clothes in his wardrobe, searching frantically through his bedside cabinet, not even sure what I was looking for. But everything seemed untouched, neat, *there*. His passport, still in the drawer where he always kept it. All his clothes, his underwear, his watch collection. No gaps, nothing missing, as far as I could tell anyway. Everything looked the way it always looked. So what *was* gone? Just his coat, his laptop, his tablet, the black backpack he carried them in, his bike and helmet. The usual things he'd go to work with. Everything else was still there, waiting for him, like I was. Like Albert was.

I slumped onto the unmade bed, breathing heavily, and Albert hesitated for a moment – he wasn't usually allowed on the bed – and then clambered up to join me, seemingly correctly assuming that I was currently too distracted to tell him off.

Is Danny's stuff all still being here a good thing or a bad thing? I didn't know, couldn't think straight, panic taking hold, and suddenly I felt very alone. If we'd still been in London at least I'd have had old friends nearby, people who could just pop round, people who could support me, but here, in this new city …

I took a few deep breaths, my heart racing again, and wondered if I should reconsider my decision not to burden the couple of new friends I'd made so far in Bristol with all of this. I'd met Clare on Clifton Down just days after we moved in. I'd actually arrived in the city a week before Danny, who'd had work to finish up in London before he joined me, and I'd abandoned the mountain of unpacked boxes for an hour to clear my head and give Albert a decent walk. Clare had a Standard Poodle, a white curly bundle of energy who had bounded up to Albert, nuzzled him enthusiastically and then run off again, looking coyly over her shoulder. Albert had hesitated for a moment and then raced gleefully after her, leaving me and Clare standing helplessly, leads dangling from our fingers, awaiting their return.

'She's called Winnie. Winnie the Poodle. Get it?' She'd grinned, and I'd liked her immediately. Clare was tall, five eleven in her bare feet and slender as a hazel twig, with a mass of blonde curls.

'And yes, I did choose a dog who looks just like me,' she added.

We'd sat on a bench and chatted for a full half an hour on that first day and, when I told her I was new to Bristol and was planning to look for a yoga class somewhere nearby, she insisted I come to hers the following evening.

'I go twice a week with my friend Tai. It's Ashtanga and it's quite full-on, but you feel great afterwards. And we sometimes go for a drink in the wine bar across the street when we're done, if you fancy it?'

I did fancy it, and I'd loved the class, although I'd only returned to it twice in the few weeks since, too busy with trying to get the new house sorted out in the evenings when Danny was back from work. I'd met up with Clare and Tai – a beautiful, petite Chinese woman with an infectious laugh, who'd moved to the UK to attend university and never gone home – several times for drinks or coffee though, and I could already sense a solid friendship beginning to form. They were my kind of women, feisty and strong, kind and funny, and I could tell they liked me too. But it was still early days, and to call them and land something like this on them, to tell them my husband had suddenly gone missing and ask for their support? No, I just couldn't.

I groaned. Where *was* he? And how soon could you officially report somebody, an adult, missing? Wasn't there some rule? I dragged myself off the bed and back down to the lounge and grabbed my iPad, checking my email inbox again – empty – before doing a Google search.

No, there wasn't a rule.

It's a common belief that you have to wait 24 hours before reporting, but this is not true. You can make a report to the police as soon as you think a person is missing. Most people who go missing return or are found within 48 hours, with only around 1% still remaining missing after a year ...

A year? Fear swirled in my stomach. But most people came back within forty-eight hours. I checked the time. Nine o'clock. That was forty-six hours then. Forty-six hours since I'd last heard from my husband.

Come on, Danny. You've got two hours. Be like most people. Come home. Please, Danny.

And if he wasn't, if he *didn't* come home? What then? I'd have to do it, wouldn't I? Yes, I thought. I'd do it, first thing in the morning. I'd go to the police and report him missing.

Chapter 4

'Boss, sorry to disturb but there's somebody just called in downstairs you might want to have a quick chat with.'

Helena dragged her eyes reluctantly from her computer screen, where she was once again reading through the latest on the two murder cases. The usual incident room buzz had dulled to a low hum on this grey Sunday morning, and she suspected that she wasn't the only one feeling disheartened and exhausted. It had been a long, and largely fruitless, weekend, and she'd slept badly the previous night, waking every hour, her mind racing. In the end she'd crawled out of bed at 5 a.m. and gone for a long run on The Downs, making sure her route took her past the scenes of both murders, hoping for some flash of inspiration, some inkling as to why on earth two young men had been bludgeoned to death for no apparent reason. She rubbed the aching small of her back – *I really need to go and see an osteopath or someone if I'm going to be able to keep running*, she thought – and sighed. Forensics had come up with nothing on the latest killing, and while she still didn't know for sure if the two deaths were linked, the similarities between the two men were just so damn striking ...

She knew it wouldn't be long before the papers picked up on it too, and she was dreading the possible Monday morning headlines:

TWO SLAIN – TERROR ON THE DOWNS
DOUBLE MURDER: THE LOOKALIKE VICTIMS OF THE
DOWNS KILLER

She shuddered. She needed sleep, and a decent cup of tea, but neither seemed to be forthcoming any time soon.

'What is it, Devon?'

She turned to her DS, trying to keep the irritation out of her voice.

'It's a woman who wants to report her husband missing. She says—'

'A missing person? Shit, Devon, I've got a double murder on my hands here. Why the hell would I be interested in a missing person? Give me a break.'

She saw him flinch, and immediately felt guilty.

'Oh, mate, I'm sorry. Knackered, you know. Go on, tell me.'

He gave her a small smile.

'No worries, I had the same reaction when the front desk called me. But I've had a quick chat, and honestly, there's something ... look, can you just trust me on this, and come down and have a quick word? It'll take five minutes, tops.'

Helena stared at him for a moment and then sighed. He was a good copper, Devon – a good friend too – and she trusted his judgement. He'd been through a bit of a tough time in his personal life recently, but not once had it affected his work, and she wondered if he realized how much she appreciated that, and him. Probably not. She'd have to tell him, one of these days. For now though, if he thought she needed to see this bloody woman, then fine. It would do her good to get out of the overheated incident room for a few minutes, if nothing else. She pushed her chair back from her desk and stood up.

'OK, you win. But you're buying me a large mug of the canteen's finest on the way back up.'

He grinned, his teeth white and even.

'Deal.'

The woman, waiting in an interview room, was probably in her early thirties, slender with shoulder-length, wavy brown hair, her pretty face pale and drawn. She shook hands nervously, her palm clammy, and introduced herself as Gemma O'Connor.

Across the table, Helena smiled, trying to put the woman at ease, noticing that despite her obvious distress she'd made an effort with her appearance, a slick of crimson lipstick matching the oversized red leather bag on her knee, her smart black wool coat accessorised with a leopard print scarf draped around the neck.

'And you want to report a missing person? Your husband?' she said.

Gemma nodded.

'Yes. His name is Danny. Full name Daniel Ignatius

O'Connor.' She grimaced slightly. 'His parents are Irish, Catholic. Ignatius is some obscure saint, apparently.'

Helena smiled again.

'I got Muriel as my middle name, after my grandmother. I feel his pain. Go on.'

Gemma gave her a small smile back, then took a deep breath.

'Right, well, I was away on a business trip on Thursday night; we had breakfast together that morning, and last thing that night he emailed me to say goodnight. When I got home on Friday evening he wasn't there, and I thought at first he'd just had to work late, because he sometimes does, you know? Has to pull an all-nighter. But I couldn't get hold of him, and when I woke up on Saturday morning, yesterday, and he still wasn't home and I still couldn't contact him I started to panic. I spent all day calling everyone I could think of, his work, the hospitals, friends ... even took Albert out and we walked along his route to work, to see if I could find him, in case something had happened. That sounds silly, I know, but he cycles to work, and this is just not like him, not at all, and he hasn't taken anything with him, just his bike and his laptop and the usual stuff he'd go to work with, and now it's Sunday and I still can't get hold of him and I'm just ... I'm just so *scared* ...' Her voice cracked, and her eyes filled with tears.

Helena, feeling for the woman but still wondering why Devon had asked her to leave her double murder investigation for this, looked around for tissues, saw a box on a side table and got up to retrieve it.

Offering it to Gemma, she said gently: 'OK, try not to get

upset. We'll need to take some more details, if that's all right, and then we can start looking into it for you. But there's every chance he'll turn up in a day or so, most missing people do, OK? So take a breath, and then we'll do a bit of paperwork. Who's Albert, by the way? Your son?'

Gemma, who'd ignored the proffered tissues and had started fumbling in her handbag, looked up with a surprised expression and shook her head.

'Oh, sorry, no! We don't have kids yet, we've only been married less than a year. Albert's our dog. He's a black Miniature Schnauzer. Bit like a child though, I suppose. They're super clever.'

Helena smiled.

'Ahh, I see. Cute dogs, yes. A friend of mine has one.'

Gemma, who was rooting in her handbag again, didn't seem to be listening.

'Where is it, dammit! This bag ... sorry. I wasn't sure what you'd need, but I thought a photo ...'

She raised her eyes to Helena, finally pulling an envelope from her bag and sliding a picture out of it.

'I showed your colleague here when he came down earlier. I don't know why I put it away again, I can never find anything in this stupid bag at the best of times. This is the first one I could find. I'm in it too as it's a wedding photo, obviously, but I can get you a better one, one of him on his own, later, I have loads on my phone, I just need to look through them and find a good one, but I thought you might need a hard copy one and I just wanted to get the ball rolling, do *something* ...'

Her words came out in a rush, tumbling over each other, and she stopped talking abruptly, eyes still glistening with tears. Devon reached out and took the photograph, placing it on the table between himself and Helena.

'Thanks, Gemma. Guv, take a look.'

He looked meaningfully at Helena, and she glanced at the photo, then looked again, properly. Shit. SHIT. *Now* she understood. Her stomach lurched. There was Gemma, glowingly pretty in a simple white satin shift dress, hair piled high in an elaborate up-do, one hand clutching a bouquet of white lilies, the other gripping the hand of a smiling young man. Dark hair, curly. Thick dark eyebrows, dark brown eyes. A man who appeared, like his wife, to be in his early thirties. A man called Danny O'Connor. But a man who, at a quick glance, could quite easily have been Mervin Elliott. Or Ryan Jones. Or their brother, at least. The same build, the same colouring, the same *look*. *Christ, what's going on here?* She took a deep breath, trying to stay calm. *No point in jumping the gun*, she thought. Danny O'Connor was, according to his wife, missing. Not dead. There was no body, no evidence he'd come to any harm. *So, treat this as a standard missing person, then. For now, anyway.* She pushed the photo aside and turned to Devon, nodding slowly.

'Thanks for calling me down, Devon. OK, Gemma, let's get some details. You said you last saw him on Thursday morning, the twenty-eighth? What time did you leave?'

Gemma took a deep breath.

'About seven. We had breakfast together at six, got up extra-early to make it a special one, before we both went off to work ... Danny cooked a fry-up. I had to go on a press trip, to a new spa hotel in the Cotswolds. I'm a journalist, a feature writer, freelance. I used to do hard news, but I prefer mostly lifestyle stuff nowadays. You know, fashion and beauty and travel, that sort of thing? I have a monthly column in *Camille* magazine but I do other bits and pieces too. It's mostly from home but a few times a month I get a chance to get out for a bit, go away for a night, so I'd really been looking forward ...' Her voice tailed off, and the animated expression that had appeared briefly on her face as she talked about her work faded, the anguished look back in her eyes.

'OK, great. So you said goodbye and headed off and then what? When did you next speak to Danny?'

Helena was scribbling in her notebook.

'Well, I didn't *speak* to him, not exactly. We only moved into our new place a few weeks ago, we just moved down here from London, and we haven't got a landline phone, and there was a delay with Danny's new company getting him a mobile, so he hasn't got a phone at all at the moment. So we've been communicating by email for the past few weeks. Bit of a pain, but it works most of the time. He emailed me late on Thursday night, about eleven, just to say goodnight. Reminded me he'd be cooking dinner when I got home on Friday, that sort of thing. Just a normal email. I replied, told him I loved him, and that was it. I haven't ... haven't heard from him since.'

The tears were back. She reached for a tissue, her hand shaking.

Helena nodded.

'Right. So you came home on Friday night, that's the first of March, and there was no sign of him? And you said as far as you know he hasn't taken anything with him? Passport, clothes? Nothing he wouldn't normally take on a work day? No note left or anything, I presume?'

Gemma shook her head.

'No note. And yes, everything's still there, passport, clothes, the lot. So he probably hasn't skipped the country at least.'

She smiled weakly.

'And you said you've called his office, his friends, family? And the hospitals too?'

Gemma nodded.

'Yes, everyone I could think of. I couldn't get hold of anyone at his office, it's closed, and I don't have numbers for all his friends, but I called all the ones I had. Nobody's seen or heard from him. I didn't call his family though. Most of them live in Ireland and his mum's elderly and ... well, I didn't want to worry them, not yet.'

'Yes, probably a good idea not to panic his family, for now at least.'

Helena gave the woman a brief smile.

'I'll get a list of the hospitals you've tried and Danny's work address from you in a moment, Gemma, and we'll need his date of birth, what he was wearing when you last saw him, your current address and where you recently moved from, some specifics like that, OK? But first just a few more general questions, if you can bear it? Did Danny's behaviour change at all recently? I mean, did he seem worried about anything, distracted, anything like that? Was he having any problems

– medical, financial, that sort of thing? Was he misusing drugs, or alcohol?'

Gemma was shaking her head and frowning.

'No, nothing like that at all. We've been really happy – it was his idea initially to move here from London, and I can work from anywhere so I was fine with it too, delighted in fact, and he's been really excited about his new job, and a better lifestyle. We've been busy non-stop since we moved in, of course, just getting the house sorted, but it's really lovely. We're renting for now, just until we decide exactly where we want to live, but it's such a great place, big rooms and this beautiful courtyard, we both love it, and ... well, no. None of those things. He was fit and healthy and happy, and I honestly can't think of a single reason why ... why ...' She stopped talking and swallowed hard.

Helena was still making notes.

'Does he use social media? Facebook, Twitter, Instagram? Any of them?'

Gemma shook her head again.

'No. Neither of us do really. He doesn't at all, and I have an Instagram account for work purposes but I don't post very often. Danny's quite anti-social media actually. Says it's damaging, that people end up comparing themselves to all these other people who seem to have these perfect glamourous lives, and it's all rubbish really. I'm not so extreme – I think it can be quite useful, if you follow things you're really interested in. And it's kind of part of the job when you work in the media, it's expected. But to answer your question, no, I've never known Danny to have a social media account.'

Devon, who'd been sitting quietly, cleared his throat.

'How long have you been together, Gemma? You said you've only been married a year or so?'

She turned to look at him.

'We haven't been together long at all really. It all happened quite quickly. I hate the term "whirlwind romance", but it was, kind of.' She gave a little laugh, her cheeks flushing. 'We met online, about eighteen months ago. We'd only been dating for four months when he proposed, and we got married three months later, in March last year. It'll be our first wedding anniversary in a couple of weeks. So, as I said, all pretty quick really. But when you know, you know, I guess.'

'I suppose so, yes.' Devon smiled, then his face turned serious again.

'So ... well, I hate to ask this, but ... is there any chance that he was seeing somebody else, having an affair? It's just that sometimes when people go missing ...'

Gemma was shaking her head again, vehemently this time.

'Absolutely not. One of my friends asked me that too, and I've really thought about it, you know; even though it's an awful thing to think, I've tried to genuinely consider it as an option. But no, no way. He was at work all day, sometimes until quite late, but he pretty much always came straight home afterwards, and we haven't had a single night apart since we moved, or a single weekend – I didn't have a press trip booked until Thursday, so that was the first night since we came to Bristol. And we were together most of the time in London too. I mean, we'd both have the odd night out with friends, separately, do the occasional thing on our own, you know;

he'd go off on his bike and so on, he's a keen cyclist. But we spent the vast majority of our time together. I'd *know*, too. I just would. Nothing's changed between us, we're the same as we've always been, *better* in many ways since we moved ...'

The tears were back, sliding down her cheeks, leaving streaks in her foundation.

'All right, and so sorry to have to ask these questions, I know it's very difficult for you.'

Devon pushed the tissue box towards Gemma again, and she sniffed and nodded.

'It's OK. I understand. I just want him to come home,' she whispered.

'We'll do everything we can,' Helena said. She turned to look at Devon for a moment, and he gave a small nod.

'OK, let me just get those other details, addresses and date of birth and things, and then we'll let you go.'

For a few minutes, she listened as Gemma ran through home and work addresses, Danny's contact details and other basic background information, until she was satisfied she had everything she needed for now. She made a final note on her pad, put her pen down and leaned back in her chair.

'Look, we're going to start making some enquiries. The best thing you can do is go home, and let us know the second you hear anything from him, or if you hear anything about his whereabouts from a friend or relative, anything like that, OK?'

'Thank you.' Gemma stood up slowly and held out a hand first to Helena and then to Devon, a delicate silver bangle glinting on her wrist.

'Thank you,' she said again. 'I really appreciate this.'

'You're welcome. And I know this is an easy thing for me to say but try not to worry too much. As I said, most people who go missing do turn up, and usually pretty quickly. We'll let you know if we find anything. Devon will see you back out to reception. Take care now, OK?'

Gemma gave her a watery smile, and Devon led her out of the room.

When he returned, Helena was still sitting at the table, staring at the wedding photograph.

'So – what do you think?' he said.

She turned to look at him.

'I don't know. Yes, he fits the pattern, if there is one. Age, appearance. And they live in Clifton, very close to The Downs in fact, so the location fits too.'

She tapped the page where she'd written Gemma and Danny's address. Devon sat down beside her, and there was silence for a few seconds as they both gazed at the smiling man in the picture, then Helena sighed.

'Oh shit, I just don't know, Devon. I mean, this guy's only just moved here from London, there's no way he can have any connection with the other two. We haven't even found any connection between *them* yet, have we, other than their physical appearance? They worked in totally different fields, didn't know each other, no friends or associates in common, nothing. This Danny works in IT, different again, and as he's only just moved in ...'

She sighed again.

Devon nodded slowly, eyes still fixed on the photograph.

'I know, I know. It's just so fricking weird that our murder victims look so alike, and now this guy too ... but you're right, guv. We have nothing at all to go on at the moment, do we? So, what do we do with this?'

She paused for a moment, thinking, then decided.

'Right. Look, we don't have a third body right now, do we, just a missing man. For now, anyway, and please God it stays that way. But at the same time, the similarity in appearance, the fact that he's not contactable ... so let's run this as a sidebar to the main investigation. Mervin Elliott and Ryan Jones must be our priorities, OK? But can you take this on, just for twenty-four hours or so initially, until we see what's what? And let's keep everything crossed that he turns up, and that this is all a big coincidence.'

'Sure. I'll get onto it right away. Oh ... and by the way, *Muriel*? Really?' He grinned widely.

'Shut up. And if that gets out, I'll know exactly where it's come from. Now get out of here.'

'I'm going, I'm going. And your secret's safe with me.'

Still grinning, he stood up and left the room. Helena's eyes returned to the photograph on the table in front of her. Yes, it might well be just a coincidence that a man who looked like Danny O'Connor did had now gone missing. But there were suddenly too many damn coincidences floating around, and she didn't like coincidences. Didn't like them one little bit.

Chapter 5

I typed a full stop, then read the sentence I'd just written. *Urgh, what a load of rubbish*, I thought. It didn't even make sense. I tapped the backspace key furiously, deleting the words, then pushed my wheelie chair back from my desk in frustration.

The room was stuffy, too warm, and I felt nauseous, my stomach churning, another night of little sleep leaving my head muzzy and my eyes sore. I'd dragged myself into the spacious bedroom I was using as a home office an hour earlier, really needing to get my article finished by lunchtime, but how could I concentrate on writing about the heavenly massages and delicious, fresh food I'd experienced at the spa on Friday when I was so desperately worried about my husband? I'd still heard nothing from him, my phone silent, my email inbox empty, and when I'd called the police first thing that morning, desperate to find out if they'd come up with anything, I'd been told, gently, that there was no news as yet, but that they'd be in touch as soon as they had something to report. And so I'd taken Albert out for a quick walk and then come home and tried to work, to distract myself, but it was impossible. I just *couldn't*. I stood up, running my hands through my hair, thinking. Would Rebecca, the editor at *Fitness & Style* magazine, extend my deadline if I told her what was happening? Maybe. I walked back to the desk, grabbed my phone and, before I could change my mind, dialled her number. Two minutes later, I ended the call, relief flooding through me. She'd been lovely: shocked to hear that Danny was missing, and totally understanding my panic about my deadline.

'Honestly, Gemma, don't worry about it at all,' she said. 'I can easily move that piece to next week's issue or even the week after that. Do it when you can. And if you need anything, anything at all, give me a buzz, OK? I'm sure he'll come back soon though. Keep me posted, yes?'

I turned my laptop off and headed downstairs to the kitchen, thanking my lucky stars that I had such an understanding boss. Well, she wasn't *technically* my boss – I was freelance, so I didn't really have one – but for the past six months or so about fifty per cent of my work had been for *Fitness & Style*, which had been great. That, combined with the monthly column I wrote for *Camille* magazine, was more than enough to pay the bills, and I was lucky enough to pick up other commissions here and there too – the occasional travel feature for *Red*, or a health piece for *Woman & Home*. I hadn't been sure about working for *Fitness & Style* at first; it was an online magazine, which made me a little nervous, having spent my career to date on 'real world' newspapers and magazines, publications you could hold in your hand. I'd been silly to worry though – with a rapidly growing readership, and a host of celebrity contributors, *Fitness & Style* was one of the biggest publishing success stories of the past few years, and I loved the variety of the work. Regular boxes of beauty samples arrived for me to test and review, and a few times a month there was a trip somewhere, maybe a new Pilates studio, the launch of a new fashion brand, or – the most coveted invitations – an overnight visit to a spa hotel or retreat, to try what they had to offer and write about my experiences. It was all a far cry from my early days as a news reporter, when I'd worked my way up through the regional press and finally landed my dream job at *The Telegraph*. I'd thrived for a while, adoring the buzz of chasing the big stories and landing the major interviews, but after a few years, the long hours and endless stress had begun to take their toll. Unexpectedly, I'd found myself becoming increasingly anxious, developing insomnia so crippling that I'd go days without sleep, panic gripping me as I stared at my blank screen, unable to write a single word. It all came to a head the day I was pulled into the editor's office for a dressing-down for the second time in two weeks for failing to meet a deadline. That night, I staggered, sweating and shaking, off my tube train home two stops early, gasping for breath and convinced I was having a heart attack. When my doctor informed me the next day that it had most likely been a panic attack and told me frankly that I looked dreadful and needed to take some time off work for the sake of my mental health, I rang the paper and handed in my notice that same afternoon. It had been as if a huge, heavy weight had been lifted off my back, and I'd slept soundly that night for the first time in months. And I'd got lucky. A few high-profile stories during the previous year had boosted my profile, and when I decided to try going freelance and started looking around for work, I'd quickly been signed as a columnist for *Camille*, one of the UK's biggest selling women's monthly magazines. It paid well, very well, and the kudos the job gave me meant that other magazines were keen to commission me too. All the same, the transition hadn't been easy, not in the early days. I missed the newsroom banter and my work friends, terribly at first, but we'd kept in touch, and very soon the freelance life began to suit me so well that I'd never regretted my decision. And OK, so writing about lipstick and wallpaper wasn't quite the same as interviewing the Home Secretary or covering a murder trial, but I'd been there and done that, and I realized that I *needed* this quieter life, one where I could sleep and breathe and *live* instead of being chained to a news desk, on call twenty-four hours a day, always on alert for the next big story.

It had been when Albert had come into my life too. Before, my hours had been too long and unsociable to even think about dating, never mind consider having a pet. But suddenly, anything was possible, and getting a dog seemed to be the perfect way to celebrate my new lifestyle: a companion at home, lying at my feet as I wrote, and an excuse to get outside daily and walk in the fresh air. Albert had brought me so much joy, and fortunately when Danny had arrived on the scene, he'd instantly fallen in love with my gorgeous, clever puppy too.

'Gemma, he's feckin' perfect,' he'd said, crouching down to get a better look. Albert had promptly rolled over for a tummy rub, and Danny had laughed and obliged.

'We always had dogs growing up in Ireland, but since I moved to London I haven't been able to, you know, with work and everything. Can we take him for a walk, now? He can come to the pub with us!'

His enthusiasm had sent a ripple of happiness through me, and the attraction I was already feeling towards Danny had doubled, instantly. Eighteen months later, I'd never been happier. Well, never been happier until Friday of course. Danny's face floated into my head again and my throat tightened. Trying to write had kept me from obsessing for an hour or so, but now the fear was returning. It was Monday morning. Day four without a word, my repeated emails unanswered, attempts to Skype him failing, his status still showing as offline.

Where are you, Danny? For God's sake, this isn't funny anymore!

I'd thought hard about when to tell my and Danny's families what was going on, and had decided to leave it just a few more days, a week maybe. Surely he'd be back by then anyway, I reasoned, and I'd have freaked everyone out for no reason at all. Trying to deal with the freaking out I was doing myself was quite enough. Purely for something to do, I flicked the kettle on for what must have been my fifth cup of coffee of the morning and, realizing that, although I'd fed Albert, who was snoozing in his bed, I hadn't eaten anything myself since the previous day, since before my visit to the police station, pushed a slice of bread into the toaster. I needed to dig out another photo of Danny, I remembered – they'd asked me for one of him on his own, a recent one if possible. They'd been nice, those two police officers, the woman – DCI Dickens, was that her name? – petite but formidable at the same time, her body lean and taut, hair tightly cropped into a blonde pixie cut and those intense, dark blue eyes. And her sidekick, her deputy, DS Clarke, a little quieter and gentler, tall and solid, good-looking with his neatly trimmed facial hair, white even teeth, smooth dark skin. A right handsome pair. *Are they romantically involved?* I wondered idly, then pushed the ridiculous thought aside. They were police detectives, in Bristol and not in some TV cop drama. They were probably so busy they barely had time to pee, never mind have illicit workplace affairs.

I took my coffee and toast into the sitting room and sank onto the sofa. It was a lovely room – big and bright and high-ceilinged, with a huge working fireplace, cushioned window seats and a polished, dark wood floor. We'd bought a new sofa in yellow velvet and, after checking that the owners wouldn't mind us doing a little decorating, had found a delicate, trellis-patterned wallpaper in the softest dove grey to cover two of the walls. I'd put it up myself in an afternoon, and I loved it. The place was in immaculate condition but if we were going to live in it for a year or more, we wanted to put our own stamp on it.

'It's a parterre pattern,' I'd explained to Danny, when the wallpaper sample had arrived. 'You know, you see it in Victorian-style gardens? When they plan the flower beds so that they form a beautiful pattern. It's in keeping with the house, but sort of a modern interpretation.'

He'd frowned at me in an exaggerated fashion, clearly bemused, and I'd laughed and given up. To say that Danny wasn't very interested in home décor was an understatement, but the upside of that was that I could basically do what I liked. He'd help, happily, if I asked him to, but I called the shots, and that was fine by me.

I sat there for a moment, gazing around the room, then remembered what I'd gone in there to do and pulled out my phone. I clicked onto the photos file and started to scroll, looking for a decent snap of Danny. He'd never really liked having his photo taken – for such a gorgeous man he was remarkably camera shy – but we'd taken a few pictures since we'd moved and I thought one of them would be perfect for the police: a close-up shot of Danny lost in thought, standing in the middle of the lounge, staring at the wall as he tried to help me work out which of our several large pieces of art would look just right above the fireplace. I'd taken the photo before he'd even noticed I was there, and he'd growled and leapt on me, pulling me down onto the Persian silk rug, telling me I was 'worse than a bloody paparazzo' and then kissing me so hard I could barely breathe.

Oh Danny, I miss you so much. Please come home.

I paused, finger resting on the screen of my phone. I'd gone back through a month's worth of pictures without finding what I was looking for, and I frowned and started scrolling forwards again. Where was it? In fact, where were *lots* of the photos we'd taken since we'd come to Bristol? There were a few of my work ones from recent weeks, shots of pots of moisturisers and faded jeans and a vibrant pink orchid in a glass bowl. And there were a couple of the house, pictures of some of the rooms, images I'd taken to try to visualize the walls in different colours, to plan my decorating. But where were the photos of Danny gamely attempting DIY, putting up a decidedly wonky shelf? Or the selfies we'd taken, the two of us crashed out on our bed after a full day of trying to sort the bedrooms out and lugging boxes up and down the stairs, sweaty and exhausted but grinning ear to ear? The picture of us both cuddled up in one big armchair, clinking glasses of champagne? I tapped each photo in turn, slowly now. I must have been going too fast, missed them. But no – once again, I was back onto pictures from London, shots I'd taken before we moved. Where the hell were the photos I wanted, the ones from the past few weeks? And why were only *some* of the recent pictures missing, and not all of them? Some sort of blip with my camera app? They'd all be backed up though, on the cloud, wouldn't they? I tapped the cloud storage app and started scrolling again, but it was the same photos, the ones I'd just gone through several times in my photos file.

'What? This makes *no* sense,' I said aloud. I put the phone down on the cushion beside me and sat still, thinking. They must be somewhere, but where? Had they been saved into a different file or something? But didn't photos automatically get saved into the photos file? Something had clearly gone wrong, and while I wasn't too bad with technology, I didn't know enough to know where to look next. And the police had asked for a new photo *today*, if possible. What was I going to do? Give them one from our London days, I supposed. I had a few of those on my phone, and they'd be recent enough. I took a deep breath, trying to quell the anxiety, then picked up the phone again, checking for emails this time. *Maybe, just maybe.* But just like the previous twenty or fifty or a hundred times I'd checked, there were no new messages in my inbox. Tears suddenly sprang to my eyes. I couldn't take this much longer. Four days. FOUR. Where was he? Was he lying injured somewhere, unable to get help? *Had* he just left, without saying a word? Left me, for somebody else, as people kept suggesting? Or ... was he ... was he *dead*? My heart began to pound, my breath suddenly coming in ragged gasps.

Stop it. Stop it, Gemma.

Thinking like that wouldn't help anyone. My hand shaking slightly, I scrolled down my messages, looking for the last email Danny had sent me, the one from Thursday night, feeling a sudden desperate urge to read his words again, wondering if I'd missed something, some sub-text, some clue as to where he might have gone. Shit, where *was* his last email? I couldn't find *that* now. Surely I hadn't deleted it by mistake? Pretty sure I hadn't – soppily, I never deleted messages from my husband – I clicked onto my deleted messages folder, putting Danny's name into the search box.

No messages found.

I *knew* I hadn't deleted it. But where was it then? I returned to my inbox and did the same search. This time, a string of emails from Danny appeared, but the most recent was dated

Wednesday, the thirtieth of January, weeks ago. What was going on? We'd exchanged dozens of emails since we'd moved to Bristol, since Danny had been phone-less. Where were they all?

'Oh, for God's sake!' I threw the phone hard onto the carpet, and sat back, covering my face with my hands, the tears flowing freely now. I needed to read Danny's last email, I *needed* to. What was wrong with my phone? Or was it my email provider? Was it having some sort of problem? I'd have to phone, ask ...

I jumped as a sharp ringing sound interrupted my frantic thoughts. The doorbell. *Danny?* Could it be Danny, back home, keys lost somewhere? From the kitchen, an excited yelp seemed to imply that Albert was hopeful too.

'Danny!' I rushed from the room, pounding down the hallway, almost tripping over Albert who was suddenly scampering past me, my fingers fumbling with the keys, my heart thumping painfully against the wall of my chest.

'Dann— oh!'

'Mrs O'Connor, we're sorry to disturb you ... are you OK?' DS Devon Clarke was standing on the doorstep, broad-shouldered in a black coat, his brow creasing as he looked at me quizzically. Beside him, a smaller, younger man with a sharp nose and small rectangular glasses was also staring at me. I took a step backwards, catching a glimpse of myself in the hall mirror, suddenly aware that I was still crying, yesterday's un-washed-off mascara streaking my cheeks, my hair wild and unbrushed.

'Oh, gosh, I'm so sorry. I thought ... I thought you might

be Danny. I still haven't heard anything, and I was getting myself into a state … and oh no, please, *please* don't tell me you're here with bad news, please …'

I suddenly realized that two police officers on my doorstep was probably not a good thing, and the panic began to rise again.

'*Please* …'

DS Clarke was shaking his head, stepping into the hall and reaching out a hand towards me, patting me on the shoulder.

'No, no, nothing like that. Don't worry, OK? We've just been making some enquiries and discovered something a little odd we need to talk to you about, and we thought it would be easier to chat face to face. But it's nothing to panic about, so calm down, all right? Come on, let's go and sit down. This is DC Stevens …' he gestured behind him at the smaller man, who nodded, giving me a hint of a smile, 'and if you point him in the direction of the kitchen he'll go and make us a nice cup of tea and then we'll have a chat, OK? Is your dog all right with strangers, by the way?'

I looked down at Albert, who was standing protectively in front of me, gulped in some air and nodded.

'Sorry, I'm just … yes, he's fine. Albert, go to your bed. It's not Danny. *Go*, Albert. Kitchen's down there, just follow the dog. I was just in the sitting room, I'll show you.'

After a moment's hesitation Albert obeyed and trotted off down the corridor, his head low, his disappointment clear. DC Stevens followed him as instructed, and I staggered back into the lounge and slumped onto the sofa again, my legs feeling weak and wobbly. DS Clarke perched on the chair opposite, and for a couple of minutes made small talk, asking me if I'd heard anything at all from Danny, then changing the subject entirely, admiring the large bay windows, commenting on the bronze sculpture that sat on a side table and asking me to remind him how long we'd lived in Bristol. But when DC Stevens reappeared, bearing three steaming mugs balanced on the tray we kept on the kitchen counter, the mood suddenly changed.

'Mrs O'Connor, we've been making some enquiries this morning, into your husband's disappearance, as promised. We started by visiting his workplace, ACR Security?'

His tone was suddenly serious, and a chill ran through me. I nodded.

'OK? And?'

He paused. 'Well, this is the weird thing. It's *not* his workplace.'

I stared at him, not understanding.

'What do you mean? Of course it is. I mean, he hasn't been there long, but certainly a few weeks. He would have started on the ...' I thought for a moment, trying to remember the exact date. 'Well, I actually moved down to Bristol a week before Danny did, because he had stuff to finish up in London; I can't remember if I told you that? But he came to join me on the evening of the eighth of February, that was a Friday. He started at ACR on the Monday, so that would have been the eleventh. I'm sorry, I don't understand what you mean by it not being his workplace?'

DS Clarke glanced at his colleague for a moment, and then both turned back to look at me.

'What I mean, Mrs O'Connor, is that ACR say your husband was offered and did accept a job with them, which he was indeed due to start on the eleventh of February. But a couple of weeks before that date, he emailed them to say that he wouldn't be taking up the position after all, due to a change in circumstances. Needless to say they weren't very happy about him changing his mind, especially at such short notice, but there wasn't much they could do about it. Therefore, you see, ACR Security was *not* your husband's workplace. So ... can you help us out with that, at all?'

Chapter 6

'And she had no explanation for it whatsoever? She really didn't know?'

Helena, sitting on the edge of Devon's desk, looked down at him and frowned. He swallowed a mouthful of tea, grimaced, and put his mug down carefully on the coaster next to his computer keyboard.

'Nope. She looked absolutely gobsmacked, to be honest. She said as far as she knew he was excited about the new job and really enjoying it. Left for work early every morning, came home usually after six, sometimes a lot later. Been doing it every weekday since they moved. Which begs the question, if he wasn't going to work at ACR Security, what was he doing?'

Helena nodded slowly.

'Another job somewhere, that for some reason he didn't tell his wife about? Or was he doing something else entirely? We need to check his bank account, Devon. See if he was being paid by someone else? Although if he'd only been working in Bristol for three weeks, he may not have had a payday yet, I suppose. It would probably be end of the month, wouldn't it?'

'Probably. But I'm already on it – well, Frankie is, anyway. We should have his bank records this afternoon.'

He gestured at the neighbouring desk, where DC Frankie Stevens was chatting animatedly on the phone.

'OK, good. Did we get hold of a more recent photo of him, by the way?'

Devon nodded.

'She's emailed one over, yes. Couldn't find any from the past few weeks – says her phone's playing up, her recent emails and pictures haven't saved or something. But it's only a couple of months old. I've printed a few copies off. Should be fine.'

'OK. All right, well, stay on it for a little bit longer, and keep me posted, OK? And I want this kept quiet for now – no missing person appeals in the papers or on social media or anything. This possible connection to our other two cases is still worrying me, and I don't want any more speculation out there. Today was bad enough.'

She glanced at the front-page splash on the copy of that morning's *Bristol Post*, which was lying on Devon's desk, and sighed. It had been just as she'd feared.

SERIAL KILLER FEARS AFTER DOUBLE MURDER ON THE DOWNS

'Bloody reporters. So hush, hush, right? And I know you're working really long hours at the moment, Devon. I do appreciate it, thank you.'

'Sure boss. Got nothing better to do these days, so that's fine by me. Joys of being young, free and single, eh?'

Helena gave him a sympathetic smile, pushed herself off the desk and straightened her jacket. Poor old Devon had been dumped by his girlfriend of the past year just weeks ago, and while he didn't seem outwardly broken-hearted, she had the sense he was feeling the loss far more keenly than he was letting on. She'd take him aside, maybe for a drink, at some point and have a chat, but there was too much work to be done at the moment, and now with this added complication ... she shook her head slightly as she crossed the room, weaving her way between the desks piled high with scruffy stacks of paperwork. She was starting to get a feeling that there was something strange about the disappearance of Danny O'Connor, especially with the revelation about the job that never was, but without a body he was still just a missing person, and right now she had more important things on her mind, namely two *actually* dead men whose murders may or may not be connected, and a distinct paucity of leads. With a sigh, she reached her own desk and sat down, pushing aside a plastic container of half-eaten mozzarella and tomato salad and tapping her keyboard to wake up her computer screen.

The files for both sets of forensic results were open on her desktop and she flicked backwards and forwards disconsolately between them for the tenth time. There was nothing there, basically; the killer had either been very careful or very lucky, leaving no trace of his identity on either of the victims. Or *her* identity, Helena thought. No assumptions, not at this stage, even though right now her money was on a male killer. Although no murder weapon had been found in either case, both Mervin Elliott and Ryan Jones had been attacked with some considerable force with some sort of heavy object – both, it had now been confirmed, had died from their head injuries. Both were young, fit men, and it seemed unlikely that a woman would have been able to take either of them down so easily. *Although* ... Helena thought about some of the women she saw at her local gym, on the rare occasions when she chose indoor exercise over running. Those bodybuilder types, the ones who entered those Miss Bikini Fitness contests or whatever they were called – they'd definitely be able to take a man down if they wanted to. *So, don't rule anybody out*, she thought. It was far too early in the investigation to start doing that. *Keep an open mind, about all of it.*

She stood up again and crossed the room to the incident board, hands massaging the aching small of her back as she walked. Maybe she'd ask Charlotte to give her a back rub later, if she was still awake when she got home, she thought, then smiled wryly to herself, realizing how unlikely that was. Her wife, head teacher of a fairly challenging city centre secondary school, came home from work as exhausted as she did.

'Will you be home for dinner? Or is that a stupid question?' she'd asked sleepily as Helena had tried to slip noiselessly out of bed at six that morning, wanting to get a run in before what would undoubtedly be another long, frustrating day. She'd leaned across and kissed Charlotte softly on the forehead. She smelled of rose oil and sleep.

'Sorry, did I wake you? And honestly ... I don't think so. This is a tough one, and I've got nothing to go on, Char, nothing. Probably better to assume I won't be home for dinner for the foreseeable. I'll make it up to you when it's all over, promise.'

'Yeah yeah. Heard that before.'

Charlotte had squeezed her arm and rolled over, eyes closing again, and Helena had dressed quickly and headed out into the dark, frosty morning, guilt nibbling at her guts. Charlotte was patience personified, but sometimes she wondered how long that would last. The job, as poor Devon had recently discovered, was a relationship killer. And Charlotte wanted children – well, they both did, really, but with them both being so busy ...

Helena sighed. Charlotte would never put pressure on her, she knew that. But there'd been a few comments recently, a few occasions when babies had suddenly come up in an unrelated conversation. She'd changed the subject, dodged the discussion, but she couldn't do that forever, she knew that. Maybe, when this was all over ...

She sighed again and stared at the incident board. They had had *one* breakthrough that morning – after struggling for days to find any connection whatsoever between the two victims, a young detective constable had come to her a couple of hours ago, pink with excitement, to announce his discovery that both Mervin Elliott and Ryan Jones had used the same dating app.

'It's one of the new trendy ones, nowhere near as big as Tinder and so on, but getting more and more popular among people wanting something a bit more discreet,' he'd said, his words tumbling over each other in his eagerness to share his news. 'It's called EHU – it stands for Elite Hook Ups. It's not cheap – you have to pay quite a lot even for the basic version. A lot of the others allow you to use them for free at a basic level, and then have a subscription fee for the premium service. This one, well, you have to pay a hefty monthly fee up front to use it at all. Hence the "elite" bit, I suppose.'

The breathless DC – his name was Mike Slater, Helena remembered – had paused for a moment, turning the pages of his notebook, then looked up at her again, eyes bright.

'But they'd both subscribed to it, and what was really interesting, ma'am, is that for some reason the app had actually been deleted from both victims' phones. I started looking into it because both Mervin's and Ryan's friends said they definitely used a dating app – they didn't know which one – to meet women, yet there was no sign of one on their mobiles when their bodies were found. I didn't really know where to start, I'm married, so I'm not an expert, but I asked around, did a straw poll of all the singles in the office,' he gestured vaguely around the room, 'asked them which dating apps were big at the moment, and almost all of them mentioned this EHU one as being really popular. It only launched about a year and a half ago, and lots of people have apparently left the old favourites and joined it instead. Well, not everyone – Frankie sticks to Grindr; he's addicted, says it's the one with the hottest men and he's not switching for anyone ...' He grinned and glanced across to where DC Stevens was sitting, then looked back at Helena. 'Sorry. Anyway, I made a list of the top five apps everyone seems to be using, including this EHU one. I knew it was a massive long shot, but, well, I got lucky.'

'I started contacting the various companies and asked if there was any way I could find out if Mervin and Ryan had signed up to them. The first few wouldn't play ball, even when I explained that the two men had been murdered, but then I called EHU and they had a think about it and then came back to me and agreed to release some very basic data. And it turns out they were both signed up to it. Mervin and Ryan I mean.'

He paused again.

'Both had been registered with the site for a few months ...' He consulted his notes. 'Mervin since last September, and Ryan since November. So a bit weird that the app wasn't on either of their phones when their bodies were found. I can't explain that. I mean, obviously this all might just be a coincidence and not get us anywhere, but I asked EHU if there was any way they could give us details of anyone either of our victims hooked up with via the app. Then we'd have a list of new people to talk to, seeing as none of their mates were much help. Neither Mervin nor Ryan had introduced a woman to their friends in months, none of their dates had got serious enough for that. So I just thought, maybe if we could find any of the women they were in contact with through the app, it might just give us a new angle, and you never know, one of them might have some information that might help us. Or they might not, of course, but ...'

Helena, who'd been sitting in her chair and listening with increasing interest, stood up suddenly and clapped her hands.

'Amazing work, Mike! So will they do that, then? The app people? Can we get that information?'

The DC shuffled his feet, looked down at them for a moment, then back at her, the smile fading from his face.

'Ah, well, that's where the problem started. Because it's an expensive, paid for app, it works in a bit of a different way. There's none of this "swipe right if you fancy me" or anything. Each person who registers has to provide an email address, which is listed on his or her profile. Users are advised to set up a new email address specifically for the site, and not to use their personal address, but that's up to them. Then you just search for people with traits you're interested in – profession, body type, age, hobbies and so on, the usual – and if you find someone you like the look of, you just drop them an email, effectively taking the app out of the picture. It's a feature of the site – it ensures much more privacy than most, because only the two people emailing each other know they've decided to take it further. In other words, the people who run the app have no knowledge of who contacts who. They just provide a private, discreet platform for people to find people they might be interested in meeting.'

Helena felt her heart sinking. *Damn. Bugger it.*

'OK, well that's a massive shame. But still, excellent work, Mike.'

She paused for a moment, thinking rapidly, her brow furrowed.

'Look, what about their phone and email accounts? Mervin's and Ryan's, I mean? If these dates were arranged by email, initially anyway, can't we just find the women they dated that way?'

Mike was nodding rapidly.

'The IT guys are having another look. I mean, they looked at emails and phone records straight away, for both victims, but didn't find anything that seemed significant, though I suppose they were looking for threats and stuff like that, not stuff about making dates. They're looking again in the light of this app thing. And yes, I'll get back to EHU, see if they can help any further. They might have some sort of search data that could at least help us narrow the field – like, I don't know, say Mervin had a thing for tall redheads and searched for women fitting that description a lot, that might help us track down some of his dates. Or not. I mean, I could be totally wrong about this, it probably doesn't mean anything at all.'

'But it might, it just might. Thank you, Mike. You've done a great job. It's finally something our two murder victims have in common, and it's about the only lead we have at the moment, so it's definitely worth following up. Send me anything else you can on this as soon as humanly possible, OK?'

That had been a few hours earlier, and there'd been no updates since. Helena stared at the board for another moment, then wandered back to her desk, thinking. Dating apps. It seemed to be the way everyone met their partners now. In her day, you met people on nights out, in bars, clubs; she'd met Charlotte in a gay bar in Bristol a decade ago. But times had changed, and as far as murder investigations were concerned, the fact that everything was online now was often a good thing, making the movements of victims and suspects so much more traceable. The fact that the two victims had been registered with the same dating site didn't *necessarily* mean anything, she knew that. If it was as popular as Mike had said, thousands of people would be using it, which probably made the coincidence meaningless. And how likely was it, after all, that they'd both somehow had the enormous misfortune to fix a date with the same female psychopath, who'd then proceeded to batter them both to death? No, the deaths might not be linked at all, but at least it was *something*, a lead they could investigate, and that made a pleasant change after days with nothing at all to go on.

I wonder …?

Halfway to her desk Helena suddenly stopped dead as an idea struck her. Devon, who was coming the other way carrying a fresh tea, stopped too just in time to avoid walking straight into her, and groaned as the hot liquid slopped over the edge of his mug, splashing his pristine white shirt.

'Ahhh, shit! What's up, boss?'

He dabbed ineffectually at the spreading brown stain with a paper napkin he held in his other hand, looking quizzically at Helena.

'Oh Devon, I'm so sorry. It's just … I just had a thought. A random one, and probably a stupid one, but …'

She turned on her heel, scanning the busy room.

'Mike?'

At his desk near the window, DC Slater raised his head.

She gestured at him. 'Can you come over here for a minute?' She turned back to her DS.

'And Devon, can you give Mike a copy of that new photo of Danny O'Connor, the one Gemma sent across earlier? It's just an idea, but ...' she looked at the eager face of Mike Slater, who had joined them, 'Mike, DS Clarke is going to give you a photograph. It's of a man called Danny O'Connor, who seems to have gone missing in slightly strange circumstances. He's very, very similar in physical appearance to our two murder victims which is just making us slightly nervous, and he's not single, he's fairly recently married, but it's just a thought, something I'd like to rule out ... could you just humour me and have a look to see if he's on that EHU site too? I mean, I'm sure he won't be, but can you access it to search it, without paying to join?'

Mike nodded.

'Yes, the general public can't, but they gave me a code so I could look at Mervin's and Ryan's profiles, and it gives me access to the search facility. I'll give it a go.'

They didn't have to wait long. Ten minutes later there was an elated yell from across the room. Helena and Devon stood simultaneously, and in seconds were peering over Mike's shoulder, Helena aware her heart had started beating uncomfortably quickly.

'Well ... what have you found?' she asked. On Mike's screen was a search page, where he'd clearly been filling in details of Danny's physical appearance, hair colour and so on.

'OK, well I searched for his name and nothing that matched him came up, although that's not unusual, lots of people use nicknames and so on, on sites like this. So I put in all the basic info from his missing person report instead. And when I hit search ...'

He clicked on the red search button at the bottom of the

screen. Immediately the screen changed, a dozen or so photographs of dark-haired young men flashing up. Helena scanned them, looking for a familiar face, and then gasped.

'There! Middle of the second row. Is that ...?'

Devon leaned closer to the screen, hand on Mike's shoulder. Mike was grinning widely.

'That's him. That's bloody him. Holy cow,' Devon said slowly.

'I think it is too. He's on there under a different name, calling himself Sean, look. Not much personal info in the profile, but it does say he works in IT. I'm pretty sure it's him too, from comparing the two photos. What do you think, boss?'

Mike looked up at Helena. Her eyes were glued to the image on the screen, her brain trying to process what she was seeing and what it could possibly mean. It had only been a stab in the dark, a wild hunch. She hadn't expected to actually be *right*. She cleared her throat.

'I think, Mike, that you're bang on. I have no idea what's going on here, or why on earth an apparently happily married man has a profile on a trendy dating site, but that's *definitely* Danny O'Connor.'

Chapter 7

I was slumped on the sofa, shivering violently despite the warmth of the room. *What was going on?* My head throbbed, and I felt disorientated, dizzy, as if I'd had too much to drink, although not a drop or morsel had passed my lips since the police had left that morning. The thought of food made me feel ill. How could I prepare a meal, sit down and eat it like a normal person, when everything I thought of as normal seemed to be crumbling around me? Danny hadn't been going to work, hadn't even *started* his new job. How was that even possible? For three weeks, he'd been leaving the house in the morning, dressed for the office, heading off on his bike and returning long after dark in the evening. He'd seemed to be enjoying his new role enormously, seemed so happy, so ... so *Danny*. Nothing different about him whatsoever. And now I'd been informed that all of it, *all* of it, had been a lie. *Why?* Why would he make something like that up, pretend to be going to work when he wasn't? And if he wasn't working at ACR Security, where I thought he was, where he *said* he was, then where the hell had he been spending his days? The police had asked me that too, and I'd simply gaped at them, shaking

65

my head, unable to think of anything, anywhere he could possibly have been going. Of course, now that I was alone again, I'd managed to come up with all sorts of wild scenarios in the past few horrible hours – he'd taken another job, some sort of top secret one he wasn't allowed to tell anyone about. He was sick, suffering from some terrible illness, and had been having clandestine daily treatment, not wanting to worry me. He had another family, a second wife, children maybe, who lived in Bristol, and that's why he'd been so excited about moving here, finally able to spend time with them. But as each theory slammed into my brain, and was then instantly dismissed as ludicrous, my fear grew. I had no idea, no clue at all.

Danny, what have you done? Why would you do this to me? I love you, Danny, and you love me. Don't you?

But suddenly, the doubts were creeping in.

If he's lied to me about this, what else might he have lied about?

There were little white lies in every relationship, of course there were. But you didn't lie to somebody you loved about the *big* things, did you? Not the huge, massively important things like your work, your *life*. The job, the daily routine, the annoyance he'd shown at the delay of his new work phone's arrival when, in reality, it appeared now, there *was* no work, no imminent phone. Lies, lies, lies. And then to just *vanish*, leaving me so confused, so frightened ... who would treat someone they loved like that?

A little sob escaped me and, at my feet on the carpet, Albert, who was curled up, asleep, opened his eyes briefly, looked up at me, glanced around the room as if to check if Danny was back yet, then shut his eyes again with a heavy sigh. There was a faux fur throw on the back of the sofa and I dragged it off, wrapping it around my legs and pulling it up to my chin, trying to stop the shivering. We'd snuggled under this velvety softness so many times, Danny and me, watching films, talking, kissing. The flash of memory made my eyes sting with sudden tears. This made no sense. None of it *made any sense*. And yet, I thought, had increasingly been thinking in the past few hours, how well did I really know my husband, when you looked at the facts? We'd met on Tinder only eighteen months ago, as I'd told the police officers when I'd gone to the station. We'd liked the look of each other, exchanged a few flirty messages, then it was phone calls, long and late into the night. His soft Irish burr had enthralled me, and I'd found myself opening up to him before we'd even met in person, telling him about my work, the anxiety that had led to me packing in my newspaper career, the emotional trauma it had left me with. He'd been so kind, so supportive, so understanding, right from the start. And then, when we'd finally had our first date, when I'd looked into those chocolatey brown eyes, there'd been a connection so immediate, so deep that it had almost frightened me. I'd had boyfriends before, even a few serious ones over the years, but not for a while and not like that. Not like Danny. That was September; on Christmas Eve, he dropped to one knee in our favourite little Italian restaurant and proposed, amid the whoops and cheers of the waiters and other diners. We got married just three months later, on the seventeenth of March, St Patrick's Day.

'Always a day for celebrating. And I can't think of a better reason for celebrating than marrying you,' he'd said, as we left Marylebone register office, holding hands, grinning crazily. We'd kept it small, simple, just us and a few friends, plus my parents and, representing the O'Connors, Danny's cousin Quinn, his only relative who lived in London. His mum hadn't flown over from County Sligo for the wedding – Donal, Danny's father, had died just six weeks or so earlier, at the beginning of February, after being ill on and off for years, and his mum was full-time carer for their other, disabled, son, Liam, Danny's younger brother.

'Mum hates travel, and Liam isn't good with changes to his routine, it freaks him out. Even before Dad died, they'd rarely left the county for years, never mind the country,' Danny had told me. 'It's a shame, but I'll send her pictures and videos. She's not that bothered anyway, you know what she's like. And I've told her it's just a modest do, and she's not missing much.'

I'd only met Bridget once, but I knew what he meant. Danny had told me he'd never really got on well with either of his parents, and I had seen why when I'd met them. Bridget was definitely an odd one, and I hadn't warmed to his father at all. And he was right, it *wasn't* much, our wedding reception, but it was perfect for us and I loved it: a knees-up at the local pub, champagne and fish and chips, photos snapped on friends' phones, to be collated and put into an album later. It was really how Danny had wanted it – he hated *fuss*, as he called it – but I'd been happy to go along with it, as long as a few key people were there: Mum, Dad, my closest friends.

I still wore white though, a beautiful Chanel sheath, and insisted he wear a suit and cut his wild locks into something resembling a hair style. He'd moaned, but he'd complied, and I'd never seen him look more gorgeous than he did that day. I'd never felt more in love, or happier. Never dreamt that just a year later ...

There was a lump in my throat, and I swallowed hard, feeling the nausea rising again. We'd been happy, we *had*. We *fitted*. And I hadn't lied when I'd told the police we'd been virtually inseparable most of the time. OK, so Danny, very occasionally, would become a little withdrawn, wanted to be alone, would head off on his bike for a couple of hours, but that was natural; he loved cycling, and he had a stressful job, cooped up in a stuffy office, staring at a screen. It was a bit like that for me too, with my writing, and I'd always understood his need for a bit of solitude. He'd always come back a few hours later, smiling, relaxed, rejuvenated. So this, this complete disappearance – this wasn't Danny. Or not the Danny I thought I knew, certainly.

He lied to me, I thought again. *He lied. And not just a little white lie, a* massive *one.*

And if Danny had lied to me about something as huge as his job, hadn't told me what was really going on in his life, it suddenly seemed to me that it was much more likely that he *had* just left me, just walked out, despite my previous insistence that he wouldn't do that. *Could* he have been having an affair? Were those solitary cycle rides not what I thought they were – had he been meeting up with somebody after all? Had he now gone off to be with her, whoever she was? And yet, I thought, rubbing my throbbing temples, even that didn't make much sense, for why had he taken nothing with him? His passport, toiletries, clothes – everything was still here. If you were leaving your partner, and wanted to do it quickly while they were away for a night, surely you'd still take the basics? One bag, with a few clothes, bits and pieces to keep you going until you could come back and collect the rest? *I* would. Why leave with nothing ...?

BRRRRR.

I jumped as the doorbell rang, Albert instantly awake and on his feet, running across the room, yelping excitedly. I groaned. Now what? Police, again, with news this time maybe? Had they found him? I pushed the throw off and followed my dog to the front door. I was right. It was them again, DS Clarke and DC Stevens and, feeling suddenly shaky, I showed them into the sitting room, sending Albert to the kitchen again. We sat down in the same positions we'd been in that morning, me on the sofa, DS Clarke on the armchair opposite, his colleague remaining standing, hovering. I had the sudden, almost irresistible urge to cover my ears with my hands and sing '*la la la*' like a child. The police officers' faces were serious, and whatever they were about to say, I could already tell I didn't want to hear it. I didn't think I could take much more.

'Mrs O'Connor, Gemma ... is it OK, if I call you Gemma?' DS Clarke's voice was gentle, his eyes kind, and I nodded.

'Yes, fine. Please ... is there any news?' My voice sounded shrill, reedy, not like me at all.

He paused, glanced at DC Stevens, then looked back at me. 'Well, sorry to disturb you twice in one day, but there is news of sorts, yes. We haven't found your husband though, not yet. I'm sorry.'

I nodded again, feeling tears pricking my eyes once more. 'OK. So – what's the latest?'

DS Clarke looked down at the notebook he had pulled from his pocket and placed on his lap when he'd sat down.

'Well, we've done a little more digging, since discovering that Danny hadn't started his new job in Bristol after all. Checked out his finances a little. His final salary payment from his previous company, Hanfield Solutions, went into his bank account at the end of January, as it seems to have done every month for the past few years – correct?'

'Yes. He'd worked there for, I don't know, four years maybe?' At least *that* hadn't been a lie, I thought.

'Right.' DS Clarke cleared his throat then continued. 'So that money went in as usual. And we noticed some other big payments into the account too, a few times a year over the past few years, also from Hanfield Solutions. Would that have been bonuses, maybe?'

I nodded.

'Yes, he got bonuses every few months. A few thousand at a time, they were pretty generous. The company was doing well and they shared the profits with their staff.'

'OK, well that's all fine then.'

The DS paused for a moment.

'The thing is, since that last salary payment at the end of January, there've been no further payments into his account of any kind. And – and this is the really interesting bit – no money taken *out* either. Other than a direct debit to a letting agency, which we've assumed is the rent payment on this house ... actually, can I confirm that? It's rented via Pritchards?'

My head was starting to spin again, but I blinked and replied.

'Pritchards Lettings Agency, yes. Danny was covering the rent and I was doing the bills, electricity and so on. But what do you mean, no money's been taken out? Do you mean since Friday, when he went missing?'

DS Clarke shook his head.

'No, Gemma. I mean no money's been taken out of his account for weeks. Since ...' he looked back down at his notes, running a finger across the page, 'since Thursday the thirty-first of January. So that's, what? Four, four and a half weeks ago. Does that make sense to you?'

I stared at him. *What? Of course it doesn't make sense. That can't be right.*

'No. No, that's not possible. He took money out, of course he did ... he paid for lots of things since we moved in.'

I looked around the room, starting to feel frantic.

'That, look.' I pointed to the coffee table in front of the sofa, its dark oak top piled high with interiors magazines. 'He paid for that, for example. I saw it in an antiques shop in Clifton Village a couple of weeks ago. I took a photo of it and showed it to him when he came home from work that night ...' I paused, realizing what I'd said. 'Well, when he came home from wherever he'd been. And he said he'd buy it for me, if I liked it that much, told me to order it, get them to deliver it. I mean, I could have bought it myself, but he insisted. He gave me the cash right there and then. It was a hundred and fifty pounds, but he said he'd just been to the cash machine.'

DS Clarke was listening carefully.

'There haven't been any cash withdrawals, Gemma, not for weeks as I said. No debit card purchases either. Not a single one, not from his current account. He has a savings account too, and we've checked that, but it's empty ...'

'Well, yes. We both emptied our savings accounts to pay for the move, and buy new furniture, stuff like that. We haven't really saved that much up until now, we spent Danny's bonuses on trips away and nice dinners and stuff, treated ourselves, but we were going to start saving seriously from now on, get a deposit together to buy a house. Look, Danny *must* have been using his bank account. I don't understand. He paid for loads of stuff ...'

I raked my fingers through my hair, my mind racing, aware of two pairs of eyes fixed on my face.

'I mean, takeaways. He always paid for those with cash when we had them. And he came home with a new cycle helmet he'd bought only last week. He *was* making withdrawals, paying for things, of course he was. The bank must have made a mistake. I'm sorry, but you're wrong, DS Clarke.'

His dark eyes were still glued to my face, and for a moment we just stared at each other, my brow furrowed with fear and confusion, his expression calm, unreadable. Then he turned to DC Stevens again.

'Can you show Gemma the app, Frankie?'

He looked back at me.

'We'll forget about the bank account for now. I'm not sure

73

what that all means, but we'll come back to it later. DC Stevens is going to show you something on his tablet, and I want you to tell me if you're familiar with it.'

The DC, who'd been clutching the tablet under his arm since he'd arrived, was opening it up, tapping the screen. He crossed the room and sat down beside me on the sofa. He smelled faintly of cigarettes, and I began to feel sick again.

'What is it?'

He angled the screen towards me.

'It's a site called EHU. Have you heard of it?' he asked. He had a soft Scottish accent, and I realized that this was the first time I'd heard him speak more than a couple of words.

'EHU? That's that dating app, isn't it? The one everyone says is going to be as big as Tinder soon?'

I leaned forwards, puzzled. Why was he asking me about a dating app? He tapped the screen and a myriad of smiling faces began to spin around a logo, and then a log-in box appeared.

'Hold on, I'll just ...' the DC tapped in a password, 'and you're right, yes, it's a dating app. EHU, acronym for Elite Hook Ups. I want to show you something.'

'OK.'

I frowned, squinting at the screen. DC Stevens had clearly logged in and was now swiping rapidly up and down a list of what looked like dozens of profiles. Photographs of men, some close-up head shots, others full-length, men in football kit, in tennis whites, in suits. The ...

'Oh my GOD. What ... that's ... that's *Danny*!'

DC Stevens stopped swiping, and tapped on the photograph, enlarging it, then turned to look at me. I ignored him, my heart beginning to pound, staring at the screen, my whole body suddenly feeling weak. The name next to the photograph said it was somebody called Sean. But ... it was Danny. My Danny, smiling at me from the tablet, wearing his favourite red T-shirt. A selfie, by the look of it, the top of his arm visible, outstretched, chin tilted towards the camera. My husband, Danny.

'I-I-I'm sorry, I just don't understand. Why is he on there? I mean, we met online, on Tinder, but that was the only site either of us had ever used, and we both came off it as soon as we started dating ...'

Even I could hear the desperation in my voice. I swallowed hard. *Please, please, let all this be a horrible mistake. A joke. Call it a joke. It's not funny, but I'll laugh anyway. Just tell me ...*

DS Clarke was talking again, quietly, his tone soothing.

'Gemma, we know all this is a lot to take in. I need to explain something to you, and it's going to be worrying, OK, but I don't want you to panic, because we don't know anything for definite, right? It's just one avenue we're going down, just something we're looking into. So just stay calm, OK? Take a deep breath.'

I tried to do as he'd asked, but my breath caught in my chest, jagged and painful. I rubbed my eyes, trying to focus.

'I'm OK. Just tell me, please, whatever it is. I'm having a hard time trying to process all this ... the job, the bank account stuff, and now this website ... it's just making no sense. None.'

The DS grimaced.

'Trust me, we're struggling almost as much as you must be. OK, so this is our concern. Have you heard about the two recent murders in the Clifton area? One about a month ago, one last week? Two young men?'

I frowned, trying to think, my mind blank. I hadn't watched the television news in weeks, and I rarely checked the online news sites anymore. I shook my head.

'No, sorry. I don't keep up with the news as religiously as I used to – I used to be a news reporter, but it just makes me anxious now, with all the horrible things going on in the world. And we've been so busy, since we moved in ...' I gasped, as my brain finally took in what he'd said, and what it might mean. 'Hang on – two murders? Men? Do you think Danny's been *murdered*?'

The shivering had started again, my hands suddenly freezing cold.

No. Please, no.

DS Clarke was shaking his head.

'No, look, honestly, it's just a theory, a possibility. We've just discovered that the two men who died, who were killed, were both users of this EHU app. That could just be a coincidence, we have nothing concrete to link the two murders at the moment, other than a few vague similarities between the two crime scenes. But ...'

He was fumbling inside a flap at the back of his notebook, pulling out two photographs. He held them up. They were pictures of two men, both maybe early thirties, both with dark hair, dark eyes. I stared, the cold creeping up into my chest now, and then dragged my eyes back to the tablet, to Danny's face.

'Is that them?' My voice was barely a whisper.

'Yes. Do you see why I'm showing you these?' DS Clarke's voice was low too, compassionate. 'It's because they look ... well, they all look quite similar, don't they?' he said. 'A certain ... well, a certain *type*, I suppose. And when we saw the photo you gave us, of your husband, well, we noticed the resemblance immediately. So, even though it was a long shot, we thought we'd just check, just in case. Check the website I mean, to see if Danny might be registered too. To see if it might be more than a coincidence. And, as you can see ...' He gestured towards the photo of Danny on the screen.

I swallowed again. My throat felt as if it were closing up, as if, if they told me anything else, piled any more of this incomprehensible information into my brain, I might actually stop breathing.

'Hang on, so you think ... you think that somebody might be killing men who use this app? Men who look like that ... who look like Danny? And two have been killed already, and now Danny's gone missing, and you think that he might ... might have been killed too? Why though? Why would some-body do that?'

DS Clarke was shaking his head, splaying his hands in a vague gesture I somehow interpreted as *who knows?*

'As I said, we just don't know. We have no proof, no evidence. And, of course, no third body. Danny is, we hope, still alive and well and out there somewhere. But it's a possibility, that's all. It's not something we'd normally ... well, normally I wouldn't worry the family with something like this. But this is such an unusual case, and we thought that maybe, if you knew, you might be able to shed some light ...' He sighed. 'I'm so sorry. Don't dwell on it, please. There's every chance your husband will still turn up. And until we can find anything that says otherwise, we have to assume he hasn't come to any harm, OK? But, just to confirm ...' he pointed a finger at DC Stevens's tablet, now closed and resting on his knee, 'you didn't know, then? That he had a profile on that site?'

He had the good grace to look a little sheepish as he asked the question, not quite meeting my eye. DC Stevens was staring at his own shoes.

I took a breath.

'No, I did not know that my husband had a profile on a dating website,' I said, with as much dignity as I could muster. *Of course I didn't bloody know. What's going on, Danny? What the hell is going on?* 'And I don't understand it, any of it. Danny wasn't ... wasn't shagging around, I'm sure he wasn't.'

Even as I said the words, I felt new doubts creeping in. *Were you, Danny? Were you?* But I couldn't think about that now, couldn't let myself.

'Look, maybe somebody else put his profile on there. One of his mates? For some sort of silly joke? Danny probably doesn't even know his picture is on there,' I said.

The two police officers exchanged looks again, and both nodded.

'That's true, it certainly could have happened like that,' DC Stevens said.

'I suppose so, yes. Certainly a possibility. This case gets curiouser and curiouser,' DS Clarke replied unexpectedly, then stood up abruptly.

'Right, we'll get out of your way. I'm sorry, again, that we've had to land all this on you. But we're a little bit stuck on this one, Gemma, I don't mind telling you. We simply can't work out what's happened to Danny, and what was going on in his life in the weeks before he vanished. The job, his bank account, this app ... look, if you can think of anything, anything at all, that might explain some of it, please call, OK? Any time. And maybe, can I suggest, get someone to come and stay with you for a few days? A friend, a relative? It's a lot to cope with on your own.'

Still a little stunned by his *Alice in Wonderland* reference, I gaped up at him. DC Stevens was on his feet now too, shuffling towards the door, seemingly anxious to leave now that he'd thrown a live grenade into my living room and let it explode, leaving me to deal with the agonizing aftermath. What the *hell* was I supposed to do now?

'Yes,' I said. 'I think I might do that.'

Chapter 8

'This is just getting more and more bizarre.'

Helena was standing in front of the incident board, cradling her second cup of tea of the morning and frowning. Next to her, Devon popped the final sliver of his pain au chocolat into his mouth and turned to put his plate down on the desk behind them.

'And where did you get that anyway? Surely not downstairs? It actually looked edible. Although you eat far too much sugar, Devon. It's not good for you, you know. Your diet's gone to pot since Jasmine left you.'

He shrugged, swallowing.

'Don't care. Needed something to cheer me up. Picked it up on my way in. That little bakery round the corner? It opens at six. You should try it, instead of eating all those boring salads. Might help.'

Helena grimaced.

'Charlotte makes them for me. I don't like to say no. But even I might have to turn to comfort food one of these days, the way this is going.'

She rubbed the small of her back as she spoke, and winced.

'And sorry. I shouldn't have mentioned Jasmine. I'm an idiot. Are you OK?'

He shrugged again.

'I'm fine. Don't worry about it. I'll be back on the horse soon. And when are you going to see someone about that back?'

'Soon. When this is all over.'

'Yeah, yeah. And I just saw a cute little piggy flying past that window over there.'

He turned away and began picking up the sheaf of papers he'd dumped on the desk earlier, shuffling them into some sort of order, and Helena watched him, her heart twisting suddenly. For all his bravado, he was definitely hurting. He'd fallen hard for Jasmine, a bright, ambitious medical registrar he'd met while interviewing a stabbing victim at Southmead Hospital, and who he'd been dating for the past year or so; he'd even, when Helena had joined him and some of the other detectives for a rare night in the pub a few months back, confided in her after several vodkas that he was considering proposing, once Jasmine had completed her training.

'Maybe on the day she qualifies, something like that. What do you think, guv? Think she'd say yes?'

Helena had smiled.

'She'd be mad not to. Catch like you? Course she'll say yes.'

What had actually happened was what so often happened in relationships between two people with such demanding jobs; the long hours, the constant weariness and the repeated enforced cancellation of plans to meet up that came as standard with both police and big city hospital work had taken their toll. Devon and Jasmine, it seemed, had simply drifted apart, until she had finally called time on the relationship.

'Ready, guv?'

Devon had finished organizing his paperwork and was looking at her expectantly.

'Ready, yes. Let's take stock.'

She gestured at the board.

'And we all need to get our thinking caps on, because this lot is doing my head in. Do we have a potential serial killer, or just two separate murders? Is someone targeting men who look alike and finding them by using a particular dating app, although I can't for the life of me think why, or is that app irrelevant, just a coincidence? Why was the app not on either of our victims' phones, even though they were both users of it? And is Danny O'Connor just a missing person, or a third victim? Frankly, I have no clue.'

Devon shrugged.

'Me neither guv. Let's do this.'

He turned to the room.

'Guys! Gather round. Meeting.'

When everyone was settled, Helena nodded at the DS.

'Go ahead.'

'OK, let's run through what we have so far,' he said. 'First – our two murders. No new leads in the past couple of days, on either Mervin Elliott or Ryan Jones, other than the intriguing discovery that both of them used the same dating app, EHU. Great work on that, Mike.'

Perched on the edge of a desk towards the back of the room, DC Mike Slater flushed and nodded.

'Any progress on getting the EHU people to provide us with any more details on women our victims might have dated?'

Mike shook his head. 'I've asked, and they're being very helpful, but they said they've had a few system crashes recently, probably due to the site getting more and more popular. They're not sure all the search data has been saved. But they've also said they'll have to check it all out with their legal people, even if this is a major double murder investigation. You know, the new data protections laws and all that? Should know in the next day or so though. I'll keep chasing. And our tech guys are still going through the victims' emails and texts again to see if they can trace any of the women they dated through the site. I'll let you know if they find anything.'

'Cheers, Mike.'

Helena, who was standing to the side of the board, leaning against the wall, smiled at the DC and said: 'Yes, well done again, Mike. And we're keeping this EHU app thing from the press for now, guys, OK? I mean, we still don't know if the two murders are linked, as we need to keep reminding ourselves. Anyone have any theories on that, by the way? Shoot, if you do.'

She paused, as a low murmur ran around the room.

'I might have one. I mean, it's probably bollocks, but hey ...'

DC Tara Lemming, a tall woman with striking coal-black hair pulled back into a bouncy ponytail, and deep green eyes, had raised a hand.

'OK Tara, let's hear it.'

Tara stood up.

'Well, it's just with both of our victims, and now this missing guy as well, Danny, all using the EHU app, and all looking so alike, well ... we all have a *type*, don't we? A type we go for? Mine, for example, is tall and blond.'

She turned to look at DC Matthew Shawcross, who was sitting beside her and who also happened to be six foot five inches tall with cropped, white blond hair, and winked. There was a ripple of laughter, and Matthew blushed.

'OK, OK, let's stick to the topic at hand. Go on, Tara.'

Helena waved a hand, and the room fell silent again.

'Sorry. But my point is, our victims, plus Danny O'Connor, well, they're all a definite *type*, aren't they? I mean, if someone was on a dating site searching for dark-haired, dark eyed, fit, slim but sporty men in their thirties, they'd all pop up, wouldn't they? So what if our killer is a woman, who for some reason has a violent dislike of men who fit that description? Maybe she was a victim of domestic abuse or just badly treated in a relationship by someone who looked like that or something, I dunno. What if she's a member of that dating site too, and she's hunting them down and killing them, one by one? I mean, that's just me wildly speculating, and I know most serial killers are men, that is if we *are* dealing with a serial killer of course, but, well ... it was just a thought,' she finished lamely.

There was silence for a moment.

'It's certainly a theory. And one that would mean our killer also has a profile on the EHU app,' said DC Slater from the back of the room.

'How many people are registered, Mike?' Devon asked.

'They wouldn't tell me. Data protection again blah blah blah. But tens of thousands, I'd say. It's growing by the day. And if we can't access any of their data to narrow it down ...'

There was silence again.

'Yeah. Impossible. Probably a bollocks theory anyway, as I said,' said Tara.

She sat down again, and Helena stood in silence for a moment, thinking. Her gut feeling was still that this was a male killer, despite telling herself firmly not to rule anything out. But women did kill too. She wondered if she should consider the possibility a little more closely.

'Possibly bollocks, but maybe not. We can't discount anything at the moment. Thank you, Tara,' Helena said. 'We have to keep an open mind about this entire investigation, until hard evidence takes us in a particular direction. Anyone else?'

She glanced around the room, at a sea of blank faces.

'OK. Carry on, Devon.'

'Sure.'

Devon turned back to the board and pointed at the photograph of Danny O'Connor, which had been pinned to the far right-hand side.

'So – Danny O'Connor. Sounded like a straightforward misper at first, despite his strong physical resemblance to our two murder victims. But now that we've discovered he also had a profile on EHU, despite apparently being happily and fairly recently married, we're looking into his disappearance a little more closely ourselves, instead of handing it over to Missing Persons.'

He picked up a piece of paper from the desk in front of him.

'Obviously, we have no evidence he's come to any harm, not at the moment. He does seem to have pretty much vanished into thin air though, and our efforts to trace him so far have drawn a blank. He doesn't have a mobile phone currently, according to his wife, so that stops us being able to find him via that, and there are definitely a few oddities here. With regard to the EHU app, Gemma was pretty horrified when we told her about it yesterday. She flatly denied any possibility that he could have been, as she put it, "shagging around". She suggested that somebody, one of his mates, might have put his profile on the site as some sort of joke. And she's right, that could be what happened. We don't really have any way of knowing how it got on there – did Danny register himself, or did someone else do it for some sort of stupid wind up? We need to talk to his friends, ask them if they know anything about it, and try to find out if Danny has been up to anything his wife might not know about. Mike, can you take care of that too? Be discreet though, don't mention the app. We don't want anything about that discovery getting out at the moment. Just ask them if they think there's any possibility he might have been playing around. And also check out the email address he used on his profile on the site, see what we can get from that?'

From the back of the room, DC Slater gave him the thumbs up sign.

'No problem.'

'Great, thanks. We'll continue to leave his family in Ireland out of it for now, don't want to panic them unnecessarily. We'll obviously need to speak to them at some point fairly soon though if he doesn't turn up. OK, a couple of other strange things. The fake job – where did Danny go every weekday between Monday, the eleventh of February when he said he was starting his new job, and Thursday, the twenty-eighth of February, which was the last day his wife saw him? He didn't drive, so wherever he went he was using his bike. Gemma O'Connor says she has absolutely no idea. But the guy couldn't make himself invisible. Somebody, somewhere must know where he was spending all those hours every day.'

He pointed to two new photos on the board, under the image of Danny.

'We took these yesterday afternoon when we visited Gemma. They live in a very nice house in Clifton, and this is the back courtyard, where O'Connor kept his bike. And this is the alleyway that runs behind the row of houses, so he would have gone out through that back gate and cycled along there every day to access the main road. Our problem is that there aren't any CCTV cameras in the immediate vicinity, so we're trying to pick him up on private cameras, those used by homes and businesses in the area. Not knowing which direction he was going is problematic of course, because we're going to have to cast the net wide, which will take time.'

Helena spoke again.

'And again, where he was going every day might well be irrelevant to our enquiry. It could be anything, and if he was just having an affair or whatever, taking some time out from work, having some sort of breakdown, well, all very sad but none of our business. Tough thing to say, but it's really only if he's dead too that he's any concern of ours, otherwise we can hand him back to Missing Persons. But with the dating app connection, we do need to pursue it for now, see if it can throw up any leads. Was he meeting someone? He's now vanished, so did that person hurt him in some way? Kill him? And maybe kill the others too? We need to find out ... yes, what is it?'

Another hand had been raised, that of a short, ginger-haired officer whose name escaped Helena.

'I was just thinking – I mean, we don't want to panic anyone, obviously. But just assuming for now that the two murders *are* connected, and Danny O'Connor *is* a third victim, well ... there were what, another nine, ten men on that EHU site who all came up in the same search, weren't there? Isn't it possible that they're all at risk too, if someone really is bumping them off one by one for some weird reason? Should we be warning them?'

Helena ran a hand across her forehead. She could feel a headache starting.

'It's far too early for anything like that. We still don't know what's going on here, and if the dating app really has any link to the murders. So, no. If we made an announcement like that, there'd be mass hysteria ... every man in Bristol with dark hair and dark eyes would be after police protection.'

There was silence in the room, and Helena sighed.

'Look, I hope I'm not making the wrong call here. But there may be something else that connects our victims that we haven't discovered yet, and of course we still don't know if

Danny is dead or alive. We could be barking up the wrong tree entirely, and until the picture becomes clearer I don't think it would benefit anyone to start warning people about a potential serial killer who's using a dating app to pick his, or her, victims. Everyone OK with that, for now?'

There was a murmur of assent, heads nodding. Helena turned to Devon again.

'Go on, finish what we have so far on Danny.'

'Right. So, there's the non-job and the mystery about where he was spending his days, and his appearance on the EHU app. The other strange aspect is the financial one. No money's gone into his bank account since his final pay check from his job in London, which is as expected as it seems now he probably wasn't working in Bristol, so we wouldn't expect any deposits. But no money has left his account either, not since the thirty-first of January. No cash withdrawals, no purchases, nothing. And yet his wife says he paid for any number of things since he joined her in Bristol – takeaways, furniture and so on. If he wasn't taking money from his bank account, where was it coming from?'

There was silence for a moment, the assembled officers clearly thinking. Then:

'Another bank account, a secret one his wife didn't know about?'

'Maybe he was working cash in hand for those three weeks? Something dodgy, off the books?'

Devon nodded, acknowledging the suggestions.

'Yes, both possible. We can definitely look into the alternative bank account theory right now ... Tara, do you want to take that on? Call around as many as you can? The current and savings accounts we know about are with NatWest, so try the others. Whether they'll release confidential information at this stage though, I don't know. Danny O'Connor isn't a criminal – well, not as far as we know anyway – and we don't have any evidence he's actually in danger. Still, give it a go.'

Tara nodded, her ponytail bobbing.

Devon turned to Helena.

'And that's where we are, for now. We're going to search the O'Connor house, this afternoon probably, just in case that throws up anything, and then—'

'Boss!'

The door had just opened, and a young officer was striding across the room towards them, an excited expression on his face.

'Yes, David? What is it?'

Devon and Helena took a simultaneous step forward.

'Got something to tell you. Something very odd indeed.' He was slightly out of breath, and he paused, gulping in air.

'OK, go on.' Helena moved closer.

'Right. Well, we've been checking private CCTV footage for any sign of Danny O'Connor, as you know. There aren't many cameras in the area, and nothing's come up as yet, but we're still working on it. But while we were at it, we thought we'd check out the neighbours, just to see if any of them had seen him cycling past every day, you know – if they noticed which direction he went in, help narrow it down?'

'Good idea,' said Devon. 'And?'

David took another deep breath.

'Well, that's the thing. We managed to speak to the people who live either side of the O'Connors. And they said – *both* lots said the same thing – well, they said something we didn't expect.'

He paused again, turning to the room and looking from one expectant face to another.

'They said that as far as they were aware, they only had *one* new neighbour. They've never seen a man at the property, not even once. They said that, as far as they knew, Gemma O'Connor moved into that house alone.'

Chapter 9

'They won't be much longer. Sorry, I know this isn't very nice. It's important though, you know? They might find something that might help find your husband.'

The plain-clothes police officer sitting opposite me smiled, looking at me kindly with her dark eyes, and I nodded, slipping my hands around my coffee mug again, seeking comfort from its warmth. We were at my kitchen table, and through the open doorway I could hear drawers being opened in the lounge, heavy footsteps crossing the master bedroom upstairs, the low rumble of voices as the three officers who were currently searching my house conferred.

'Like what?' I asked, more out of politeness than from a real desire for information. I'd had enough, more than enough, unexpected and unwanted information from the police about my husband in recent days and if I heard much more I thought my head might actually explode.

Earlier that morning, desperate to get out of the house which suddenly felt suffocating and claustrophobic, I'd finally decided to call Clare and Tai, telling them something horrible was going on and asking if they happened to be free for coffee.

Despite it being a Tuesday morning, I'd been hopeful; Clare was a freelance bookkeeper, who'd told me she preferred to keep her mornings free and settle down to work after lunch, while Tai was a piano teacher who tended to only be busy from three o'clock onwards on week days, when her pupils were released from school. Clare had immediately invited us both to come to her place, a beautiful three-storey Georgian villa not far from the south end of The Downs, with a stunning view of the Clifton Suspension Bridge. I'd been there once before, when I'd called in to pick Clare up for the second yoga class I'd gone to with the pair of them, and had only seen the long, tiled hallway and huge, clearly recently modernized, gleaming white kitchen, but it had immediately struck me as being incredibly stylish and, almost definitely, worth a fortune.

'This place is AMAZING!' I'd hissed to Tai, who'd also met us there before the walk to yoga, when Clare ran upstairs to grab her mat and handbag.

'I know,' she'd whispered back. 'Her husband, Alex, has family money. Something to do with banking. He only works part-time too, he's a strategy consultant, whatever that is. But they bought this without a mortgage. Lucky, eh?'

'*Very*. Wow.'

That morning, I'd pulled on a thick sweatshirt and jeans and walked to Clare's with Albert, shuddering as I approached Clifton Down, remembering what DS Clarke had told me about the two murder victims. I'd googled them, of course, staring with horror at their photographs in the news articles, seeing their unmistakable similarity to Danny. The previous night, I'd even dreamed about them, dreamed that I was standing, shaking and terrified, over the bodies of two dead men, their corpses stiff on damp grass, mist swirling around us, their sightless eyes fixed on my face, hands rigidly outstretched. I'd woken in a cold sweat, gasping, screaming Danny's name, and had had to run to the bathroom to throw up. Their faces had swum across my vision again as I walked across The Downs to Clare's, my stomach tightening and my footsteps quickening until I was almost jogging. Albert ran alongside me, glancing up at me now and again in what looked like bemusement, unused to such a rapid pace. When we arrived at Clare's though his joy at seeing Winnie was unrestrained, his whole body wagging, little yelps of happiness escaping him, the poodle bouncing with delight too.

Laughing, Clare opened the bifold doors at the rear of the kitchen and the two dogs bounded out and began chasing each other, first one way and then the other, around the walled garden, weaving in and out of tall ornamental grasses and red-leaved Japanese maples. I stood for a moment, watching them, supressing a shiver as images from my dream continued to float through my mind, then took a few deep breaths, forcing myself to calm down, trying to concentrate on the dogs and their antics. They were so funny together. Albert had definitely been subdued since Danny had vanished, and to see him so happy, so carefree, even for a short while, suddenly lifted my spirits a little, a hint of a smile even playing on my lips as the dogs cavorted and yelped.

'So, Gemma, what's going on?'

It was Tai, already sitting on one of the high chrome stools that surrounded the marble-topped kitchen island. She was wearing a denim mini-dress, perfectly shaped, toned legs neatly crossed at the ankles.

'We're worried. What horrible thing is going on?'

'Yes, sit down, Gemma. You look pale. Here, coffee. And I've got cake too, if you want it. A Victoria sponge.'

Clare pushed a steaming mug of coffee across the smooth marble towards me, then added hastily: 'I didn't make it. The cake I mean. My cleaner, Eleanor, dropped it off last night. She does that. Makes a big batch every now and again and then gives them all away. It's delicious, actually.'

She pushed a blonde curl back off her forehead and grinned. I smiled back.

'I'm OK. But thanks. And as for the horrible thing that's going on, well …'

I took a deep breath. Should I be doing this, when I hadn't even told my parents or Danny's mother that he was missing? I was still putting off doing that, hoping against hope that any minute I'd hear his key in the door, but now … suddenly this seemed very real.

'My husband is missing,' I said quietly.

I didn't go into too many details, didn't mention any of the weird stuff I'd discovered since Danny had disappeared; amidst horrified gasps, my two new friends staring at me wide-eyed, I simply told them that when I came back from my press trip on Friday evening my husband had vanished, and that the police were investigating. They bombarded me with questions, of course, and I answered as best I could. No, he wasn't depressed or in any sort of trouble as far as I knew.

No, I had no idea where he might have gone, and no, he'd never gone missing before. No, he didn't take any clothes or his passport. He was just gone, and I was playing a waiting game.

'God, Gemma, this is just awful. I'm so sorry. I was only reading an article the other day about how someone's reported missing in the UK every ninety seconds or something, it's crazy. Look, I know we don't know each other that well yet, but we're here for you, OK? If you need anything, anything at all ...'

Tai reached across and squeezed my arm, and Clare nodded fiercely.

'Absolutely. Call us any time, day or night. What an awful thing to happen. I can't even imagine how I'd feel, if it was Alex.'

I left soon afterwards, feeling a little less alone, a little less numb. Their kindness had brought tears to my eyes, and the hugs they'd given me as we'd said goodbye had been warm and genuine.

But back home, as the police officers arrived to start searching the house, I was still reeling from the bombshells of the previous day, shaky from another night of little sleep. It was all becoming too much, too impossible. Danny pretending to go to work. No money taken out of his bank account for weeks. Danny appearing on a dating app. And two murders. Two dead men. Two victims who looked so similar to my husband, and who had been using the same app before they died. I could no longer think in any sort of logical way, couldn't even begin to process it all. What did it mean? Where was Danny? Was he dead now, too? Why had he lied to me about *so* many things? *Was* he sleeping around, seeing other women, or was his appearance on the dating site just a stupid, juvenile joke by one of his friends? But why? What would be the point? I just couldn't work it out ... and then there was this latest thing, the thing they'd told me earlier, when they'd arrived to start trawling through my cupboards. What had it been again, exactly? That my closest neighbours, both of them, when questioned, had said they thought I'd moved in here *alone*? That they'd never seen or heard anything of Danny, of a husband, living here? I'd tried to recall the few interactions I'd had with our new neighbours, remembering brief 'good mornings', smiles and waves, little more ... but had Danny really never been with me on any of those occasions? He *must* have been, surely? I didn't know, couldn't think, and I was just so *tired* ...

I realized with a start that the police officer sitting at my kitchen table was talking to me, answering my question about what sort of thing the search of my house might throw up that could possibly help, and I tried to drag my attention back to her.

'—Not really sure until they find it, to be honest,' she was saying. 'Sometimes when someone goes missing they just walk away, but some leave evidence of plans they might have. And of course, we don't even know yet what happened in your husband's case – whether he left by choice or whether ... well, whether something unfortunate has happened to him ...' Her voice tailed off and she paused for a moment, picking at a loose thread on her dark grey jacket, then raised her eyes to mine again. 'I really hope that's not the case,' she added. 'Sorry.'

I opened my mouth to reply, to tell her it was fine, when two of the other officers appeared in the doorway. One was DC Frankie Stevens, the one who'd been here with DS Clarke, the other a new one, one I hadn't met before. DC Stevens was brandishing two clear plastic bags, and I squinted, trying to see what was in them, my heartbeat suddenly speeding up.

'We're done, I think, Mrs O'Connor. I think we've left everything pretty much as we found it, but apologies if there's any mess. We haven't found anything that throws any light on your husband's disappearance right now, unfortunately.'

He waved the bags.

'We've grabbed these though, if that's OK? Just in case ... well, in case we need Mr O'Connor's DNA at any point, for elimination purposes? We assumed the green toothbrush was his, the one on the left-hand side of the basin, and this comb? They were alongside the shaving foam and so on.'

I leaned closer to see and nodded.

'Yes, they're Danny's. Take them, that's fine. So ... so what happens now?'

DC Stevens handed the two plastic bags to his colleague and nodded, and the man turned and headed down the hallway.

'We're going to take a quick look at your previous address, in London, just to see if there's anything still there that might help. You said your husband stayed on there for a week or so after you moved down here? Don't suppose you know if it was being rented out again immediately, do you?'

'I don't know but I don't think so. I seem to remember our

landlord saying he was going to give the place a fresh coat of paint first, and I know he was going away for a few weeks after we moved out so I doubt he's got round to it yet. And yes, Danny stayed for a week after me. He had to finish working his notice at his old job and it made sense for me to come ahead, get the basics sorted here. He was due to start his new job pretty much as soon as he got here and I wanted everything to be organized so he wouldn't have to ...' I stopped talking, remembering. 'Well, that's what *I* thought, at the time. What he told me.'

Even I could hear the bitterness in my voice. I felt a sudden, unexpected flicker of anger, and looked from one police officer to the other, my chest tightening.

'I was an idiot, wasn't I? He lied to me about *everything*. What the hell is wrong with me? Why didn't I notice, why didn't I realize something was wrong?'

There were tears in my eyes now, but DC Stevens was shaking his head. He moved a step closer to the table and briefly laid a hand on my shoulder.

'Please, don't blame yourself, Mrs O'Connor. We're at a very early stage of our enquiry here, and none of us know what's behind all this. I mean, yes, there are certainly some ... well, some *peculiarities*. But please, try to stay calm. Sit tight. We're going to try to get to the bottom of it all as soon as we possibly can, OK? Are you still here alone, or is somebody coming to be with you?'

I took a deep breath and pushed a strand of hair off my forehead. I felt clammy now, my armpits damp. I needed to get these people out of my house, needed to be alone, needed to sleep, needed to *think*. I forced myself to look back up at him.

'I saw some friends this morning, and they can be here in minutes if I need them. And my friend Eva's coming to stay. She's coming down from London for a few days. She should be here in an hour or so.'

He nodded his approval.

'Good. It'll help, having some moral support. And we'll probably have to think about telling your husband's family soon too, OK, if he doesn't turn up? And maybe you should think about telling yours as well. But we'll leave that for now. Look, we'll get out of your way. Thank you for being so cooperative. As I said, we're going to go and take a look at your old apartment, tomorrow I hope. We'll keep you posted, OK?'

'Thank you. Thanks so much.'

When they were gone, I moved slowly from room to room, smoothing the Indian cotton bedding – they'd even checked under the mattress, it seemed – straightening cushions, checking that the contents of wardrobes and drawers hadn't been too badly messed up. Somehow the act of methodically restoring order to my home calmed me, my racing heartbeat slowing, my mind clearing a little. OK, so the facts around Danny's disappearance were getting weirder by the hour, but for some reason I still didn't think he was dead, murdered like the two other men. I'd know, deep down, if he was, I was sure of it, and therefore there *had* to be a logical explanation for what had happened, what was still happening. And Eva was coming. The thought buoyed me and, finally satisfied that the police search had done no lasting damage, I headed for the kitchen to check the contents of the freezer. I hadn't been shopping in days and we were all but out of fresh food, but there were a couple of pizzas and wine in the wine rack. We'd manage, for tonight. And Eva ... surely Eva would help me work it out?

We'd been friends for years, since early in my newspaper reporter days, and even when I'd quit hard news, we'd remained close. Eva was still in the job, now a crime reporter for *The Independent*, and she'd covered some hugely complex stories in her time. She'd think of something, wouldn't she? Because there was clearly something, some huge something, that I was missing. Something I hadn't thought of yet, something that would explain why Danny had lied to me about his new job, explain why he'd gone away. Explain all of it.

I picked up my phone, checking once again for a text or email from Danny – nothing, of course – then looked at the time. Nearly five. Eva's train was due in at Temple Meads station at seven, and she'd told me she could probably stay until Thursday or Friday, having just finished a major story and being due a few days off. Two hours – what was I going to do for two hours? Go to bed, try to catch up on some sleep? But I was feeling more awake suddenly, more alert. I put the phone down on the kitchen table and wandered restlessly into the hall, then stopped, horrified, as I caught a glimpse of myself in the big wall mirror. When had I last actually looked at myself properly? My hair, normally falling to my shoulders in soft, natural waves, looked greasy, flat; my skin, free of any make-up, looked deathly pale, except for dark circles like angry purple bruises under my eyes. I looked dreadful and, suddenly knowing exactly how to fill the time until Eva arrived, I headed for the bathroom.

I stood under the blissfully hot water for a long time, letting it massage my painfully tense shoulders, my eyes closed, mind wandering. For some reason, the trip Danny and I had made to Ireland to visit his parents a couple of weeks after we'd got engaged drifted into my thoughts, and for a moment I was back there, in the old farmhouse in Sligo, overlooking the shores of Lough Gill. Always a W. B. Yeats fan, I'd been thrilled to discover that not just the lake, but its tiny island of Innisfree, little more than a rocky outcrop, were visible from our cramped little room under the eaves, Danny's childhood bedroom.

'"I will arise and go now, go to Innisfree",' I'd chanted, as Danny, unpacking his suitcase, frowned, bemused.

'"And a small cabin build there, of clay and wattles made",' I continued, then sighed dramatically. 'Honestly, Danny, you're the one who grew up here! How can you not know one of Yeats's most famous poems? 'The Lake Isle of Innisfree'? Come on!'

He'd grinned at my exasperation.

'I do know it, of course I do. We did it at school. I just don't remember the words, not to just reel them off like you do. I haven't got that sort of brain.'

'You haven't got much of any sort of brain,' I'd muttered, and then squealed as he'd dragged me onto the bed and tickled me until I was helpless with laughter.

The laughter had been in short supply for most of the trip however, and I'd been glad we'd only decided to stay for two nights, citing work we needed to get back to. Danny didn't talk about his childhood much, but I'd definitely got the impression it wasn't the happiest time of his life.

'I don't get on great with my parents,' was all he would ever say, and I hadn't pushed it. If he wanted to tell me about it one day, I'd be there for him, but he clearly didn't want to talk about it then and that was fine. And when I finally met his parents, the animosity between them and their son was immediately obvious. Bridget, a thin, downtrodden-looking woman with a deeply lined face and white hair tied back tightly in a low bun at the nape of her neck, gave me a quick peck on the cheek and a half smile when we arrived, but merely nodded at Danny, her face stiffening again as she looked him up and down. Donal, visually an older version of Danny with thinning grey hair, simply waved at both of us from his armchair, eyes barely moving from the hurling game he was watching on the small television that sat on the sideboard next to him. He was frail from a recent string of illnesses, but nonetheless was a brusque, stern man, a cold look in his eyes as he snapped orders from his corner of the farmhouse kitchen, his wife jumping to do his bidding, her expression hard, as if she was permanently angry at everything and everyone. I'd felt sorry for her, and taken an instant dislike to him, at the same time feeling guilty for feeling like that about my fiancé's elderly, clearly unwell father.

At dinner on our first evening both parents engaged in a little stilted conversation with us, but after that they paid us scant attention; Danny, meanwhile, while virtually ignoring his father and being equally ignored in return, seemed almost pathetically eager to please his mother, repeatedly offering to help her with meal preparation or washing up, and looking crestfallen when she told him she didn't need his assistance. The look on his face at each rejection hurt my heart and made me even more eager to leave the farmhouse at the earliest opportunity.

They were a staunch Catholic family, although Danny had told me not long after we'd met that *he* had lapsed years ago, and had made me giggle when he'd explained the reason for his rather unusual middle name.

'It's after Saint Ignatius,' he'd said. 'He was wounded in some battle and while he was in bed recovering he wanted to read adventure stories, but the only thing available in the hospital was religious stuff and books about saints. So he read those instead, and decided he wanted to do what they had done. Bloody git. Means me and thousands of other poor sods got lumbered with his stupid name.'

The O'Connor family house, spotlessly clean and cosy enough with its dated furniture, sagging sofas and the big old Aga in the kitchen, didn't have a picture of Saint Ignatius that I could find, but it was certainly full of religious imagery. In the hallway, a plaster statue of Jesus, arms outstretched, greeted visitors, while the rest of the house was dominated by paintings and figurines depicting the Madonna and Child, Saint Bernadette ('patron saint of illness', Danny had hissed, one eyebrow raised, as he'd given me the tour), Saint Jude ('he's for desperate causes') and Saint Clare ('eye diseases. And, weirdly, patron saint of laundry and television,' he'd said). Wildly sceptical, I'd googled Saint Clare at the first available opportunity, only to find out he'd been absolutely right. Laundry? Why did laundry need a patron saint?

The reason for the choice of saints soon, however, became clear – Liam. Danny's kid brother was twenty-eight, partially sighted, and suffered from learning difficulties.

'They had kids late; Mam was well into her forties when Liam was born, although maybe that had nothing to do with his problems, who knows,' Danny had told me on one of those early, getting-to-know-you dates. 'He's always lived at home – he's not able to work; he can't even look after himself, not really. I mean, he's a good lad, and he tries – he can just about make a cup of tea, but he can't be trusted with the cooker or anything. Combination of his learning difficulties and his eyesight. I worry, you know, about what will happen to him when Mam and Dad die. I suppose it will work itself out though. Maybe I'll be in a position to look after him by then, or there are some good residential units nowadays. It's not like the old days in Ireland, when those places were like the kind of prisons you'd see in your worst nightmares.'

Having heard so much about him, I'd been looking forward to meeting Liam, but it seemed that Danny was the only O'Connor blessed with warmth and a sense of humour. Liam was definitely more like his parents in personality, and although he threw his arms around his brother, clearly delighted to see him, he barely acknowledged me, grunting a sullen 'Hiya,' when Danny insisted he say hello to his new sister-in-law-to-be. I noticed, though, that Liam was the only family member who seemed to actually like his father, patting

Donal's hair as he passed him, Donal yelling: 'Will ya STOP!' but with a hint of a smile.

'Yeah, they've always got on,' Danny said when I remarked on the fact as we'd snuggled together in bed later that night, trying to get comfortable in rough cotton sheets and scratchy blankets. 'Dad's a miserable bastard, but he's always had a soft spot for Liam. About his only redeeming feature.'

I didn't ask any more questions. Donal was, it seemed to me, simply an unpleasant man who ruled the house with an iron fist, and Bridget, while clearly unhappy, seemed to have a heart of stone. But if Danny didn't want to rake up the past, which he very obviously didn't, then that was fine. Some things were better left alone, I thought, and if Danny had had a tough time at home growing up, well, that was a long time ago and he seemed happy enough now. It wasn't as if we'd be seeing his family regularly, and it was all about the future now, about me and him. That was all that mattered.

Even so, a few weeks later when the news came in the early hours of a cold February morning that Donal had died from a massive stroke, it seemed to hit Danny hard. For weeks afterwards, in the run up to our wedding, he seemed grief-stricken. I never saw him cry – that wasn't Danny's style – but he was quieter, sadder, needing more time alone or, when we *were* together, regularly becoming lost in thought, his face rigid, fists clenched, relaxing only when I wrapped my arms around him, muttering soothing words. That was why I'd been so surprised when he'd announced that we wouldn't be going back to Ireland for the funeral.

'No point,' he said. 'I said goodbye to him when we were

there last month. I don't need to go back again just to see his body being put in the ground. And Mam will be OK, she's got Liam, plenty of extended family. And you know how things are between us, she'd probably prefer it if I wasn't there anyway. I'd be a hypocrite if I went and cried at his funeral, Gem. He's no big loss.'

And so we didn't go, but despite Danny's cold words I could see that the loss of his father had affected him deeply and that it continued to do so, even more than a year on, the same anguish still flashing across his face at odd moments. They're complicated sometimes, family relationships, aren't they? Love and hate, hate and love, so tightly entwined that they almost become one.

None of this was helping me work out where Danny was now though, and with a sudden new sense of resolve I climbed out of the shower and started to towel myself dry. I'd blow-dry my hair, maybe even put on a little make-up, some clean clothes, and then Eva would be here. Two of us, two investigative reporters, even if one of us was somewhat out of the swing of things. Two heads, focused on one problem. Danny hadn't just vanished into thin air, and we could work this out. We *had* to work this out. Somehow, *somehow*, we were going to get to the bottom of it.

Chapter 10

'Should be there in about twenty minutes. Traffic permitting, of course. Might get a bit heavier as we get nearer to junction two.'

DC Frankie Stevens, who was driving, turned his head briefly to glance at Devon, then fixed his eyes on the motorway again.

'Quite possibly,' Devon replied. The M4 had been remarkably quiet, and although they hadn't left Bristol until just before nine, they now expected to arrive at the O'Connors' former home in Chiswick before eleven fifteen, traffic permitting, as Frankie had said. The easy journey had been the one bright spot in a so-far frustrating morning. Before they'd even left police headquarters, the team checking all the private CCTV camera footage from around Gemma and Danny's Bristol home had finally reported their findings.

'Nothing. We've checked the entire forty-eight-hour period around him going missing and we can't see a single person who looks like him, either on a bike or on foot. Although of course that doesn't necessarily mean much. Loads of routes he could have taken that have no cameras on them at all.'

Even so, it had been a blow. The fact that Danny's immediate neighbours had never laid eyes on him had been frustrating enough, but maybe not that surprising in the modern age – Devon didn't think he'd recognize his own next-door neighbours if they came up and punched him. It was another small oddity to add to the growing list of oddities in the Danny O'Connor case though, and another possible lead which had drawn a blank. Devon had been desperately hoping for something, *anything* to come of the CCTV search, and now that had led them down a dead end too.

Is it too much to ask for one little lucky break in this bloody case? he had thought, as he and Frankie left the incident room and headed out to the parking bay where the pool cars were kept. Seemingly, it was *far* too much to ask, as they'd barely reached the Bath junction of the M4 when Devon's mobile trilled. It was DC Mike Slater, who'd been tasked with accessing the search data from the EHU dating app.

'Remember they said their system had been crashing recently?' he'd asked. 'Well, it's back up and running again. But they've lost *all* their search data. Can't get it back. They've apologized, but it looks like there's no way of retrieving it. So that's that. No way of finding who might have searched for men who look like Mervin, Ryan or Danny. Really sorry.'

'Shit!' Devon had replied. Then: 'Sorry, Mike. Not your fault. Thanks for trying anyway. We'll just have to come at this from another angle, although don't ask me what that is right now.'

'OK. Oh, and the tech guys can't find any EHU date related emails on either of the victims' phones either. Must have been deleted, which is bloody annoying, but I suppose people do delete old emails. I know I do. I also checked out the email address on Danny's profile. It doesn't exist, seems to be a fake one, or maybe one that's since been closed down. So maybe adds weight to the theory that his profile was put up on the site as some sort of weird joke?'

'Maybe. Anything else?'

'Oh yes ... Tara checked into the bank account thing. Couldn't find any other accounts in his name with any UK bank. Plenty of Daniel O'Connors but no Daniel *Ignatius* O'Connor, pretty unusual name. She had a closer look at his NatWest account too to see if there've been any unusual transactions or anything in recent months but nothing stood out. No big withdrawals or deposits. Dead end on that too, for now. Sorry.'

Devon had hung up feeling despondent. The investigations into the murders of Mervin Elliott and Ryan Jones had now completely stalled, with no new witnesses or evidence emerging. And now with Danny O'Connor still missing, the whole team was starting to feel helpless. He sighed. Maybe he needed a good night out, a few drinks to take his mind off things, maybe even a date. He thought about that for a few seconds, then changed his mind. He was still in love with Jasmine, that was the problem. He couldn't imagine being with somebody else, and even if some miracle happened and he did meet someone he was interested in, wouldn't the same thing just happen again?

The job isn't getting any less demanding, the hours aren't getting any shorter, he thought. *How does anyone in this profession manage to hold down a relationship, when work's so all-consuming? But they do, don't they? Helena and her wife Charlotte are OK; Frankie's not seeing anyone right now, but he's had more than one long-term relationship over the years. Even Mike Slater's managed to get married, and he seems happy ...*

'Here we go,' Frankie said suddenly, and Devon dragged his attention back to the situation at hand. Up ahead, red tail lights had suddenly flashed on and the traffic slowed.

'Bugger,' said Frankie, and braked.

'Bugger,' agreed Devon.

He leaned back in his seat, trying to focus on the case again. He didn't have time to think about relationships at the moment anyway, not if they really had a serial killer on their hands. The theory had definitely gained ground among the team since the discovery of all three men's profiles on the EHU app; there'd been much talk of historical cases in recent days, and not just those from the UK. The classic serial killer was male, and targeted the vulnerable – the elderly, sex workers, hitchhikers, young women. But there was another, significant group of male serial killers too – those who targeted other men, although they tended to be homosexually motivated murders. Dennis Nilsen, who killed at least twelve men in the UK in the late seventies and early eighties, and the American serial killer Jeffrey Dahmer who murdered seventeen men and boys, were two of the best-known examples. Although they only had two bodies so far, the thought that they might, just might, now have a serial killer on the loose in Bristol had sent a ripple of horror through the incident room, and the DCI had been quick to quash the theory.

'Come on, get a grip, guys,' she'd said. 'We have zero evidence at the moment that the deaths of Mervin and Ryan are linked, and we don't even have a third body yet. Yes, the dating app connects the three, but it's the only thing that does, and that could still be coincidence. Probably is, in fact, seeing as tens of thousands of people seem to be using the flipping thing. So calm down on the serial killer theory, OK? We deal in facts, and facts only.'

Her tone hadn't been entirely convincing though, and Devon knew Helena well enough to know that, deep down, she was thinking the same as the rest of them. The team had stopped their discussions, but the sense of unease had remained. They all knew, from the latest available research on serial killers, that most had a vision of their ideal victim, and that that was often based on characteristics like gender and physical appearance. In America, the so-called 'Green River Killer' chose prostitutes as his victims, because he felt the police 'wouldn't look for them as hard as they'd look for other women'. Anders Breivik, the man who killed seventy-seven people at a Norwegian summer camp in 2011, selected victims who had a 'leftist' look, in his own words. Was it so far-fetched, then, to think that somebody in Bristol was, for some bizarre and unknown reason, tracking down and bumping off dark-haired, dark-eyed men in their thirties, when they already had two victims who fitted the bill and another who had vanished?

But then again, some of them had argued, would Danny O'Connor really turn out to be victim number three? His disappearance had some distinctly odd elements to it, Devon thought, as he gazed out of the window at the stationary lorry in front of them on the motorway, 'WASH ME' smeared in the grey dirt that covered its chassis. Yes, Danny's disappearance had features that the previous two cases didn't, and nobody could quite put the pieces together just yet. He'd clearly been up to something in the weeks before he vanished, but what? Why lie to his wife and pretend to be working in a new job when he wasn't? Where had he been spending his days? And he'd obviously been keeping a very low profile even when he *was* at home, if both sets of immediate neighbours had never laid eyes on him, and assumed that Gemma had moved in alone. Was he hiding from somebody? Was he in some sort of trouble that he couldn't share with his wife, with anybody? Why had he not been using his bank account in recent weeks? And, the biggest question of all in some ways, why was a man who was fairly recently and seemingly happily married popping up on a dating website? Using phone numbers provided by Gemma O'Connor on the missing person information sheet, Mike had managed to speak to a few of Danny's friends the previous night, and each one had expressed first amusement, and then absolute bafflement, at the very idea of him 'playing away' as Mike had delicately put it.

'As requested, I didn't mention the EHU app,' he'd told Devon. 'But I did ask them if he might ever have been unfaithful to Gemma, if he was a bit of a lad, you know? Emphatic "no" from every one of them. They all said that, like most blokes, he'd had his share of girlfriends and one-night stands in the past, but that as soon as he met Gemma that was it, he was ready to settle down. Interestingly none of them has spoken to him in weeks though – said they assumed he was busy with his new job and the move et cetera. Looks like this low profile he seems to have been keeping extended to his mates too.'

No, none of it made any sense whatsoever, but Devon knew from years of experience that, eventually, it was possible to unravel most mysteries. It was just a matter of perseverance, and that elusive lucky break. As he thought that, the traffic suddenly started moving again, and ten minutes later Frankie was sliding the car into a parking space outside number 10 Homefield Avenue, just off Chiswick High Road.

'This is it,' he said. 'Landlord should be meeting us here with the keys any minute now.'

Number 10 was halfway along a tidy looking Victorian terrace. Period houses lined one side of the street, but the other was a mix of old and ultramodern, and the former home of Danny and Gemma O'Connor was a two-storey, white-painted apartment block with chrome-framed windows and a large number ten in shiny stainless steel fixed to the wall. The railings that separated the property from the street had been painted red, and aluminium planters filled with yellow crocuses lined the short path to the front door.

'Nice place,' muttered Devon.

'Gents? Good morning!'

There was a tap at the passenger side window, making him jump. He turned to see a short, rotund man in a black leather jacket, the zip straining over a rounded belly. He was clutching a large bunch of keys, which he waved at Devon.

'I'm Edgar Evans, the landlord?' he said loudly.

Devon and Frankie got out of the car, and for the next thirty seconds or so were subjected to a monologue delivered in a broad Welsh accent by a slightly breathless, pink-cheeked Edgar Evans.

'I've not been in at all since they left – been on a few weeks' holiday. I wasn't worried though – they were model tenants, the O'Connors. Place was always immaculate when I popped round, not that I did very often, I'm not that sort of landlord, but you know, if they ever had a problem, the boiler playing up or something. Oh yes, good tenants, the O'Connors. They'll have left it spick and span, no doubt about that. Now that I'm back, a quick fresh coat of paint and maybe a carpet clean and it'll be ready for some new renters. I've got two nice big apartments here, one upstairs and one down, the downstairs people moved out just before the O'Connors so I thought it was a good time to smarten the whole place up, you know? I was sorry to hear about Mr O'Connor going missing though. That's a worry, isn't it? Anything I can do to help ... shall we go in then?'

'Please,' Devon said, with some relief, as Frankie smirked beside him. Moments later, Mr Evans was sliding a key into the front door and pushing it open, kicking aside a large pile of envelopes on the doormat.

'Bloody junk mail,' he said. He turned to the two officers and proffered a key, holding it clear of the rest of the bunch.

'You go on, do what you have to do. It's the upstairs apartment you want. I'll just clear this lot and then join you.'

Devon thanked him, took the keys and led the way up the

wide, carpeted stairway. Moments later they were entering the apartment, Frankie flicking on lights as they moved down the hallway, peering into each room.

'Let's do a quick sweep first, then go through each room properly,' Devon suggested, and Frankie nodded.

The place had clearly been let part-furnished; in the big, open-plan living and dining area the walls, one an expanse of exposed red brick, were bare of pictures, and no curtains hung at the floor-to-ceiling windows, but a huge, denim-blue suede sofa and low white coffee table remained in the centre of the expanse of polished oakwood flooring, and in the stylish, battleship grey kitchen three tall bar stools with red leather seats were lined up against the breakfast bar.

The bathroom had a walk-in double shower and shiny chrome fittings, and in a bedroom which had clearly been used as a home office a desk sat against one wall, opposite a large empty bookcase.

'So this last room must be the master bedroom,' Frankie muttered, as he pushed open the final door.

'HOLY SHIT!'

'What the ...?'

The two men gasped simultaneously, Frankie reflexively grabbing onto Devon's forearm, as a faint metallic tang hit their nostrils and they stared uncomprehendingly at the scene in front of them.

'Is that ... is that what I think it is? Sorry,' Frankie stuttered, and slowly released Devon's arm.

Devon was still staring, suddenly feeling a creeping, cold sensation like an icy hand running over his skin. The room was large and bright, light streaming in from French windows through which he could see a balcony or terrace, enclosed by glass walls. He stared out into the sunshine for a moment, then slowly, reluctantly, dragged his gaze back to ... to what? Was this ... was this what *he* thought it was too? *Could* it be? The bedroom looked like a scene from a horror film. White walls, streaked with sweeping brownish-red stains; a jagged, brown river trailing across the carpet; a dark, dry pool on the mattress. His stomach lurched, and he cast his eyes around the room, trying to make sense of what he was seeing. It was. It couldn't be anything else. He turned to Frankie, who was standing stock-still, white-faced, transfixed.

'It's blood,' he whispered. 'Blood. Pints of it. Everywhere. What the *hell* has happened in this room?'

Chapter 11

'Cereal? Oh ... hang on, no milk. Sorry, Eva ...'

Eva, who'd just plonked herself down at the kitchen table, waved a hand dismissively.

'Just black coffee for now, honestly. We'll go out in a bit and get you stocked up. Take Albert for a stroll. He was rather too full of energy this morning when he barrelled into my room and tried to lick me to death, he needs to walk some of it off. And I don't really do breakfast anyway, you should know that.'

She grinned at me, flicking her long red hair back over her shoulders, and winked one of her greeny-brown eyes.

'Yeah, I remember, sorry,' I said, smiling back at her, then turned to put the kettle on and find a clean mug. I *had* forgotten, briefly, the events of the previous few days clearly turning my brain to mush. For most of the years I'd known her, Eva had been strictly a black-coffee-and-cigarettes-only-before-midday kind of girl. The cigarettes had vanished in recent times, but the coffee habit remained.

In the end, she hadn't arrived until nearly midnight the previous night, two cancelled trains and then long delays on the one that *did* arrive making her journey from London a long and tedious one. Restless and unable to settle down to work or even watch television, I'd filled the waiting time by doing something that in retrospect I slightly regretted – I'd paid my neighbours a visit. Unable to stop thinking about what the police had said about my immediate neighbours thinking I'd moved into our house alone, I'd checked the time – just before nine, so late but not *too* late to knock on a stranger's door, I hoped – pulled on a jacket and headed out, knocking first on the door of the house to the right, where I'd occasionally seen and waved to an older woman when our arrivals and departures had coincided. She opened the door slowly, peering around it with a frown, her face relaxing as she recognized me.

'Hi, I'm Gemma – I live next door?'

She nodded, pushing a loose strand of hair back off her forehead. She looked about sixty, long greying hair pulled back into a low ponytail.

'Yes, hello. Sorry, I'm Jo. What can I help you with?'

I paused, not really knowing how to explain. *Just say it, I suppose*, I thought.

'It's just … well, I know the police have been to see you? My husband, Danny, has gone missing. I haven't seen him since last Thursday. And the police said that when they came to ask if you'd seen him around at all recently, you said … well, you said you'd *never* seen him. That you thought I'd moved in next door alone. Is that right?'

Jo narrowed her eyes slightly, then nodded.

'Well … yes,' she said. 'I mean, I've seen you coming in

and out a few times. But there's never been anyone with you. So I just assumed, you know ... I mean, I'm sorry, I just did.'

Her accent was broad Bristolian. I thought for a moment. It was true that Danny did generally come and go via the back door, because of his bike. Maybe I *hadn't* ever been with him when I'd seen Jo.

'He comes and goes through the back mostly,' I said. 'He cycles, and he keeps his bike out in the courtyard; there's a little bike shelter thing out there. You never saw him out there, or in the lane behind? He's tall, dark curly hair.'

She was shaking her head.

'I don't use that lane. Spooks me a bit, especially at this time of year – no lights, you know? Silly, I know, I mean it's a nice area and everything and nothing's ever happened to anyone along there, but it's just me. I always use the front door. I'm really sorry, I've just never seen him. I'm sorry he's gone missing, though. If there's anything I can do?' She shrugged.

'Oh, that's very kind, thank you. And sorry to knock so late. I'll leave you in peace. Do you know the names of the people on the other side, there? It's a couple, isn't it?'

I gestured to the house to the left of ours, and Jo peered out into the darkness, then nodded.

'Yes, that's Jenny and Clive's. They're away quite a lot but you might be lucky.'

I thanked her and walked the short distance down the path, along the pavement and through a creaky metal gate to Jenny and Clive's door. I'd seen them less frequently than I'd seen Jo since we'd moved in, on maybe just three or four occasions, and again it had just been a friendly wave or 'good morning'. Suddenly feeling that all of this was a little pointless, I pressed the doorbell and waited. Thirty seconds or so later a light came on in the hallway and the door was opened by a short, completely bald man in a checked shirt.

'Yes?' he said, tersely.

'Oh, hello, I'm Gemma O'Connor – I moved in next door a few weeks ago? I was just wondering ...'

'Oh, yes. Sorry, I didn't recognize you,' he interrupted. 'We've had the police round here, asking about you. Well, about somebody called, what was it? Daniel?'

'Danny. My husband, Danny. He's gone missing,' I said.

He stared at me for a moment, giving me time to note that he had very long eyelashes for a man who otherwise seemed to be distinctly follicly challenged.

'Yes, so I hear.' His tone was less terse now, warmer. 'That must be horrible. We couldn't help though, I'm afraid. We remembered seeing *you* a couple of times in the past few weeks, but not your husband, I'm afraid. To be honest, we're not around that much – I travel a lot for work and Jenny, that's my wife, she doesn't like to be in the house on her own, so she often goes to stay with her sister in Winchester when I'm away. So we couldn't recall seeing him, your husband I mean, at all. Not much help, sorry.'

'That's OK. If you're away a lot ... and we've only been here a few weeks. It's nice to meet you properly, anyway. Sorry to disturb.'

He smiled, showing crooked front teeth.

Jackie Kabler

'Not a problem. I hope he turns up soon. We'll have to get together, maybe? Have a drink?'

I smiled back, even though my stomach was twisting.

Danny, where are you?

'That would be nice. And thank you.'

Back in the house I walked straight to the kitchen and unlocked the back door, stepping out into the dark courtyard, my mind racing. How often *did* Danny use the front door? Never on a week day, when he used his bike to go to work ... I corrected myself. To go *wherever he was going*. And in February, it had still been dark when he'd left in the morning, often before seven, and was dark again when he arrived home, rarely before six, sometimes several hours later. Unless somebody was looking out of one of the rear windows of their house, and peering down into our yard, at those exact moments of his departure or arrival ... and even if they were, would they actually have been able to see him, in the dark? There *was* outdoor lighting, which would be lovely in the summer when we were sitting outside in the evenings, but we hadn't used it since we'd moved in, apart from switching it on once to check it was all working. And, as Jo had pointed out, there were no streetlights in the lane that ran behind the houses, and even if the kitchen lights were on, they cast just a faint glow into the back yard. So maybe not surprising then, that none of our close neighbours had seen him come and go. As I stood there, thinking, a movement from up above caught my eye, a shape at one of the upstairs windows next door, Jenny and Clive's house. Clive? I lifted a hand to wave at him, but the shape moved abruptly away from the window

122

again, and seconds later the light in the room was turned off. I stared at the dark rectangle for a moment – *had he been watching me?* – then turned my thoughts back to Danny.

What about weekends? Wouldn't somebody have seen him then? I walked back inside, locking the door behind me. *Although, thinking about it, Danny's only been here for three weekends so far, hasn't he?* I thought. And most of that time we had spent indoors, emptying boxes, arranging furniture, painting walls. It had been me who had gone out to do the weekly Saturday morning supermarket run, and we hadn't even been out for dinner since we'd moved in, instead trying out the local food delivery services – Mexican, Indian, Thai.

'Once this place is sorted, we'll have more time. I'll treat you to a massive blow-out in the fanciest place in Bristol,' Danny had said.

So, I reasoned, checking my phone to see if Eva had messaged again, wondering what time she'd finally arrive ... so, maybe it wasn't so peculiar at all that the neighbours had never laid eyes on Danny. And what difference did it make, really? He was missing. He was gone.

When Eva had finally appeared, practically falling out of her taxi outside the house in her efforts to haul her bag out of it with one hand and pull me in for a hug with the other, she'd been exhausted, worn out by the stress of getting her latest big story finished before her deadline and by her long, frustrating journey from London. I'd bundled her off to bed in the spare room, telling her to get a good night's sleep and that I'd fill her in on everything that had been going on in the morning, and she'd reluctantly agreed.

'We'll get to the bottom of it, Gem. I promise we will, OK?' she'd said, squeezing my hands and planting a kiss on my forehead.

After a solid eight hours' sleep, she looked refreshed, her hair still damp from the shower, cheeks glowing, her curves wrapped in a black velvet dressing gown. I handed her the steaming mug of coffee and sat down opposite her, reaching for a coaster and putting my own mug of peppermint tea down on it. I'd had so much caffeine in recent days I was starting to feel jittery.

'God, it's good to see you, Eva Hawton,' I said. 'I've missed you.'

'Missed you too, buddy. Can't believe you've moved to the wilds of the West Country. Still, it's a nice place to escape to at weekends. That's if the frigging trains are working, of course,' she said, and reached across the table to touch my hand.

'How've you been? Bloody hell, for all this to happen when you've just moved here and don't even know anyone yet, the timing is shit. Are you OK, really?'

'I'm OK. Well, hanging on in there and all the better now for seeing you. And I've somehow managed to make a couple of friends already, actually. Clare and Tai. They're nice, you'd like them.'

'Oh, great! How did you meet them?'

I told her the story; about meeting Clare and Winnie the Poodle while I was out with Albert, and about Clare inviting me to come to yoga with her. At my first session Tai, who'd been Clare's friend for years, had been warned I was coming and had saved us both a place at the back of the room. It had been an interesting first meeting; the class had only been underway for about ten minutes, all of us easing into the downward facing dog pose, when there was a loud PFFFFT somewhere in front of us.

'Oh God, somebody's farted!' hissed Clare, who was on my left.

To my right Tai snorted.

'Shhhh!' Clare hissed again, but I glanced at her and she was grinning broadly. I turned my head to look at Tai, whose shoulders were shaking, lips pressed tightly together. I felt a bubble of laughter threatening to escape my own lips and took a deep breath. Nobody else in the room seemed to have heard the cause of our mirth, or if they had they were studiously ignoring it. Tai snorted again, and next to me Clare tried to stifle a giggle. Unable to help myself, I giggled too, and suddenly all three of us were tittering away like a group of naughty schoolgirls.

'Will you PLEASE be quiet at the back?'

The booming voice of the yoga teacher, a tall, powerfully built woman with a shock of auburn hair, brought us to our senses, but we'd started giggling again as soon as the class finished.

'I knew right then that I'd get on with them,' I said to Eva, and she rolled her eyes.

'You always have had a juvenile sense of humour,' she said. 'But I love you for it. And I'm glad you've met some nice people. Sounds like you need them at the moment. Anyway ... Danny. Let's do this. Tell me everything.'

And so I did. I told her about the last email I'd had from

him on the Thursday night when I'd been away, and how I'd come home on Friday evening to find the house empty. How I'd called friends and former colleagues, asking if they'd heard from him, how I'd gone out searching for him, called the hospitals, emailed Danny repeatedly, and eventually gone to the police. And then I'd told her about the bombshells that had been dropped upon me – that Danny hadn't been working at ACR Security at all, how he'd accepted the job and then apparently changed his mind, but had still been heading out every morning, coming home every evening, lying through his teeth to me. How he hadn't been using his bank account, not for weeks, and yet still had money in his pocket whenever it was needed. How my neighbours had told the police that they'd thought I lived here alone. How his profile was currently on a dating app, and how I had no idea if he'd registered himself or if someone had put him on there as a joke. And, finally, my eyes prickling with tears, I told her about the two men whose profiles had been on the same dating app, the men who looked so similar to Danny, and who were now dead.

Eva, who'd been listening intently, gasped at that.

'Shit, Gemma. I'd heard about those murders, obviously, but I didn't connect the ...'

She sank her head into her hands for a moment, rubbing her eyes. Then she straightened up and reached towards me again, patting my arm.

'I'm so sorry, and I totally get why you're so upset. This is crazy.'

She took a deep breath.

'OK, there's a lot to take in here. So I'm going to try to look at this objectively, OK? Pretend I don't know Danny, or you. Just look at the facts, as if it's a news story. And for now, we're going to assume that those murders are just a coincidence, and that Danny's still alive. Is that all right?'

I nodded, wiped my eyes with the backs of my hands, then picked up my mug and took a gulp. The tea had gone cold, and I grimaced as I swallowed.

'Of course. The police have already done a quick search of the house to see if they could find anything that might help – they didn't. And they're going to Chiswick today for a look around our old place, although I can't imagine they'll find anything of any use there either. So if you can think of *anything*, Eva, anything at all ... because honestly, I'm stumped here. I just can't think of anything that would explain any of this.'

'Well, I'll certainly give it a try.'

She'd put a notebook and pen on the table when she'd sat down, and she reached for them.

'OK, let's brainstorm. First, the job thing. Why would somebody do that, lie to their wife about something like that? Have you come up with anything so far?'

'A few things, but they're all a bit mad.'

'Shoot.'

'OK. Well ...'

I told her about the crazy theories I'd come up with – Danny had some sort of top-secret job he couldn't tell me about; he was secretly ill and having daily treatment somewhere in Bristol; he had another wife and family nearby and was spending his days with them, returning to me at night. She wrote them all down, an increasingly sceptical expression on her face.

'Hmmm,' she said. 'Top-secret job, unlikely. Although very, very vaguely possible I suppose, given his line of work. Ill? Did he look or seem ill?'

I shook my head. 'No. He's looked great recently, actually. Really fit. I don't really think he's ill. I was just desperately coming up with theories, you know?'

'OK. And another wife? And kids? Seriously?'

The wide-eyed, disbelieving look on her face almost made me laugh.

'No, I don't really think that either. But what else, Eva? I can't think of any other reasons he'd lie about where he was going every day.'

Eva was nodding slowly, looking at her notes. She stared at the page for a few seconds, then looked back at me.

'Well, I can think of one more possibility. Look what we have here. A man who doesn't start the new job he was supposed to start, but still disappears every morning and comes home every evening. A man who isn't using his bank account. A man whose new neighbours have never seen him. And now, a man who's disappeared without trace, overnight. Sounds like a man who's laying low, to me. A man who's in trouble. A man who's trying to keep a very, very low profile. A man who's scared of somebody or something. A man with a secret. A man who doesn't want to be traced, so he lies about where he's working, goes and hides away somewhere every day instead, even hides where his money is being kept? Moves house, and makes sure even his new neighbours don't know he lives here?'

I stared at her. Bizarre as it sounded, what she was saying made some sort of sense.

'OK, but ... but *who*, Eva? What? Who would he be scared of, who would he be hiding from? I mean, I've never had the slightest inkling that he's in any sort of trouble. He seemed totally normal at home, surely he wouldn't be so relaxed if something like that was going on? At the same time, well, it's a good theory – better than any of mine, that's for sure.'

I stopped talking, thinking. Thinking again about the times over the past year or so that Danny would seem stressed and distracted, would say he needed to be on his own for a while, would head off for a few hours and come home looking better, behaving like himself again. It had happened more frequently after his dad had died, but I'd put that down to grief, to him trying to handle his loss, even if he didn't want to admit that his father's death had hit him harder than he'd expected it to. But maybe I'd got that all wrong. I'd wondered over the past few days if he might, after all, been having an affair. But maybe it wasn't that at all. Maybe he *had* been worried about something, something else. Maybe he *had* been in some sort of trouble. Could Eva be right?

'Eva. The EHU app thing. How would that fit in?'

Eva sat back in her chair, her smooth brow crinkling.

'Mmm, good point. That doesn't really fit with the rest of it, I suppose. A man who's trying to keep a low profile isn't very likely to put himself on a dating app.' She sighed. 'Damn. Thought I'd cracked it there for a minute. OK, let's just look at that separately for a minute. As you said earlier, somebody could easily have stuck him on there for a silly joke, although I'm not sure who would think that was funny. Still, you know how childish men can be, especially after a few drinks maybe. And yes, it's kind of freaky, very freaky in fact, that two other men who used the same app have been murdered. But that could just be a horrible coincidence. Billions of people use those apps. So, leaving that aside for a moment, well ...' she paused, her eyes fixing on mine, 'well, I hate to ask this again, I really do, and I know you told me when he first went missing that there was absolutely no way he was seeing anyone else, but things have changed a bit now, so I'm going to ask you again. *Could* he have been seeing other women, Gem? I mean, how were things between you, really? How's your sex life been?'

I looked back at her, squirming slightly inwardly. How *had* our sex life been? It had started off fine, even great. And recently ... well, we probably had sex less frequently than we had back in the early days, there was no doubt about that. But that was normal, wasn't it?

'Our sex life ... it's fine. I mean, we've been together a while now, we're not tearing each other's clothes off every ten minutes. But it's OK, we're still doing it. Now and again. I mean, not so much recently, with the move and all the work we've been doing trying to sort this place out. But ... oh, I just don't know anymore, Eva. The police asked me this too. I've wracked my brains, I really have, trying to think of anything that should have made me suspicious. And other than him heading off on his bike every now and again, wanting some alone time ... I mean, he *could* have been seeing someone. But I've never seen any real evidence ...'

My voice tailed off. I wasn't being entirely truthful, was I? Because there had been *one* occasion, just one. It had been the previous summer, just a few months after we got married, when I – and, as my plus one, Danny – had been invited to a party thrown by the fashion editor of *Camille* magazine to mark her fortieth birthday. It had been during the heatwave, several weeks during July and August that year when the temperature in London had soared into the mid-thirties and stayed there, and even though the party hadn't started until seven, the sun was still beating down, the ice cubes that clinked in our glasses melting within minutes, sweat beading on our brows. From the glass-roofed kitchen, guests drifted slowly into the shady garden at the back of the chic terraced house in Notting Hill, chatting and laughing, languid in the heat. I'd been networking, of course, as usual – so many editors to chat to, from all of the big magazines! – but I never worried about Danny at parties, knowing he was happy to wander from group to group without me, sipping his drink, joining in easily with the varied conversations, letting me do my thing and waiting for me to re-join him. That night though, as I glanced around, looking for him, checking he was OK, I noticed that he seemed to be deep in conversation with a pretty, blue-eyed woman with dead straight, almost waist-length blonde hair. I vaguely recognized her from another event – a fashion stylist called Sylvie, I seemed to remember – and when I looked for Danny a second time twenty minutes later and he hadn't moved, head bent towards her, her hand on his arm, the sound of his laughter floating through the humid air – a shiver of apprehension ran through me. What were they talking about, and why was he spending so much time with just her? When I looked again just a few minutes after that the spot where they'd been standing, next to a slender silver birch tree, was empty. I'd excused myself from the conversation I'd been having with a group of art directors and weaved my way around the garden, between the women in their floaty, brightly coloured cocktail dresses, the men with shirt sleeves rolled to the elbow, ties discarded. The music had been turned up as the light had faded, the air muggy and heavy with perfume, the bodies I brushed against hot and sticky. Unable to see Danny anywhere, I'd made my way back into the kitchen, where catering staff were laying out canapés on big platters, but he wasn't there either, nor was he in the hallway where a small queue had formed for the downstairs loo, two gently swaying women in matching slinky jumpsuits leaning against each other for support as they waited. Uneasy about searching the house any further, I'd returned to the garden, accepting a glass of champagne from a waiter with a tray as I stepped outside, anxiety building. And then, suddenly, there he was, hands slipping round my waist from behind, lips soft on my neck.

'Danny! Where did you go? I was worried!'

'Work called. Went out the front to take the call, couldn't hear myself think back here with all the music and chat. Managed to sort it out on the phone though, so nothing to worry about. Right – where's the beer?' he'd said, with a grin.

Suddenly weak with relief, I'd let it go. He was allowed to

chat to other women, after all – I'd been chatting to plenty of men that night, hadn't I? – and I trusted him, trusted him implicitly. I hadn't seen Sylvie again that night and I'd forgotten all about it. But as I repeated the story to Eva, I wondered. Had I been *too* trusting? Was Danny all I thought he was, or had he been making a fool of me all along? How long had he *been* on that dating website, if his profile on it wasn't a joke by one of his stupid mates ...

'Well, I wasn't at that party, so I just don't know, Gem,' Eva was saying. 'But, well ...' she hesitated, then shook her head. 'Oh nothing. Look, it's probably just ...'

'No go on. What were you going to say?'

She shook her head again.

'Nothing. We don't know anything at this stage, Gemma, that's all. Maybe he has gone off with some other woman, but maybe it's something else entirely. There's no point in working yourself up and jumping to conclusions until we know, OK?'

I sighed.

'I know. I'm trying, I really am. But I just *can't* understand it. Cheesy as it sounds, I thought we were the perfect couple, you know? Well, clearly not; he's been lying to me for weeks, and now he's vanished. He could be *dead*, Eva. Dead like those other two men. Or he could have just upped and left me. Or he could have been abducted by bloody aliens for all I know. I have no idea what's happened to him, none at all.'

Eva closed her notebook, pushed it to one side and put her pen down.

'I think aliens are unlikely. But, you know what, I don't think I have any proper idea either,' she said. 'This is going to take more thinking time, a lot more thinking time. So we're going to go out now, get some fresh air, walk Albert, go to the supermarket. Get you some supplies in. And then we're going to put our heads together, and we're going to work this out, OK? The two of us, together. Because whether he's alive or dead now, he's definitely been hiding *something*, your Danny. That much is pretty clear. We just need to figure out what it was.'

Chapter 12

D S Devon Clarke was staring at the glazed doughnut on the plate in front of him. Normally, he'd have wolfed it down in a matter of seconds, but today, weirdly, it held no appeal whatsoever. It was the room that had stolen his appetite; since the moment he'd walked into that nightmarish, blood-soaked bedroom in Chiswick some twenty-four hours previously, he had barely eaten, or indeed slept, missing Jasmine more than ever, needing her arms around him, the comfort of her body next to his. He'd seen crime scenes like that before, of course he had, many, many times, some with the bodies, mangled and macabre, still in situ. So why had this one stuck in his mind, haunted his dreams, taken away his desire for *doughnuts*, for goodness' sake? Was it the unexpectedness of it, maybe? After all, they hadn't been expecting to find much at all in Danny O'Connor's former home, so to open a door and see ... and see *that* ...

He shuddered and glanced at the clock in the corner of his computer screen. Just after two. The forensic report should be arriving any minute.

'No sign of it yet?'

Helena suddenly appeared at his elbow, peering over his shoulder.

'Are you reading my mind? I was just thinking about it. No, not here yet. They're fast-tracking it for us though, so it should be here soon. Want that doughnut?'

He pointed at the plate, and Helena wrinkled her nose.

'Thanks, but I'll pass. Charlotte would kill me. She wants me healthy, if we're going to have a baby ...'

She stopped talking abruptly, and Devon raised a quizzical eyebrow.

'Is that definitely on the cards then? I know you mentioned it before, but that was ages ago and you haven't said anything since.'

Helena shrugged. There was an empty chair at the next desk and she reached for it, pulled it across and sat down next to him.

'Nah, nothing definite,' she said, glancing around the room and keeping her voice low. A couple of dozen officers were milling around, some chatting, some on the phones, a small cluster of them standing around the incident board, pointing at the new pictures that had been pinned there and clearly discussing them animatedly.

'But she's certainly keen, and I can't put it off much longer. I've told her that once this case is done, we'll sit down and make a decision. I mean, I'm keen too, don't get me wrong. It's just ... could I make a good parent, Devon? Seriously, when the job's like it is? The kid would never see me. I'm really scared that I'd be shit at it ...'

She suddenly looked so vulnerable, so insecure, that his

heart twisted a little, and he reached over and patted her hand.

'You'd make a brilliant parent,' he said. 'Coolest mum on the block, look at you! Hunting down the baddies ... kids love all that stuff. And other cops make it work, loads of them. You would too.'

He paused, watching her, and was rewarded with a flicker of a smile.

'She wants to carry it though, which is fine by me,' she said. 'I'm not sure pregnancy and me would get on.'

'That's a relief. You're bad enough first thing. Can't imagine you with morning sickness as well,' he said, and she laughed and punched him lightly on the arm.

'OK, back to business. What are you thinking, Devon?'

He glanced at his computer screen again – still no report from the lab – and turned back to face her.

'I'm thinking, guv, that things have taken a pretty dramatic turn in the past few hours, that's what I'm thinking. I'm thinking that when Danny O'Connor vanished last week, for some reason he went back to London to his old apartment. And I'm thinking that now, well, he's probably dead. Almost certainly dead, in fact. I can't imagine whoever lost all that blood in that room walked out of there alive. I mean, obviously we don't know yet if it *was* his blood, but seeing as it was his former home, and he's missing and everything ... shit, guv, if it's his blood, I'm dreading telling his wife.'

He ran a hand across his face. When he'd looked in the bathroom mirror earlier his eyes had been bloodshot, his dark skin tinged with grey. The images of that damn Chiswick bedroom were suddenly back in his head again, making his stomach churn. He wondered if he might actually throw up. He took a deep breath, and then another, trying to focus.

Helena was silent for a moment, clearly realizing he was struggling. She rested a hand on his knee briefly, then said: 'I know, that's going to be tough. And I'm so sorry you had to see it. It's always shitty, coming across things like ... well, like *that*, especially when you're not expecting it. Are you OK?'

He nodded, the nausea subsiding a little.

'I've seen worse, you know. Not sure why this one has got to me so much. Been thinking about it all night, playing out scenarios. I'm assuming the apartment keys had been returned to the landlord when the O'Connors moved out, so did Danny have a spare set cut? And why go back there anyway? How would he know the place was still empty?'

Helena shrugged.

'Don't know. Lots of unknowns right now. You're right, we still don't know if the place is covered in Danny's blood or someone else's. But assuming for now it *is* his, we're thinking what? What would send him back there? If we go with Tara's theory for a minute, a date maybe, with someone he met online, taking advantage of the fact his wife's gone away on her press trip? And then what ... the date goes horribly wrong and she slashes him to death?'

She was looking doubtful.

'It's one theory. Long way to go for a hook-up though.'

'It is. And of course, a very long way from our first two murder scenes. Although of course we've been assuming our killer is local, seeing as we have two bodies in Bristol, but that's not necessarily the case, is it? Could be London based.

Could be from anywhere, and willing to travel. That's if there's any connection at all between these three cases, which is something we've yet to establish, as we all know.'

Devon had picked up a pen and was poking the doughnut, cracking the shiny glaze. Helena watched him for a moment, then closed her eyes and started swinging her chair slowly from side to side.

'This is BLOODY DRIVING ME MENTAL. It just *feels* as if there's a connection though, doesn't it? Even if we don't have the evidence to prove it yet. If they didn't all look so similar, and if they weren't all on the EHU site, it would be different.'

'I know, I know. If Danny O'Connor *has* been murdered though, which is now very likely, it's a very different MO. The other two scenes were really clean – this one was a freaking bloodbath. And where's the body?'

Helena stopped swinging and opened her eyes.

'No idea,' she said flatly. She was silent for a few moments, then said: 'The papers don't know about Danny yet, but they're bound to get hold of it any minute, you know. If they keep up with the news, one of Danny's friends is bound to notice the similarity between him and our two murder victims any day now, and could easily go to the papers, even though we've asked them not to. And we've been talking to Ryan Jones's and Mervin Elliott's friends and families over the past day or so too, even shown some of them Danny's photo, trying to see if our victims might have known him. No joy there at all, but one of *them* could easily speak to a reporter too, let it slip that there's another possible victim. If we really do have three dead men, the serial killer stuff is going to go through the roof.'

Devon poked the doughnut again, watching as the glaze cracked further, little pieces of it slowly dropping onto the plate in a manner he found strangely satisfying.

'Hope not. That's all we need,' he said.

PING.

'Shit. It's here.'

At the sound of the email notification Devon dropped his pen and sat bolt upright, grabbing his mouse and clicking on the message that had just dropped into his inbox.

'Forensic report in!' Helena raised her voice, and the room fell quiet, all heads turning towards Devon's desk.

He tapped the cursor to move down through the report, aware that Helena had moved closer, her breathing quickening, conscious that he was breathing more heavily too, his hands shaking slightly.

'Come on, come on ... where is it?'

He scanned the screen, looking for the crucial line of information. Then:

'SHIT. And ... what? Seriously?'

Helena had seen it at the same time he did. Frowning, she leaned in closer, reading the line again, then looked at Devon.

'How can that be right?' she said softly.

He shook his head.

'No idea. But ... well, it's there in black and white. And they very rarely get it wrong, boss.'

She looked back at the computer screen, then slowly stood up and turned to the room.

'Right, well, we have a development. First, as we suspected, it's a match – the blood all over that bedroom in Chiswick *is* Danny O'Connor's. They used the DNA they found on the toothbrush and comb taken from his current address to confirm it. So we know now that something terrible happened in that room, which must have left Danny very seriously injured or, very possibly, dead.'

A low murmur ran around the room, officers exchanging glances. Helena raised a hand.

'But there's something else. And this is the bit that doesn't quite make sense. Because Danny O'Connor has only been missing for seven days. But the forensics guys have dated the bloodstains, and they say – wait for it – they say that blood has been there for approximately five weeks. *Five weeks*. Whatever happened to Danny O'Connor in that room happened right back at the end of *January*.'

For a few seconds there was complete silence. Then, from his desk on the far side of the room DC Frankie Stevens said: 'But ... boss, that's not possible. He only disappeared last Friday. He was living here in Bristol from the eighth of February, alive and well. At least that's what his wife ...' His voice tailed off.

'Exactly, Frankie. That's what his *wife* told us.'

Helena's tone had turned hard, and there was a steely look in her dark blue eyes.

'So, I think we need to have a rather urgent chat with Mrs Gemma O'Connor, don't we?'

Chapter 13

The interview room was small, and far too hot. A table, old-looking, rickety, with four chairs. Another, smaller table against one wall, upon which were a glass jug full of water and a tower of brown paper cups. They'd made me wait, on my own, for a good half an hour before they finally came in and sat down opposite me, and in that time I'd started to feel headachy, my temples beginning to pulsate. Why was it so hot? I couldn't see any radiators – was it underfloor heating, maybe? There was a cup of water on the table in front of me but when I'd taken a cautious sip it tasted stale, tepid. I'd put it down again, aware that my palms were beginning to sweat. I was so tired too, my head fuzzy. I hadn't told Eva, but I'd had another bad dream the previous night, another nightmare. The details had faded now, the dream melting away with the daylight, but I could still remember running, running fast in the dark, stumbling, picking myself up and running again, gripped by a terrible fear, heart pounding, breath catching in my throat. I could hear, somewhere far behind me, the terrible sound of wailing, a low keening sound, the sound of somebody in dreadful pain, and yet I kept on running, terrified, desperate to get away. When I woke up I was again drenched in sweat, the bedclothes twisted around my legs, and my sleep for the rest of the night had been fitful and disturbed. The last thing I needed now was to be sitting in a police station, especially when I had no idea what this was about. Why did they need to talk to me again so urgently, and – and this was what was making me feel so anxious – why had their attitude towards me seemingly changed suddenly, from sympathetic and concerned during our previous encounters to abrupt and matter of fact?

When DS Clarke and another officer – yet another I'd never met before – had arrived at the house earlier Eva and I, supermarket run done, had been curled up on the sofa, picking at some cheese and crackers, trying with little success to come up with new explanations for Danny vanishing, for his lies. The police had simply told me that new information about my husband's disappearance had come to light, and that I must accompany them to the station immediately for questioning. But they'd spoken to me in brusque tones, DS Clarke informing me that no, it wouldn't be possible for Eva to come with me, the other officer simply suggesting tersely that I get a coat and put some shoes on and asking me if I had a solicitor I wanted to call.

'A ... a solicitor? Why would I need a solicitor? What's happened? No, I don't have one, does that matter?' I'd asked, my stomach starting to flutter uneasily.

The officer had muttered that no, it didn't matter, that a duty solicitor would be made available to me if I wanted one, but I shook my head, telling him that wouldn't be necessary.

My husband was missing – maybe, as Eva and I were now thinking, in some sort of trouble, maybe in hiding because of something *he* had done, someone *he* had upset, or maybe, just maybe, he'd run off with another woman, something I was still barely allowing myself to think about. So why on earth would *I*, his wife, the one he'd abandoned for *whatever* reason, need a solicitor? Had they found out what he'd been up to, and thought we were in it together, maybe? If so, what was it? What the hell was I about to find out about my husband?

It seemed I wouldn't have to wait much longer for the answer, because there they were, finally sitting in front of me – DS Clarke and his boss, DCI Helena Dickens, formalities concluded, about to start the interview. It was being recorded, videoed too, and the thought made me even more anxious. I felt scruffy in jeans and trainers and a sloppy sweatshirt, my hair scraped back into a messy ponytail; *not* how I would have dressed if I'd known I was being interviewed by the police today. Would they sit down together later, maybe a room *full* of police officers, and scrutinize it, scrutinize me? And yet, I thought, did it matter if they did? I had nothing to hide, whatever they thought, for it seemed clear to me that they thought *something* now, something they hadn't thought before. DS Clarke was looking at me with a new interest, the gentleness I'd seen in his eyes previously replaced with something more piercing, as if I was a fascinating exhibit in a museum. DCI Dickens wasn't looking at me at all, instead staring intently at a page of notes in front of her. Suddenly, she cleared her throat, the rasping sound in the silent room making me jump. She raised her dark blue eyes to mine.

'Gemma, as you know, yesterday morning DS Clarke here, and another colleague, DC Stevens, who I know you've also met, visited your previous address, at number 10 Homefield Avenue, Chiswick.'

She paused, looking at me, and I nodded.

'Yes, I know. I haven't heard anything though, so I assume ... well, was it any help?'

DCI Dickens glanced down at her notes again, then returned her cool gaze to my face.

'It was certainly *interesting*, Gemma. I'm now going to show you some photographs, OK?'

'Errr ... yes, fine.'

The DCI reached for a large envelope which had been lying on the table to the left of her notebook and slid two prints out of it. Slowly, she pushed first one and then the other across the smooth wood.

'These were taken in the master bedroom of the apartment yesterday. Can you take a look please, and tell me about what you see?'

I glanced down at the two photographs, confused, for a moment not sure what I was supposed to be looking at. Then my stomach lurched.

What the ...?

Yes, this *looked* like our old bedroom, the one we'd spent those heady, early days of our relationship in, wrapped around each other, planning our lives together. But at the same time, it wasn't the same room at all. The pictures showed some twisted, nightmarish version of our cheerful bedroom, the walls, carpets, even the bed streaked and stained and polluted with something dark and sinister, something that looked viscous and evil. My vision blurred, and I gripped the edge of the table for support, my stomach contracting violently. I was going to be sick, I was sure I was, but first I had to ask, had to know …

'Is that … is that *blood*?'

My voice was a strangled whisper. There was a brief silence, then the cup of tepid water was pushed towards me.

'Have a drink, Gemma.' DS Clarke's voice.

Slowly, eyes still glued to the horrific images in front of me, I let go of the table edge with my right hand, reaching for the cup, trying to steady it as I moved it to my lips, swallowing a little water, the liquid spilling over the sides as I shakily put it down again.

'Are you all right to continue?' DS Clarke again.

I nodded, the nausea subsiding a little as the water slid down my dry throat.

'I'm OK, but … these pictures. What … please, what happened there? Has something happened to Danny?'

There were a few moments of silence. Then DCI Dickens spoke, her voice low and calm.

'That's what we'd like to know, Gemma. Because, yes, that *is* blood. A lot of blood. And we know now that it's *Danny's* blood. So, the question is, do *you* know what happened in that room?'

Danny's blood? I dragged my gaze away from the photographs. *What does she mean, Danny's blood?*

'What? How would *I* know? I moved out weeks ago, I haven't been back … oh God, what's happened? Please …'

My chest was tightening, a trickle of sweat running down my back, my stomach rolling again. What were they trying to tell me? My brain felt fuzzy. *Danny's* blood? Did that mean …?

The DCI was speaking again.

'Yes, we know you moved out weeks ago, Gemma. On Friday the first of February, you said? And you also told us that your husband stayed on in London and moved here to join you a week later. The thing is, we have a very, very good forensics laboratory here, Gemma. And they've told us that that blood, *Danny's* blood, was most likely splattered all over your former bedroom approximately five weeks ago.'

She paused, as I stared at her. *Five … what?*

'Five weeks ago, Gemma. Which, by my calculations, would mean that Danny did a hell of a lot of bleeding in that room on or around the first of February. Around the time *you* packed up and moved to Bristol, in fact.'

I shook my head, aware that a low hum had now started up inside my skull. Was I going to faint, instead of vomiting? It was so hot, unbearably hot, and my brain didn't seem to be working properly, DCI Dickens's words not making any sense.

'No. No, that didn't happen,' I said. I was finding it hard to move my mouth, I realized; as if some external force was slowing the movements of my lips, my tongue. 'It must be a mistake. Danny was fine, when he moved down here. He wasn't hurt … I don't understand, what's going on?'

Sweat was beading on my forehead now, running into my eyes, and I wiped it away with my sleeve, wondering as I did so why I was the only one who seemed to be feeling the heat in the small, stifling room. The two officers weren't sweating. *Why aren't they sweating? What's wrong with me?*

'We're confused too, Gemma.' DS Clarke this time.

I looked at him, trying to focus.

'We spoke to your former landlord, after we discovered the blood in the bedroom. Mr Evans? He was kind enough to come and let us in to the place. He told us that you both vacated the apartment on the same day – that Mr O'Connor *didn't* stay on for a week after you left, as you claim. He says he thought that *was* originally the plan, but that in fact the keys were left at his office – posted through the letterbox, so he wasn't sure which of you left them – sometime on Friday the first of February, with a note saying that you'd both moved out after all. Unfortunately, he didn't keep the note, and there aren't any CCTV cameras on his premises, so we haven't been able to verify which of you dropped off those keys, or at what time. But we believe it was you, Gemma. Because it's pretty clear that something terrible happened in that apartment, on or around that date. And it's Danny's blood. So whatever that terrible thing was, it happened to him.'

He stopped talking and leaned back slightly in his chair, but his eyes were still locked to mine. The humming in my head had grown louder. I stared back at him for a moment, then looked at DCI Dickens. She was watching me too, and I realized they were both waiting for me to speak.

'I-I.' I swiped at my damp forehead again. My heart was

pounding, as if I'd just sprinted up a long, steep staircase. What was I supposed to say, when everything *they'd* just said was wrong, was ridiculous? Of course Danny had stayed on in London. Of course he hadn't been hurt. How did I get them to understand that? I took a deep breath.

Just tell them. Tell them calmly, and firmly.

'Look, I'm sorry, but none of this is making any sense to me,' I said at last, trying hard to make my mouth cooperate, to enunciate each word clearly. 'Danny stayed on in London, at our apartment, for a week after I left, like I told you. And when he arrived in Bristol, he was fine. He wasn't hurt, or cut, or anything. I'd have noticed – we shared a bed, for goodness' sake. I don't what else to say. This is wrong, all of it. None of it is true. Somebody's made a huge mistake, or is lying to you. That's the only explanation.'

DCI Dickens stared at me in silence for a few moments, then sighed.

'Right. Well, let's look at what else we have here, shall we?' She tapped a finger on her notepad.

'None of your Clifton neighbours have ever laid eyes on Danny – they say they believe you moved into the house alone. He accepted a new job in Bristol, and then mysteriously pulled out of it. We've now checked his main email account, the one you gave us details of when you first reported him missing, and he sent the email to ACR Security to tell them of his change of plan on the thirty-first of January. No further activity on that account since that date. His bank account also hasn't been touched since the end of January.'

She turned a page.

'We've also checked *your* email account, Gemma. You say you last heard from Danny via email on the night of Thursday, the twenty-eighth of February, when you were away on your press trip. There's no sign of that email, or indeed, as I just said, any other emails between you and Danny after, again, the end of January. I know you mentioned to my colleagues that you were having some trouble with your phone, that some photographs and emails had gone missing, but ... well, as well as *no* recent emails, you also don't seem to have *any* photographs of your husband since the move, just photos from your time in London. And nobody we've spoken to so far – his friends, his former colleagues – have heard anything from him, also since the end of January. We're planning to speak to his family today, but I strongly suspect that it will be the same story there.'

She paused, regarding me coolly.

'Do you see a bit of a pattern developing here, Gemma?'

I swallowed. 'Yes, but there are explanations for all that. I mean, the job thing, I still haven't got to the bottom of that. Or the bank account. But he doesn't have a phone at the moment, so that's why he hasn't been in touch with people much. And my phone's just playing up, not saving stuff, I'm sure I'll track those photos and emails down ...'

DCI Dickens was holding up a slender hand. She wore a wedding ring, I noticed for the first time, a narrow gold band.

'In addition, Danny seems to have vanished but taken absolutely nothing with him. His passport, clothes, everything is still there, correct?'

I nodded.

'Yes. That's why I'm so worried, so scared ...'

'Well, we're worried too, Gemma. Very, very worried.'

DCI Dickens leaned towards me across the table, and I smelled a faint scent, a soft floral perfume.

'We're very worried indeed,' she said. 'Because, looking at all of the evidence, it does very much seem now that Danny has actually been off the scene for quite a few weeks. Since the end of January in fact. Since just before you packed your bags and moved to Bristol, Gemma. Did you discover his profile on that dating app, is that what happened? Because it can't have been very nice, discovering that your husband was on the hunt for other women to have sex with. Not nice at all, is it, Devon?'

She leaned back in her seat again, turning to look at her colleague. He nodded slowly.

'Not nice at all, boss. Nobody would blame you for losing your temper, Gemma, after discovering something like that. Is that what happened? Did you and Danny get into a fight, and it went too far?'

The humming in my head faded to a low buzz, and then stopped. Suddenly, with growing horror, I understood. I understood perfectly. They thought ... they thought that Danny's disappearance was down to *me*. Me. They thought I'd ... what? Seriously injured him – *killed* him – in our London apartment, and then calmly moved to Bristol on my own? And then what? That I'd waited a few weeks, and then reported him missing, when all the time I knew exactly what had happened to him, because it had been me that had done it. That was what they thought, wasn't it? It was ... it was *insane*.

'No,' I said. '*No.*'

They both sat in silence, watching me, waiting. Waiting for what? A confession? I felt a sudden surge of anger. How could they think me capable of something like that?

'NO.' I practically shouted the word this time, banging both fists on the table. 'That's not true. *None* of it is true. Danny's been here, in Bristol, living with me for the past few weeks. He was fine, everything was fine. Or I thought it was fine, until last week when I came home and he was gone. I know it looks bad, none of what you've told me makes sense and I don't understand any of it either. But I'm telling you the truth ...'

I paused for a moment, my voice suddenly thick with tears, my chest contracting, my breath coming in shallow gasps.

Then I said: 'You have to believe me. Nothing can have happened to Danny in that room, not five weeks ago or whenever you said it did. Because he's been here, with me. *He's been here with me ...*'

I stopped, unable to continue speaking, the tears pouring down my cheeks, my whole body starting to shudder. This couldn't be real, could it? Could the police really think I'd hurt, I'd *killed*, Danny? It was like some sort of sick nightmare. And now DCI Dickens was leaning towards me across the table again, her voice low and hard.

'He's been here, with you? Here with you, since early February? OK. Prove it, Gemma.'

Chapter 14

The Friday morning papers bore the headlines Helena had been dreading.

BRISTOL SERIAL KILLER – IS THIS A THIRD VICTIM?

FEAR IN BRISTOL AS A THIRD MAN VANISHES

'SHIT,' she said. 'And where did they get that photo of Danny O'Connor? It's not one we've seen before, is it?'

Devon, who'd been adding some notes to the incident board, put his marker pen down and turned to face her.

'Nope. It looks as if it was taken at a party or a night out, so my guess is one of his mates got in touch with the press about him being missing, as we feared, and the journos have put two and two together and made ... well, made their serial killer theory stand up even more.'

'Probably. It's so frigging frustrating. Just fuelling the fire when we don't even know if any of these cases are connected yet. Or if Danny's even bloody dead, although that does seem highly likely now. I wish we could find his body. Where the hell is it?'

She groaned and ran her hands over her hair. It was getting long, she thought distractedly, little curls beginning to snake over her ears. She needed to make an appointment at the salon, but who knew when she'd have the time to do that. She'd look like bloody Rapunzel before this case was solved at this rate. And her back was still killing her too. Another appointment she needed to make. She looked around the room. It was only just 8 a.m., and not everyone was at their desks yet, but she decided she couldn't wait any longer. This enquiry needed to be stepped up, urgently.

'Can everyone gather round please? Guys?'

When all the officers had shuffled themselves forward, some still in outdoor coats, others clutching coffee mugs, all with tense, weary expressions, she began.

'OK, so as you all probably know we released Gemma O'Connor on bail late last night. Yes, there's a lot of circumstantial evidence, and the quantity of blood in that Chiswick bedroom is extremely worrying. But at this point we have no body, and no proof that Gemma has done anything to harm her husband. There are a lot of things that don't add up in her story though, so we'll be keeping a very close eye on her and I'm ready to haul her in again if we find even the *slightest* ...'

She took a breath.

'However, what I do want to do now is stop thinking of Danny O'Connor as just a missing person. This is now significantly more likely to turn into another murder enquiry, which I want to run alongside our current two cases. The Met will probably want to get involved with the London end at some point, but for the moment I'm hoping we'll be able to keep it ourselves as it does seem to tie in somewhat with what we have here.'

She turned to point at the board behind her, where the gruesome photographs of the Chiswick bedroom sat next to the image of Danny.

'All the evidence we *do* have points to Danny either being very seriously injured or killed in that room approximately five weeks ago, which is a bit of a time gap but still doesn't rule out it being linked to our other two cases. It looks to be a very different type of killing though – all that blood – but we need to keep an open mind on that. And, of course, we have the added complication of his wife claiming he was alive and well and living with her until a week ago. She also claims that she's going to prove that to us, despite the fact that nobody else seems to have laid eyes on him in weeks, et cetera et cetera.'

She waved a hand at the board, and to the list of the things they'd discovered about Danny's recent past.

'We await that proof with interest,' she continued. 'But in the meantime, Danny O'Connor is still missing. Whether that disappearance has anything to do with his wife, is connected to our other two killings or is down to something else entirely, we don't know yet. But there's something not right about his wife's story, that's for sure.'

Devon, who'd been leaning against the wall to her right, stepped forward, a questioning look on his face. Helena nodded.

'Go ahead, Devon.'

'I just wanted to point out a few things that came out of our questioning of Gemma O'Connor,' he said. 'For the benefit of those who weren't there.'

'Of course.'

She moved aside, taking his place against the side wall, and Devon turned to study the board for a moment, where a photograph of Gemma had been pinned next to that of her husband. Then he cleared his throat.

'OK, so yes, Gemma O'Connor is now a person of interest. But there are a few things which don't entirely add up. First, when we showed her the photographs of the bloodstained room, she seemed genuinely shocked. In fact, she looked like she was going to pass out for a bit, didn't she guv?'

He looked at Helena and she shrugged and nodded.

'If she did attack Danny in that room then, which has to be one of our major lines of enquiry now, she's a very good actress. In addition to that, she knew we were going to search that apartment a few days ago and didn't react at all when we told her that. If she knew what we were going to find when we got there, I'd expect at least some reaction from her, some attempt to stop us going until she could cover her tracks, maybe.'

'Could just be the good actress thing again though. Or, if she has done something to her husband, maybe she's in some sort of denial, post traumatic shock, something like that. She was certainly in a bit of a state last night, sweating, crying, the lot, wasn't she?' Helena said.

'She was. And it could be PTSD, possibly, yes. I've started

the ball rolling to access her medical records by the way. See if there's any history of mental illness, violence, anything like that. She has no criminal record, but it would be interesting to see what else we can find out about her background.'

'Good.' Helena gave him a thumbs up sign. 'OK, go on.'

'As we already know, and we put this to Gemma last night, there's no evidence of any email exchanges between her and Danny since the end of January, despite her claims to the contrary. However, there are a number of emails from Gemma's account to Danny's in the past week, in the days after she claims he went missing. A number of attempted Skype calls too, all of which have gone unanswered. She's told us she tried numerous times to contact him after he went missing, in a desperate attempt to track him down. If she knew he'd died five weeks ago, would she be trying to email and Skype him like that?'

'Could easily just be an attempt to throw us off the scent, make it look like she thought he was still alive. Just like all her calls to his mates, and to the hospitals and so on. Could all be part of her act.'

This came from DC Tara Lemming, sitting on the edge of a desk in the centre of the room. Devon nodded an acknowledgement.

'That's true. So let's just look at the timeline for a moment, and assume for a moment that Gemma did seriously assault, or kill, her husband. It would have to have worked like this.'

He turned to the board, placing his finger at the left-hand end of a long red line, above which had been written various dates and comments.

'A message was sent from Danny O'Connor's email address to ACR Security on Thursday, the thirty-first of January, informing them that he would no longer be taking up his position with them in Bristol. Did Gemma actually send this message, and not Danny himself, because she was planning to kill him, or indeed had *already* killed him, and didn't want alarm bells to ring when he failed to turn up at his new place of work?'

He ran his finger a little further along the line.

'Sometime on Friday, the first of February, somebody dropped the Chiswick apartment keys off at the landlord's office, with a note saying there'd been a change of plan and that the apartment had now been fully vacated. The land-lord had already told the O'Connors that he was heading off on holiday for a few weeks and wouldn't be able to check over the place until he got back. As it turned out, he didn't actually get back to it until this week when we visited. So, if Gemma did kill Danny in the apartment, she most likely did that on the thirtieth or thirty-first of January. Knowing the landlord was away, she wouldn't have been worried about being disturbed. But then – and this is the bit I'm struggling with – she'd have had to somehow move the body out of that apartment and hide it somewhere where it still hasn't been found. And then she'd have had to calmly move to Bristol without even bothering to clean up after herself. Doesn't quite add up, does it? Unless she's totally psychotic, and hiding it very, very well. Which she could be, I suppose.'

'Or maybe she had an accomplice, someone who helped

her move the body? But yes, leaving that mess behind is a bit odd, to be fair.'

Helena had moved back across to join him as he was speaking.

'Anyway, to extend that theory, she moves house, bringing all *his* stuff with her too, to make it look as if he'll soon be moving in with her. Then she claims he joined her here a week later, and has been living with her ever since, until he vanished a week ago,' she said. 'That bothers me too. Why wait so long? Why not just wait until the day he was due to move to Bristol to join her, for instance, and *then* report him missing when he allegedly didn't show, if that's the route you want to go down? I'd love to be able to pin Danny's disappearance on her, it would make our lives a lot easier. But I agree, there are definitely some things that don't really add up.'

There was silence in the room. Then Devon spoke again.

'We swabbed her yesterday, of course, and overnight the lab compared her DNA to that found in the Chiswick apartment. They say the only DNA found in the bedroom was hers and Danny's, as you'd expect. But that doesn't rule out somebody else being there, of course, if they were careful.'

'Indeed. Hard to imagine whoever carried out that attack getting away without being covered in blood though, even if they did manage not to leave anything of themselves behind. We're getting the forensic team into her house in Bristol today, by the way. We've already searched it, but now we've found what we've found in Chiswick, we need to tear her new place apart. If Gemma *was* responsible, there may well still be traces of blood on some of her clothing and so on, even if she's tried to wash it off in the meantime.'

'If it was me, I'd have dumped the clothes though,' DC Mike Slater said from the back of the room.

'I would too, Mike,' Helena said. 'But we also need forensics in there to check out Gemma's claim that Danny has been living there for the past few weeks. They'll know if he hasn't.'

'Good point,' said Devon. 'On that note, Frankie spoke to the letting agent, Pritchards, last night while we were interviewing Gemma – thanks Frankie.'

From his perch next to Tara, DC Stevens nodded.

'They couldn't tell us much of any use though. They said that Danny did come to Bristol with Gemma when they initially viewed the house, and that the two of them were here again in mid-January to pay the deposit, sign the rental agreement and pick up the keys. They brought a van with a few bits of furniture with them that time and stayed in the house overnight before returning to London the following day. But the agents haven't been round to the house since Gemma moved in on February the first, so couldn't say whether Danny has been there again or not.'

'OK.'

Devon sighed.

'Well, those enquiries continue,' Helena said. 'But let's not forget that we have two other murders which still remain unsolved too. And interestingly ...' She moved closer to the board, studying Devon's red timeline, then looked up at the photographs of Mervin Elliott and Ryan Jones. 'Interestingly, both of our killings happened *after* Gemma O'Connor moved to Bristol. What do we think about that, then?'

A murmur ran round the room. She turned away from the board and shrugged.

'Oh, highly unlikely, I know. Look, I know we don't have a third body, not yet. And the first two murders were very similar – clean killings, with some sort of heavy weapon. The crime scene in Chiswick is totally different, as I said earlier. Speaks of a much more frenzied, passionate attack. But ... could that be the difference between killing a relative stranger, and killing your own husband? I'm just saying. We can't rule anything out.'

Devon was staring at her.

'You seriously think Gemma O'Connor could have killed *three* men, boss?'

She shrugged again.

'I don't know. The thought's only just occurred to me, if I'm honest. But I'm clutching at straws here, in the absence of anything more solid. And what possible motive would she have for killing our two local victims?'

She paused, and blew out some air, staring at the photograph of Gemma O'Connor, and thinking. Then she turned back to Devon.

'Ridiculous, eh? I know. Far too many ifs and buts. But just do me one favour, Devon? Talk to her again and see where she was on the nights Mervin and Ryan were killed. And while you're at it, check and see if there've been any similar, unsolved murders in London in the past year or so. Humour me, OK?'

Devon nodded slowly.

'Sure. You're the boss.'

Chapter 15

Friday dawned bright and mild, the birds singing joyously outside my bedroom window, the clouds little white powder puffs in a baby blue sky. It was as if spring had suddenly decided to arrive in all its glory overnight, something which would normally fill me with delight after a long cold winter. Instead, I felt numb, low, my head and limbs aching. Albert, who usually slept downstairs, had somehow crept onto my bed during the night, his warm body stretched across my feet, tiny snores emanating from his glossy black nose. I'd stayed still for as long as I could, not wanting to wake him, trying to organize my thoughts, grateful that at least I'd somehow managed to sleep for a few hours, undisturbed by any more nightmares. Finally, my right foot beginning to cramp, I'd gently shaken my dog off it, and he'd yawned and stretched and licked my face, then suddenly leapt from the bed, running through the half-open door and back downstairs as if remembering he shouldn't have been up there in the first place.

When I'd finally arrived home from the police station late the previous night Eva had been anxiously waiting in the living room, but I'd brushed her questions aside, telling her I was too tired to speak, and that I'd fill her in on everything in the morning. When I finally crawled out of bed and made it, still in my pyjamas, hair a tousled mess, to the kitchen, she simply handed me a mug of tea and a newspaper.

'Popped out while you were sleeping. He's on the front page, Gem. Someone's obviously been talking. There's not much detail, nothing about all the weird stuff about his job or his bank account or anything like that, it just says he's missing and remarks on his resemblance to the two murder victims. But still, it's out there now. I'm so sorry.'

FEAR IN BRISTOL AS A THIRD MAN VANISHES

I read the headline, the knot which had begun to form in my stomach again the moment I'd woken up tightening painfully. Then I looked at the big photo of Danny, instantly recognizable as one taken at a friend's wedding about eight months ago. Where had they got that one from? And 'Fear in Bristol'? Fear? *Terror* was closer to what I was starting to feel now. Fear wasn't a big enough word for this, not big enough for this all-consuming anguish, this confusion, the growing sense that everything around me was spinning faster and faster, completely out of control. Knowing I couldn't hide what was happening for much longer, and that the press were bound to get hold of it, I'd finally called my parents on the way home last night, trying to play things down, telling them only that Danny had gone missing, trying to reassure them that I was certain he would be home soon and not to believe anything they might hear or read in the papers. They were distraught, of course, my dad offering to get on a train first thing in the morning, but I eventually persuaded him to stay put.

'I'm fine,' I lied. 'My friend Eva's here, and it'll all blow over in a few days, don't worry. I'm sure he'll turn up. I'll keep you posted, OK? I love you both. It'll all be all right.'

My parents lived in Cornwall, where I'd been born, neither of them in the best of health. My dad had been diagnosed with prostate cancer a year earlier, and although his treatment had gone well and was keeping the disease at bay, he had aged noticeably in recent months, his frail appearance a shock when I had last visited just before Christmas. My mother had always been a delicate woman ('I suffer terribly with my nerves' was her constant refrain), and not for the first time in my life I wished I had a sibling, a brother or sister who could share this load with me. At least Danny had Liam – if not someone he could share his troubles with, at least someone to distract his mother from what was going on. I couldn't bring myself to ring Bridget though, and I hadn't heard from her, even though I assumed the police would be calling her any time now, if they hadn't already. Would she even care that Danny was missing? She didn't seem to even *like* her son very much. The thought of speaking to her about Danny's disappearance ... I didn't think I could, couldn't face it, and I couldn't read the article in the newspaper Eva had handed me either, and so I didn't. Instead, I pushed the paper aside, and I started to talk, telling Eva everything the police had said to me. Told her about the pictures, the blood. Danny's blood, in our old bedroom.

'Blood that's five weeks old? *Five?* But that doesn't make any sense.'

Eva was wide-eyed, gaping at me as I recounted the story.

'I mean, you'd have noticed if he had any injuries that severe, wouldn't you? Surely?'

'Of course I would. He was absolutely fine when he arrived in Bristol. Shit, Eva, what's going on? I feel like I'm stuck in one of those horrible dreams where everything's back to front and upside down and nothing makes sense. And that's not all. Apparently our landlord said we *both* moved out on the first of February, because the keys were left at his office that day with a note. That's the day *I* moved down here, but Danny stayed on in London for a week to finish up his final project for Hanfield Solutions. Or at least, that's what he *said* he was doing. He certainly didn't stay in the apartment though, it seems now. So where the hell did he go?'

Eva shook her head slowly, eyes even wider.

'Whaaat?'

'I know. And it gets worse. They accused *me*, Eva. They think *I* hurt Danny, attacked him, even killed him maybe. In our bedroom, back at the end of January. And they think I'm making it up about him moving down here. They don't believe he was ever here, because the neighbours never saw him, and he hasn't used his bank account, and he didn't start his new job, and all the other stuff. But he *was* here, Eva. He was *fucking* here, until last week ...'

I stood up, feeling panic rising, my heartrate speeding up. Eva stood up too, reaching a hand out towards me.

'Gemma ... Gemma, calm down, come on. We can sort this,

this is ridiculous. How can they think that? There'll be loads of ways of proving it, there must be. I mean, it was three weeks, wasn't it, that he was here? There must have been heaps of people who saw him and can vouch for the fact that he was fine. Sit down, come on.'

Her tone was soothing, and I took a deep breath, trying to regain control. Slowly, I lowered myself onto my chair again, and nodded.

'OK. But I need you to help me make sense of this. My brain is all ... muddled. The stress ... I can't think properly. They've got no real evidence, not against me, not yet, other-wise they'd have arrested me, charged me. I've been released on bail, and they haven't put any restrictions on me or anything, for now. But they're coming here again later, to do forensic stuff or something, and I'm just so scared, Eva. What the *hell* is Danny playing at? Where is he? And all that blood? What's that all about? I just can't ...'

Hot tears were burning their way down my cold cheeks, and Eva grabbed my hands, rubbing them hard.

'I don't know. I don't understand any of it any more than you do. And the blood thing is weird, bloody weird, no pun intended. But you know he was OK when he moved to Bristol, so don't think about that for now. Go and get your diary. We need to go through every day, every single day, from the day Danny moved down here to the day he disappeared. Because he didn't have an invisibility cloak, Gem. This isn't some sort of Harry Potter fantasy story, it's the real world. And he was out of this house all day every day, pretending to go to work, and you must have had things delivered to the house, and done lots of stuff together over the past few weeks, right? Somebody will remember seeing him, there'll be *somebody* who can prove to the police that Danny was here with you and alive and well until last week, OK? Come on. Game face on.'

I managed a small smile. 'Game face on' – it was what we used to say to each other in our early newspaper days, when we were half dead from lack of sleep and the stress of deadlines, and had just had yet another assignment thrown at us.

'Game face on. We can do this.'

And so, I put my game face on. I even got dressed, brushed my hair, moisturized my skin, ate a bowl of cereal, fed Albert, promising him as I did so that I'd take him out for a nice long walk later. And then I brought my diary to the kitchen table, and we began, as the morning sun streamed in, dust motes dancing in the air around us.

An hour later, I pushed the diary aside, feeling something close to despair.

'There's nothing. *Nothing.*'

Eva steepled her fingers together, eyes fixed on the diary.

'OK, well as far as I see it at the moment – and leaving the mystery of the blood in the bedroom aside for now, as that makes no sense whatsoever – there are really only two possible scenarios here. One – and I know this is one you don't want to think about, love, but I'm sorry, we have to consider it as a possibility – one, he's vanished because he's gone off with someone else, someone he met on that app. He might have stayed with *her* that week after you moved down here. It doesn't explain all his odd behaviour, I know, but still. The other one … well, I now think it's even more likely that we were on the right track with that vague theory we came up with before. Because what this increasingly sounds like to me now is that he was being very, very careful to make sure that nobody would see him here in Bristol. But he was clever about it, really clever, so you wouldn't notice. I don't know why yet, but now I'm really starting to think he was hiding, Gemma. He was hiding right here, and you didn't even realize it,' she said slowly.

She tapped her notebook with her pen.

'Let's look at it all again with that in mind. For a start, when you lived in London he always took his turn doing the weekend supermarket run. Or else you did it together, right?'

I nodded.

'But since you moved here, he decided he'd stay in and clean the house on a Saturday morning, and that *you'd* go out and do the shopping.'

'Well, yes, but that was because I always moaned about having to do all the cleaning, and he was just being nice …'

My voice tailed off.

'OK, maybe. But seriously …'

'You did every dog walk since you moved here. Every single one, on your own.'

'Well, yes, but that's just because of his working hours … well, I *thought* he was working. I generally did most of it in London too, not all, but most; he used to come out with us at weekends. I'm sure he would have started doing that again here soon.'

'Every time you got food delivered, *you* went to the door to get it, not him,' Eva interrupted.

'He said he'd get the plates out, pour the wine ...'

'Exactly. Making sure the delivery guy didn't see him. Did he *ever* go to the door, to take in a delivery? Of *anything?*'

I thought. I couldn't remember, but he must have, surely?

'I don't know,' I said quietly.

'When you went out with your new friends, he never asked if he could come. Fair enough, maybe, as you'd only known them a few weeks. But even when you went round to ... Tai, is that her name? ... to Tai's house for a drink after yoga, and Clare's husband joined you too, and you called Danny and asked him if he wanted to pop over for a quick one as well, and meet them all, he said no. So they never met him, either.'

I'd told Eva about that night earlier. On the spur of the moment as we'd left the third yoga class I'd been to, Tai had suggested that it might be nice if her husband, Peter, and Clare's husband, Alex, met Danny.

'I've got some very nice sauv blanc chilling in the fridge; shall we have an impromptu midweek drinkies?' she said, with a cheeky grin. 'Are they all free? We could just have a couple, it would be nice.'

I'd called Danny, but he told me he'd had to bring some work home with him that needed to be done for first thing in the morning.

'Any other night ... look, give them my apologies and tell them we'll have them all over here soon instead, OK?' he'd said. And so I'd done just that, and gone for drinks at Tai's stunning penthouse apartment in the Cathedral Quarter on my own, admiring the three-hundred-and-sixty-degree views of the city from the floor-to-ceiling windows and wishing Danny was there to enjoy them, and the wine and the company, with me.

Eva was still talking.

'And you stayed in, every weekend. I mean, I know he was only living here for three weekends, but still. Didn't it strike you as weird that he never wanted to go out? Not once? To explore your new city?'

I was staring at the diary myself now and starting to feel very stupid. What Eva was saying was starting to make more and more sense. How had I not realized it, any of it, at the time?

'It just ... it just didn't occur to me. He was working long days ... well, I *thought* he was working long days during the week, and I had loads on too. So when the weekends came we just wanted to get this place sorted, get the walls painted and put up shelves and stuff. We were *planning* to go out soon; we'd even made a list of all the restaurants and bars we wanted to go to. We just hadn't got around to it yet ...'

I stopped talking. *Shit*. Eva waved her hands in a 'see what I mean?' sort of gesture.

'And he cut all communications too, didn't he? He deliberately didn't have a phone. He didn't call or email a single friend or family member since he moved here, if what the police have told you is true. Maybe he thought whoever he was scared of could track him via his mobile. Or via his job, which is why he didn't start it. Look at all the evidence,

Gemma. He was *hiding*. It's obvious. He was hiding. From everyone, except you,' she said.

'Yes, OK, OK.'

I rubbed my eyes, my brain racing. It made sense, finally. Something about this big fat mess made *sense*.

'But the blood ... what about the blood, Eva?'

She shrugged.

'I don't know. I can't explain that. And honestly, I don't know if he's dead or alive right now, nobody does. But what we *do* know is that you didn't kill him, and we also know that, despite what the police think, nothing terrible can have happened to him five weeks ago in London either, because he was here with you, alive and well, for the past few weeks. Somehow, we need to prove that. So if we forget the blood thing for now, assume it's some sort of forensics cock-up or something, the rest of this theory makes sense, right? That he'd maybe got himself in some sort of trouble, and was laying low?'

I nodded slowly.

'Maybe. I mean, I never thought of it before but now ... except for the fact that he *did* go out, Eva, every day, for hours, Monday to Friday. Yes, he left in the dark and came home in the dark, but there were hours of daylight in-between. He must have been somewhere. And wherever that was, people must have seen him. So maybe he *was* hiding from someone. But he couldn't hide from *everyone*, not in a busy city like this. So how do I find out where he went every day, and what he was doing? Because that must be the key to all this. How on earth do I find out?'

Eva grimaced.

'Well *that*, my dear, is the million-dollar question.'

She paused, and shifted on her seat, suddenly looking uncomfortable.

'Look, we can't totally discount the other theory though. He did have a profile on a dating site after all. Maybe both theories work, maybe he *was* in some sort of trouble *and* he's run off with someone else to get away from it. It's just that, well ...'

She took a deep breath, looking even more uneasy now, and I stared at her, my chest tightening.

'What? What is it? Eva, if you know something, you have to tell me!'

'OK, OK. Look, I didn't want to tell you this, I really didn't. You seemed so happy, and I just didn't see the point, it was nothing really ...'

'Shit, Eva, TELL ME!'

'OK. I'm telling you. It's ... well ...' She paused and blew out some air, then covered her face with her hands. 'Danny made a pass at me once,' she mumbled through her fingers.

'Danny ... he *what?*'

I suddenly felt light-headed. What? Seriously. WHAT? Had she really just said that Danny, my husband Danny, had made a pass at her, my best friend? Eva dropped her hands from her face again, looking anguished.

'I'm so sorry. So, so sorry. I should have told you about it ages ago, but I just didn't see the point. I mean nothing happened, nothing whatsoever, OK? I would never have done that to you, even if I did fancy Danny, which I didn't. I mean, there's nothing wrong with him, he's very attractive, but he just isn't my type ...'

Her voice tailed off, her face flushed. I stared at her.

'Well, go on. When, how? What happened?'

She ran a hand across her eyes, then leaned forwards in her seat.

'OK. It was at that crazy space restaurant opening in Soho, do you remember? Back in September. The one where robots served the pre-dinner nibbles?'

I did remember. I'd actually been given four tickets for the opening night of Space Soho at pretty short notice, and only Eva and Danny had been free to come with me; it had been on a Tuesday night, as far as I could recall. The restaurant, with glow in the dark menus, a slowly rotating dining area and small white robots moving jerkily between tables holding aloft trays of finger food, was owned by the brother of one of my *Camille* magazine colleagues, and although it was all as tacky and cheesy as hell, it had been a really fun night. But, I thought, casting my mind back, the three of us had been together all evening, hadn't we? When would Danny have ...?

'It was towards the end of the evening, when you were invited into the kitchen to talk to the head chef, remember?' Eva said, anticipating my question.

I nodded. Yes, I remembered that too. But I'd only been gone for ten minutes, fifteen tops ... 'So what happened?' I said.

She sighed.

'We were all really drunk, weren't we? All those cocktails

173

at the beginning, and then the champagne, and the espresso martinis, and ... anyway, you went off, and we just chit-chatted for a few minutes, and then I think I said something about it getting late and needing to get home, because I had work early the next morning, and he just ... he just said something like, "I wish *I* could take you home".'

She stopped talking for a moment, looking at me with a wary expression, but I nodded at her. I was beginning to feel sick.

'Carry on. It's OK.'

'Right. Well, I just laughed it off at first, you know? I said, well, that's kind of you, but I'll be fine, I can get a cab right outside. And then he ... well, he slipped his hand under the table and started stroking my knee, Gemma. And he told me that wasn't what he meant. He told me I was gorgeous, and that what he actually wanted to do was take me home and ... take me to bed.'

She stopped again, her face flushing an even darker shade of red. I swallowed hard.

'And ... what did you say? What happened next?'

'Well, obviously, I told him to bugger off. I didn't want to make a scene, especially as I knew you'd be back any minute, but I asked him to get his hand off my leg and told him I was going to ignore what he'd said, just this once, because you were my best friend and I knew he loved you and he was only saying what he said because he was drunk. When you came back a few minutes later it was all over, and he was acting normally again, laughing and joking like nothing had happened. I felt dreadful the next day, and not just because of the hangover, which was a stinker. I just didn't know what to do, didn't know whether to tell you or not. But then the next time I saw him, a few weeks later, when we all went to the pub, he took me aside as soon as he got a chance and he apologized, told me he didn't even really remember what had happened but he knew he'd been inappropriate, and he seemed really genuine, Gemma, really, really sorry and really embarrassed about it. So I thought about it a bit more, and I decided to just let it go. I mean, we all do and say stupid things when we've had too much to drink, don't we? And nothing happened, after all. It would just have upset you, and caused a big row, and for what? It never happened again, either. So ... well, that's it really. I just thought that now, with all this going on ...'

I nodded. This was horrible, *horrible*, but it wasn't her fault. Would I have told *her*, if the situation had been reversed? Probably not, if I thought it was a one-off. Why potentially wreck somebody's relationship over a drunken, unwanted advance? No, I'd probably have done exactly the same in her shoes. It didn't stop it hurting, though. It was shit, SHIT.

How could you have done that, Danny? Eva's my friend.

'It's OK, honestly,' I said. 'I'm glad you told me. I just don't know what to make of it, though, Eva. I don't know what to make of any of it, and I can't even think straight anymore, I feel sick all the time and I think my brain is turning to mush—'

BRRRRR.

The doorbell rang, making us both jump. The police, to do whatever forensic stuff they needed to do in the house. They filed in past me, four of them, led by DC Frankie Stevens, the other three clutching cases of equipment, as Eva watched silently from the kitchen doorway.

'You're welcome to stay around while we work, but it will take a couple of hours. You might prefer to go out, maybe have a coffee or something. It's a nice day out there,' DC Stevens said, and the unexpected kindness in his voice almost made me burst into tears. The previous day had been so horrible, the way DCI Dickens and DS Clarke had looked at me ... maybe they didn't *all* think I was some sort of lying, husband-attacking witch then? We took his advice, and went out, Eva and I, Albert trotting along beside us, walking towards Clifton Village under a sky so bright we wished we'd thought to bring sunglasses. On a cobbled side street, we found a little coffee shop that sold almond croissants and pains au chocolat, and we ate at a tiny outside table, Albert stretched out at our feet, the sun warm on our faces, any awkwardness that hung between us after Eva's revelation quietly dissipating.

'Let's talk about other things. About anything. Just not about Danny, just for a little while,' I begged, and so we did, Eva regaling me with tales of newspaper life, stories that made me smile, even laugh out loud once, before I remembered again, and the hollow feeling that had been building in my chest for days now threatened to engulf me, smother me.

Where are you Danny? What are you doing to me? Come home, Danny. Please, please come home.

After coffee, we wandered around for a while, peering into quirky little homeware shops and flicking through the rails in trendy, independent boutiques. But our hearts weren't in it, and by mid-afternoon we were heading back to the house. As we turned into Monville Road, I stopped abruptly.

'What's going on? Shit, Eva, are they for me?'

Halfway up the street we could see a little cluster of people, a large white van parked a few yards away, a satellite dish on its roof.

'Press,' she said. 'Bugger. OK, just walk quickly, and keep your head down. And get your door keys out now.'

I did as she said, but as we got closer a shout went up.

'Gemma! Gemma O'Connor? Any news about Danny?'

'How do you feel about him being the third man to go missing, Gemma?'

We were almost at the house now, and I lowered my head, pushing my way through the assembled group, Eva close behind me. They moved aside to let me pass, but the questions kept coming, and there was a sudden flash, then another. They were taking photos. As we reached our gate I could see somebody at next door's window, the curtains pushed back, a face peering through the glass. Clive? Oh God, what would the neighbours think of all this?

'Gemma, do you think your husband's dead too?'

I gasped at that, turning to look at the journalist who'd asked the question, catching a glimpse of a slender, pale man with a neat goatee beard, a mobile phone thrust towards me.

'He's *not* ...' I said, but Eva was pushing me forwards towards the front door, grabbing the keys from my clenched fingers. Moments later we were inside, the door slamming behind us.

'SHIT,' Eva said. 'Not nice being on this side of it, is it? I might be nicer in future, when I'm doorstepping people.'

I nodded, breathing heavily. We'd both spent many hours in press packs like that one, outside so many homes, over the years. It was horrible, *horrible*, to be on the receiving end. Was this a punishment for my days as a tabloid hack? Some sort of divine retribution? Was it ...?

'Mrs O'Connor.'

DC Stevens was walking down the hall towards us.

'We're just about finished here. Sorry about that outside. We think one of your husband's friends must have talked to the press about him being missing, because it certainly didn't come from us.'

I took a breath, then another, trying to calm myself.

'It's OK. They're only doing their jobs. Not a pleasant experience though.'

'I can imagine. And I'm afraid ...' he paused, looking from me to Eva, then back again, 'I'm afraid we're going to have to ask you to brave it again in a minute. DS Clarke wants you back at the station. He has a few more questions for you.'

Chapter 16

'Bugger.'

DCI Helena Dickens picked up the Saturday edition of the *Bristol Post*, scowled at it and dropped it into the wastepaper bin beside her desk.

WIFE QUESTIONED IN BRISTOL SERIAL KILLER MYSTERY

The headline was accompanied by a photograph of a distressed-looking Gemma O'Connor being led through a crowd of reporters by DC Frankie Stevens. It had been taken outside her home the previous afternoon when they'd brought her in for further questioning, and while Helena knew there'd been nothing Frankie could have done to stop the press taking pictures, the paper's front page had instantly put her in a bad mood.

'This damn "serial killer" thing is really starting to piss me right off. And the nationals have got in on the act now too. Have you seen the front of the *Mail*?' she said, turning to Devon, who'd just got in and was perching on the edge of a neighbouring desk, stuffing the last of what looked like a sausage bap into his mouth.

He nodded and swallowed.

'Yeah, and it's bloody annoying,' he said. 'Doesn't seem to matter how many times we tell them there's no evidence the same person's responsible for both of our murders. They don't listen. Serial killer sells papers, I suppose.'

He'd been rolling the brown paper bag that had held his breakfast into a small ball as he spoke, and he raised his hand, aimed at the bin and threw. The paper ball landed on top of the newspaper with a small thud.

'Yes!' he said, sounding victorious, then looked back at Helena.

'And now they seem determined that Danny O'Connor is victim number three, even though the press office has been very clear that there's no body yet. We've managed to keep the bloody scene in Chiswick out of the public domain for now, thank the Lord. And all the stuff about his weird behaviour in the run-up to his disappearance.'

'Well, that's something I suppose,' Helena said morosely. She sighed heavily. She had slept badly, waking in the early hours and worrying about Charlotte and parenthood and what to do about it all. At five, she'd once again given up on sleep and gone out for a run, but even that hadn't helped to clear her head, and it had made her sodding backache worse again. Once this case was over, she could think about babies and the future properly, but for now ... she dragged her focus back to Devon.

'Any news from the lab yet on the O'Connor house?'

He shook his head.

'They promised by ten. It's a bit early yet. How are you feeling about Gemma now, after seeing her again yesterday?'

Helena thought for a few moments, swinging her chair slowly from side to side.

'I'm not sure. I know we have nothing concrete on her, not yet. It's all circumstantial, and not everything makes sense. But I absolutely think she's lying to us. She knows way more than she says she does. And all this rubbish about him living with her here in Bristol for the past few weeks? I reckon if we keep the pressure up, she'll cave.'

They'd questioned her together again after Frankie had brought her in, and Helena had noted with interest the deterioration in the woman's appearance. Less than a week ago when she'd come in to report her husband missing, she'd looked well groomed, smartly dressed, face neatly made-up, even though she'd clearly been distraught. On Thursday, when they'd confronted her with the photographs from Chiswick, it had been like looking at a different person, her hair greasy and pulled back off her face, eyeliner smudged, clothing creased. On this most recent meeting, she'd looked even worse, a pale, exhausted shadow of the Gemma O'Connor they'd first met just days ago. Grief over her missing husband, or guilt because she knew exactly what had happened to him? Helena couldn't decide, but there was just *something*.

'I agree, I do think there's something extremely weird about her story,' Devon was saying. 'But I thought her reaction seemed genuine. When we asked her about the other murders, I mean. She looked ... dumbfounded.'

'Mmmm.'

'You sound a tad sceptical, boss.' Devon looked amused. 'Tea?'

'Yeah, go on. Thanks.'

He gave her a thumbs up sign and headed for the door. Helena stopped swinging and tilted her head backwards, staring at the grey ceiling tiles and thinking. When she'd asked Devon after their last team briefing to check and see if there'd been any similar, unsolved murders in London recently, she hadn't really been expecting him to come up with anything. When he'd rushed over to her desk just half an hour later, a tingle had run along her spine before he'd even shown her what was on the piece of paper he was excitedly waving.

'Shit! Look at this!' he'd said. 'Look at these pictures!'

She'd looked, and then looked again. Two photographs, two men. Two men with thick dark hair, dark eyes. One clean-shaven, one with a small goatee beard. Two men who looked to be in their thirties. Two men with a striking resemblance to Mervin Elliott, Ryan Jones, and Danny O'Connor.

'You're not serious? In London?'

'In London. This one ...' he tapped the left-hand picture, 'was found in Richmond Park pretty much exactly a year ago, in early March. He died from a head injury inflicted with a blunt object, and his killer has never been found. He was a user of dating apps, although we don't know if he used EHU. It wasn't on his phone when he was killed, at any rate, just like our Bristol victims, and as the company seems to have lost all its data now we won't be able to find out if he used it or not unfortunately. This one ...' he tapped the second photograph, 'was murdered in the car park of Hounslow West tube station a few weeks later. April last year. Similar injuries. He wasn't a dating app user though, had a long-term girlfriend. Again, nobody ever done for it. There are cameras in that car park but the body was found in a blind spot unfortunately. The Met say they didn't link the two cases at the time, didn't have any reason to, but in the light of our two here and the similarities in appearance and cause of death, they're going to have another look at the files. They'll let us know if they come up with anything.'

Helena let out a long, low whistle.

'Wow. Devon, I'm starting to think that EHU app thing is leading us down the wrong path. If tens of thousands of people use it, it doesn't mean much. There must be some other way our killer is finding lookalike victims. I mean, look at these two new ones! There *has* to be a connection with our three here, there *has* to be. And Richmond and Hounslow? Both west London. Neither very far from Chiswick in fact. Not far at all from Gemma O'Connor's former home. Well, well, well.'

'Crazy, eh? Do you really think it could be her, though? I just can't see her being able to ... well, to kill four, or five or whatever young, fit men, can you? She's not a big woman. And why? What on earth would be the motive?'

Helena had shrugged. 'I don't know. But this is potentially huge, Devon. Christ, if we do have a serial killer on our hands, and if it's a *woman*, after all ...'

They had stared at each other then, Devon slowly shaking his head. Female serial killers weren't unheard of, but they were much less common than the male variety; if a hundred serial killers were put into a room, only around seventeen of them would be women, Helena had told Devon, a fact she remembered from some long-ago research she'd read. And they tended to be so-called 'quiet' killers, generally avoiding mutilating their victims' bodies, less likely to abduct or torture them. Did that pattern fit with these murders? *Maybe*, she thought. And there *were* instances of female serial killers choosing male victims – Aileen Wuornos in the US, for example, although she'd shot her seven victims, not bashed them over the head or slashed them with a knife. But even so …

By the time Gemma O'Connor had arrived at the station, both Helena and Devon had been feeling twitchy. Once they were settled in the interview room, Gemma still refusing any legal assistance despite the offer of the services of the duty solicitor, Helena had begun with something that had come to light just an hour earlier.

'Mrs O'Connor, you told us that you believed your husband was staying on at your Chiswick apartment for a week after you left, to finish up some work for his previous employer, Hanfield Solutions?'

Gemma nodded.

'Yes, that's right. That's what he told me he was doing.'

'Well, as we all know now, he didn't stay on in the apartment after that Friday the first of February, as the keys were handed back to the landlord. So today we made a call to Hanfield Solutions to see if they could shed any light on this. And they said there was no work to finish up. Your husband's final day in the office was Thursday, the thirty-first of January.

Which makes sense, being the last day of the month, doesn't it? They all said their goodbyes to him then and wished him well in his new life in Bristol. They didn't see him again, or indeed hear from him. Anything to say about that?'

Gemma was listening, a frown furrowing her brow.

'But ... he told me he needed a week to finish a project. That's why I moved down here first. He joined me the following week, and he said it was all done ...'

She shook her head, her eyes darting from Devon to Helena and back again.

'So that's yet another thing. I'm sorry, no, I can't explain that. Unless he was seeing someone else after all, someone he met on that app, and went to stay with ... with her. That's the only thing I've been able to think of.'

Helena waited a few moments, but Gemma had stopped talking, eyes still flitting from one of them to the other. Helena gave it another few seconds, then started again.

'OK. Now I want to ask you about some specific dates. First, can you remember where you were on the evening of the third of March last year?'

She glanced down at her paperwork, checking she'd got the date of the Richmond Park murder correct. She had. She looked back at Gemma, who was frowning again.

'The ... the third of March?'

'Yes. It was a Saturday evening.'

'Well ...' Gemma paused, still frowning. 'Well no, of course I don't. That was over a year ago, and the date doesn't ring any bells. Why are you asking me?'

She sounded faintly exasperated.

'I just need you to answer the question, Gemma. Please try to think.'

'Well ...' Gemma gave a small sigh. 'Well, OK, we got married on the seventeenth, St Patrick's Day. So that would have been two weekends before that, is that right?'

Helena flipped a page to the calendar she'd printed off earlier, checked the dates and nodded.

'That's right, yes.'

'OK, well in that case, that was the evening Danny had his stag do. His dad had died just a few weeks before that and he was still pretty upset, so it wasn't a wild night out or anything, just a few drinks with some of the guys from work and one of his cousins. He was home by midnight, and I just stayed in on my own that evening because I had some work to finish up for the Monday. I remember because I was still up when he got in, which was quite unusual for me. I'm normally crashed out by ten.'

Helena was making notes.

'You're sure about that? That date?' she said.

'Positive. Danny had his stag two weeks before the wedding, and I had my hen do one week before, so the following weekend.'

'Right. And can anyone verify that you were at home alone on the evening of the third? Anyone come to the door, maybe a takeaway or something?'

Gemma was frowning again.

'No, not that I can think of. It was over a year ago, so obviously I don't remember what I ate. I probably cooked something, I wouldn't normally order a takeaway if it was just me. Look, why are you asking me about that date? How is it relevant to Danny's disappearance?'

The exasperated tone was back. Helena ignored the question, instead flipping to the next page of her notes to check the date of the Hounslow West tube station car park killing.

'Just another few questions, if you don't mind. Another date for you – can you remember what you were doing on the evening of Wednesday, the fourth of April last year? So that would have been a few weeks after you and your husband married.'

Gemma stared at her for a moment, then sank her face into her hands, letting out a little groan. She stayed like that for several moments, fingers clawing at her scalp, and Helena and Devon exchanged a brief glance. Then Gemma straightened up again.

'Look, what's going on? What's this about? I don't understand any of it,' she said. 'You're supposed to be looking for my husband. Yes, I know you clearly think I had something to do with his disappearance, but I didn't, OK? You need to find him, you need to be out there looking for him. How is this helping, asking me about what I was doing a year ago? This is *ridiculous*.'

Her voice was becoming louder and louder as she spoke, a flush spreading across her cheeks.

'I mean, how am I supposed to know what I was doing on a random Wednesday last April? Would you remember what *you* were doing? This is pointless, all of it, and in the meantime Danny is out there somewhere and he could be dead, or injured, and you're wasting time with this ... with this *bollocks*.'

She banged a fist on the table, and her eyes filled with tears. There was the usual box of tissues at the end of the table, and Devon pushed it towards her.

'There's no need to get upset, Gemma. This is all part of our investigation, I promise you. Please try to answer the question. The sooner you can do that, the sooner you can get out of here, OK?'

There was silence for a moment, then Gemma sighed.

'Sorry,' she said. She pulled a tissue from the box and wiped her eyes, then looked from Devon to Helena and back again.

'I'm sorry. I just get so ... so frustrated, you know? I don't understand any of this, it's like some sort of horrible nightmare and I'm just so scared about ... about where Danny is and what's happened to him. I shouldn't take it out on you, I know you're just doing your job, but it's just ... it's just so hard, you know?'

'Of course.' Devon turned to Helena. 'It was the fourth of April we wanted to know about, right?'

Helena nodded.

'Yes, Gemma. I know it's not easy, but if you could just cast your mind back. It would have been about, what? Two and a half weeks after you got married. Can you remember anything about that period?'

Gemma took a deep breath, held it for a moment, then let it out. The flush in her cheeks had subsided but her eyes were still wet, and she dabbed at them again.

'OK. Let me think. Can I see that calendar?'

Helena slid it across the table, and Gemma studied it, running a finger across the dates.

'Right, well, we got married on the seventeenth of March as I said. We stayed in London until the Monday, the nineteenth, and then we flew to Paris for a week for our honeymoon, so we would have been back on the following Monday, the twenty-sixth. Danny took the rest of that week off work and I didn't have much on so we just sort of hung out for a few days, kind of extended honeymoon but at home kind of thing. Then we both went back to work properly on the following Monday, the second of April. So that week you're asking about would have just been a normal one. I remember Danny had a few late nights at work, catching up on stuff he'd got behind on while we were away, and I was busy again so pretty much chained to my desk. But we didn't go out that week, as far as I can remember, because we'd spent a lot of money on the wedding and in Paris and everything, so we thought we'd better be good for a while. So, to answer your question, I would have been in the apartment on the night of Wednesday, the fourth. All night.'

Helena, who'd been scribbling again, put her pen down.

'Alone?' she asked.

'Well, until Danny came home from work. Then it would have been the two of us.'

'OK.' Helena paused for a moment. 'Two other dates. Recent ones this time. We need to know where you were on the nights of Tuesday, the twelfth of February and Wednesday, the twenty-seventh of February this year. The nights Mervin Elliott and

Ryan Jones were murdered. The two men Devon here mentioned to you in a previous meeting?'

'What?' Gemma sat still, looking stunned, for a moment, then stood up suddenly, pushing her chair back so violently that it toppled over and crashed to the floor.

'WHAT?' she said again, her voice tight and angry. 'Are you serious? You really think I could be involved in those deaths, just as you think I'm involved with whatever's happened to Danny? I mean, look at me. Come on, look at me.'

She put both hands on the table, angling her body across it towards them.

'I'm a journalist. I work from home, writing articles about woolly hats and Pilates and lip glosses, for fuck's sake. I've never been in trouble with the police in my life, not once. So do you seriously believe that now, at the age of thirty-four, I've suddenly decided to take up murder as a hobby? That I've spent my time in Bristol popping out every other night to kill some random man? Why? Why would I do that?'

She straightened up again, backing away from the table and taking a deep, shuddering breath.

'I was at home, on both of those nights, OK?' she continued. 'Danny and I didn't go out together at all since we moved here, because we were too busy sorting out the house. I went to yoga a few times, and for drinks in the evening *once*, with some new friends, but that wasn't on either of those nights. Otherwise we stayed in. And yes, I'm saying WE, because despite what you think Danny was here in Bristol, alive and well, living with me for the past few weeks, until he disappeared exactly a week ago today, OK?'

She was breathing heavily now, her face red again. Helena sat in silence, watching her, but Devon held out a placatory hand and stood up.

'All right. Let's take a moment. Gemma, I know this is difficult, but getting angry isn't going to help, OK? Sit down.'

He moved around the table to pick up the fallen chair and gestured for her to sit in it. She did, still panting slightly, her fists clenched.

'Are you all right to carry on?' Helena asked.

Gemma nodded, eyes fixed on the table in front of her.

'Sorry, again,' she muttered.

'It's OK. We understand that you're going through a lot right now,' Helena said. 'But you must also understand that we are now very, very concerned for your husband's welfare, and on all of these dates we're asking you about, men who bear a striking resemblance to Danny were killed in what so far remain unsolved cases. So as you see ...'

Gemma's head had snapped up, her eyes locking onto Helena's.

'All of them? What, those two London dates too? Men were murdered in London as well? So that's ... that's *four*?'

Helena paused for a moment, then nodded.

'Four, yes. We don't know if any of them are connected, not yet. But there are certain distinct similarities, and as Danny is now missing ...'

Gemma was shaking her head, an incredulous look on her face.

'Oh my GOD,' she said. 'You really do think I've got something to do with all this, don't you? OK, so if you really don't believe me about Danny only being missing a week, what exactly did I do then? Show me some proof that I hurt him, that I hurt *any* of them. Tell me how I overpowered my big strong husband, slashed him to death with a knife and then ... well, then what? Carried his body out of our apartment all by myself, and hid it somewhere? Buried it? All without anyone else noticing a thing? Where is it then? And again, look at me, for *fuck's* sake. I'm five foot four, and Danny's over six foot. I don't know why his blood is all over that room, I can't explain that. But I didn't hurt him. He was absolutely fine when I last saw him. I didn't do anything, to any of them. This is crazy, all of it. You're *crazy*.'

She was still in her seat but looked as if she was about to leap out of it at any moment, her hands shaking, her face suddenly drained of colour, ashy white. There was silence in the room for several moments, then Helena cleared her throat.

'OK, we'll leave that for now,' she said. 'Just one more thing. We've accessed your medical records, and we've noticed that you suffered from a period of anxiety and depression a few years ago. Can you tell us a bit about that?'

Gemma sighed wearily. She looked drained, Helena thought, the dark rings under her eyes even more pronounced now that she was looking so pale.

'It was work-related. I was working as a newspaper reporter back then and it was really high pressure. It all got on top of me, so I quit my job and got help. I'm fine now. Being freelance is much better because I'm in control. I can turn down jobs if I have too much on. And again, how is that relevant to Danny's disappearance? It was before I even met him.'

Her words were defiant, but she just sounded sad now, her voice low and monotone. Helena looked at Devon, who gave her a small nod. It was time to wrap things up. And so they'd let Gemma O'Connor go home, not really any further forward than they'd been when she'd arrived.

'Here you go.'

Devon was back, carrying two steaming mugs. She accepted hers gratefully, desperate for the small caffeine hit the tea offered. After a couple of sips she put the mug down again.

'Right, so now we wait for the forensics on the O'Connor house. Maybe that will tell us what to do next, Devon, because I don't mind telling you, I'm struggling here.'

He sighed.

'I know, boss. And I know what you mean about Gemma O'Connor. There's a lot there that points to her, but things don't entirely add up. By the way, notice how she still talks about him in the present tense? I was just thinking about that when I was getting the drinks. "I'm five foot four, he's over six foot", remember that? It's a little thing, but the psychs would say that means she believes he's still alive. Otherwise it would have been more like "he *was* over six foot".'

Helena picked up her mug again.

'I know. I noticed that too. And if she did kill him in that apartment, she had a point – she's not very big, or very strong looking. Unless she did have help, how would she have been able to overpower him? When he was asleep, maybe? And how would she dispose of the body? I just don't know. But she's a clever woman, Devon. She's a journalist, remember, and they're tricky. We can't let her fool us.'

She took a sip and put the mug down.

'And also, that episode of mental illness she had a few years ago? She says she's OK now, but how do we know it's not back and worse this time, making her do things she might not even be aware of? We can't take anything for granted, there's too much at stake here. I mean, now it's potentially *four* murders we're talking about. Four, and maybe five. We need to find Danny O'Connor's body. Because he's dead, Devon. I know he is. And I still think his clever little wifey knows a lot more than she's letting on.'

Chapter 17

'Well, thanks a lot. Thanks for *nothing*.'

I cut the call and flung my phone down onto the sofa, then sank onto it myself, a sudden wave of shame rushing over me to replace the surge of anger I'd just felt. *Shit*. What was wrong with me? I'd just lost my temper with the police *again*, just like I had in that interview room the previous night when they were asking me all those ridiculous questions. I needed to get a grip.

'Who was that? They're still out there, you know. In fact, I think there are more of them now than there were last night.'

Eva appeared in the doorway of the living room, long hair in a plait down her back, a half-eaten apple in one hand. Albert scampered in behind her and ran across the room to sit at my feet, resting his head on my knee.

'Hello, you,' I said, and stroked his soft nose, then turned back to Eva.

'It was the police. I rang them to tell them we were under siege by the press, that we couldn't even open the front door without a billion flashbulbs going off, and the desk sergeant or whoever it was just said there was nothing they could do, not unless they were trespassing or there was damage to property or something. I got mad and just put the phone down on him. I feel really shitty about it now.'

Eva crossed the room, dropped the remains of her apple onto a plate that was sitting on the coffee table, and sat down beside me.

'Oh sweetie, they'll understand. You're under massive pressure, especially after last night. And you've been on the other side of things often enough in the past to know that he was right – the press are perfectly entitled to stand outside someone's house on a public road as long as they obey some basic rules. Nothing we can do, sadly.'

She squeezed my arm, and I sighed.

'I know. I just can't bear it, Eva. This whole thing … it's just getting more and more bizarre. I don't think they're even looking for Danny alive anymore, you know. I think they're absolutely convinced he's dead, and that I had something to do with it. And with those other murders too. I mean, seriously? Two murders in London, and another two in Bristol? They seem to think that because I once suffered from a bit of anxiety that I'm some sort of psycho. *Me*, Eva. If it wasn't so bloody nightmarish it would be funny.'

'I know. It's crazy. I'm so glad you've got some new friends here, you know. I'll feel so much better about leaving you here and going back to London. I did really like them.'

'Good. I like them too.'

Earlier, Tai and Clare had come round for coffee. They'd obviously heard the news, seen my picture on the front of the paper, and Tai had rung first thing, asking if I was OK and if she and Clare could come over.

'We'll bring cake. Sounds like you might need it,' she said.

An hour later they were on the doorstep, looking anxious and flustered after pushing their way through the press pack in the street.

'God, that was horrible! This *is* horrible, I can't believe what's going on here,' Clare had gasped as I closed the front door behind them.

'Welcome to my world,' I said drily. 'And yes, it's not much fun. Come in and meet Eva, she's dying to say hello.'

True to her word, Tai had brought cake; not just one, but a selection of cupcakes from one of the bakeries in Clifton Village.

'There's lemon, banoffee, carrot, rocky road and, errrm, salted caramel, I think,' she said, as she lifted the beautifully decorated mini-sponges carefully out of their white box and laid them neatly on a plate, Albert hovering nearby, eyes following her hands, hoping for some dropped crumbs. Clare had arrived without Winnie and Albert's disappointment had been clear, his frantically wagging tail drooping as the door closed and he realized that it was just two humans standing in his hallway, no poodle in sight.

I smiled at Eva.

'Told you they were nice,' I said, and she grinned back as Tai and Clare laughed. The cake had lifted the mood a little, and for a few minutes we sat and ate and chatted about not very much.

Then Clare said: 'Gemma, I know you probably don't really

want to talk about it, it must be so awful with Danny still missing, but are you OK? I mean, when we saw in the paper that *you'd* been questioned, and that the police seem to be linking Danny's disappearance to the two murders on The Downs, well, we were just horrified.'

I hesitated for a moment, wondering how much to tell her, then decided to keep things simple. What had been in the papers was enough for now.

'I'm OK. Well, as OK as I can be under the circumstances,' I said. 'The police just brought me in to get some more background stuff on Danny, that's all. The press outside, they're just hoping for a new angle on the story. If Danny *is* dead ...'

I swallowed hard, trying not to cry, and Tai who was sitting to my left on the sofa immediately slipped an arm round my shoulders. She smelled, as always, of oranges and bergamot, a fragrance she imported from a tiny *perfumerie* in Paris twice a year. She'd told us she'd discovered it on a weekend trip to the French capital years ago, and had never worn another perfume since.

'Oh Gemma, I can't even imagine what you're going through,' she said. 'We are so sorry, honestly.'

'I just wish you'd met him, before he went missing,' I said quietly. 'You'd have liked him. Hopefully, one day ...'

'*Definitely* one day,' said Clare, who was on my right. 'Positive thinking, right?'

We all fell silent for a few moments, then Eva said: 'It's such a shame that you didn't meet him. We've sort of been struggling to find people who did, you know, since he moved here with Gemma? It might have been useful to see if anyone had picked up anything that Gemma might not have noticed, about how he was behaving and stuff before he went missing.'

Clare nodded.

'Well, we tried!' she said, with a little laugh. 'We invited him to join us for drinks but he couldn't make it, could he, Gemma? So the mysterious Danny remained a mystery.'

'Seemingly so,' said Eva. She glanced at me as she spoke, and I thought I saw a strange expression cross her face. A shiver ran through me. Surely Eva wasn't starting to doubt me now, too? Surely *she* wasn't beginning to think I was making it up about Danny being here with me in Bristol, like the police did?

Tai and Clare left soon after, hugging me hard in the hallway and grimacing as they prepared to face the camera flashes once again. When it was just me and Eva again, I turned to her and asked her straight.

'Eva – you do believe me, don't you, that Danny was here? It's just that when Clare talked about having never met him, you looked ... I don't know, you looked a bit strange.'

Was I imagining it, or was there a moment of hesitation before her reply came?

'Gemma, of course I believe you! Don't be ridiculous. All this is making you paranoid. I've got your back, OK? Always had, always will.'

She'd wrapped her arms around me then, and I'd taken a deep breath, burying my face in her shoulder. Of course Eva would never doubt me, of course she believed me. She was right, I *was* getting paranoid. But if only my new friends *had* met my husband. It would have meant *four* people, four people who could tell the police they'd seen him here in Bristol a couple of weeks ago. Four people who could confirm that he couldn't possibly have been badly injured in Chiswick back at the end of January, because he was *fine*. How could the police think I'd hurt him, *how*? It made no sense, any of it.

We'd done some googling on the London murders earlier, using the dates the police had mentioned to me, and had found various news articles, although at the time it appeared the two deaths hadn't been linked. I could see why they were trying to connect them in retrospect though, and why they were being looked at in connection with the Bristol murders too; the photographs attached to the news stories had given me shivers. Men with dark hair, dark eyes. Men who looked alike. Men who looked like Danny.

Eva gave me a small smile.

'My friend, the serial killer,' she said. 'Now *that* would be a story.'

I couldn't help smiling back.

'Oh, shut up. Seriously though, what am I going to do, Eva? I feel like I'm in some sort of nightmare. And do you really have to leave today? It's going to be so awful being here on my own.'

'I know. I'm so sorry, I really am, I hate to leave you like this, but you're not totally on your own, are you, and I've stayed too long already. I'm needed back in the newsroom, just for a few days. I'll try and come back on Friday night though, OK? Stay for the weekend. And I need to go and get dressed, *now*. The train leaves at one.'

'Go on. I'm OK.'

She leant over and dropped a kiss on my cheek, then leapt from the sofa and ran from the room. I leaned back on the cushions, trying to ignore the low hum of chatter from just metres away outside the front gate. We'd closed the lounge curtains so they couldn't snap any photos through the window, and I'd made sure the back gate was locked so they couldn't sneak into the courtyard, but even so, their continued presence was hugely unsettling. Karma, I thought yet again. The number of times I'd been part of a press pack, staking out the home of a politician or a paedophile, desperate to get that shot, that interview. I'd barely given a thought to how awful it must be for those trapped inside their homes. Well, I knew now, didn't I?

We'd turned on the radio as we'd eaten breakfast in the kitchen first thing, tuning in to the Saturday morning news show on BBC Radio Bristol. They'd talked about me of course. I was all over the front of the papers, and not just the local ones. The nationals were reporting the story too.

WIFE QUESTIONED IN BRISTOL SERIAL KILLER MYSTERY

THIRD MAN MISSING – WIFE 'HELPING' POLICE ENQUIRY

No mention of the London murders yet, but surely that was only a matter of time, I thought. My phone, which had been buzzing with messages for the past couple of days, and which I'd largely ignored, had started ringing again at 8 a.m.

Friends, former colleagues, of both Danny's and mine. And finally, Danny's mother, as well as my own parents. I'd answered each call this time, each message, fobbing them all off, telling them, as I later told Tai and Clare, that the press had put two and two together and come up with seventeen, that I was simply giving them more background information about Danny in an effort to help them track him down. My friends, many of them journalists themselves, were aggrieved that I'd found myself in the papers, sympathizing and offering help if I needed it. Our families though were a different matter. Bridget had been icily polite, weirdly so, as if she was ringing to enquire about something mundane like the times of a theatre performance, not about her eldest son who'd seemingly vanished into the ether.

'And have the police any theories as to where he might be?' she said.

Clearly whoever had called her from the police station hadn't given her many details.

'Not yet, Bridget,' I said. 'I'm just hoping he'll come back, and all this will be over. It's just been so awful.'

There was a pause on the line, then she said coldly: 'Right. Well, fine. Goodbye, Gemma.'

The line had gone dead, leaving me staring at the phone feeling slightly stunned. What sort of reaction had that been, from a woman whose son was missing, possibly dead? OK, so she and Danny didn't get on well, weren't close, but even so. She was his *mother*. What the hell was wrong with her? Why wasn't she in tears, in a panic, offering to come over here to support me, to help find him? I shook my head in bewilderment, but then a thought struck me. Was there any way ... could she possibly be so casual about it because she wasn't actually worried at all? Because she *knew* where Danny was? Was there any chance at all that he might have gone home to Ireland? But no, he couldn't have, could he? His passport was still upstairs in the bedroom. Was there any way of getting to Ireland without a passport? I wasn't a hundred per cent sure, but I didn't think so. And anyway, surely however bad things were, whatever trouble Danny might be in, his mother would be the last person he'd turn to. And so I dismissed the theory, beginning to feel too overwhelmed by the barrage of callers and messages to think about Bridget for too long. It was my own parents I was more concerned about. Moments before I'd spoken to Bridget they'd been on the phone too, both of them together, my mother sobbing quietly, my dad's voice wobbly with emotion.

'Darling, your mother and I can't understand it. If Danny has walked out on you, why are *you* the one who's in trouble now, being dragged into the police station? Why didn't you mention it when you called last time? You haven't done anything wrong, have you Gemma, please tell us you haven't? And what about these murders, these men who look like Danny? Your mother's in a terrible state about this, she's had the neighbours knocking on the door and the WI women phoning, and she doesn't know what to tell them, neither of us do ...'

'Dad ... Dad, it's OK, I promise.'

I'd tried to explain that I hadn't been arrested, that the police had simply invited me to come in for routine questioning, but when I finally ended the call I could tell he was still distressed, uncomprehending. I felt a sudden fresh wave of anger. It wasn't just me under siege now, my parents were too.

'It's wrong, just *fucking* wrong,' I'd shouted, making Eva jump, her freshly poured coffee slopping over the edge of her mug and onto the table.

As I slouched on the sofa waiting for her to pack her bags, eyes closed, exhaustion taking hold, the images the police had shown me of the blood-soaked bedroom in Chiswick floated into my mind yet again, making my stomach churn. If that really was Danny's blood, blood from many weeks ago, as they claimed, there had to be an explanation. But what? How could it have happened, *how*? Come on, Gemma, think. *Think*.

I stood up, and started pacing the room, my mind racing.

OK, so let's forget about the other murders for now, the other dead men. Let's just concentrate on Danny and assume that he's in some sort of trouble, big *trouble. What if the person he's in trouble with came to see him the day I moved out of the apartment? And then got violent with him, really violent, hence all the blood? Danny didn't join me until a week later, so maybe his injuries had time to heal? But there was so much blood, and no serious injury could heal in just a week …*

I stopped pacing, suddenly feeling a little dizzy, and reached out a hand to lean on the mantelpiece to steady myself.

Think, Gemma, think.

Had I actually seen Danny naked, totally naked, since he moved down to Bristol to join me? We hadn't had sex in the three weeks he'd been here, I knew that. It hadn't bothered me at the time, not really – we'd both been tired, busy, and we'd had dry spells in the bedroom before when things were a bit crazy. But had I seen him with his clothes off? Could he have had injuries after all, ones I hadn't seen because he'd kept them covered up?

I started walking again, up and down, up and down, my temples starting to throb. The central heating hadn't been working properly in the house for the first ten days or so, so we'd been bundled up in jumpers, sleeping in tracksuit bottoms and T-shirts. Even when the letting agent had finally arranged for someone to repair the boiler, the bedroom was still chilly enough to stop us going to bed naked. I'd definitely seen Danny with his top off, I could remember that, but ... I stopped dead, staring at myself in the mirror over the fireplace. He *could* have been hiding an injury, or even more than one, if it was below the waist. His legs, his lower belly ... he *could* have been. My stomach lurched. Was I completely on the wrong track here? There had been so much blood in those photographs, and Danny hadn't seemed to be in any pain, had never flinched noticeably when I'd touched him, had been walking and riding his bike normally. But didn't injuries on some parts of the body bleed a lot, even when they weren't very serious? Head injuries tended to, I thought I vaguely remembered someone saying once, but did the same apply to cuts on other parts of the body?

Feeling decidedly wobbly now, I staggered back to the sofa. *So, continue this line of thought.* How would the timing have worked? I left Chiswick early on the morning of Friday, the first of February, and the keys were dropped off at the landlord's office later that day. So this attacker, whoever he was, must have come round to see Danny not long after I left, that morning in fact. Something went wrong, and he attacked him. Danny somehow survived, fought him off, but he was scared. Maybe the guy threatened to come back and finish him off? So instead of staying on in the apartment for a week as planned he moved out that day, went to stay with someone else, went to hospital even, or possibly stayed in a hotel or bed and breakfast? And then, a week later, he moved down here to join me, and didn't tell me a thing about it. He didn't want me to know about the trouble he was in, so he simply kept quiet about all of it.

I took a deep breath. Did this work, as a theory? Almost. It didn't explain everything – why Danny had pulled out of his new job on the thirty-first of January, for example. That would have been the day before any of it had happened. But even so ... I knew I was speculating crazily, but on most levels, it did make some sort of sense. Danny had been through something horrifying and was scared something even worse was going to happen to him, and he needed to hide, and so he did. He hid, in plain sight, hid without me even realizing what he was doing, because he was terrified. Terrified that this man, this person who'd attacked him so viciously in London, was going to track him down in Bristol. And then, maybe it all got too much, so he ran. Or ... nausea rose again, my body growing clammy, little beads of cold sweat running down my face. Did he run? Or was he caught? Had whoever he was so scared of finally found him?

I swallowed hard. I didn't know if any of this was true, but it *worked*. It made some sort of weird, twisted *sense*. But who could I tell? Could I take this to the police? How would I get them to believe it, to start investigating my version of events, when they thought Danny died weeks ago, in our Chiswick bedroom? When they didn't believe he ever moved to Bristol at all? How could I prove he was here? How could I get them to stop looking at me, and start looking for the real perpetrator?

I could hear Eva banging her suitcase down the stairs. I needed to talk to her about this, run all of it past her again with all the detail I'd just added. And then I needed to find some sort of evidence that I could show the police. Somehow, I *had* to prove to them that Danny had been here, living in this house with me, until just over a week ago. I needed to find out where he'd been spending his days, work out what he'd been doing. Where he'd been hiding. And I needed to do it myself, because the police were, it seemed, on completely the wrong track and unless I could somehow prove all this, unless I could convince them ... and I *could* do this, couldn't I? I'd been an investigative journalist for years, and a good one. And after all, Danny was *my* husband. I knew him better than anyone, didn't I? I stood up, walked slowly to the door and stepped into the hallway. Then I stopped again, gripping the doorframe for support as a fresh wave of dizziness struck. Who was I kidding? *I knew my husband better than anyone? I didn't know him at all, did I?* I had absolutely no idea what had been going on with him, for months. Maybe longer. Maybe, for as long as I'd known him, Danny had been lying to me. He was getting himself in trouble, he was using a dating app so presumably seeing other women while he was married to me, he was making passes at my friends. And now he was gone, and now it was *me* that was in trouble. Potentially huge, life-changing trouble. As I stood there, my whole body starting to shake, Eva appeared, walking down the hall towards me, her smile fading as she got closer.

'Bloody hell, Gem, you look terrible! Has something else happened?'

I shook my head. My lips felt dry, cracked, and I moistened them with my tongue.

'Gemma? What is it, you're scaring me?'

She reached towards me, her hands warm on mine.

'I think my whole life with Danny has been a lie,' I whispered.

Chapter 18

On Sunday, the headlines were still all about the so-called serial killer, but the press had finally made the London connection, the photos of the four lookalike men emblazoned across the front pages.

TWO MORE VICTIMS OF WEST COUNTRY KILLER?

LONDON MURDERS – WAS BRISTOL SERIAL KILLER
RESPONSIBLE?

Helena pushed the *Mail on Sunday* and the *Sunday Mirror* off her desk with a groan. They landed on the worn carpet with a soft thump, and Devon, who'd been scribbling some new notes on the board, crossed the room and picked them up.

'Shit. They've linked the four murders. How?' he said.

'Don't ask me. There's a leak somewhere now, presumably, because this certainly hasn't come from anywhere official.'

Helena ran both hands through her blonde crop, her eyes narrowing.

'And that leak had better be in London. Because if I find out that one of our team is talking to the press ...'

'It won't be from here. No way. They wouldn't.'

She sighed.

'I bloody well hope so. What were you putting up just then? Anything new?'

He shook his head and began tossing the marker pen he was still holding from one hand to the other.

'Nope. Just adding what the Met told us this morning. Which is sod all.'

Helena sighed again. A senior detective from the Metropolitan Police had called an hour ago, to inform the team that they had now taken a fresh look at the two murders in London and, other than the previously unremarked upon fact that the two victims did indeed closely resemble each other physically, they could find no other connections between the two cases.

'The two men didn't know each other, lived in different parts of London, had no friends or hobbies or anything else in common,' Mike, who had taken the call, had said.

'The victim in Richmond Park – his name was David Reynolds – had no criminal record. But the Hounslow tube station car park guy, name of Anthony Daniels, had a bit of a past – a few burglaries, some low-level dealing. That was one of the reasons they didn't even think to link the two cases at the time last year – they thought Daniels's death was probably related to his drug connections. Both *did* die from head injuries, attacked with some sort of blunt object which was never found in either case though. So similar MO to our two cases here. And obviously, there's their physical appearances.

The guy I spoke to didn't sound entirely convinced though, and they can't help us with any forensics or anything – they didn't have any. But they say they'll keep an open mind about a possible link. We've agreed to keep in touch.'

Now that the press had decided to link the cases regardless though, and had splashed their unsubstantiated musings all over the front pages, Helena knew that the pressure on her to come up with some sort of result would become intense. She'd already had a terse phone call from her boss, Detective Chief Superintendent Anna Miller, earlier that morning.

'Miller's been on,' she said morosely to Devon, who was still skilfully juggling his pen. 'She's a very angry Geordie today. She wants an arrest, pronto. Wondering why we haven't got Gemma O'Connor in custody. I told her we just don't have enough on her ... well, anything really. Nothing that would stick.'

'Agreed. Nowhere near enough for the CPS, that's for sure,' Devon agreed. 'Pity the forensic report on her house wasn't more conclusive. That would really have helped if it had backed up the theory that she's lying about Danny ever having made it to Bristol.'

Helena nodded. The Crown Prosecution Service would want a lot more than they currently had to make a charge stick to Gemma O'Connor, and the forensics report had been another blow. Traces of Danny O'Connor's DNA, along with his fingerprints, had been found in numerous parts of the Clifton house, although in vastly smaller quantities than those of Gemma's. They had already known from speaking to the letting agency that Danny had spent a night there with Gemma in mid-January, so that wasn't unexpected. But the lab had been unable to give any firm answer on exactly how much time he'd spent in the place.

'It's impossible to say. Depends how often the house is cleaned, what cleaning products are used. He's been there, that's all we can say for definite. Can't tell you how recently, or for how long, unfortunately.'

It was something they wanted to speak to Gemma about, but as they'd been about to contact her earlier, she had unexpectedly phoned the incident room, saying *she* needed to speak to *them*. She was due to arrive any minute, and just as that thought crossed Helena's mind, her desk phone rang.

'She's here,' she told Devon when she'd replaced the handset. 'You coming?'

'Definitely.'

When they were settled in one of the interview rooms, Helena decided to let Gemma speak first. The woman looked better than she had on their last meeting, she thought – a little more rested, hair freshly washed, and a determined expression on her face.

'Look, I've been thinking, really thinking, about Danny's behaviour over the past few weeks,' she began. 'And I've been talking it over with my friend Eva too. Eva Hawton? She's an investigative reporter on *The Independent*, and she's really good at getting to the bottom of stuff like this. She's been a big help.'

'Has she indeed?' said Helena. 'So what does Miss Hawton make of all this then?'

She tried to keep the scepticism she was feeling out of her voice. *Bloody reporters*, she thought, thinking again about the latest newspaper headlines.

'Well, she thinks – and so do I now, it just didn't occur to me before, but the more I think about it the more it makes sense – well, she and I *both* think now that Danny must have been in some sort of trouble, and maybe had been for a while, before he ... before he disappeared.'

'What sort of trouble?' asked Helena, glancing sideways at Devon and raising an eyebrow.

'Well ... I don't know, not at the moment. But our theory is that whoever Danny had got himself in trouble with met him at our place in Chiswick that morning after I moved out. And this guy attacked Danny, didn't manage to kill him but hurt him somehow. I still don't know how there could have been *so* much blood, but I've thought about it and in retrospect I don't think I actually saw Danny totally naked after he moved to Bristol. We didn't have sex ...'

'Ohh-kaaay.' Helena couldn't help it – her scepticism was growing exponentially.

Gemma ignored her and carried on.

'We didn't have sex after he moved down, and I just wonder now if he might have been hiding an injury on the lower part of his body. He didn't *seem* hurt or in pain, but it's the only thing I can think of to explain the blood.'

'Unlikely, but go on,' said Helena, resisting the temptation to roll her eyes. She wasn't buying this 'theory' for a minute.

Gemma flushed.

'I know this sounds far-fetched, but please, bear with me.

I don't know how it ties in with the other murders, or why the victims all look so alike, and so like Danny, I can't explain that. But leaving that aside, it does make some sort of sense, honestly. So Danny got hurt, and went somewhere to recover for a week before joining me here as planned. I don't know where – maybe a hotel or something. Or, if he *was* seeing someone else, some other woman, which I don't really want to think about, but you know ...'

She paused and swallowed hard, then took a breath.

'And then when he did move here, he was terrified that this guy would track him down, finish him off. So he hid, basically – never answered the door to deliveries, made sure the neighbours never spotted him, didn't even get a new mobile phone. I still don't know why he pulled out of his new job before any of this would have happened, or where he was spending his days when I thought he was at work. But ... can you not see that it's *sort of* logical? He'd have been scared. Really scared. And then, maybe he just got so scared that he ran. And he's still running. Either that or ...' She paused again. 'Either that or he got caught, and he's dead now too,' she said quietly.

For a few moments there was silence.

Then Devon said: 'Just assuming for a minute that this *is* what happened – and there are a lot of holes in this theory, as you've just pointed out yourself. But just assuming ... so you really think your husband could have been going through all this, I mean being literally scared for his life, without you noticing a thing? Without you noticing any change whatsoever in his behaviour? Nothing?'

She stared at him for a moment, dropped her gaze to the table, then raised her head again.

'I don't know. But I didn't. I didn't notice anything. He was acting perfectly normally, and I'm struggling with that too. And I know, I *know* how unlikely this all sounds. But all I know is that I didn't do anything to hurt my husband, that he *did* move to Bristol and lived with me here for three weeks despite what you think, and that now he's gone. And there has to be a reason, and with everything that we know so far, this is the only thing that makes even half sense to me. Can you not ... can you not go with me on it, even a little bit?'

There were tears in her eyes now, and the earlier determination Helena had seen in her face had been replaced by an expression of deep distress.

'Look, Gemma ...' She paused, unsure of quite what to say. 'It does sound highly unlikely, yes. It's a very elaborate theory, with nothing to back it up, I'm afraid. And the only way to prove or disprove your theory – well, *any* of the theories we have about this case really, is to find Danny. Alive or dead.'

Gemma nodded, and a fat tear rolled down her cheek.

'I've tried to tell myself he's still alive. Tried not to give up hope. I thought I'd somehow *know*, deep down, if he wasn't alive anymore. But I honestly think he *might* be dead, now,' she said, her voice barely a whisper. 'Just in the last day or so. I just don't think he'd go this long without contacting me, if he was still alive. Because, and this is going to sound stupid, really stupid, after what I've just said, after he's obviously lied to me and probably cheated on me ... but I do think he loved me, despite all this. And he'd know how desperately worried

I'd be. He'd have found a way of getting in touch, if he could.'

There was silence for a few moments again, then Helena cleared her throat.

'Well, we'll bear in mind what you've told us. However, now I just want to share with you the outcome of the forensic examination of your home on Friday.'

Gemma wiped her eyes with the backs of her hands.

'OK,' she said.

'We did find some of your husband's DNA and his fingerprints throughout the house. You are still claiming he lived there with you for three weeks, which as you know we aren't sure is true. However, we are aware that you and he spent a night together there in January, before you moved down here properly. So that alone might account for the presence of his DNA and fingerprints there. But the report does say that the quantity of your DNA present outweighs the quantity of his found many times, which adds some weight to our theory that he didn't spend much, if any, time here in Bristol since January. Any thoughts on that?'

Gemma shook her head and groaned softly.

'He lived here for three weeks,' she said wearily. 'But he was out all day, and I work from home so there'd naturally be more of my DNA around, I suppose, wouldn't there? I don't really know how it works, but that would make sense, wouldn't it? And well, I mean, he's been gone now for what, nine days? I've obviously cleaned the place since then, several times. Maybe I cleaned his away? I don't know how it works with DNA – *can* you clean it away?'

She looked at Helena, who didn't respond.

'I don't know then. I can't help you,' Gemma said.

They let her go soon after that, and as Helena and Devon walked slowly back upstairs to the incident room, Helena sighed.

'Her theory is bollocks, isn't it? I mean, she's just tried to come up with something that vaguely works with what we already know. Trying to make it fit in with her lies. Isn't she?'

'Probably.' Devon didn't sound quite so sure. 'I mean to be fair it does sort of work. But only sort of. There are big holes. Like, why would he pull out of his new job in Bristol before he was even attacked? That just doesn't fit.'

'Because *she* attacked him. And it was planned, so it was *her* who sent that email pulling out of the new job, not him at all,' Helena said firmly. 'And yes, I know I still don't have any proof of that. Damn that DNA evidence from the house. It's just not strong enough to help us. But I'll get there, Devon. She'll slip up one of these days, you just wait and see. And when she does, I'll be waiting right there to catch her.'

Chapter 19

I wiped the cloth one more time across the cooker top and stood back, satisfied. Cleaning the house again had, for a few minutes at least, focused my mind on something other than Danny, and even that brief respite from the constant, confused clamour in my head had made me feel calmer, more in control. The press were outside my door again, and although I'd kept the curtains closed, I could still hear them, the low hum of their chatter, the occasional shout and burst of laughter. I was trying to ignore their presence and keeping busy helped. I had now temporarily given up on work altogether, calling the various editors who were waiting for articles from me, all of whom had been in touch in recent days anyway as the news about Danny had hit the newspapers, and telling them that the situation still hadn't been resolved and that I needed a few more weeks without a commission. I had somehow managed, in snatched moments here and there over the past few days, to finish the spa feature for *Fitness & Style* – definitely not my finest work, but it was done – but writing anything new seemed impossible. All of the editors had been understanding, and I was deeply grateful, but I assured them

I wouldn't be unavailable for long. I had to. The world of freelance journalism was a fickle one, and I knew I'd be replaced as a regular if I was away for too many weeks, maybe even lose my *Camille* column, although thankfully that was always written several issues ahead of time. But surely, this would all be over soon? How much longer could it go on, for goodness' sake? And how long would it be before my neighbours came round to complain about the press invasion of their street?

Earlier, I'd swept the courtyard, whipping the broom backwards and forwards, sweat beading on my forehead from the physical effort. I'd stopped for a moment to wipe my sleeve across my face, and had seen Clive again, standing motionless at an upstairs window next door, looking down at me. Unsure what to do – would a wave look too cheerful, too casual, in the circumstances? – I nodded at him, then looked away and started sweeping again. Thirty seconds later when I glanced back at the window, he was gone. I hadn't spoken to him or his wife – or indeed to Jo, my other neighbour – since the night I'd popped round to ask them if they'd seen Danny. It was just too awkward, too impossible, with the press camped on my doorstep: what on earth must they think of me? *They'll be ruing the day I moved in, and who could blame them?* I thought, as I picked up the wire basket I used to cart cleaning products around the house and headed up to the bathroom, my thoughts drifting back to the previous day and my latest encounter with the police. They'd humoured me, but I had the feeling they hadn't believed my theory about Danny's disappearance at all, and in many ways I didn't blame them.

Faced with a bizarre collection of facts and odd behaviour, I'd pieced them together as best I could to come up with something that sort of, vaguely, made sense. And yet, when it was said out loud, in the cold light of a police interview room, it did sound like something a half-crazed person would say to cover up a crime. It *wasn't* really logical, and there *were* big holes in it. It was all I had though, for now, I thought, as I sprayed cleaning foam around the hand basin and vigorously wiped it off again. I loved this bathroom, with its huge double walk-in shower and the clawfoot, cast iron bath in front of the window, trailing plants cascading down one wall from a high shelf and scented candles dotted around. Since Danny had gone, the pleasures of our bathroom had passed me by, a cursory swipe of a toothbrush and quick, joyless shower all I'd been able to manage in the past few days. Yes, the half-baked theory I'd shared with the police was all I had, but it was something to cling onto now, something to work on, on my own if I had to. At least they hadn't kept me in custody.

'Thank goodness for forensics,' I said out loud to my reflection in the mirror, as I wiped a spot of toothpaste off the smooth glass. 'At least they know you were here at *some* point, Danny. At least they know I'm not making *everything* up.'

Their findings bothered me though – the fact that they'd found so little of Danny in the house. Yes, he'd been gone for a while, and yes I'd cleaned the place since he'd vanished, as I'd told them. But was it that easy, to destroy DNA? I didn't know much about it, but I'd always somehow thought that it was harder than that – that DNA was tough stuff that could hang around for years. And then, as I twisted the cap off the bleach bottle and poured some of it into the toilet bowl, I stopped dead, staring at the bottle suspended in mid-air. *Bleach.* That Friday night, when I'd arrived home to an empty house. Danny had cleaned the place, hadn't he? I remembered the shiny surfaces, the clean bed linen, the used bedding damp in the washing machine, the bathroom towels in there too, the faint smell of bleach in the air. What if ...? But why would he?

I slammed the bleach bottle down onto the cistern and ran from the room. In the kitchen I found my iPad, opened Google and tapped in 'can you clean away DNA?'. And there it was.

... oxygen-producing detergents destroy all DNA evidence ...

... oxygen bleach tested on bloodstained clothing for two hours completely destroyed the DNA ...

Oxygen-producing detergents? I did another quick search. There were dozens of them on the market. I ran my eye down the brand names, recognizing most from the cleaning aisle at the supermarket, then ran back to the bathroom. Our bleach was on the list. Our innocent-looking household bleach could destroy DNA. And Danny had, it seemed, cleaned the house from top to bottom before he left. Did he know that, about the DNA? Yes, he wanted to disappear, that much was abundantly clear now. But did he want to disappear to that extent? To literally try to wipe away all evidence of his very presence in his own home? Or was he just carrying out a final act of kindness and leaving the place clean for me? Was I totally overthinking this? I groaned and slumped down onto the closed toilet lid. For a few moments I simply felt sad, worn down, exhausted. And then, unexpectedly, a shiver of anger. Yes, Danny was probably dead now, because surely, surely, he wouldn't have let me go through this agony alone, without some sort of contact, some sort of apology, some sort of explanation. But if – IF he was still alive …

'You BASTARD!'

I screamed the words. Did he know that I was getting the blame for his disappearance, was the police's prime suspect, was likely to be dragged into custody any day now? That I'd been questioned, not just about him but about four other murders? That I'd been humiliated, stalked by the press, photographed? If he was alive, he knew it, he knew all of it. How could he not, when it had been front page news for days? And still, to do nothing?

'Bastard. FUCKING BASTARD.'

I was on my feet now, and I kicked the waste bin next to the basin so hard that it flew into the air, landing with a clatter on the tiled floor, disgorging its contents. I stared at the plastic wrapping, toilet roll tubes and cotton wool balls stained with mascara scattered across the floor for a moment, then turned and walked out of the room. I thought Danny had *loved* me. I would have sworn it on my life, on my mother's life. We had spent days, weeks, months, planning our future, totally wrapped up in each other. Could he have been that good an actor? Was I really that stupid, to have let him fool me for so long? And then, just as quickly, the anger subsided. Because however he felt about me, however much he'd lied to me, the simple truth was that *I* loved Danny. And, regardless of what he'd done to me, I was scared for him, so terribly, horribly scared.

I don't care if you're in trouble, or what you've done. I don't even care about what you've done to me. I just want to know where you are, Danny. I just want you to be alive and well and safe and here.

And so I sat down at the kitchen table, taking deep breaths to clear my head, and I began to think. Danny had been here, with me, for three weeks, but for hours every day he'd been going somewhere. Somewhere, presumably, that he felt safe. Where? Where would he go? Where can you spend hours, every day, without anyone questioning you? Somewhere you can just do your own thing, and be left alone? A park? But it had been February and freezing. No, somewhere indoors. A library? Maybe. People sat all day and worked in libraries, didn't they, without anyone thinking it was weird? But Danny, in a library? I couldn't see it. He wasn't a reader, and I'd never known him to even contemplate walking into a library. So what else? What about a gym? You could spend all day in a gym, couldn't you? The big ones nowadays had pools, saunas, coffee shops – was that a possibility, even if he *was* nursing a hidden injury? Danny had always liked to look after himself. In London he'd been a member of a local gym in Chiswick and had worked out several mornings a week, squeezing in an early session on his way to work. I often told him he put me to shame – forever thankful that I was naturally lean, I'd always said I got enough exercise walking Albert, and although I enjoyed my yoga or Pilates sessions, that was only once or twice a week maximum. Working out really wasn't a big priority in my life, but Danny loved it.

I reached for my iPad again, pulling up a map of Bristol, then zooming in on our street. Then I slowly zoomed out again until I had an area of about one square mile of the house on my screen. Something told me that if Danny was trying to keep a low profile, had essentially been hiding in plain sight, he wouldn't have wanted to travel too far. Were there any gyms that close to the house? I typed 'gym near' into the search box and added our postcode. Yes! Two pins appeared on the map, one just a couple of streets away, one about half a mile to the south. I clicked on the first one, then clicked again to open its website.

Fit4U Gym – a small, friendly independent gym in Clifton, Bristol.

I scrolled through the photographs; a compact but well-equipped gym, a steam room, a spin class, a small café. Would Danny have felt comfortable there? Or was it *too* small? I wasn't sure, so I clicked onto the second pin.

GYMCITY. A big city gym at small town prices.

This one looked huge – a spa with hydrotherapy pool, personal trainers, an Olympics standard weights room. Shit. If Danny had to choose one of these, which would he go for? I wasn't sure. I'd have to try both of them.

* * *

Assuming dogs weren't allowed in gyms, I left Albert behind, muttering apologies as I slipped out of the front door, and headed for the big one first, bracing myself for the barrage of questions from the reporters as I left the house, only to find that they'd suddenly disappeared. Called to a press conference, maybe, I thought, then realized I didn't care. As long as they weren't bothering me, they could go where they liked. In the reception area of GymCity, a harassed-looking man with a shaven head and a dark, bushy beard glanced at the photographs of Danny I was holding and shrugged.

'Don't recognize him. That doesn't mean he hasn't been here though. We get hundreds of people coming in every day and I'm only part-time. There are eight of us on this desk, we work shifts ... hang on.'

The phone on his desk was ringing and he picked it up.

'GymCity. Can you hold please?'

He looked back at me.

'Look, I'm really busy, sorry. If you want to leave a photo and your number, I'll stick them on the desk here with a note, see if any of the others remember him. We'll call you.'

I thanked him and left, a now-familiar feeling of hopelessness creeping over me. This was a waste of time. My legs felt heavy as I trudged slowly to Fit4U, wondering why I was bothering.

There was somebody already chatting to the man on the desk when I walked in, so I wandered around the small lobby, reading the posters advertising 'cardioblast' and 'bodypump' classes, studio cycling and body balance sessions.

'Hi, can I help?'

I turned to see the receptionist smiling at me.

'Yes, sorry. I was just wondering ... well, the thing is, my husband has gone missing. And I was just wondering if you might have seen him in here, any time over the past few weeks? It's been tricky, trying to track his recent movements, and well, I brought a photo, just in case. You probably won't have seen him, I know how busy these places always are, but I was just hoping that maybe if you could take a look at this picture ...'

I was gabbling, already feeling embarrassed for wasting his time. The young man, who had cropped dark hair and was wearing a very tight, white T-shirt, looked at me quizzically.

'Missing? Sorry to hear that. Sure, let me see.'

I pushed the photograph across the desk.

'His name is Danny. Danny O'Connor. He's thirty-three, six foot one. Do you recognize him at all?'

The man – he wore a name badge which said 'Gerry' – was staring at the picture, his eyes scrunched into narrow slits.

'Well ... I'm not sure actually. At first glance I'd have said no ...', he picked up the photo, angling it towards the light, 'but ... well, he does look a bit like someone who's been coming in. His name isn't Danny though. Hang on. Paul? PAUL!'

A head poked out from behind a half-open door to the rear of the reception desk.

'What?'

'Come here a minute, will you? Does this look like Patrick to you?'

'The Patrick you had the hots for?'

Paul emerged fully from behind the door, grinning. He was short and muscular, biceps bulging.

'Shut up!' Gerry had turned pink. 'Just look. Could that be him?'

Paul glanced at me then at the photograph. He frowned.

'Could be,' he said, but he sounded unsure. 'I mean, he definitely has the *look* of him. But Patrick has a beard and specs and he always wears that beanie, so I've never seen his hair. Could be though. Why?'

'He's this lady's husband.'

He gestured towards me.

'He's gone missing, and she wants to know if he's been in here recently.'

'Husband!' Paul laughed, then looked apologetically at me.

'Oh, sorry. I'm not laughing about him being missing, that's shitty. Just laughing at Gerry here. He has the right hots for him.'

'Shut up!' hissed Gerry.

Paul hooted and headed into the back room again.

'Hope you find him,' he called over his shoulder.

Gerry rolled his eyes.

'Sorry,' he said, and tapped the photo of Danny with a manicured finger. 'I do quite fancy him, if I'm honest. He *is* hot. Sorry.'

I smiled and waved a hand dismissively. I needed to get this back on track.

'So – you *do* think you might have seen him? In here? I'm confused.'

Gerry looked back down at the picture, nodded slowly and then looked up again.

'I think so. There's a guy who started coming in about a month ago. Didn't join as an annual member, just paid for a weekly pass and kept renewing it. His name ... well, he said his name was Patrick, not Danny. Patrick Donnelly. He's Irish?'

I nodded. 'Danny's Irish, yes.'

'He said he was a freelance writer who'd just moved to Bristol and he was waiting for new office space, said it was being renovated or something. Asked if it was OK to use the gym in the morning and then hang out and do some work in the café in the afternoon. We were cool with that – as long as people pay for the pass they can use the facilities as long as they like, we're open eighteen hours a day. And he was nice, no trouble, just got on with it. He started coming in Monday to Friday, just in the daytime. Stayed all day. Worked out for a couple of hours then had lunch and got his laptop out and sat in a corner of the café for the rest of the day. Did that for a few weeks. Then he just stopped coming. I presumed his new office was ready. Gutted.'

He smiled sheepishly. My heartbeat had been quickening as I listened. Could this Patrick be Danny? The timescale fitted. The Monday to Friday fitted. It *fitted*.

'Did he seem OK? I mean, did he look like he was injured at all, when he was in the gym?'

Gerry frowned.

'Not that I noticed. Looked fine to me.'

'But ... you said he had a beard? Danny didn't have a beard. And glasses?'

Gerry nodded.

'Yes. And he always wore a little black beanie, even when he was working out.' He paused. 'Not that I was spying on him lifting weights or anything. But, you know, we're always running about, in and out of the gym, and you notice,' he added hurriedly, his face flushing again.

I nodded distractedly, my mind racing. If Danny had been trying to keep a low profile, it might have made sense for him to try to disguise his appearance a bit when he was outside the house. Would it be outside the realms of possibility for him to have stuck on a hat, a pair of glasses? A false beard seemed faintly ludicrous, but maybe, if he was that desperate to avoid being recognized …

'You know, the more I look at this the more I think it *is* him,' Gerry was saying. 'His body shape, and those eyes – you can't disguise eyes, even in glasses. I'm pretty sure that's Patrick. Are you saying he was wearing a stick-on beard though? Why?'

'I don't really know,' I said honestly. 'Do you know how he got here every day? Did he walk, or drive?'

'Cycled,' Gerry said immediately. 'Always came in carrying a bike helmet.'

My heart was racing again. It *was* Danny, it had to be. But how could I prove it?

'Look, you said he paid for a weekly pass. Did he use a credit card, a bank card, anything like that? I can't really explain, but I need some sort of proof that he was here, that he'd been coming here for the past few weeks. Do you have anything like that?'

Gerry was frowning, shaking his head.

'As far as I can recall he always paid cash,' he said. 'I always work Mondays and that's when we renew the weekly passes, and I remember him pulling out a wad of notes each time. I remember thinking he must be loaded, to carry that much cash. Made him even sexier. Oh shit, sorry.'

He slapped himself on the forehead, and I smiled.

'It's fine, honestly. OK, so no credit card receipt ...'

I looked around, eyes searching for cameras. Yes! Two of them, one angled towards the gym's front door, the other pointing at the desk we were standing at.

'But you have CCTV, right?'

I pointed at the closest camera, and Gerry nodded.

'Just here in reception though. We're a small, friendly place. Nobody wants to be watched when they're working out or getting changed, so there aren't any in the gym or exercise areas.'

'The café?' I asked.

Gerry shook his head.

'Never felt the need. We're well-staffed so if there's ever any trouble or anyone gets injured on one of the machines or collapses or anything, there's always someone around to deal with it. We only have cameras here, where we take the money, just in case, you know?'

'OK. But if Dann ... er this Patrick guy, was coming in here every day he'd be captured by these cameras here, right?'

'Sure. We don't keep the footage for long though. Gets wiped after two weeks if we don't need it. Want me to look?'

'Yes! Yes please.' I thought quickly. Today was Monday, the

eleventh of March. Two weeks would take us back to Monday, the twenty-fifth of February.

'Can you look at the week of the twenty-fifth of last month?'

'Sure,' he said again. 'I can get it up on this screen here. You'll have to come round for a minute.'

I made my way behind the reception desk and watched as he tapped various keys, suddenly feeling excited.

'OK, so he usually came in quite early, around seven,' Gerry was muttering. 'So if I start it *here* ...' He moved the mouse a couple of times, then stood back. 'There. That's Patrick. I've zoomed in and frozen the image.'

I leaned forwards. On the screen a man was standing at the front of the reception desk I was now behind. He was wearing, as Gerry had described earlier, a dark beanie hat and small round glasses, the outline of his jaw obscured by a fluffy beard. His jacket was dark, anonymous. But Danny had a black jacket, simple like this one. His shoulders were broad, like this man's. If only I could see his face more clearly. I leaned even closer, squinting, but the picture just wasn't clear enough. Was it him? I didn't know. I just couldn't tell.

'I don't know if it's him,' I said. 'Can you let it play for a minute? Maybe if I see a bit more ...'

Gerry had already hit 'play'. The man on screen was moving now, pulling something from his pocket – cash? – and as he lifted his arm again I saw a flash on his wrist.

A watch.

I stared at it, then gasped.

'Can you zoom in? On his wrist, there?'

I jabbed at the screen, and Gerry obliged. The picture froze,

231

and I stared. Stared at the now surprisingly clear image of a square-faced, steel-cased watch with a bright red seconds hand. A sleek, elegant, very distinctive watch. The watch I'd bought Danny as a gift on our wedding day. The watch that had cost me the equivalent of a month's salary but which I knew had been worth every penny when I'd seen the delight on his face when he opened the box and slipped it onto his wrist. That was Danny's watch. That was *Danny*.

Chapter 20

'I bloody hate Mondays. I've always bloody hated Mondays, but today has been The. Shittiest. In. A. Long. Time.'

Helena punctuated the words by throwing a small rubber ball hard at the wall. She caught it for the sixth time then flung it onto her desk, where it landed with a plop in the handle-less mug which doubled as a pen holder.

'Nice shot.' Devon sounded impressed.

Helena grunted and flung herself petulantly into her chair. 'That's meant to be a stress ball. Charlotte gave it to me. I'm going to tell her to demand her money back, because it doesn't bloody work.'

Devon laughed. 'I feel sorry for your poor wife. Agreed though, it hasn't been the best of Mondays.'

He walked a few steps closer and leaned against the edge of her desk.

'It was grim, wasn't it?' he said.

She nodded, closing her eyes briefly. It really had been. After the on-call press officer had been forced to deal with numerous and increasingly demanding calls from journalists over the weekend about the so-called 'Bristol serial killer',

Detective Chief Superintendent Anna Miller had been on the phone to Helena at seven that morning, ordering her to call a press conference.

'If you can't make any arrests, if you really don't have enough evidence, knock this serial killer nonsense on the head,' she demanded in her broad Tyneside accent. 'Tell them there's no proven link even between the Bristol cases, never mind the London ones. But give them something. *Anything*. We're being accused of doing nothing and getting nowhere, Dickens, and I won't have it. Sort it out.'

And so, with the greatest reluctance, Helena had called a press conference for midday. She hated press conferences with a passion; not normally a shy person, she always wanted to curl up under a rock when forced to endure the glare of television lights, the flash of cameras and the volley of questions being fired from the press pack. It wasn't that she wanted to be obstructive; she totally understood the need for the public to be kept informed, especially with rumours of serial killers floating around.

'They're just so ... so *relentless*,' she said, opening her eyes again and looking up at Devon. 'And if they don't get what they want, they just make stuff up half the time. Or speculate and exaggerate at least, and dress that up as fact. It drives me mad.'

'I know.' He sighed. 'They're totally fixated on this serial killer thing now though, aren't they? No talking them out of it, no matter what we say. And their fascination with Gemma O'Connor seems to have grown too. Plenty of questions about her and whether we think she's involved.'

Helena's eyes widened. 'Well, I can't blame them for that. They know she's the only one we've called in for questioning so far. And I still think she might have done it, Devon. Killed Danny, at least. Even if I did insist rather firmly this morning that she's only ever been questioned with regards to background information about her missing husband. I don't want *them* focussing on her too much, not right now. I know they've been hanging around outside her house, and we can't stop them doing that, but I don't want to give them anything more than we have to on her for now. She'll clam up, and at the moment she's still talking to us. Talking bollocks, but still talking. And I still think one of these days she'll talk too much, let something slip.'

Devon shrugged. 'Maybe. I still can't make up my mind on that one.'

PRRRR.

There was a low purr from the breast pocket of his shirt. He slid his mobile phone out of it, looked at the screen and gave a short laugh.

'Talk of the devil,' he said, and answered the call.

'Mrs O'Connor? How can I help you?' he asked.

Helena sat up straight, suddenly feeling a little less gloomy. Gemma O'Connor, calling Devon direct? What did *she* want then? To confess, maybe, finally? She leaned a little closer to Devon, but he was giving little away.

'Really? OK. OK. Well, I suppose it won't hurt to take a look. Sure. OK. I'll try to get someone down there tomorrow morning. Around 10 o'clock? OK. Someone will meet you there unless you hear otherwise. Great. Bye.'

He ended the call then grabbed a pen and a pad from Helena's desk and scribbled down an address.

'Well?' she said impatiently. 'What was all that about?'

He put the pen down and ripped the page from the notepad.

'Not sure, really. She says she's seen some CCTV footage from a gym in Clifton and she thinks it's Danny. Apparently she decided to try and find out where he'd been spending his days while he was apparently here in Bristol ...'

'Pah!' Helena couldn't help herself.

'Yes, yes, I know you don't believe he ever made it this far. But *she's* still insisting, so ... anyway, she says she had a brainwave that he might have been hanging out in a gym because he was always into his fitness and so on, so she checked out a couple nearby, and at one of them the staff said there was a bloke who came in every weekday for a few weeks. He said his name was Patrick, not Danny, but she asked to see CCTV and she says this guy's wearing some sort of disguise so she can't be totally sure, but what she *is* sure about is that he's wearing her husband's watch, which has convinced her that it's hi—'

'A disguise?' Helena snorted. 'And you're sending someone down there? Are you sure? It sounds like a load of old—'

'Boss! BOSS!'

DC Tara Lemming was running across the room towards them, her black ponytail bouncing. She skidded to a halt, slightly out of breath, her eyes bright.

'You're not going to believe this,' she said.

'What now?' said Helena. 'Are you OK?'

'I'm fine. And you will be too, when you hear what's just happened.'

She looked from Helena to Devon, then back again. Helena felt a little shiver of excitement.

'Go on.'

'Boss, a man's just walked into reception downstairs. He says he wants to speak to whoever's in charge of the so-called serial killer case. And – wait for it – he says he's here to hand himself in. He says he killed them. All of them. The two in London, Mervin Elliott, Ryan Jones *and* Danny O'Connor. He says *he's* the serial killer.'

Chapter 21

I walked back from the gym on Tuesday morning feeling close to despair. As DS Clarke had promised, I'd been met there at 10 a.m. by DC Frankie Stevens, but he'd seemed distracted, glancing at his watch as he waited for Gerry to load up the CCTV footage. Gerry had taken his time, clearly rather taken with the police officer and giving him coquettish sidelong glances as he tapped keys and clicked on files. When we were finally able to show the detective the shots of the man I was now, on second viewing, even more convinced was Danny, he studied them for a few moments then said doubtfully: 'They're not very *clear* pictures, are they? I mean, that could be anyone really. I know he's your husband, Gemma, and you'd be the one most likely to recognize him, but with a hat and glasses and a beard ...'

'But that's his watch, I know it is. Look, there.' I jabbed a finger at the screen. 'It's really unusual – it's a Nomos Tetra, I bought it for him as wedding gift. And I know the way he moves, the way he walks – look, as he heads away from the desk. It's *him*, DC Stevens. This is where he was coming every day when I thought he was going to work. This proves it, can't you see? It proves he was alive and well until twelve days ago when he stopped coming here and he vanished. It proves I'm telling the truth, you must believe me now? I didn't bloody kill him in London, did I, because he was here, safe and well!'

My voice was getting louder and louder, my frustration growing. At the words 'kill him' Gerry took a step back, a shocked expression replacing the genial one he'd been sporting previously.

'You ... you killed Patrick?' he said, his voice tremulous.

'What? No ... no, of course I didn't!' I reached out a hand to touch his arm, but he backed away, looking scared.

'He's just missing, like I told you. And it's Danny, not Patrick, remember?' I said. Gerry just stared at me, edging even further away, so I turned back to DC Stevens. I was starting to feel a little panicky. How could I get him to believe me?

'Please, DC Stevens,' I began, but he was looking at his watch again.

'Look, I'm sorry, but I need to go. We have something ... well, I just need to get back. But, er ... Gerry, is it? Gerry, can you copy that footage onto a disk or whatever and send it to me at the station? Just so we have it on file. Here, my details and the address ...'

He reached into his jacket pocket and pulled out a business card which he handed to a now grinning Gerry.

'No problem, Frankie,' he said. 'I'll deliver it myself.'

'Well ... thanks. That would be great, if it's not too much trouble.'

The two men smiled at each other – *are they* flirting? I

thought. *Oh, for goodness' sake!* – and then the police officer turned to me.

'I'm sorry,' he said again. 'I really need to go. I don't think this footage is very helpful, to be honest – it's just not clear enough. But I'll show it to the high-ups, OK? Someone will be in touch.'

And then he was gone. As I left the gym, it began to rain; the sky looked bruised, pale with angry violet patches. The weather had turned cold again over the past few days, and I shivered as I trudged towards home, Albert tugging on his lead by my side: I hadn't had the heart to leave him behind again. Suddenly, I felt desperately alone. Yes, I had my beloved dog, and I could call Tai or Clare, I knew that, but otherwise ... I was on my own. When Danny had been around, I'd never felt lonely, even in a new city where I hadn't yet had time to make many friends. But now ...

Even the press had gone, having not returned since they vanished the day before, the street quiet and empty when I'd tentatively opened the lounge curtains earlier. Relief had swept over me at the time, but now I felt curiously abandoned. How had things ended up like this? How could a life, a nice, normal life, unravel so quickly? Less than two weeks ago I was so happy – a new home, a lovely husband, a steady freelance income, and now ...

How would I ever be able to trust a man – trust *anyone* – ever again? Would I ... oh God! Would I now even ever have *children*, become a mother? The thought slammed into my brain with such force that I almost stumbled, reaching out to the nearest lamp post for support, leaning on it heavily, my breathing suddenly laboured. Albert whimpered, looking up at me anxiously, and across the street, a man walking briskly along with his dog slowed for a moment, staring at me, then sped up again, his Labrador pulling at the lead. I stood there for a minute, staring at a stain on the pavement, trying to focus, trying to calm myself. *Children.* It was the first time I'd really thought about that, since Danny had disappeared. We'd talked about having children, talked about it more than once, but I was only thirty-four, and we hadn't felt the need to rush into anything.

'We have time,' Danny had said. 'Sure you're only a spring chicken. Let's give it a couple of years, enjoy being married for a bit, buy a house, get properly settled. Then – babies!'

I'd agreed, happily. I knew plenty of women who'd fallen pregnant in their late thirties, even early forties. It would be absolutely fine. But now ... the police, no matter what I said, no matter what evidence I tried to show them, still seemed to think that I had killed Danny. They clearly didn't have enough to arrest me, not yet. But what if somehow they did, eventually? What if I went to prison? It could be for years. Or, even if that didn't happen, if I got through all this, what if I never met anyone else? What if Danny had been it, my one chance of love, of happiness, of a family? What was *wrong* with me? How could I have been so stupid, so gullible? There *must* have been warning signs, there had to have been. How could I have missed them? And – the thought suddenly struck me for the first time, and I gasped, horrified – what about *diseases?* If Danny had been sleeping with other people, possibly *many* other people ... I needed to get tested, didn't

I? Find a clinic, where I'd have to tell them. Tell them that I strongly suspected that my husband had been unfaithful to me, and possibly with multiple partners.

Albert whimpered again, pawing at the leg of my jeans, but I ignored him, my mind racing, yet another thought striking me. How was I going to cope financially, if Danny really was dead, if he really wasn't coming back? I made good money, and I could probably afford the rent on our current house on my own, just. But to save for a deposit, to buy a house, to have a secure future ... it was over now, all of it. A tear rolled slowly down my already-damp cheek. The rain had grown heavier, running down under my collar, drops clumping on my lashes. I blinked and looked up. An elderly woman was approaching, white hair peeking out from under a bright red headscarf, rheumy eyes looking at me curiously.

'Come on, Albert. Let's go,' I whispered.

I pushed myself back to a fully upright position and walked on, suddenly desperate to get home, away from people, out of the rain.

As soon as we got indoors I called Eva.

'Shit, Gemma. And you're sure the footage is of Danny?'

'I'm pretty sure. The police officer just didn't seem interested though. He asked for a copy, to keep in their files, but it was like he couldn't wait to get out of there. I just don't know what to do next, Eva. I'm out of ideas, and I feel like I'm going mad. What am I going to do? What am I going to *fucking* do?'

I was crying again, my voice cracking.

'Oh darling, stay strong. I'll be back down there on Friday

evening, OK? Keep thinking. There's something you've missed, something we've both missed, there has to be. Don't give up. We'll find a way to prove you didn't hurt Danny, OK? We *will*, Gem. That's all we need to do. The rest of it, working out who killed those other men and whether Danny's case is connected or not, is down to the police, so forget all that. Just concentrate on this one thing, OK? We can do it.'

Her words were reassuring, but when I put the phone down I sat very still for a long time, the rain pounding against the window, the sky darkening, the room growing cold around me. What was it? *What* were we missing? I had a horrible feeling time was running out, and I still had simply no idea. No idea at all.

Chapter 22

The incident room was quiet, but the air crackled with tension. DC Frankie Stevens, who'd just returned from meeting Gemma O'Connor at a gym in Clifton, was briefing Helena on what had happened there, but she could tell even he wasn't particularly interested in what he was saying, and she was having a hard time forcing herself to listen. They had bigger fish to fry, and the interview room was being readied for the man who could well turn out to be the biggest catch of her career so far. George Dolan, the man who'd walked in the previous day claiming to have killed five men, had told officers he was originally from Bristol but had moved around a lot and was currently of no fixed abode, sleeping on friends' sofas and picking up occasional shifts as a bar and club bouncer. He had been fairly seriously intoxicated when he'd arrived, stumbling and mumbling, and had been put in a cell to spend the night sleeping it off. When they'd checked his record, they'd found a history of arrests for violent behaviour, including a six-month prison sentence for common assault ten years previously following a brawl outside a nightclub. When, after breakfast, a by-then-sober Dolan had stuck to his story about committing the murders, the news had raced around the building like a greyhound around a track, and Helena's insides hadn't stopped churning since.

'So I asked the bloke at the gym – quite cute, actually – to send us a copy of it anyway. But honestly, I'm pretty sure it's of no use whatsoever. Too unclear to be admissible, in my view,' Frankie was saying.

'Err ... cute? Mind on the job please, DC Stevens!' Helena said, but she smiled. 'Look, thanks for doing that, it's a box ticked. But Gemma O'Connor has strangely suddenly stopped seeming like such a high priority. Christ, Frankie, I'm nervous.'

'You? Really?'

He looked genuinely surprised, and she raised her eyebrows.

'Yes, me, really! I am actually human, you know. And if this Dolan guy is the real deal, well ...'

'I know. Massive,' he said. 'Good luck, boss. You'll smash it. DS Clarke doing it with you?'

She nodded.

'Yep. Think he's on his sixteenth builders' tea of the day over there. I've been drinking herbal tea, some sort of calming mix Charlotte brought home for me last night, thought I might need it. Smells vile and tastes worse and hasn't worked at all. And Devon, who should be wired to the moon after all that caffeine, seems calm as you like.'

She gestured with a hand, and Frankie turned to look at Devon, who was sitting at his desk, elbows on the desk, fingertips steepled, eyes closed.

'Looks very zen,' said Frankie. 'Right, good luck, again. See you later. We'll all be waiting. Oh – and when I came in just now the press were outside, by the way. Loads of them. All shouting questions about the serial killer suspect we have in custody. How do they know?'

Helena sighed. 'Bloody parasites. Can't blame a leak this time though. When Dolan came in last night, pissed as a parrot, there were half a dozen scallies in reception, and they'd all have heard him claiming to be the Bristol serial killer – apparently he wasn't exactly being quiet about it. It was on social media within ten minutes. Not much we could do this time, Frankie.'

'Arse,' he said.

'Arse indeed,' she replied. It would all be worth it though, if Dolan really was their man. *If.* A case like this, so high profile, so well documented in the press, often attracted the crazies, the attention seekers, the false confessors; but generally when they came in drunk, their story changed dramatically in the cold light of dawn without the buzz of alcohol in their system. Dolan's hadn't.

Please, she thought. *Please, be the one. Be the killer.*

An hour later she was sitting across the table from him, Devon to her right, two other officers guarding the door, one inside, one out in the corridor. The duty solicitor, a young woman in a bright red jacket which looked two sizes too big for her, sat next to the suspect, back rigid, her pen tap-tapping on the pad in front of her. George Dolan was fifty-three, a short, shaven-headed brute of a man in a stained blue shirt who lumbered into the room bringing with him the smell of stale sweat and bacon. He looked as though he may once have been a bodybuilder or a boxer, a ripple of muscle still visible under a layer of blubber, the knuckles of his meaty fists scarred.

When the formalities had been completed, Helena cleared her throat, and then for a moment there was silence. George Dolan looked calm, his small eyes, so dark they were almost black, giving nothing away.

'So, Mr Dolan. Last night you walked into this police station and made a confession. Because it was clear that you were in an inebriated state, we allowed you to sleep it off and then spoke to you again this morning, when you made the same confession. For the benefit of the recording, can you repeat that again now?'

Dolan shuffled in his seat, then leaned forwards, both hands flat on the table in front of him.

'Sure,' he said, and his voice was guttural, roughened by cigarettes, the accent strong West Country. 'What I said was, I killed 'em.'

He paused, looking from Helena to Devon, then sideways at his solicitor. All of them stared back at him, and his lips twitched.

A smile? thought Helena. *Christ, he's enjoying this.*

'I killed all of 'em.' Dolan was speaking again.

'The two lads in London, and the two 'ere on The Downs. And the other one too. The most recent one, O'Connor, the one you lot 'aven't even found yet. I did it. I did 'em all. I'm the one you've been looking for. I'm the serial killer.'

For a moment nobody spoke, moved, breathed. Then Dolan leaned slowly back in his chair, and the smile that had been threatening to appear finally crept over his face.

247

'So go on, you've got your confession. Arrest me. Bang me up. I'll keep on doing 'em if you don't,' he said.

Helena swallowed, and glanced at Devon, who raised an eyebrow. She turned back to Dolan, who was gazing at her, a quizzical expression on his bloated face.

'OK, Mr Dolan. Thank you for that. However, now we need to ask you some questions. The first of which is … why? Why did you kill five men? And why those five men, in particular? What was your motive … your reason?'

'My motive?' George Dolan laughed, a short, hoarse sound that reminded Helena of a barking dog.

'You want to know what my motive was?' He leaned forwards again, his head jutting out across the table, and she could smell his breath, acrid and sour.

'I'll tell you what my motive was.'

His voice was low, and full of menace. Then, suddenly, and quite unexpectedly, he grinned widely, showing a mouthful of yellow, rotting teeth.

'I just didn't like the look of 'em,' he said.

Chapter 23

On Wednesday morning, sitting at the kitchen table with a half-drunk coffee and untouched bowl of porridge, I listened to the latest batch of voice messages I'd been ignoring. The police, it seemed, had held a televised press conference on Monday, and my name had come up numerous times, the assembled journalists grilling the panel of officers about whether I had been questioned about the London murders as well as the Bristol ones and Danny's disappearance. I'd missed that completely; I hadn't been online or watched or listened to any news bulletins for days. Eva hadn't mentioned it when I'd spoken to her either – obviously trying to spare me the grief, bless her, I thought, as I played voicemail after voicemail. Some of the messages were kind, as usual; this time even a couple from friends of Danny's, hoping that I was OK, telling me that it would all sort itself out, and not to worry because nobody who knew me could possibly think I was guilty of anything like the press were suggesting. Tears sprang to my eyes as I listened – I seemed to be making a habit of bursting into tears pretty much on an hourly basis in recent days – but this time they were tears of gratitude. Not everybody was against me then. The messages from family were different though; my father again, still distraught, but with more than a hint of anger in his voice this time.

'You have no idea what this is doing to me and your mother, Gemma. It's a disgrace, what's going on there. We know you haven't done anything wrong, but there must be something you can do to stop your name ... *our* name ... being dragged through the mud like this. I mean, to be linked with *murder* ... *multiple murder* ... have you got a solicitor yet? Get one, please. Get him to sort this out. We can't take it much longer, your mother doesn't even want to go out now, she even missed bridge last night, everyone's staring ... look, I've got to go. Bye.'

He's embarrassed, I thought. *Embarrassed. My life's falling apart and my parents are worried about what their friends at the bridge club think. Thanks, Dad. Thanks so bloody much.*

The next and final message was from Bridget. She sounded bored, as if she was just calling me for something to do.

'Don't suppose there's any update on the police investigation,' she said. 'I assume you'll let me know if there is.'

Her tone was calm, disinterested, and it struck me again how strange her reaction to all this had been. She didn't seem concerned about Danny at all, no hint of emotion in her voice. Fleetingly, I resurrected the possibility I'd briefly considered that Bridget knew where Danny was, that somehow he'd made his way to Ireland and that she was helping him to stay hidden, calling me to see if the police might somehow be on his tail. Then I put the theory out of my mind again. I couldn't for a second imagine Danny turning to Bridget, or indeed her agreeing to help him if he did. Still, her reaction to his disappearance was weird. *Weird, weird, weird.* I put the phone down, picked up my cold coffee mug and slowly made myself a fresh drink. I felt lethargic, unmotivated, exhausted, but I knew I had to somehow snap myself out of this, keep going, find some other way of proving that I had nothing to do with whatever the hell had happened to my husband. The street outside had again been empty of press when I'd looked earlier, a fact which, combined with the apparent complete lack of interest from the police in the footage from the gym, was starting to concern me a little. Had something else happened, something I didn't know about? Was their attention – press *and* police – currently being directed elsewhere, I wondered? I was pretty sure that if it was to do with *my* case, with Danny, that somebody would have told me, but I'd have a quick look at the news websites later, I thought, as I poured boiling water into my mug and stirred. But first, there was something I needed to do.

I sat down again, picked up my phone and started scrolling through the address book. I'd had a sudden thought earlier – Quinn, Danny's cousin. Having now accepted that I hadn't really known my husband at all, I'd lain in bed that morning wondering if there was anyone out there who really did, someone who might be able to shed some light on his recent behaviour, someone who might even know the truth behind some of the secrets he had clearly been keeping. His mother? No, definitely not. His brother Liam? Danny was probably far closer to him than he was to his mother, but Liam would clearly not be capable of being a reliable source of information. And then it had come to me – Quinn. As his first cousin, son of his late dad's brother Michael, and of a similar age to Danny, they'd known each other all their lives. Quinn had moved to London from Ireland around the same time as Danny had, and although their careers and lifestyles had been very different – Quinn worked on building sites and spent most of his spare time drinking in west London pubs – the two had remained close. Quinn had been on Danny's stag night and had been the only one of his family to attend our small register office wedding. If anyone knew Danny, he did.

It had struck me, once or twice, especially after Danny's family had finally heard about his disappearance, that it was slightly odd that Quinn hadn't been in touch with me. Living in London, surely he would have seen the newspaper headlines? Then I'd realized that although he obviously had Danny's old mobile number, and our old apartment landline, he wouldn't have had a number for me. He could have got hold of it if he'd tried, through Danny's mother, but maybe the family were keeping him up to date with developments, I'd thought, and let him slip from my mind. I probably should have called him myself, really, but I'd never been a hundred per cent sure what to make of Quinn. I knew, from Danny, that he'd regularly got himself into trouble with the police growing up, minor stuff like vandalism and pilfering from shops, although he'd apparently grown out of that in his late teens, training as a bricklayer, moving to the UK when work in Ireland proved hard to come by. He was currently single, as far as I knew, having split with a girl he'd been seeing for a while the previous summer, and although Danny had always described him as 'great craic' and 'a real decent fella, deep down', on the few occasions we'd met he'd seemed pleasant enough but always a little reserved, chatting mainly to Danny and seemingly reluctant to engage in any form of lengthy conversation with me.

'He's a bit intimidated, I think,' Danny had said, as we'd walked to the tube hand in hand after an evening spent with Quinn at a pub near Victoria station a few months before we'd decided to leave London. 'He left school with no qualifications, failed all his Leaving Cert exams. He doesn't really hang out with brain boxes like you. He doesn't know what to say.'

I'd squeezed his hand, laughing.

'But you're even more of a brain box than I am, and he chats away to you! How does that work then?'

'Ahh, sure we've known each other since we were kids, it's different. We're family. He's like a second brother to me. He likes you fine though, don't be worrying about that.'

I hadn't been worried, not really. You can't get on brilliantly with everyone in life, I reasoned, and Quinn was just a very different sort of guy to the ones I was friendly with – a gruff, macho in an old-fashioned-sort-of-way *bloke*, who had four sugars in his tea and had looked slightly horrified at the sight of the pink rose buttonholes I'd organized for the male guests at our wedding. But he'd always been there for Danny, a link to his past, a solid, hardworking, loyal presence, and that was fine by me.

I had his number in my phone – I'd asked Danny for it before the wedding, wanting to make sure I had contact details for all of the guests, just in case of any last-minute changes – and, after a moment's hesitation (*What if he has seen all the press coverage, and thinks I'm responsible for Danny's disappearance? What if he just puts the phone down on me?*) I hit the call button.

'Hello?'

'Hi – Quinn? It's Gemma. Danny's Gemma.'

For a few seconds ... three, four ... there was silence on the line. But just as I'd opened my mouth to speak again, he said:

'Gemma. Howah ya?'

'I'm ... well, I'm not sure how I am, really, to be honest. I presume you've heard, about Danny?'

Another couple of seconds' silence.

'I have, yeah. I was sorry to hear ... Bridget told me da, he's been keepin' me up to date. I was going to call, but I didn't know what ... well, you know, it's hard, isn't it?'

'It is, yes.' I paused for a moment. 'Although Bridget didn't seem too bothered when I spoke to her. She was acting a bit weird, like she just wasn't very interested.'

There was another silence, a longer one this time.

'Quinn? Quinn, are you there?'

'Yeah. Yeah, I'm here. Look, you know what Bridget's like. I wouldn't worry about her.'

He sounded gruff, an edge to his voice suddenly.

'I'm not, really. Just thought it was strange,' I said. Was he being short with me because he thought I had something to do with Danny's disappearance, as I'd feared he might, I wondered?

'Look, Quinn, whatever the papers have been saying, you

know I have nothing to do with this, right? I'm heartbroken, I miss him so much, and I have no idea what's happened to him.'

'Yeah. No, I'm sure it must be shite. Listen, I need to go in a minute, I'm at work.'

'Sure, of course, sorry,' I said quickly. 'Look, Quinn, I need to see you. Can we meet? I'm happy to hop on a train and come to you. It's just that since Danny's been gone I've found out a load of weird stuff that I didn't know about him, and he was doing some kind of odd things in the weeks before he vanished. I need to speak to someone who's known him for a long time, and you're the only one I could really think of. Please, it won't take much time. I could meet you for lunch maybe, or after work? Tomorrow?'

The silence again, and then the sound of muffled muttering. *Is he talking to someone else?* Then he said:

'OK, well, I don't know what I can tell you, but if you can come here ... I'm busy in the evening but if you meet me at one, I get an hour for lunch. There's a pub just down the road from the site, we can go there.'

He gave me the address and we ended the call. *Good,* I thought. Suddenly, and quite unexpectedly, I felt a pang of hunger. Had I eaten yet that day? Or even the previous night? I couldn't remember. I'd even gone off wine in the past week or so, coffee about the only drink I'd been able to stomach, and I knew I'd lost weight; I'd had to look for a belt that morning, my jeans loose around my waist. Food, then. I needed to start looking after myself. The police were clearly still completely on the wrong track about Danny, and so it was down to me to get to the bottom of it, and quickly. I'd eat, and then I'd make a list of everything I wanted to ask Quinn. And maybe, just maybe, I thought, I'd be coming back from London with some answers.

Chapter 24

'How much longer are we going to keep him?'

Devon's question made Helena jump, even though she'd been quite aware he'd been standing next to her for a full minute.

'I don't know. I just don't know. I think we're right ... but what if we're wrong, Devon? Can you even *imagine* ...?'

He grimaced and shook his head.

'Don't even want to think about it,' he said.

They were both leaning on the sill of the window that ran the full length of the incident room. Outside the sky was grey, a light rain spattering the pavement three storeys below. It was rush hour, the traffic crawling past, pedestrians scurrying, umbrellas bobbing, the occasional irate blast of a horn penetrating the Victorian building's ancient single glazing with its peeling wooden frames. For a moment, Helena wished she was out there, hurrying to work in a shop or an office, somewhere safe and easy, somewhere where her toughest decision of the day would be whether to have a cheese or a tuna sandwich for lunch, or whether to put the black dress or the red one in the window display. Or maybe that she'd chosen a career like Charlotte's. Being a teacher wasn't easy, she knew that. But at least Charlotte didn't generally have to make life or death decisions during the working day. The decision *she'd* have to make today could, if she got it wrong, mean even more men could die.

She turned away from the window, arched her aching back and walked slowly back to her desk, leaving Devon still staring down at the street. They had questioned George Dolan for hours the previous day and, technically, having applied for the full ninety-six hours permitted to hold someone suspected of a serious crime without charge, they still had until the following evening before they'd need to charge or release him. During the entire time they'd been in the interview room, Dolan had continued to sneer and belittle the dead men, while still giving no real reason for killing them other than that he 'didn't like the look of them' and 'they were a fucking *type*; poncy looking wastes of space'. His words and attitude towards his alleged victims had chilled and disgusted them both; at one point, Helena had had to ask for a break, rushing to the toilets down the corridor feeling physically sick.

'How can there be people in the world like him?' she'd hissed at Devon, who had followed her out, concerned.

'He doesn't seem to care at all that these men are dead, that their families are distraught. He's laughing about it. What's wrong with him? *Jesus* ...'

Devon had nodded, face tight, mouth set in a grim line.

'I know. He's scum, pure and simple.'

Earlier, when Dolan had requested his own comfort break, Frankie had popped his head into the interview room. He'd been watching proceedings from the viewing room, along with some of the others.

'Sick, sick bastard,' he said. 'You're doing a great job. Well done, both of you.'

Helena had nodded, suddenly unable to speak, a lump forming in her throat. But after the initial thrill of Dolan's confession, it hadn't been long before the doubts had begun to creep in. She'd felt the first niggle when they'd started to drill down into each murder separately, deciding not to begin with the earlier, London killings they were less familiar with but with that of Mervin Elliott, the man found dead on Clifton Down in February.

'Fucking smarmy bastard. Worked in a poncy clothes shop, probably only because he liked touching up all the poor fuckers who came in to try the gear on,' Dolan had spat. 'I followed him up to The Downs and gave him a good kicking.'

'A good kicking? Could you elaborate, Mr Dolan? How exactly did you kill Mervin Elliott?'

Dolan had stared back at her, a pale pink tongue snaking between his lips and moving slowly across them. Helena's stomach had rolled, but she'd forced herself to keep her eyes on his.

'Battered him. A few kicks, a few good hard punches. Didn't take long,' Dolan said, then leaned back in his chair, which creaked ominously.

Helena felt Devon's elbow press ever so gently against hers, and she nudged him back. Mervin Elliott had died from a blow to the head, and no other significant injuries had been found on his body. *Battered? A few kicks, a few good hard punches?* That didn't tally, and a little knot began to form somewhere deep within Helena's chest.

'OK, let's move on to Ryan Jones, whose body was found on the morning of the twenty-eighth of February. You claim you also killed him, Mr Dolan. Can you tell me how you did that?'

'Same way,' he said immediately, and with satisfaction. 'Good battering. Kicked his ass into the middle of next week. Nice quiet lane that was, nobody to disturb me. Took my time. Enjoyed every minute.'

He leaned his bulk back heavily once again, and the chair creaked loudly in protest. And so it had continued. When they'd asked him about Danny O'Connor, he'd told them he too had died after a 'good beating' and had simply shrugged when asked where the man's body was.

'You'll find it. Eventually,' he said, with a sly grin.

After two hours, they had taken a break. Helena and Devon had walked quickly and in silence down the corridor away from the interview room. When they reached an empty conference room at the far end, Helena marched in, Devon following and closing the door behind them.

'You're clearly thinking what I'm thinking,' she said.

He nodded. 'He's a bloody fantasist, isn't he? He's told us absolutely nothing that's not been in the public domain for weeks, and when we do ask for more detail he's getting it wrong. The way he claims he killed them – it's just not what the post-mortems showed. Those two murders on The Downs, for example, were quick and clean. He's describing frenzied attacks, beatings. And as for Danny O'Connor, all that blood

– his reply to that didn't match the facts either. He's making it up, boss, I'm sure of it.'

'I know. Shit. *SHIT.*'

She groaned and thumped a fist against the nearest wall. Then she turned back to Devon.

'I just don't know. My gut's telling me this isn't our man after all. His motive just doesn't make any sense. I mean, who kills people because they just don't like the look of them? And how did he manage to track down people who all look so similar – luck? It doesn't add up. But ... what if we're wrong? What if he *did* kill them, and he's just embellishing his story? Maybe he'd *liked* to have given them a good kicking as he described it, but they died too quickly for him to do that? And we let him go and he goes straight back out there and kills someone else? And then goes to ground, and we lose him? The press ...'

'Don't. Just don't.'

They'd carried on questioning Dolan for another couple of hours before returning him to his cell, by which time the gnawing doubts had grown into fully fledged disbelief. George Dolan, Helena was now convinced, was telling them an elaborate lie. Why, she had no idea, other than he was currently unemployed and homeless, and maybe a couple of days in a warm police cell with all meals provided was a better option than trying to find somewhere to sleep and scrabbling around for work. It had happened before; there were many in his position who were happy to be charged with wasting police time and suffer its maximum penalty of a six-month prison sentence if it meant guaranteed accommodation for a while.

At her desk, Helena suddenly made her decision. Her gut feeling had rarely let her down, and right then it was telling her that George Dolan was not their killer. They could release him on bail on the murder charges, pending further investigation. They could keep tabs on him, make him surrender his passport if he had one, make him report to the station daily. It was a risk, possibly, but only a small one. He wasn't their man, she was almost certain of it. It just didn't fit, and Dolan had been a distraction, someone who'd taken her eye off the investigation for too many hours. She needed to focus. And despite the lack of hard evidence, she still felt that focus pulling her in only one direction. Towards Gemma O'Connor.

Chapter 25

I emerged from Victoria Underground Station feeling hot and anxious. The tube had been packed, and I'd been forced to stand, hands clammy as I clutched onto the overhead rail, body pressed between a tall, bearded man who smelled strongly of cigarettes and an equally tall woman who was wearing far too much perfume. The combination made me feel ill, and out on the street I took huge gulps of the traffic-polluted air, trying to steady myself. It was already ten to one, but the pub I was due to meet Quinn in was just around the corner, and I found it easily. It was small and half-empty, a dark little bar with a beer-stained, seventies-style swirly carpet and mismatched wooden tables and chairs, the ceiling and paintwork – clearly not redecorated since long before the smoking ban – nicotine yellow. A quick glance around showed me that I was the first to arrive, so I ordered a diet Coke and found a corner table from where I could see the door. I sipped my drink, wondering why I was feeling so nervous. It was only Quinn, and it had been me who'd requested this meeting, after all, I reasoned, but the anxiety remained.

Maybe it was because I'd finally caught up with the news

on the train on my way to London. Flicking between the websites of Sky and BBC News, I'd discovered that for the past two days the police had been questioning a man who'd walked into the police station of his own accord, claiming to be the serial killer. That would explain the sudden disappearance of the press from my front door, I thought, my chest tightening as I'd speed-read the articles. Then I'd groaned quietly in frustration as I clicked on the latest update.

At midday, the suspect was released without charge, pending further enquiries. A spokesman for Avon Police said that the investigation into the murders of Mervin Elliott and Ryan Jones remained their highest priority, alongside that of establishing the whereabouts of missing man Danny O'Connor, who vanished from his home in Bristol two weeks ago.

'Gemma? Howah ya?'

I jumped as a man suddenly sat down in the chair opposite me, pint in hand.

'Quinn! Sorry, I was miles away. How are you? Thanks so much for coming.'

I leaned across the table, and we exchanged awkward pecks on the cheek.

'No hassle. Haven't got long though, as I said. Big job on today and the boss is a right bastard.'

I smiled and told him I wouldn't keep him long. He looked tired, I thought; a short, muscular man with closely cropped dark hair slightly receding at the temples, he was normally clean-shaven but had a couple of days' worth of patchy stubble on his chin, and his denim shirt was faded and creased, the large tattoo of a skull and crossbones on the right side of his neck creeping above the grubby collar.

'So, you're worried about Danny?' He asked the question and then looked away, eyes flitting around the bar before returning to mine.

'I'm worried sick, Quinn. I just know he'd never deliberately go off without telling me where he was, even if he was in terrible trouble. He just wouldn't. And that's why I'm so scared. The police think he's dead, and *I'm* starting to think he might be too. But they think I had something to do with it – I mean you know I've been questioned, don't you, you've seen the papers? And this hasn't been made public yet, but Quinn they also think that whatever happened to him happened weeks ago ... they found blood, you see, in our old apartment in London, lots of blood, and I have no idea what happened there, he seemed fine when he moved down to Bristol, but the police think he never made it to Bristol at all. They think I'm lying about everything, and I'm not, they're looking in completely the wrong direction, and if they keep looking at me they're never going to find him, because I don't know where he is. The whole thing is just ludicrous, that they could even think I was capable of killing my husband, and maybe the others too, it's just insane, but that's why I need to try and find Danny, or find out what might have happened to him, not just for his sake but for mine too.'

The words had spilled out of me in a torrent, and I stopped talking suddenly, aware that Quinn was sitting in silence, staring at me, an odd look on his face.

'You don't ... *you* don't think I had anything to do with it, please tell me you don't?' I said desperately. 'I mean, you know how much I love him, right?'

He said nothing for a moment, still looking at me with that odd expression, then his face cleared.

'Course I don't,' he said. He picked up his pint and drank slowly, then put the glass down again and wiped the back of his hand across his mouth.

'But what do you want me to do? I'm as gutted about him going AWOL as you are, but I don't know where he is, Gemma. I don't know anything.'

I took a deep breath.

'I don't know. I don't know if you can help, but you know him so well, and you've known him for so long, and I just thought ... look, there's been a lot of weird stuff that's emerged since he vanished, and I just wanted to run it past you, see if you can shed any light on it. Can I do that? I actually made a list, because there's so much.'

I rummaged in my bag which was lying on the table in front of me and pulled out my notebook, flicking through the pages until I found the list. Quinn looked vaguely amused for a moment, then nodded.

'Sure. Shoot.'

And so I told him. I told him how careful Danny had been not to bump into any of our neighbours after he moved to Bristol, how he never answered the front door, how he always seemed to make sure he left in the dark and came home in the dark, and how I'd realized, too late, that he must have been lying low, in some sort of serious trouble. I told him

266

that Danny had lied to me about starting his new job, and how I now thought he'd been hiding out in a local gym every day instead. How his bank account had remained untouched since the end of January, fuelling the police view that something had happened to him back then, and how none of his friends or family had heard a word from him since January either.

'Have *you*, Quinn?' I asked. 'When did you last hear from him, can you remember?'

He took a few moments to answer, eyes flitting around the bar again. Then he shrugged.

'Dunno. It's been a while though. Probably January, yeah.'

He was looking down at his pint as he spoke, running a finger around the rim of the glass. I suddenly felt uneasy – *is he telling me the truth?* I wondered – but I ignored the feeling and carried on talking, telling him next about what the police had told me about Danny appearing on EHU, the same dating app as the two Bristol murder victims. I knew that, like the stuff about the blood in our old apartment, this information hadn't been made public, so I wasn't surprised when Quinn's face twisted, his eyes widening.

'Do you ... do you know if he was seeing other women, Quinn? I'm struggling with it, but it might explain some of—'

'I don't know,' he said sharply. 'And he probably wouldn't have told me if he was. I don't agree with that sort of messing around. You're either with someone or you're not. Danny was brought up Catholic, and adultery's a sin. He'd know I'd hold no truck with that.'

I couldn't hide my surprise at his answer.

'Well, yes ... I mean, I agree with you, but most people don't think like that nowadays, do they? But, well ... look, he was definitely using that EHU dating app. Whether he actually went through with any actual dating, I don't know.'

I suddenly felt a tiny bit better. Surely if Danny had been seeing other people, he'd have shared that with Quinn, his closest confidant? OK, so he'd flirted with that woman at that party, and made a pass at Eva, but maybe that was as far as it had gone ...

'He saved my life, you know.' He said the unexpected words loudly, almost angrily, his face suddenly flushing, and at the closest inhabited table an elderly man with a small dog stretched out on the floor by his feet turned and frowned.

'He ... what?'

Quinn looked down at the table, one bitten fingernail scratching at a spot of dried paint on the antique wood. Then he looked at me again.

'He saved my life. It was when we were kids, messing around in the lake at home. It was summer, hot, and we were in and out of the water all day long. I was showing off, holding my breath underwater, and I went too deep, got my foot stuck in something, dunno what, and suddenly I was drowning, panicking ...' He paused, an anguished look in his eyes, as if he was back there again, reliving the horror. 'I thought I was a goner, you know? Thought it was all over. And then, just when everything was going black, and my lungs were bursting, and I thought that was it, I was going to die, there was Danny, like some sort of miracle. There he was, divin' down and pulling my foot free, and draggin' me back up to the surface, and I was alive and … well, that was it. That's the story. He saved my life. I'd have died that day, if it wasn't for him.'

His tone had softened, and I stared at him, a lump in my throat, strangely moved.

'I … I didn't know. He never told me,' I said.

He shrugged.

'So, you know, I owe him. I'd defend the man to me grave. But if he was messing around on ya, Gemma, that's bad. I'd batter him for that.'

I didn't know what to say. He was a strange man, I thought.

'Thanks … thanks, Quinn. Look, another thing. Bridget … you don't think she could possibly know where he is, do you? Every time I've spoken to her, well … as I said to you on the phone, she doesn't seem that bothered. By Danny being missing, I mean. Is there any chance that's because she knows he's alive and well somewhere?'

Another odd expression crossed his face, his eyes widening, then he stood up abruptly.

'No, I don't think that. No way. Look, I need to go now. Sorry I can't help you. I don't know where he is. I'll let you know if I hear from him.'

He nodded at me, then turned and walked quickly away.

'But Quinn …'

He was already gone, the pub door swinging shut behind him. Shit, I thought. SHIT. Did he really not know anything? Why had he left as soon as I'd mentioned Bridget? And what had he said about what he'd do if Danny *had* been 'messing around'? *I'd batter him for that?* A chill ran down my back, as if someone was running a cold hand slowly along my spine.

269

There'd been something else too, something which was only now dawning on me as I remembered the garbled explanation I'd given him when he'd first sat down. When I'd mentioned Danny using a dating app, Quinn had looked visibly shocked. But earlier, when I'd told him one of the other things that the press didn't know, one of the other things that had been kept out of the public domain, the thing about the blood in the Chiswick apartment, he hadn't reacted at all. No reaction, no questions. It had almost been as if he already knew all about it.

Chapter 26

'His name is Quinn O'Connor. Says he's Danny O'Connor's first cousin and he wants to come in and talk to us about Danny's disappearance. He's getting on a train from London now, says he'll be in Bristol by midday.'

'And he didn't want to just tell us whatever it is he wants to tell us on the phone?' Helena looked up at DC Mike Slater, who'd just appeared at her desk to tell her the news.

'Nope. Says he has some photos to show us and he'd rather talk in person. Sounded quite anxious.'

Helena frowned. 'We spoke to him, right, when we were contacting Danny's friends and family after he vanished? He said he hadn't heard from him?'

'Yep. I checked, he says he still hasn't. But he was pretty keen to talk to us today. He wouldn't tell me anything else, boss, sorry.'

'OK, fine. Let me know when he arrives. Devon's off today so you can come and see him with me.'

'Sure.' Mike wandered off, and Helena broke off another piece from the Twix she'd been eating and popped it in her mouth. She tried her hardest to keep away from chocolate

271

but she'd been so despondent earlier about the events of the past few days that she'd succumbed on her way in to work that morning, stopping at the local corner shop to stock up. Charlotte wouldn't allow chocolate in the house, one of the very few things Helena found annoying about her wife.

'You're so bloody *saintly* when it comes to food. It's beyond irritating. A bit of sugar won't kill us. Dark chocolate's actually good for you. For your heart or something, same as red wine,' she'd snapped a few days previously, when she'd reached for a packet of dark chocolate digestives in the supermarket and Charlotte had practically slapped them out of her hand.

'Well fine, we'll get a bar of organic seventy per cent cacao then. But you won't eat it, will you?' Charlotte had snapped back, so loudly that an elderly woman who'd just stopped next to them and was perusing the shortbread section actually jumped.

Charlotte lowered her voice.

'You just want to eat that shitty cheap chocolate crap which is full of fat and sugar. Fine, go ahead. But don't blame me when all your teeth fall out and your arteries are all clogged up.'

The old woman backed slowly away from the biscuit shelf and hurried away down the aisle, and Helena glared at her wife.

'Well, I pity our kids,' she hissed. 'Great fun they'll have at Easter, when all the other kids are stuffing down the chocolate eggs. What are you going to give them instead? Brussels sprouts dipped in bloody couscous?'

She'd instantly regretted the remark, but the damage had

been done, and the shopping trip had been completed in stony silence. They'd made up since, but the row had left Helena feeling guilty and low. Work was tough enough at the moment without strife at home too. Now, she suddenly felt a little cheerier.

'Just when you think all your leads have dried up, along comes another one. Maybe,' she said out loud to nobody.

When Quinn O'Connor arrived in reception at twelve thirty he was shown into a side room and given a cup of tea. When Helena and Mike entered the room three minutes later, they saw a pale-faced, stocky man in a tight black T-shirt, a large skull tattoo visible on his neck. A black jacket lay balled up on the floor next to his chair. He stood up quickly as the two police officers approached him and offered a hand.

'Thanks for seeing me, appreciated,' he said. He sounded Irish, but Helena wasn't familiar enough with the country's regional accents to know what part of the country his came from.

'I thought I needed to see ya as soon as possible, so I took the day off work,' he continued. 'My cousin Danny ... well, I thought I might have some information that might help.'

'Great.' Helena sat down on the chair opposite him, and Mike slid into the seat beside her. 'So, what have you got for us, Mr O'Connor?'

He cleared his throat.

'Well, yesterday Gemma came to see me.'

'Gemma O'Connor? She came to London?' Helena was immediately interested.

The man nodded. 'Yes. She said she was worried about Danny and how the cops ... sorry, you, the police ...' He coloured slightly but carried on. 'How you seemed to think she might have done somethin' to him. To Danny. And she wanted my help, to persuade you that she'd never do anythin' like that.'

He paused and licked his lips.

'Go on.' Helena smiled encouragingly, realizing that he was nervous.

'The thing is, she says she'd never hurt him, she said it again to me yesterday, but she has a history, you see. Of hurting him. And he never went to the police about it, well you wouldn't would you, as a man, it's embarrassing, telling anyone a woman's been beating you, but he told me. But that's why you probably don't know about this, because he never got her charged, so I thought I'd better tell you ... I have pictures, look.'

He bent down to lift his jacket from the floor and fumbled in the inside pocket, pulling out an envelope.

'Hang on, do you mean domestic violence? Gemma O'Connor was violent towards her husband?' said Helena. She could hear the excitement in her own voice.

'Yeah. Look.'

Quinn opened the envelope and removed two photos from it, sliding them across the table. Helena and Mike leaned forwards simultaneously. The pictures were of a man they both instantly recognized as Danny O'Connor, standing shirtless against a white wall. In one shot he was facing the camera, in the other facing away. In both pictures, a large area of livid bruising could be seen across the right side of his torso, stretching from just under his arm to below his ribs.

'Ouch. Looks painful,' said Mike. 'What happened?'

'That was just a couple of months before they were planning to leave London,' Quinn said. 'He said she started kicking him in the ribs for absolutely no reason when he was lying in bed one night. Well, they'd had some sort of minor row a few hours earlier, but he didn't think it was a big deal, like. She obviously thought differently. The next time I saw him he asked me to take photos, just so he had the evidence, like, if he ever decided to use it. But he always said he could handle it, and he didn't want to go to the cops ... sorry, to you guys. Embarrassing, like I said.'

'And this would happen how often?' asked Helena, eyes still on the photographs. 'Are there any other pictures?'

Quinn shook his head.

'Happened every now and again. But those are the only pictures to prove it, as far as I know.'

'OK.' Helena looked at Mike, who raised an eyebrow.

'Why didn't you tell us about this before, Mr O'Connor?' he said.

Quinn hesitated. 'Well, as I said, it made Danny sound a bit soft. If he'd just gone off on a jolly, and he was going to come back, I didn't want to go back on my promise to him to keep my mouth shut about it. But it's been a while now, and maybe he's not coming back, and after yesterday, well, I just thought ...'

Helena nodded.

'I understand, but there's no shame in it, Mr O'Connor.

Domestic violence is domestic violence, no matter who the victim is. But thank you very much for bringing this to our attention.'

She paused.

'Can I just ask you one more thing? In your opinion, would Gemma O'Connor be capable of *more* than punching or kicking her husband? Do you think she'd have the capacity to hurt him badly? To actually inflict fatal injuries?'

Quinn sat up very straight in his chair and looked her straight in the eye.

'Do you mean kill him?'

She nodded.

'Well then yes, I do. I think she'd be very capable of that.'

Chapter 27

I spent Friday at home, cleaning the house, making up the spare bedroom for Eva's return, baking some bread for Saturday morning's breakfast, sweeping the front porch. As I'd emptied the dustpan into the bin by the front gate, Clive had emerged from next door, shouting a 'bye, Jenny', over his shoulder, then stopping abruptly halfway down the path as he spotted me.

'Err ... hi, Clive,' I said awkwardly.

He opened his mouth, then shut it again, his face reddening. Then he grunted something unintelligible and turned away, stumbling and almost tripping over an uneven flagstone in his apparent rush to make it down his path and into his car, revving the engine loudly and speeding off down the street.

Shit. I'm the neighbour from hell, aren't I? They just don't want to know me, and why would they? I've turned their nice quiet street into a circus over the past couple of weeks.

And so I went back inside and carried on cleaning and baking and tidying. I needed to keep busy, because if I stopped, even for a minute, the thoughts came crowding in, thoughts which even I was no longer sure were logical or rational.

Thoughts about Quinn, the man who was Danny's only relative in the UK, and one of his closest friends. The man who I, after our meeting the previous day, had increasingly begun to think might know more than he was admitting about Danny's disappearance.

I kept replaying our conversation in my head.

They think that whatever happened to him happened weeks ago ... they found blood, you see, in our old apartment in London, lots of blood ...

The blood in our Chiswick apartment, and the fact that it had been identified as *Danny's* blood, was something the police had never told the press about, something that had never appeared in the newspapers. I didn't think Bridget knew about it either; she'd certainly never mentioned it to me during our phone calls. So why had Quinn not reacted to that, in any way, when I'd told him about it? Why hadn't he asked me to elaborate, to explain? Instead, he'd just watched me as I spoke, with that slightly odd expression on his face which I still couldn't quite work out. And then there had been the surprise and distaste on his face when I'd asked him if he thought Danny might be cheating on me. What had he said?

I'd batter him for that ...

It was a pretty extreme thing to say, wasn't it? Surely, even if Quinn didn't agree with 'adultery' as he put it, he wouldn't actually beat Danny up over it? It wasn't as if Quinn was particularly fond of me, and would feel affronted on my behalf. But even so, the fact that he'd said it, and the fact that he hadn't reacted at all when I'd told him about the blood, was

The Perfect Couple

making me think. *Could* it have been Quinn who had attacked Danny in our old apartment? Could Danny have hidden his injuries from me because he didn't want me to know that his cousin, his friend, had turned on him, and the reason why he'd done so? And ... another thought suddenly struck me. Quinn had acted oddly, had left immediately, when I'd mentioned Bridget. Could she somehow be involved in all this after all, but maybe not in the way I'd first considered? I'd originally wondered if she was protecting Danny, helping him to hide away in Ireland possibly. But what if it was *Quinn* she was actually trying to protect? If he had attacked Danny, did she know about it? Is that why she'd asked me about the police investigation when I'd spoken to her, trying to find out if they might be on to Quinn? But why would she protect Quinn if he'd hurt her son – did she dislike Danny that much? Or was all this in my imagination?

Even if I was right, it still didn't explain where Danny was now or why he'd disappeared, I thought, as I kneaded the dough, mechanically pummelling it, flipping it back and forth on the flour-covered table. But if I went to the police, told them about my fears about Quinn, that might at least divert their attention away from me, and help them get closer to the truth of all this.

I needed to talk it all through with Eva first, I thought. And would the police even listen to me this time? They certainly hadn't seemed to have given my previous theory any serious consideration; they still appeared to think every word I said to them was a lie, an attempt to mislead them and stop them looking at me as prime suspect. Maybe if Eva came with me though ... she was a respected crime reporter, surely they'd listen to her?

BEEP.

I jumped at the sound of my mobile phone text alert. Wiping my floury hands on my jumper, I leaned across to the worktop and picked the phone up, tapping the screen to open the message. I read it, and a chill ran through me. What? WHAT?

It was from a withheld number, and the message was short and to the point.

I know what you've done. Time to confess. Or else.

Chapter 28

On Saturday morning Devon was in the process of dialling Gemma O'Connor's number to ask her to attend the police station yet again for further questioning following the visit from Quinn O'Connor when, across the room, somebody called his name and told him the woman had just walked into reception downstairs and had asked to speak to him.

Weird, he thought, as he headed down to meet her. She just keeps on turning up, doesn't she? Is she here to tell us where her husband is, or where she's buried the body?

He snorted. Chance would be a fine thing. He needed to confront her about the domestic abuse allegations made by her husband's cousin, and Helena would be joining him shortly to carry out that interview, but he'd see what Gemma wanted first, he decided. Despite the increasing quantities of circumstantial evidence, he still couldn't quite make his mind up about her. Helena was out for her blood, more and more convinced that she was responsible for Danny's disappearance at the very least, and very possibly for all four murders too, and while he could definitely see why she thought that, despite the lack of any logical motive, he was still clinging on to the

281

fence he'd been half-sitting on, reluctant to entirely give up on other possibilities just yet. The evidence against her was becoming increasingly compelling though, he thought, no doubt about that, and if she really was the perpetrator of domestic violence on top of everything else ...

Gemma was waiting in reception, bundled up in a black wool coat, her face pale and tired looking. Unexpectedly, she wasn't alone, accompanied by a woman with long red hair and arresting green-brown eyes who she introduced as: 'My friend and former colleague, Eva Hawton. Eva's the crime reporter for *The Independent* I mentioned to you before. Is it OK if she comes in with me?'

Devon had shrugged and nodded, seeing no reason to refuse the request and, if he was being honest with himself, feeling for the first time in months a small flip of the stomach – that undeniable sign that he was physically attracted to someone – when he looked at Eva Hawton. She'd looked back with a cool gaze and then given him the smallest of smiles, and his insides had somersaulted.

Wow. She's gorgeous, he thought, as he led the two women into the interview room. Was this a good sign? Did it mean he was finally starting to get over Jasmine? He certainly hadn't even looked at another woman with the slightest stirring of interest since his relationship had ended, so he hoped it was, and he began to wonder how he could discreetly find out if she was single. Then his heart sank a little. After such a long dry spell, trust him to suddenly find his interest sparked by a woman who was best friends with a possible serial killer.

When they were settled at the table, the two women sitting side by side opposite him, Gemma reached into her coat pocket and pulled out her mobile phone. She tapped at the screen, and Devon noticed that her hands were shaking.

'It's this ... I need to show you this,' she said. 'It arrived yesterday, from an anonymous number.'

She held the phone out, and he took it and read the message.

I know what you've done. Time to confess. Or else.

Interesting, he thought instantly.

'OK. And it's from a withheld number. So who do you think sent this?' he said.

'Well that's just the thing, I have no idea. But it's threatening, isn't it? That bit – "or else"? It sounds like someone is planning to hurt me, doesn't it? And I'm scared, DS Clarke. I'm suddenly really scared. I haven't done anything, nothing at all, but with all the press and the publicity and everything, clearly there are people out there who think I have, and ... and I'm just scared. Pictures of my house have been on TV, in the newspapers, it wouldn't be that hard to find me, and I'm alone there most of the time, anyone could ...'

Her voice, which had become more and more hysterical as she spoke, suddenly cracked and she burst into tears, sinking her face into her hands. Her friend slipped an arm round her shoulders, then looked at him.

'Look, this is unacceptable,' she said, and Devon was struck again by how beautiful her eyes were. 'You can see how terrified she is, and she's right, if some nutter's got hold of her phone number, what next? Is there any way you can give her some protection, put an officer outside her home for a few days? Come on, DS Clarke. This isn't fair. If you really do think Gemma has committed a crime, provide the evidence and arrest her. But if not ...'

Devon nodded, eager to please her. 'OK, I'll discuss it with my superiors. Leave it with me. Is there anything else?'

Gemma was still sobbing quietly.

'Shall I tell him?' Eva asked her gently.

'Please.'

Eva turned her attention back to Devon, and he felt that tiny flicker of desire again. Then he checked himself. There'd be plenty of time to think about women when all this was over. *Concentrate, Devon.*

'Well, on Thursday Gemma went to London, to meet up with Quinn O'Connor, Danny's cousin,' she began.

'Yes, I know,' said Devon. 'And in fact, when you arrived I was just about to get in touch with you to discuss Mr Quinn O'Connor, Gemma. You saved me a job.'

'You ... you know? How? Did you have me followed or something?'

Gemma, face still tear-streaked, looked up at him, clearly alarmed. Devon shook his head.

'No, we didn't. But ...'

He turned as the door opened and Helena walked in, brown envelope in hand.

'Ready?' she said.

'Yes,' replied Devon. 'Mrs O'Connor, we need to ask you some more questions with regards to the disappearance of your husband. Miss Hawton, I'm afraid we'll need you to step out now. Are you still declining legal representation, Mrs O'Connor?'

The two women looked stunned.

'But ... but we wanted to tell you ...' began Gemma.

'Oh, come on, now what?' said Eva, sounding exasperated.

'Legal representation?' Devon repeated.

'No, I don't need any, I haven't *done* anything ...'

'Gemma, maybe you should, this time? If they're questioning you yet *again* ...'

Eva sounded concerned, but Gemma shook her head vehemently.

'I'm fine, Eva. Go. I'll see you outside.'

Eva frowned, clearly reluctant to oblige, but Gemma waved her hands in a shooing motion.

'Go, honestly.'

She did, and when they were ready Helena began.

'Mrs O'Connor, some allegations have been made against you, and we'd like to put them to you. It's been alleged that on at least one occasion, and reportedly on numerous occasions, your husband Danny was the victim of domestic abuse. And that you were responsible for that abuse. What's your response to those claims?'

Gemma stared at her, wide-eyed.

'Domestic ... domestic *what*? What are you talking about?'

'Domestic abuse. Or domestic violence, as it's commonly known. We have evidence that, on at least one occasion as I said, you punched and kicked your husband so severely that he was left with significant bruising ...'

'I did *what*? That is absolutely ludicrous. I love Danny. I would never ... who told you that? And what evidence?'

Her face was flushed with anger, her voice getting louder with each word. Devon raised a hand.

'Mrs O'Connor, please try to stay calm. We want to show you a couple of photographs.'

She took a couple of deep breaths, obviously trying to regain control, and he waited a moment then slid the two photographs Quinn O'Connor had presented them with out of the envelope Helena had brought with her. He placed them on the table in front of Gemma.

'What can you tell us about these pictures, Gemma?' Helena asked. 'Are these the injuries you inflicted on your husband on one of the occasions when you attacked him?'

'I *never* ...' Gemma leaned forward, staring at the photos. Then a look of relief crossed her face, and she straightened up again.

'Those aren't injuries inflicted by me,' she said firmly. 'I know exactly how and when Danny got those bruises. It was back in early November, during that really icy spell? He was cycling home from work and a car pulled out of a side road right in front of him. He braked but the bike slid on the ice and he went over the handlebars, straight onto the bonnet of the car. He cracked a rib and got that awful bruising all down his right side. It lasted for weeks. Who on earth said this was domestic violence?'

She sounded calmer now, the flush in her cheeks lessening.

Helena reached across and picked up the photographs, then said: 'And this accident was reported to the police?'

'Well ...' Gemma hesitated. 'No, it wasn't actually. By the time Danny had managed to get himself up the car had driven off, and it was all so quick he didn't get the number plate or even the make or model. And it was dark and quite late – he'd been doing a late shift at work. There was nobody else around, no witnesses. He thought about reporting it anyway, but in the end he didn't bother. He said he didn't see the point.'

'I see.' Helena raised an eyebrow.

'Look, what's going on here? Who told you ... oh, hang on. Hang on.'

Gemma shook her head slowly, a look of incredulity on her face. She turned to Devon.

'When I mentioned going to see Quinn in London, you said you already knew about it. And you said you didn't have me followed, which means the only way you could know about my meeting with Quinn is if *he* told you about it. Shit, it was him, wasn't it? *He* told you I'd been abusing Danny! Why on earth would he?'

Suddenly, she was on her feet, her face bright red again. Devon made a move to stand up too, but Helena put a restraining hand on his arm.

'Just a moment,' she whispered.

Gemma had begun pacing up and down the small room, muttering under her breath.

'What is it, Gemma? Is there something you want to share with us?' Helena asked. Her tone was low and steady, but Devon could tell exactly what she was thinking.

Come on, Gemma. Now's the time. Tell us. The truth, this time.

Jackie Kabler

Gemma stopped her pacing. She looked at Helena for a long moment, then at Devon. And then she laughed.

'I give up,' she said simply. 'No, I have nothing to share with you. You don't believe a word I say anyway. What's the point, in any of this? Is there anything else? Anything else I can do for you? Any more ridiculous accusations you want to throw at me, without a shred of evidence? Because if not, and if I'm not under arrest, I'd like to go home now please.'

When she was gone, to his chagrin her friend Eva glaring at Devon as he showed a clearly very upset Gemma back out into the reception area where she'd been waiting, he and Helena retired to the canteen for a tea and a regroup. When he filled her in about the threatening text message Gemma had received, Helena pursed her lips.

'Somebody else thinks like I do then. That she did it, and it's time she confessed. Either that, or she sent it to herself. She'd do anything to draw our attention elsewhere, that one. That random guy on the CCTV footage at the gym that she tried to convince Frankie was her husband? And now that hasn't worked she's trying to make herself into a victim, trying to make out someone's out to get her. She was right when she said we don't believe a word she says – I certainly don't believe that flimflam about Danny having a bike accident. Very convenient that it was never reported, wasn't it?'

Devon swallowed the piece of chocolate brownie he'd just put in his mouth.

'The alleged domestic abuse was never reported either

though. So yet again, we can't prove it. We can't prove any of it, boss.'

Helena stretched her arms above her head, arching her back, and groaned.

'Bloody back's killing me again. Still haven't managed to find the time to make an appointment with anyone to sort it out,' she said.

Then she reached out and broke a large chunk off Devon's brownie.

'Oi!' he said, with mock outrage. 'You said you didn't want anything to eat! And you don't even eat chocolate. Get your own, Muriel!'

She scowled.

'I hoped you'd forgotten about my delightful middle name.'

He stuck his tongue out at her, and she grinned.

'As for not eating chocolate, I do today. Share and share alike, boy. And as for not being able to prove any of it ...'

Her face grew serious.

'Well, maybe we won't have to,' she said.

Chapter 29

BEEP.

I jumped, a jarring sound rousing me from an uneasy sleep. The luminous digits on the alarm clock on my bedside table told me it was 4.25 a.m., and I whimpered. I hadn't fallen asleep until gone two. I groped behind the clock for my phone, wondering who on earth was trying to get hold of me at this hour. My alarm clock – a white, chunky, old-fashioned thing with big yellow numbers on its display – had always been a great source of amusement for Danny.

'Who uses an alarm clock nowadays, you mad woman? Use your phone like everyone else does!' he'd say, but I always ignored him. I liked my clock; I liked being able to see at a glance what time it was when I opened my eyes, without having to fumble for my phone. Finally, I found it, and squinted at the screen. My body stiffened, and a surge of adrenaline rushed through me, making me jerk upright in bed.

'No! Not again, please!'

I stared at the screen. It was another text message, sender's number withheld.

Tell them what you did. If you don't, you'll be next.

There was a sudden movement at the door and for a moment I stopped breathing.

'Gemma? What's wrong? I just got up to go to the loo and I heard you shouting.'

Eva. I exhaled, my body sagging with relief.

'Sorry. It's another text, look.'

She crossed the room and sat down on the bed next to me, reaching for my phone.

'Shit, Gem. This is getting out of control. You need to go back to the police and make them take this seriously. They haven't even bothered to put anyone outside, have they? If anything happens to you ...'

I shivered, and she grabbed my hand.

'Oh bugger, I'm sorry, I'm no help, am I, scaremongering like this. But I'm worried, Gem. Come on, let's go and make a hot chocolate or something. We're not going to sleep now. Where's your dressing gown?'

'On ... on the back of the ... the door.'

My teeth were chattering, even though the room was warm, and I had a sudden urge to hide, to crawl under the bed or into the wardrobe, to stay there until all this was over. But when would it be over? This nightmare was never-ending, a dark stain spreading through my life, slowly obliterating all that had ever been good and right and happy.

I've lost everything, haven't I? I thought suddenly. All of it was gone, *all* of it. My sense of security, my feeling of being loved, belonging. My self-esteem. My marriage. My *life*. So what did it matter what happened to me now? I'd lost everything worth living for. The police might as well arrest me, lock me up. I was beyond caring. I was done.

As if in a trance, I let Eva slip my robe around my shoulders and lead me to the kitchen. But as my body slowly warmed up, and I watched my friend as she bustled around, spooning chocolate into mugs and heating milk, I felt a tiny ping somewhere deep inside my brain, and one word began to run through my head over and over again. Quinn. *Quinn.*

Eva and I had talked for hours when we'd got back from the police station, trying to make sense of it all, and we'd both come to the same conclusion. If it *was* Quinn who had given the police those photos of Danny – and it must have been, who else? – and if it was Quinn who'd told them I'd been physically abusing my husband, then he was doing it for one reason only. Quinn was trying to frame me. He wanted to make it look as if *I* was the one who had hurt Danny. To lay a false trail, because in reality it was he who was responsible.

I'd batter him for that …

The more I thought about it, the more I thought it had to have been Quinn who attacked Danny in our Chiswick bedroom. I still didn't really understand the reason behind it – him finding out that Danny was cheating on me just didn't seem cause enough for such extreme violence. But the fact that he didn't react in any way when I mentioned the blood, as if that wasn't news to him, as if he already knew all about it … could Quinn and Danny have fallen out over something else, something much bigger? Danny had, apparently, saved Quinn's life many years ago, and maybe that explained why he had always seemed so devoted to my husband. But maybe some-thing had happened that made even that pale into insignificance. Maybe Danny had got himself into trouble, and somehow dragged Quinn into it too, and Quinn had attacked him out of revenge. Maybe – and we thought long and hard about this, until we convinced ourselves that it was a real possibility too – maybe it was *Quinn* Danny was hiding from in Bristol. Maybe it was Quinn who had driven him away. Maybe he'd even caught up with Danny, and Danny was now dead at the hands of his own cousin. The dating app, the other murders, they were all a big coincidence, nothing to do with Danny's disappearance at all. And now, after I'd gone to see Quinn, he'd suddenly decided to reinforce the police's suspicion that *I'd* hurt Danny. He wanted them to think it was *me*.

'He knew, Eva, about that bike accident. He knew all about it. I remember us meeting up with him not long afterwards, and Danny pulling up his shirt to show him the bruises. I have no idea why they took pictures, but Quinn *knew* what had really happened. So why tell such a different story, unless he's trying to make the police think I killed Danny?'

She'd nodded slowly, picking a piece of jalapeno off the slice of pizza on her plate and rolling it between her fingers. And then she'd said what I'd already started to think but hadn't yet dared to voice.

'And if he's done that ... I think it might have been him who sent that text message too, Gem. He *wanted* you to show it to the police. It reinforces their theory that you killed Danny. It implies that you did it, and that somebody knows you did it, and they're trying to make you confess.'

I swallowed hard.

'I was just thinking the same thing. But it's just ... it's just so *horrible*, Eva. I mean, if Quinn really has hurt – or even killed – Danny? They were like brothers ... so why turn on him like that?'

We both sat there for a moment, looking at each other, my despair reflected in her eyes. Then Eva said:

'You should have told the police, you know. This theory about Quinn being the one who attacked Danny. Even if they didn't believe you, you should have told them. Got it on record.'

'I know. I know. It just suddenly seemed so pointless, all of it. They can't prove anything, and neither can I. It's all just theories.'

We both sat in silence then, the pizza growing cold and greasy on our plates. Finally, Eva spoke.

'Gem. Look, I don't want you to freak out or anything, but you said just now that the police can't prove anything against you. You do realize, don't you, that with all this circumstantial evidence mounting, well ... it's like building a jigsaw. And if they get enough pieces, and they all fit together neatly enough, well, sometimes that can be enough.'

'What? What do you mean?'

I pushed my plate aside, the sight of the uneaten food beginning to make me feel queasy.

'Well, it's just ... look, remember Barry George? The man convicted of shooting Jill Dando?'

I nodded. The BBC television presenter had been murdered on her doorstep in west London in 1999. Barry George, a local man, had been convicted of killing her two years later. It had been a huge story.

'Of course. He got out though, didn't he? Served eight years, something like that?'

'Yep. Was released on his second appeal. But my point is that he was convicted basically on circumstantial evidence. They said they found a tiny speck of gunpowder in his pocket, but everything else was circumstantial. They found witnesses who said he was obsessed with celebrities and with guns. They found women who said they'd had unwanted approaches from him. He was a loner, and he stalked and photographed women, and he had a grudge of some sort against the BBC. None of it proved he'd killed Jill, but the prosecution built a successful case on all that stuff, Gemma. No hard evidence. Yes he was cleared in the end, but he went to prison for years. And all this stuff that the police keep hauling you in for ... it's making me nervous, Gem. I'm wondering if any day now they're going to think they've got enough. That they'll hand it all over to the CPS and charge you with murder.'

I stared at her, aghast.

'But ... but they haven't even found a body,' I said, desperately. 'We don't even know for sure if Danny's *dead*.'

'They don't need one,' she said. 'There've been loads of convictions in cases where the body's never been found.'

'Oh great. Well, thanks for that, Eva. That's made me feel loads better.'

I slumped backwards in my chair, feeling utterly defeated.

'Oh shit, sorry, darling.'

Eva leaned across the low table, her long hair trailing in the pizza, and patted my knee.

'I'm sorry, OK?? But we have to get real here, and I'm just so bloody worried about you, especially after today. It was like yet another nail in the coffin. I mean, look at just some of the stuff they have on you – or *think* they have on you, so far ...'

She sat back again, frowning as she peeled a stringy piece of cheese off a strand of hair, then wiped her fingers on her jeans.

'And I'm just talking about what they think they have on you in relation to *Danny* now, leaving the other murders aside. They've found a load of blood in your old apartment. Danny's blood. They only have *your* word that he ever moved to Bristol – not a single neighbour or anyone else around here ever laid eyes on him. Since the end of January he hasn't contacted anyone he knows, he hasn't used his bank account, he didn't start his new job. You have no emails from him or pictures of him dated beyond the end of January either. And now there's photographic evidence and a witness who says you were physically violent towards him. Hell, Gemma, if I didn't know you and I was faced with that little lot, I'd be pointing the finger at you too.'

A hard knot had formed in my stomach as she'd been speaking, my nails digging into my palms.

'You're not though, are you?' My voice was a mere squeak. 'Pointing the finger? Please Eva ... I hate to ask you this again, but you're not having doubts, are you? You do believe me? Please, please say you do, because I honestly don't think I could bear it ...'

She leapt from her seat then and knelt at my feet, wrapping her arms around my knees.

'Of course I believe you, you numpty. Stop asking me that. But this is serious now, Gemma. We need to do something, to get you out of this. I just don't know what, and it's killing me.'

We'd gone to bed shortly after that, and somehow I'd finally fallen asleep, Danny's face rippling through my dreams, until the beep of my damn phone had woken me. As we sat in the quiet of the kitchen, sipping our hot chocolates, my mind clearing, the fight returning, a sudden impulse struck. I reached into my dressing gown pocket and pulled out my phone.

'I'm going to call him,' I announced.

'What? Who? It's not even 5 a.m.!" she said.

'Quinn. That sneaky, possibly murdering, little bastard, Quinn.'

My anger was growing, and I stood up, my bare feet thudding on the tiled floor as I stomped around the kitchen, clicking onto my contacts file and scrolling through it.

'I'm going to call him, and I'm going to ask him what the FUCK he's playing at. That's two texts he's sent now. It *is* him, I know it is. Does he really think he can get away with threatening me like that, the evil little shit? I'm going to tell him we're on to him, and that we're going to the police first thing to tell them everything. See what he makes of that.'

'Gemma, I really don't think ...'

I ignored her, stabbing at the phone, finding his number.

I hit the call button, and then returned to the table and put the phone on speaker.

It began to ring, and I braced myself, waiting for him to pick up. He didn't.

Hi, this is Quinn. Leave a message.

'Shit,' I said, and hit the redial button. The phone rang again, and again went to voicemail. I tried twice more, and the same thing happened.

'He's not going to pick up, Gemma,' said Eva, rather unnecessarily I felt.

'Filthy little coward,' I replied. I stared at my phone for another moment then cut off the call, the screen returning to the phone's home page, the date and time flashing. I swallowed, remembering.

'Eva, it's the seventeenth of March. St Patrick's Day. Mine and Danny's first wedding anniversary.'

She nodded and reached across the table to take my hand. 'I know. I'm so sorry,' she said.

It was after six when we finally crawled back into bed, the soft coppery streaks of dawn beginning to light up the sky. I fell asleep to the sound of birds trilling, and suddenly I was back there, in our apartment in Chiswick, in our old bedroom. The room was dim, illuminated only by the orange glow of the streetlights outside, and there was a strange, metallic odour in the air. I moved slowly across the small space, a sick, hollow feeling in my stomach, my palms damp, my legs leaden; when I reached the end of the bed I stopped, aware that I was clutching something hard and cold in my right hand, and stared at the motionless thing that lay there on the mattress, still and silent in a dark pool of something viscous and sticky.

'Danny,' I whispered. 'Danny.'

But he didn't reply, didn't move. I looked down then, down at my hands, and realized that it wasn't sweat that was making my palms clammy. It was blood. My hands were covered in blood, and the thing I was holding was a knife.

Chapter 30

The egg whistled through the air and smashed against the door, inches from Devon's left ear. He ducked back inside as a roar went up from the crowd gathered on the pavement outside.

'Shit!' he said. 'Why the hell is it taking so long to get this lot under control?'

'They're on their way. Shouldn't be long now. And I did tell you not to go out there.'

Helena was leaning against the counter in the reception area, the grim expression she'd been wearing since she'd arrived, dressed in hastily thrown on sweatpants and hoodie, replaced briefly with a wry smile.

'Should listen to you more often. Nearly took my eye out. Do they really have nothing better to do on a Sunday morning?' said Devon, running a hand down the lapels of his dark blue jacket, checking for splashes. No sweatpants for him, despite the unexpected call to work, Helena thought. Dapper as always.

'And what a waste of food. The whole front of the building's covered in flour and egg yolk. We could make pancakes.'

She rolled her eyes.

'Is there ever a single minute when you're not thinking about your stomach? Anyway, I'm going back upstairs. You staying to watch the show?'

'Yeah. For a few minutes. From the window, though. Not going out there again.'

'Good. Come up when you're done, OK? This has gone too far now. We need a plan.'

She headed for the stairs. Reinforcements were on their way, and the fifty or so protestors who'd begun to gather outside the station an hour ago would soon be sent on their way. Mostly young men, some had been waving placards bearing slogans written in large, red capital letters, streaky as if daubed in blood.

KILLER ON THE LOOSE AND THE COPS DON'T CARE

HOW MANY MORE OF US HAVE TO DIE?

They'd brought the press with them too, several photographers and three TV satellite trucks – those from Sky, ITV and BBC News – all arriving minutes after the first flour bomb hit the front door. There'd been no real damage done – a few buckets of water and a scrubbing brush would soon return the façade of the building to its usual, tatty but cleanish state – and there were unlikely to be any arrests. But Helena was already bracing herself for the phone call she knew was inevitable as soon as DCS Anna Miller heard about the fracas. The city was getting far too restless, and there was little Miller hated more than bad publicity, and her beloved police force being accused of not being up to the job. She'd be demanding answers, and making threats, and as Helena had driven to the station earlier, leaving a resigned Charlotte to finish her Sunday morning avocado on toast alone, she'd already started planning her response.

'It's time to stop pussyfooting around,' she said out loud, as she sat down in her chair and turned her computer on. Nobody responded; the incident room was empty, the team having been given a much-needed day off. Helena knew Devon needed time off too – hell, she was pretty desperate for some herself, and some quality time with her wife – but this wouldn't take long. Two hours, tops. Because, she thought, enough was finally enough. As soon as Devon came up to join her, they'd go through everything they had on Gemma O'Connor, starting with the latest piece of evidence – the statement Quinn O'Connor had given about her violent behaviour towards Danny – and working backwards. She was pretty sure they didn't have enough to persuade the CPS to even consider charging her with the four other murders, but her *husband* – they just might have enough now, she thought. OK, so there was still no body. But even so, it had been pretty damn clear for some time that something seriously bad had happened to Danny O'Connor. And now, with the public demanding action, and the pressure from her superiors about to increase tenfold, Helena was suddenly feeling a tiny bit reckless, and a big bit determined. She was as certain as she could be that Gemma O'Connor was guilty of *something*, and it was time to put her money where her mouth was. It was time to do something about it.

Chapter 31

I slept until nearly ten, waking up feeling groggy, my eyes sore and my head aching. I found Eva at the kitchen table drinking coffee and reading something on her iPad, the radio playing quietly in the background, tuned to a classical music station.

'Very civilized,' I said, as I slumped onto the chair opposite her. I felt exhausted.

She looked up and smiled.

'Hey you. Just reading about some sort of riot outside the cop shop this morning. A protest about police incompetence by the look of it – the locals are angry that there's a serial killer in their midst and nobody seems to be able to catch him. Anyway, it was something and nothing I think. All over now. How are you feeling?'

'A riot? Here, in Bristol? Bloody hell.'

I leaned across the table and she turned the tablet to show me a photograph of a sea of angry faces, placards held aloft. Then, losing interest, I rubbed my eyes, which felt as if somebody had poured sand into them.

'I'm knackered,' I said. 'Feel like an elephant sat on my head while I was asleep. And I had such a horrible dream.'

An involuntary shudder ran through me, and Eva frowned.

'What sort of dream? What happened?'

I shook my head and stood up again.

'It was just a dream. Doesn't matter. I need coffee, urgently. You?'

'Thanks, one more would be good. Look, I need to go soon, I'm so sorry. I hate leaving you, especially on your wedding anniversary and everything. But I need to be in the newsroom early tomorrow, and the flat's a tip and I haven't done any food shopping or washing in a week. I'll be going to work in my PJs if I don't get home at a reasonable hour and sort a few things out.'

'Don't worry, I'll be OK. I'm just grateful you managed to get here at all. What story are you on tomorrow, do you know?'

I'd moved to the worktop as I spoke, flicking the kettle on and opening the cupboard to find a mug.

'Eva?'

She hadn't replied, and I turned to see her staring at me, a wary look on her face.

'What?'

She clasped her hands in front of her, then pursed her lips and blew out some air.

'OK, look ... I was going to tell you this on Friday, but then with the texts and everything, and then all the Quinn stuff, it just didn't seem like ... well, you see ...'

I was back at the table, coffee forgotten.

'*What?* You're scaring me, Eva. What is it?'

'Well, it's just ... well, you know how the last time I was here I was joking about "my friend the serial killer"? They want me to write it.'

'They want ... *what?*'

I sank down onto my chair again, staring at her. She was twisting a strand of hair around a finger now, eyes downcast.

'They want me to write a piece about you. About Danny going missing, about the similarities between him and the four murder victims. And about the police dragging you in repeatedly for questioning. They want a piece about what it's like to be a suspect in a serial killer case, from the point of view of someone who's got the inside track. Me.'

My mouth had dropped open, and I was gaping at her now, speechless.

'Obviously, if anyone's charged, it all changes and we can't write anything, as you know,' she said hastily. 'But now, well ...'

'But you're not actually going to *do it?*' My voice had suddenly returned, and loudly. 'Eva, please! You can't!'

She sighed.

'I've been trying to put it off for a week, but now they're insisting. I don't *want* to do it, Gemma. But you know what it's like – if I don't, they'll do a piece anyway, and whoever writes it won't be sympathetic like I will. I don't think I have any choice. I'm so sorry.'

I groaned and sank my head into my hands. She was right, I *did* know what it was like. I could imagine exactly the pressure Eva would be under to deliver the story, picture the delight on the face of her news editor when he realized that his top crime reporter was best friends with a woman the police appeared to suspect was a serial killer. She was perfectly placed to deliver a fascinating story, but the problem was that this *wasn't* just a story, not to me. This was my life, my own personal hell, and the prospect of an in-depth article written by my best mate, my confidante ... it didn't bear thinking about.

I looked up again, tears filling my eyes, my throat constricting.

'I know. I know you wouldn't do it if you didn't have to,' I whispered. 'But please ... can you just put it off a little bit longer? I don't know if I can handle it. My family, everyone ...'

'I'll try,' she said, and I realized she had tears in her eyes too. 'I promise. I'll try.'

After she left, I forced myself to shower and dress, strip her bed and dust the spare room, vacuum the house, put a load of washing in the machine, take Albert out for a quick scamper. By lunchtime I'd run out of things to do, so I turned the TV on, finding the comedy channel and watching reruns of *Cheers*, *Seinfeld* and *The Office*, pushing the thoughts of Danny and Quinn and the police and Eva's article and all of it, every horrible, terrifying bit of it, out of my head every time it tried to wriggle its way in, refusing it entry. I was just waiting now, I realized. Waiting for what was going to happen next. Waiting for another text, waiting for the police to come and arrest me, waiting to see if I could summon up enough energy to go back to the station, to tell someone my theory about Quinn attacking or maybe even killing Danny, although what was the point? They wouldn't believe me anyway. And so I carried on, waiting, waiting, waiting.

By four, to my surprise I suddenly realized I was starving, and I boiled some pasta and threw in a jar of readymade arrabbiata sauce I found in the cupboard. I'd just settled down on the sofa to eat it when my mobile beeped. My stomach lurched. Another text. I put my fork down slowly and reached for the phone.

**Have you confessed yet? This is your last warning.
I'm coming for you.**

I read the words, and then looked to see who'd sent them, expecting as usual to see 'number withheld'. And then I smiled.

'YES! Got ya!' I yelled triumphantly, thumping the cushion next to me. Albert, who'd been lying across my feet, jumped violently and gave a short, accusatory bark.

'Sorry, Albert. But I was right. I was *right*!'

I was right. And this time, he'd made a mistake. This time, the text hadn't come from an anonymous number. He'd used his own phone. The text was from Quinn O'Connor.

Chapter 32

'Don't you see? He's trying to FRAME me! *He* sent me those other texts, as well as this one, from some sort of throwaway phone, burner phone, whatever you call it. Not *his* phone anyway. But then he sent another one, this one, and he screwed up. He used his own phone, look! You can tell the texts are from the same person just by looking at them. I think *he* hurt Danny, maybe even killed him, and don't ask me why, because I haven't figured that bit out yet, and anyway that's your job, not mine. But he did it, and he's trying to get *me* locked up for it! And threatening me too. You must see that surely, you ...'

Devon held up a hand.

'OK, OK. Slow down.'

Gemma O'Connor was standing in front of him, pink-cheeked and wild-eyed, practically jumping up and down on the spot in her efforts to persuade him that her missing husband's cousin, Quinn O'Connor, was trying to frame her for murder. He'd been shocked when the call had come from downstairs to tell him she had come in yet again and was demanding to talk to him; after long discussions with

308

Helena in the empty incident room the previous day, he knew she was almost ready to take a chance and charge Gemma O'Connor, and would be just as surprised as he was to see the woman already in the station when she got in, which should be very shortly. He decided to humour Gemma.

'Look, let me take the phone and check the number of the sender of the message against the number *we* have for Quinn, OK? Take a seat for a moment. I'll send someone in with a coffee, and I'll be back down in a few minutes.'

She glanced at the chair he was gesturing at, looking uncertain, then nodded.

'All right. Thank you,' she said.

He left her and headed back up to the incident room, where he found Helena slipping her coat off and hanging it on the overloaded rack on the back wall.

'Morning. Little lie-in today, boss?'

She turned and scowled at him.

'Oh, shut up. It's only eight thirty and I have a feeling this might be a long day. Any news?'

'A bit, yes.'

He updated her on the latest visit by Gemma O'Connor, and her eyes widened.

'And she's still here?'

'Yep. Drinking coffee in interview room number three. How do you want to play this?'

She rubbed her eyes. She looked tired, Devon thought.

'Well, what do you make of these messages? If they *are*

309

from Quinn O'Connor, does that change anything? I'm almost too tired to think straight.'

He shrugged.

'Well, if they *are* from him, he clearly shouldn't be sending threatening messages like that whatever the circumstances, and we'll have to have a word with him. I've checked his record, by the way. A handful of minor misdemeanours in his youth in Ireland, nothing for years though and nothing in this country. But the content of those messages is interesting, isn't it? It sounds like he's backing up what he told us when he came in – that he believes she's responsible for Danny's disappearance, death, whatever, and wants her to confess to it. In the meantime, she's now trying to claim *he* might have done something to Danny and is trying to frame *her*. But that doesn't ring true to me; would he really have come here of his own accord to speak to us if he was the killer?'

Helena shook her head.

'Unlikely. If *I'd* killed someone, the last thing I'd do is go to the police and put myself on their radar. So what do we think? That she's running scared now and is trying to shift the blame onto him to save her own skin?'

He thought for a moment, then sighed.

'Maybe. I just don't know. As I keep saying, boss, I just can't call this one. But even I can't deny there's a ton of evidence pointing squarely in her direction.'

'SHIT! Boss, Devon, come here, quick! You need to see this!'

They both jumped. Across the room, DC Frankie Stevens was waving frantically at them, and pointing at his computer screen. They exchanged puzzled glances and went over to see what he wanted.

'What's up, Frankie?' asked Helena, and he gestured wildly at the screen with one hand, pushing his little glasses further up his nose with the other.

'This,' he said, his voice high with excitement. 'It's just come in from our contact at the Met. It's a serious assault – an attempted murder, they believe, in London early last Thursday evening. A man called Declan Bailey was attacked in a side street off Vauxhall Bridge Road, but somebody came along and interrupted the attacker, who fled. It all happened too fast for the witness to get a look at the attacker – he says he was too concerned about the man bleeding on the ground in front of him, but wait for it ... two things. First, the EHU app was found on his phone, which may or may not be important, but worth noting. And ... and this is the most exciting bit ... the assailant *dropped the weapon* he or she was using. It was a small, heavy hammer apparently. So ...'

'Hang on, hang on. OK, last Thursday. Isn't that when ...?'

The dozen or so people in the room were all moving closer now, listening to the excited conversation. Frankie nodded, his eyes bright.

'It's the day Gemma O'Connor went to London, to visit Quinn O'Connor in a pub in Victoria.'

'And you said a side street off Vauxhall Bridge Road?' Helena was leaning closer, peering at the screen.

'I know that area. That's literally yards from Victoria station,' said Devon. His heart rate had suddenly increased. 'Bloody hell, boss. She was *there*.'

There was a mass intake of breath from the assembled detectives.

'Wow!' somebody said.

Helena straightened up again slowly, eyes still fixed on the message on the screen.

'Why are they only telling us about this now? It's Monday, for shit's sake.'

'A couple of the key people who knew about our cases here and the possible links to the London murders were away at a conference at the end of last week,' Frankie said. He sounded a little breathless. 'So nobody made the connection, until this morning, when our contacts came back and saw the crime report. Oh, and looked at his picture. They haven't sent that over yet, but apparently he's another lookalike ... it all fits, boss. It all bloody fits.'

'SHIT.' Helena spun round and grinned at Devon, then turned back to Frankie.

'So – he's alive? This Declan guy? And the attacker dropped the weapon? Holy cow.'

Frankie nodded vigorously, his glasses bobbing on his nose.

'He's got a bad head injury, but he's alive, although he doesn't remember much. But the weapon's being rushed through forensics. I'll stay across it and get the results to you as soon as they come in, boss.'

'Shit, guys. I think we've got her,' said Helena slowly.

There was a moment of silence, then somebody started to clap, followed by another and another. Helena and Devon grinned at each other, then she held up her hand.

'OK, so yes, it's looking good. But we still have a long way to go on this. If we can get DNA from that hammer though ...'

'And Gemma O'Connor? She's downstairs right now, remember?' said Devon.

She smiled again.

'Well, let's go and see her, shall we? And then let's arrest her. On suspicion of murder and attempted murder.'

Chapter 33

'Think this is it. Yep, number sixteen. Address is Flat 16B.'

DC Mike Slater, who'd just manoeuvred the car neatly into a space directly opposite number 16 Elmwood Road, pointed at the house. It was a shabby semi, the small front garden overgrown, a bicycle missing its front tyre leaning against the ramshackle wooden fence that separated the house from its neighbour.

'Right. Let me just finish these last few mouthfuls and we'll see if he's in.'

Devon raised his takeaway cup and Mike gave him the thumbs up sign. They were in Feltham in west London, after a day spent with their contacts at the Metropolitan Police, visiting the scene of the latest – thankfully, foiled – attack and then heading to St Thomas' Hospital to see and attempt to interview the victim, Declan Bailey. Unfortunately, the man had been asleep, still under mild sedation, and his doctor had been insistent that he not be disturbed.

'We're confident he'll recover, but he's still very ill, and as far as I know remembers nothing whatsoever about the attack,' Dr Mulligan had said. She was a tall, formidable-looking woman with a shock of bleached blonde hair piled on top of her head.

'You can interview him when he's better. You are *not* waking him up now.'

Suitably intimidated, Devon and Mike had obeyed doctor's orders, but they'd managed to get a look at the sleeping patient and, even though his face had been bruised and swollen and most of his hair covered by the bandages protecting his head wounds, the similarities between him and the other four victims – five if you counted Danny O'Connor – were obvious.

'He's got the same sort of hair, dark eyebrows, same general *look*,' Mike had whispered, before they'd been briskly ushered out of the room by Dr Mulligan. 'What the hell is it, Devon? I mean, if it *is* Gemma O'Connor behind all this, why is she attacking men who look like her husband? Does she hate him that much? What on earth can he have done to her to drive her to this?'

They were still waiting, though, for the forensics report on the weapon Declan had been attacked with; with profuse apologies, and mutterings about budget cuts and staff short-ages, they'd been told that there was some sort of backlog and that it might be another twenty-four or even forty-eight hours before they might have a result. In the meantime, and with Gemma O'Connor in custody since the previous morning, and still denying everything when questioned, Devon and Mike had been dispatched to try to carry on gathering as much evidence as they could. They'd stopped off in Feltham on their way back to Bristol in an effort to find Quinn O'Connor, who hadn't been answering his phone.

'Give him a warning about sending threatening text messages,' Helena had said, while simultaneously scanning the front pages of Tuesday's papers, all with excited headlines about Gemma's arrest.

IS THIS THE FACE OF A FEMALE SERIAL KILLER?

WIFE ARRESTED – IS SHE THE BRISTOL MURDERER?

'But also get a statement about last Thursday when he met up with Gemma,' she said, and pushed the pile of papers aside.

'We need details – exact timings, precise locations. We didn't get those when he came in to talk to us because it wasn't relevant then. It is now. There were no cameras in the side street Declan Bailey was attacked in but lots in the general area. Someone at the Met's looking at CCTV footage from that afternoon to see if he can spot her, but it's a massive job. We can help him a lot if we can give him more details about time and place.'

When numerous attempts to call Quinn to arrange another interview had failed, Devon and Mike decided to try his home address in Feltham, just west of Twickenham.

'Pretty much on our way home, anyway,' Mike had commented, as they'd battled through the evening traffic, heading west.

Finally parked outside the house, Devon swallowed the last of his tea.

'Lights are on. Might be in luck,' he said, as they got out

of the car. They crossed the road and opened the rusty metal gate, which creaked loudly. At the front door, Devon studied the two unnamed bell pushes for a moment, then randomly pressed the top one. Silence. They waited a full minute. This close to the house they could smell a faint odour of greasy food and stale cigarette smoke. Devon pressed the bell again. This time there was a bang from somewhere inside the building and then the thud of feet on the stairs.

'Jesus, Quinn. Did you forget your keys again?' said a male voice. The accent was Irish, and the speaker sounded irate.

Seconds later the door was wrenched open.

'Hello, we're looking for—'

Then Devon looked properly at the man who was standing in the doorway, and his mouth dropped open.

'What the ...?'

Beside him, he heard Mike gasp.

'Ahh, SHIT,' said the man.

Devon stared at him, looked at Mike, who had suddenly turned pale, and then returned his gaze to the man. The man he had instantly recognized. The man who everyone thought was highly likely to be dead, but who was actually clearly very much alive. The man who'd opened the door was, without any shadow of doubt, Danny O'Connor.

Chapter 34

I sat on the edge of the thin, plastic mattress, shivering. I'd spent the past hour pacing up and down the tiny space trying to keep warm, but now I felt sick, exhausted, my heartbeat pounding in my ears. I was terrified, I realized, as I pulled the tatty blanket the custody sergeant had given me tighter around my shoulders. I was terrified because it had finally happened, and I could see no way out of it. I'd been arrested and was sitting in a police cell. *Me*, Gemma O'Connor, journalist, magazine columnist, of previous excellent character – not even a parking ticket, for God's sake – had been arrested, on suspicion of murder and attempted murder. It would have been absolutely hilarious if it hadn't been so utterly horrifying. I'd lost track of how many questions I'd been asked, how many times I'd been walked to and from the small, overheated interview room, since that surreal moment when they'd suddenly appeared in the room I'd been waiting in and read me my rights, and I'd stood there, open-mouthed with shock, unable to believe what was happening. I hadn't uttered a word as they emptied my pockets, took my bag and shoes from me, took my photograph from different angles, took my fingerprints. *Processed* me, they told me it was called. I'd been half expecting it, the arrest, for days, but when it finally happened it was overwhelming, unreal, and I seemed to have been struck dumb, unable to form words, mutely obedient. And then, after I'd been in my tiny cell for an hour, or maybe it was two, or ten, who knows, sitting there numb and shaking, they'd finally taken me to an interview room, and it had begun.

It had been the same old stuff all over again – the blood in the bedroom, the fact that nobody except me seemed to have seen Danny since the end of January, and so on and so on and so on. My voice returned, thin and reedy, and I tried, tried so hard to argue, tried to remind them again of the CCTV footage at the gym, the footage I was convinced showed Danny, tried to tell them over and over again that he'd been alive and well and living with me in Bristol until two and a half weeks ago. They listened, and then swiftly dismissed all my arguments, their eyes cold.

If he was using the gym, if he was travelling around Bristol every day, why wasn't he using his bank account?

Why didn't he contact anyone, not even his own mother? Why do you have no photos of him, no emails from him, after the thirtieth of January? Why are you lying to us, Gemma? What did you do to Danny?

And then they asked, again, about the other men, the two killed in London, the two in Bristol. And about somebody else, somebody I'd never heard of, a man called Declan who'd apparently been attacked in London on the afternoon I'd been there to meet Quinn. I stared at them in disbelief at that, my mind racing.

'Well ... maybe it was *him*. Quinn. I *told* you I think it might have been him who's behind Danny's disappearance. Maybe it wasn't just Danny he hurt, maybe Quinn's your man for all of these murders; I don't know, I'm not a bloody detective. Maybe it was *him* who attacked this guy, if it was near where we met ... because it wasn't me, it wasn't, I couldn't, I wouldn't hurt anyone, this is ridiculous, you've got it all wrong ...'

I'd finally broken down then, huge sobs wracking my body, and they'd said we could take a break. I'd still, up until that point, declined the services of a solicitor; I was innocent, so why would I need legal representation? But as I'd been led back to my cell once again, it suddenly hit me. This had gone too far. It was real now. I'd been arrested, and the police thought I was lying, lying about everything, and that meant I was in big trouble, huge trouble, and I had absolutely no idea how to deal with it. And so I'd told them I'd changed my mind, and asked if I could call my father. Dad had been aghast, almost speechless with shock and fury, when I'd phoned to tell him what had happened, but I'd somehow got it through to him that I needed a solicitor, someone good, and he'd promised to sort it, his voice cracking with emotion as he said goodbye.

So I was waiting, waiting in my cold cell, and a day and a night seemed to somehow have passed, and I sat there, shivering, with nothing to look at but the four dirty walls and the toilet in one corner, a smell of bleach and urine in the air. They'd brought me some food earlier – a polystyrene cup of weak tea and a cardboard carton with some sort of microwaved stew – but my stomach had turned at the sight of it and I'd pushed it aside, watching a layer of grease slowly forming on top of the meat as it cooled. I sat there, huddled in my rough blanket, my whole body shaking, and a weird sensation began to creep over me, as if the coldness of my body had finally reached my brain, slowly shutting it down, rendering it incapable of thought, incapable of anything except trying to survive one more minute of this hell, and then another, and another.

And then, something so bizarre and remarkable happened that when it did, all I could do was sit there, motionless, staring at the man who'd just opened my cell door. It was the custody sergeant, and he was smiling.

'Hey Gemma. You're free to go. They've found your husband. Alive,' he said.

Chapter 35

Devon wrapped his hands around the warm mug of tea that had just been placed on the table in front of him and stared at Danny O'Connor. After weeks of looking at the man's picture pinned to the board back in the incident room it was just so – so *peculiar* – seeing him bustling around the grubby kitchen of the small flat they were now sitting in, making hot drinks, offering ginger nut biscuits from a half-empty packet. Seeing him alive, instead of finding him dead.

This is surreal, Devon thought. *And Helena is going to do her frigging nut. The amount of time we've wasted, searching for him, questioning his wife about his murder, when all the time …*

Finally, Danny sat down, the three of them close together around a table designed for two, one of those bistro-style tables more usually seen on a terrace or balcony, with two matching chairs and a small, wobbly looking stool on which Mike was perched uncomfortably. He looked as shocked as Devon felt, shaking his head every minute or so as if in awe.

'I won't ask how you found me,' Danny said. 'Pretty obvious really. Quinn, yeah? I should have known, after the stupid git told me he'd gone to see you after he met with Gemma, put himself on your radar, showing you those photos of the bruises. But he said you seemed to think I was dead, you know, weren't looking for me alive, so I thought I'd be safe here, for a few more days anyway ...'

He sighed. He had a soft Irish accent, his thick dark hair longer and even more curly and unruly than it had appeared in the photographs Devon had seen.

'Safe? Safe from what?' Devon said.

Danny shifted on his chair. He looked from Devon to Mike and then dropped his gaze to the table in front of him.

'I'd ... I'd rather not say. It's ... it's difficult. Hard to explain.'

'Well, we're certainly going to need some sort of explanation, Mr O'Connor. Let's take it slowly, shall we? You mentioned the pictures of the bruises just now – the bruises your cousin Quinn said your wife caused by beating you up? *She* said they were from a bike accident. Which account was true, Danny?' Devon asked.

'Bike,' said Danny. 'Sorry. We took the photos at the time because I was going to report the accident to the police, and then I didn't bother, didn't see the point. I didn't know Quinn was going to do that with them, make up that story about Gemma. He didn't tell me until he was back in London ... look, do I really have to tell you everything? I mean, no crime's been committed here, has it? I'm alive and well, Gemma's done nothing wrong. Can't we just leave it at that?'

He spread his hands in a placatory manner and smiled sheepishly.

Devon frowned. *Is he serious?*

'No, we can't. Do you realize how much trouble you've caused, Mr O'Connor? You do realize we thought you were possibly the victim of a serial killer, don't you? I mean, it's not an offence for an adult to vanish and not tell anyone, you're entitled to do what you want and go where you please, but you must have seen the papers, heard the news? You must have known that we thought you were a murder victim? Why didn't you at least call, text, send someone a message to let your friends and family know you were OK? They've been going through hell, Danny. And we suspected Gemma. We suspected Gemma, your wife, of killing you. Did you know that? We didn't believe a word she said, and it appears now that she was telling us the truth all along.'

Danny lowered his head, sighed, then lifted his gaze to Devon's again.

'I did see the news, yes. And I know you did, and I'm so, so sorry about that. It just seemed like the only way ...'

'The only way to *what*? Look, Mr O'Connor, you could be in trouble here, maybe even facing charges. But if you explain, at least *try* to help us understand what's gone on over the past few weeks, well, it can only help, OK? So please, start talking.'

Danny remained silent for several seconds, then nodded slowly, as if making a decision.

'OK, I get it. I'll try to explain. I don't know if you'll understand, but I'm going to try. And ... well, if I'm going to do this I suppose I'd better start right from the beginning.'

Finally, thought Devon. *Finally.*

Danny paused, shifted in his chair again, then took a deep breath.

'I've got myself in a bit of bother,' he said. 'Well, quite a lot of bother, actually. I'm an IT security specialist – well, I'm sure you know that already. A few months back, I was approached by someone to take on a private job. I wasn't supposed to take on outside work – I was working for a company called Hanfield Solutions at the time, and they had a pretty strict policy about it. But the fella who approached me was very ... very *persuasive*, shall we say. The money he was offering was insane, you know? I mean, a really *massive* amount. It would have set us up for life. The only problem was, to earn that money I had to do something ... something illegal. Something pretty bad.'

Mike and Devon exchanged glances.

Gemma was right, Devon thought. *This was her theory – that Danny had somehow got himself into some sort of serious trouble. Why didn't we listen to her?*

'Go on,' he said.

Danny looked from one of them to the other and then inhaled again and let the breath out slowly.

'Look, I can't tell you everything, I can't name names or anything, it's too dangerous. But I've spent my working life defending companies against online hacking and they were asking me to do the exact opposite. To hack *into* the system of a major company, and ... well, in the simplest of terms, to basically move some money around. To steal it, essentially. A *lot* of money. I thought about it for a while, really thought about it. I mean, it was fraud, major league fraud, and if I was caught I knew I'd go down for years. It was a huge risk, but the money was so good. So feckin' good. And so I said I'd do it. Just the once, take the money and be set for life, as I said. I was an eejit, I know that now. But how often does a chance like that come along, a chance to change your whole life? It was like winning the lottery. So I started the process. And then, I don't know why, one day a few weeks later I suddenly came to my senses, just like that. I think it was Gemma, chatting to me about babies, about our future, one day. I wanted all that, wanted a family, and I suddenly realized it wasn't the money that was important after all, it was her and our future together. I'd be throwing all that away if things went wrong, if I got caught. I'd ruin everything. So I got hold of the guy and told him I was pulling out of the job. Except, well it wasn't that easy.'

He picked up his mug, swallowed a mouthful of tea. Then he smiled briefly, his dark brown eyes crinkling at the corners, before his expression became serious again.

'I bet. How did he react?' asked Devon.

'He told me he'd kill me,' he said simply.

He paused again, running a finger around the rim of his mug.

'They said that if I didn't do the job, they'd hunt me down and kill me. I knew too much, you see? I knew everything they were planning. And even though I promised, swore on my mother's life that I'd never breathe a word to a living soul, that wasn't enough. If I didn't do the job, it would be curtains. They gave me a deadline – the end of January – and said I had to do the job by then or it would all be over. And that if I went to the police before that, they wouldn't just kill me, they'd kill Gemma and my mum and my brother Liam, too. My *brother*. He wouldn't hurt a fly, you know? Innocent as a five-year-old. I don't even know how they knew about him, about my family, but they did, they knew everything. So I had no choice, did I? If I did the job, and got caught, my life would be over. If I didn't, my life would be over too, and people I love would die alongside me. So I had no choice. I had to run, I had to disappear.'

'Phew-eeeee.' Mike let out a long, low whistle.

'I know, right?' Danny lifted his mug again, drank, then sat staring into the tea.

'So, you made a plan, to make everyone think you were dead,' said Devon.

Danny nodded.

'Look, I'm not proud of it, OK? Especially in the light of all the trouble I've caused now. But at the time ... well, I couldn't think of a better way. If everyone thought I was dead, the threat would be over, wouldn't it? So that's how it all started. Call me stupid.'

'Well, maybe not your finest idea. But no point on dwelling on that now,' said Devon. 'Tell us about it.'

Danny steepled his hands together, leaning his chin on his index fingers. He looked like a little boy about to explain his latest prank, Devon thought.

'OK, here we go. I needed to disappear, overnight. And then move abroad, get a new identity, try to start my life again. It was too risky to bring Gemma or anyone else with me ... if I got caught, they'd have killed us both. And yes, before you say it, I know what I've done was cruel, especially to Gemma. And to all of them, my family, my friends. But it would have made life so much easier, you know? Them thinking I was dead, and not just missing? It would have meant that after a while, nobody would have looked for me. Yes, I'd be alone. I'd never be able to see my friends and family again. I'd have missed Gemma so much, so bloody much. But at least I'd be free. And you know what ... Gemma's probably better off without me, anyway. I wasn't a good husband, although I tried to be. I wasn't always faithful to her. Anyway, that's not important now.'

Devon and Mike glanced at each other again.

'OK, we'll come back to that,' said Devon. 'Tell us about your plan.'

'Right, here we go,' he said, straightening up in his chair. 'We'd already decided to move away from London, to Bristol, and that turned out to be a godsend. I'd be somewhere new, somewhere nobody knew me, somewhere I could hide in plain sight, almost. Practice disappearing, before I did it for good. And I needed to buy a bit more time too, to get new ID documents and so on made up. It takes a while, if you want good ones. So I had this idea. I decided to try to make it look like I'd never been in Bristol at all, that something had happened to me in London before the move. And ... well, this is the bit I'm most ashamed of ... I knew that the easiest way to do it, by far the easiest way, was to implicate Gemma. To make it look like *she'd* done something to me, something terrible, before she left. Then, when the day came and she reported me missing, the police would look into it and find no trace of me in Bristol, and well ... think that she, or maybe somebody else, but most likely she, had killed me weeks before. Jesus, it sounds sick now, doesn't it? I didn't think it would go as far as it did, you know, there was no real evidence against her after all, because she didn't do anything wrong, but it all seems to have got a bit out of hand. I'm so, so sorry about that.'

He leaned back in his chair, rubbing both hands across his face.

It does sound pretty sick, Devon thought. And criminal, too, as Danny would soon find out when they arrested him. *How could anyone do that to his own wife, a woman who loved him?* He kept his mouth shut, but it was an effort. Beside him, Mike was silent too, but Devon could hear him breathing deeply.

He's trying to control himself too. This bastard's made fools of all of us, he thought.

'I'm so sorry, about what I've done to her. I really am, and if I ever get the chance to see Gemma again I'll tell her that too. But at the time ...' He picked up his mug, took another drink and grimaced. 'Getting cold,' he said.

'Mike, will you put the kettle on, top up these drinks?' Devon asked. 'Carry on, Danny.'

'Sure.' Mike stood up, his face expressionless.

Danny smiled at him, gesturing towards the kettle on the worktop behind them, then turned back to Devon.

'OK, so you want to know details, I assume? I started by opening a couple of foreign bank accounts, and slowly putting bits and pieces of cash into them. We never had a joint bank account, so that bit was easy; it was my money, and I just took little bits out here and there, no big withdrawals, nothing that would look odd if anyone ever checked. I had a couple of big bonuses I didn't tell Gemma about too, and I asked for them as cheques, and stashed those away as well. I put most of it away for Gemma, so she'd have something to fall back on when I was gone, you know? I'd have found a way of letting her know where to find the money, eventually. And a bit for myself too, of course – I just wanted a bit of cash in the bank to start me off, but I didn't need loads. I knew that wherever I ended up, I'd be able to find work. Beauty of my job. Everyone needs IT experts nowadays. Anyway, then the really important bit. I made sure Gemma moved to Bristol a week before I did, told her I had a job to finish up here. That bit was crucial, you see – I needed the time to stage the scene in London.'

'Stage the scene? Do you mean the blood, in the bedroom?'

Mike's voice was cold as he asked the question, turning the tap on to refill the kettle as he spoke.

Danny nodded, not seeming to notice.

He's enjoying telling his story, Devon thought.

'Yes. You found that then? I wasn't sure, but I hoped you would. OK, this sounds sick too, but I've started telling you now. No point in missing anything out. I bought this kit on the internet, needles and stuff. Started drawing off some of my blood a few times a week. A bit at a time, but it soon added up. I know, crazy right? Effective though. Quinn helped. Yes, he knew what was going on. He was the only one who did. He's my best mate in the world, Quinn is. Well, that and the fact that he owed me a debt. Not a financial one – he owed me for something that happened years ago, when we were kids. Anyway, that's not important. But he owed me, and so he agreed to help, with all of it.'

Another one who wasted our time, then, thought Devon coldly.

'Anyway,' continued Danny, 'he helped me with the blood. We read online that blood is OK for up to about forty days in a fridge, you just need some specialist bits and pieces, but we got it all online and it was pretty easy. He stored it here in that fridge for me.'

Mike, who had just opened the fridge to find the milk, visibly recoiled.

'Anyway, as soon as Gemma left for Bristol, Quinn drove the blood over and I splashed it all over the bedroom. Copied some scene of crime photos we found online. Made a pretty good job of it. And then I dropped off the keys to the landlord, making sure nobody saw me, and moved in here with Quinn for the week, laid low. When I headed for Bristol a week later I wore a disguise – a beard, a hat, glasses – and made sure I arrived after dark and used the back gate. I'd already contacted my new employers in Bristol to tell them I'd changed my mind about the job, so all I had to do then was find somewhere to hang out every day, making sure I came and went while it was dark to reduce the chance of the neighbours seeing me. I used a local gym in the end, went in disguise every day, no sweat. Used the name Patrick and paid for everything in cash. Easy.'

Gemma was right again, Devon thought, with a pang of guilt. *She tried to tell us that, and yet again we didn't listen. We thought she was lying, about everything.*

Danny was still talking.

'I stopped using my UK bank account too, used my foreign bank card if I needed to make a big purchase; I just had to make sure Gemma didn't see it,' he said. 'Otherwise I just paid cash for things, made sure I had enough stashed in my backpack for those last few weeks. And I made sure I never answered the door in the house, stuff like that. I thought Gemma would start to notice, but she didn't. I suppose we had plenty to do around the place, having just moved in. Easy to stay in instead of going out. It would have got harder as time went on, but I only ever intended to do it for a few weeks. I made sure I didn't contact anyone either, for those weeks – got rid of my phone, made up a story about a delay in my work getting me a new one. It was like a game. And it worked. My only concern was that Evans, our landlord, would find the blood in the bedroom too soon, and then I'd have to move before I was ready. But I knew he was going away, and I figured I'd have a few weeks. It all worked perfectly.'

Mike was back at the table. He'd found a teapot somewhere, and was topping up their mugs with fresh tea, eyes narrowed, listening intently. Devon was gripped too, with a sort of horrified fascination.

What a story, he thought.

'So, what about the emails Gemma said she had from you in those weeks you were in Bristol? And the photos she said she took of you? How did you get rid of those? Because I assume now it *was* you who got rid of those? She thought her phone was playing up,' he said.

'You *know* what I do for a living,' said Danny. His face wore a guilty expression. 'Pretty simple to make those vanish forever. And when I moved out, finally, I did it when Gemma was off on a press trip, so I could clean the whole place with bleach, make sure as much of my DNA and fingerprints as possible were out of there. Make it look like I'd barely been there at all. Then, in the early hours of the morning, Quinn came and picked me and the bike up in his van and drove me to London. Been here ever since.'

'Wow.' Mike exhaled heavily.

'I know. I'm a feckin' sneaky little shite, aren't I?' Danny looked contrite again. 'I tell you what though, I didn't know a serial killer was going to pop up though, did I? That was a shocker. And the fact that the victims kinda looked like me – really weird, that was. Weird, but a gift too, you know? If the guys who were after me thought I was the victim of a serial killer well, great. But then when I saw in the news that Gemma was being questioned not only about me but about those other killings too, well ... that was awful. I was really, really sorry about that. Couldn't make it up.'

'You used the same dating app as at least two of the dead men, did you know that? Elite Hook Ups? EHU?' said Devon.

Danny nodded, the guilty look back on his face.

'Yes, I was on that ... but those guys using it too? That's another weird coincidence. Or maybe not, I mean it's pretty popular these days, thousands of people use it. But still. I didn't know about that, until Gemma mentioned it to Quinn the other day and he told me. Bizarre. Look, I'm not proud of that. About being married and signing up to a dating site, I mean. As I said before, I wasn't always a good husband to

Gemma. I've always struggled to be faithful, not just to her, to all the women I dated before her too. It had got better, recently – I was trying, I really was. I love Gemma, you know? I wanted a future with her, kids, all the normal stuff. But it was like ... like an addiction.'

He ran a hand through his hair, and closed his eyes, shaking his head slowly. Devon didn't know what to say, and Mike was clearly of a similar mind, so they both sat in silence, waiting for Danny to continue.

'I needed lots of female attention, always have done. Sounds pathetic, but that's how it is,' he said finally. 'So every now and again I'd hook up with someone I met online, no strings. Just sex. Now and again it went a bit too far though. Once I shagged a bird at a party I was at with Gemma ... just skipped off to a bedroom for ten minutes when she was chatting to someone else. Sick, eh? Gemma never knew, never even suspected, and it was such a thrill, doing it with so many people just feet away. And this other time, I tried to get off with her friend, Eva. Jesus, that was a mistake. She was having none of it though, and thank God. I wouldn't have got away with that one, if Gemma had found out.'

Devon's eyes had widened at the mention of Eva's name, and he felt a small surge of satisfaction. *So the lovely Eva rejected Danny's advances? Good.*

'Can we just go back to the EHU app for a minute?' Mike was saying. 'You used a fake email address. Or an untraceable one, at least? Why?'

'I just used some software to hide my IP address. For privacy, you know? In my situation ...'

Devon's brain was beginning to hurt.

'OK. OK. There's a lot to take in here,' he said.

With Danny being alive, so much of what they'd assumed about the murders would now need to be looked at again, in a different light, but he knew he couldn't think about that right now.

'And Quinn?' he said. 'Why did he send those messages to Gemma? Did you ask him to do that?'

Danny looked startled.

'The messages? How do you ...?' He paused. 'Well, yes, I knew he'd sent some messages. I was planning to finally get out of here next week, you see. False passport, documents, the lot, they're all ready now. I wanted to reinforce the idea that I was dead, as I said, so that say someone recognized me on a plane or something, nobody would believe them if they reported it, because it would be well documented that my wife was being questioned for killing me. So Quinn said he'd send a few texts, shake things up a bit, make you guys think someone out there knew she'd done something bad to me. But he said he'd use a cheap pay-as-you-go phone, untraceable. Don't tell me ...'

'He screwed up,' Devon said. 'Sent the last message from his own phone.'

'SHITE. Feckin' eejit,' said Danny. For a moment, he looked furious. Then he shrugged.

'Don't suppose it matters now, does it? The game's up. You're going to arrest me, I assume?'

Devon nodded. 'Afraid so, yes. I'm not entirely sure what you'll be charged with yet – there's so much to unravel here, but there's trying to pervert the course of justice, wasting police time, possessing identity documents with improper intention, plus ...'

Danny raised both hands in the air.

'OK, OK! Can I just take a piss first, before we go? Too much tea.'

'Sure. And grab a coat and some shoes too. It's cold out.'

'OK. And thanks. Both of you. For listening. It was good, for someone to listen, you know? Listen, and not judge. I know I've screwed up here, badly. God knows how I'm going to keep us all safe from the nutters who are after me now though. But I guess that's not your problem.'

He stood up and walked from the kitchen, and moments later they heard the bathroom door lock. Devon and Mike sat at the table in silence for a few moments, then Mike spoke, his voice a vicious hiss.

'Listen, and not judge? The guy's delusional. I mean, I understand that he was scared for his life, and he needed to run. But there are ways of doing things. To do what he did, to that poor woman ...'

'I know. I know. But sssh, for now.'

They sat quietly again, both lost in thought. Around them, the small flat was still, the silence broken only by the low hum of the refrigerator and a slow drip-drip from the kitchen tap.

Shit, thought Devon suddenly. *It's too quiet.*

'Mike – quick!'

'What?' A startled-looking Mike leapt up and followed as Devon ran from the room.

'Danny!' He rattled at the bathroom door. Nothing,
'OK, stand back. I'm going in.'

He stepped backwards as far as he could in the narrow
hallway then launched himself at the door. It burst open, the
flimsy wood cracking, and slammed into the wall behind it.
Devon, breathing heavily, rushed into the room, Mike behind
him. The room was tiny, the shower cubicle narrow and empty.
Over the hand basin, the window was wide open, net curtain
blowing gently in the chill night breeze. And Danny was gone.

Chapter 36

I tucked my feet up under me on the sofa, pulled the faux fur throw over my knees, then reached for the plate I'd just put down on the coffee table and took a large bite of my Brie and bacon toasted sandwich. The cheese oozed out of the bread, running down my chin, and I wiped it off with my finger and then licked. It tasted divine. At my feet, Albert sat watching me, poised to fling himself on any tiny shred of bacon that might fall from my plate. I peeled a sliver off one rasher and handed it to him, and he wolfed it down noisily then resumed his hungry stare. He'd been brought home to me first thing, having been taken to a local kennels by the police to be cared for while I'd been in custody, and he hadn't left my side since, other than to gobble down a huge plate of food in the kitchen and then immediately seek me out to beg for more. I rolled my eyes – I was pretty sure the kennels hadn't been starving him – but I gave him a second helping anyway. I quite fancied double portions of everything myself, so who was I to judge?

When I'd arrived home the previous night, still feeling slightly dazed as I'd stumbled out of my taxi – *is this real?*

Danny's alive, and I'm free? – I'd suddenly realized I was starving, and other than during the few hours when I'd succumbed to a deep, dreamless sleep, I hadn't stopped eating since.

'Making up for the past few weeks,' Eva had said when I'd spoken to her on the phone earlier. 'I've been worried about you, you've hardly been eating a thing.'

'I am now,' I mumbled, through the mouthful of Mars bar I was chewing. 'I think I've put on half a stone since I got home.'

Clare and Tai had been round already earlier that morning, having heard about my arrest and subsequent release on the news. They'd arrived laden with bulging carrier bags, and told me they weren't there to ask questions, just to make sure I was all right.

'We didn't think you'd have any food in, so we went shopping for you,' said Tai, as she unpacked the bags on the kitchen table, and my heart swelled; my freedom dinner the previous night had been microwaved fish fingers and chips I'd found in the freezer, the fridge and cupboards virtually empty again. They were so kind, so thoughtful, these women I barely knew, I thought. Friends, proper friends, already, despite the short time we'd been hanging out together.

'And we weren't a hundred per cent sure what you'd want, but we knew you aren't veggie or vegan or anything so we just bought a selection,' added Clare. 'Essentials, obviously, milk, bread, butter and so on. Some fruit and veg. Cheese, salami, bacon, chicken, smoked salmon. Wine, obviously. Chocolate. And some frozen bits and pieces too. Is it OK?'

'OK? It's amazing. You're both *amazing*,' I'd said, and hugged them both hard. They left after making me promise we'd all get together very soon for dinner, and then left me to start working my way through my newly stocked cupboards.

It still seemed surreal to be sitting there, safe on my own sofa, knowing that all the accusations and suspicion that had been swirling around me for weeks had now vanished. The police hadn't told me much when they'd released me, saying simply that Danny had been found alive and well and had explained his disappearance to them. But when I'd tried to ask for more details, the officer who'd been dispatched to explain to me why I was being allowed to go home had been vague, refusing to tell me where Danny was or whether anyone would be facing any charges in relation to his disappearance.

'Just rest assured that we are no longer considering any criminal charges against *you*, Mrs O'Connor,' he had said.

I still had so many questions – why Danny had felt the need to vanish in the first place, where the blood in the bedroom had come from, why he had behaved so oddly in the run-up to his departure, what was he going to do now? And the little matter of the dating app, of course. But it seemed I'd have to wait for the answers. Eva too was bursting with curiosity.

'We need to find out what happened, this is crazy!' she said. 'Surely Danny will get in touch with you now, to explain, now that he knows *you* know he's alive? I know they have to respect his privacy but if only they'd given you some idea of where he was, we might be able to track him down. I mean, we don't even know if he's still in the UK, do we? And is he in custody, or not? I'm sure he must be facing charges of some sort.'

'No idea,' I said, and broke another chunk off my chocolate bar.

'And yes, I'm desperate to know exactly what went on too, and what his plans are now. I can only assume they don't include me, which is still heartbreaking. But for some reason right now I feel sort of OK, you know? Mildly euphoric even. It's kind of weird – I mean, my husband's still left me, and is quite possibly seeing someone else, and everything we ever had together has most likely been a lie, and all of that is totally shit, and I should be a sobbing wreck. But ... I don't know, it's the relief I think. It's just been so horrible, not knowing whether he's alive or dead, and then having the police think that I might have had something to do with it all. And with those other murders too. They said that as I clearly didn't kill Danny, the possibility that I'd killed the other men was no longer being considered either. I guess they're back to square one on those now. Danny looking so like the murder victims was obviously just some sort of weird coincidence. But honestly, Eva, I don't care. I'm just not interested anymore. Danny's alive, and for now that's enough. Everything else can wait.'

The article Eva had been asked to write about me – her 'my friend, the suspected serial killer' piece – had now been scrapped, and a peek through the lounge curtains early that morning had confirmed what I'd hoped, that the press no longer had any interest in me either. I'd flung the curtains open with a whoop, and as I sat eating my toasted sandwich the midday sunshine streamed in through the window, the clouds like fluffy white candyfloss, the sky cerulean blue.

I'd been taking, and making, calls all morning, updating friends and family on the rather extraordinary events of the past couple of days. My dad had cried with relief, my mum sobbing too in the background, and even though they, like me and all the others, had questions I couldn't answer, they were happy to let the mystery remain for now.

'As long as you're OK, darling. That's all that matters,' Dad said.

I'd decided against ringing Bridget. The police had said they would be informing Danny's family that he'd been found, and that was good enough for me. If she wanted to speak to me, *she* could call me, I thought, but I wasn't expecting to hear from her. She hadn't seemed to care that Danny was missing, and I was fairly sure she'd be equally disinterested in his reappearance. Strange, cold, horrible woman. When I turned the TV on to see the lunchtime news, there'd been just a brief mention of Danny.

Avon Police say Danny O'Connor, the thirty-three-year-old man who'd been missing for nearly three weeks, has been found safe and well. It had been feared he might have been another victim of a so-called 'serial killer', after two men were murdered in Bristol last month. Two other murders and a serious assault in London are also being linked to the Bristol killings. A woman who was being questioned has now been released without charge. A spokesman said that finding whoever was responsible for the murders remained the force's highest priority.

I picked up the remote control and turned the television

off. There was so much more I needed to know and, no doubt, so much more heartache still to come. But for now, I was content. Content to sit there, the sunlight pouring into the room, my belly full, my name cleared, my husband alive. It was over.

Chapter 37

'When we find him, I'm going to throw the bloody book at him.'

Helena threw an apple core hard at the wastepaper bin next to her desk as if to illustrate that intention. It bounced off the rim and landed on the carpet, and she cursed softly under her breath and bent to pick it up. It was late on Wednesday afternoon, and the team had gathered for an update and to regroup, after the entirely unexpected discovery that Danny O'Connor was not, after all, a murder victim but had been the mastermind behind his own successful disappearance. Successful until the previous day, of course.

'I want him done for perverting the course of justice, for a start.'

She was scowling, pacing up and down the narrow gap between two rows of desks in the incident room.

'The blood in that bedroom, the little *shit* ... fabricating evidence, letting us think Gemma was a killer ... that alone could get him years. Wasting police time ... and if he's got false ID documents too ... any news on his whereabouts yet? Or on the whereabouts of his cousin Quinn? I want him too.

Coming in here, lying through his teeth to us about Gemma, helping Danny with the whole bloody deception ... I want them both, and now. So – any news?'

'No, sadly.'

'Not yet boss.'

'Maybe whoever's after him's finally caught up with him. Good riddance.'

The answers came from different parts of the room, and she sighed in frustration. They had an all-ports warning – the bulletin circulated to all international ports and airports which aimed to identify and apprehend a fleeing suspect – out on both Danny and Quinn O'Connor, but so far no sightings had been reported.

'Probably laying low somewhere in the UK,' said Devon morosely. 'They're good at hiding, as we know.'

Helena stopped pacing and stepped towards him, punching him gently on the shoulder.

'Cheer up, mate. Stop beating yourself up for losing Danny. We'll get him, one of these days. And in the meantime, we're back to square one with these murders. We need to get our heads together. Danny and Gemma O'Connor were a distraction that's taken up far too much of our time, OK? Forget them for now.'

He sighed.

'Yeah. I know you're right, but I'm still furious with myself. I'm going for some teas, want one?'

'Please.'

Helena gave him a wry, sympathetic smile. Letting Danny escape through his bathroom window hadn't been ideal, but she wasn't about to take it out on Devon, or on Mike either. These things happened. She was more angry – extremely pissed off in fact – about the fact that the team had wasted so much time looking for Danny and investigating Gemma. There were still some coincidences that were bothering her a little – the physical similarities between Danny and the murder victims, for instance – but she knew she would have to let that go and move on. He *wasn't* a victim, and he'd been responsible for his own disappearance. She had more important things to worry about right now; the press, always quick to sniff out a negative story, were back on her case, demanding an official update on what the next step in the so-called serial killer investigation was going to be, now that the prime suspect had been released without charge. She'd wondered briefly about bringing George Dolan, the man who'd claimed to have killed all five men, back into custody, but had almost instantly dismissed the idea. He'd clearly been lying through his teeth, something that was even more obvious now that Danny O'Connor was very much alive despite Dolan's claims, and her gut told her the hours they'd spent with him had been another complete waste of time. And she couldn't afford to get it wrong again; she'd already had to deal with yet another irate call from the Detective Chief Super earlier that morning. It had *not* been a pleasant conversation.

'We just need a break. One tiny little lead. Come on, universe, help me out here,' she muttered, as she sat down at her desk and tapped her mouse. Her screen lit up, an email notification flashing in the corner. She clicked on it. It was, finally, the forensics report from the scene of the attempted murder of Declan Bailey in London, the attack which had happened, coincidentally it now seemed, so close to the pub where Gemma and Quinn had met up. Her heart skipped a beat as she started to scan the message. If they'd found DNA on the weapon the assailant had dropped ... then she stopped scrolling, frowning.

'What? WHAT?'

'What's up?'

Devon, who was still only halfway across the room, having paused for a chat with Tara as he headed towards the door on his tea mission, turned and started walking back towards her.

'SHIT! This can't be right. It can't be, it just doesn't make any sense ...'

She was standing up now, but still peering at her computer screen, unable to comprehend what she was reading.

'Boss – what? What is that?'

Devon was by her side now, trying to see what she was looking at.

'It's the forensics report from the assault in London. They've found DNA. And look, Devon. *Look.*'

He read it too, and gasped.

'What? But that means ...'

Helena took a deep breath.

'Exactly. It means we've got this wrong. We've got this *all wrong.*'

Chapter 38

'That is *so* kind of you, thank you. I really appreciate it.'
I took the fragrant-smelling casserole dish from Jo and smiled. My next-door neighbour had just popped round to tell me she'd been keeping up with the news and had been greatly relieved to hear that I was free, and that Danny was alive.

'I never met him, obviously, but you were so worried about him that time you came round, so I'm really happy it's all worked out for you,' she said. 'We didn't really know what to do, me and Jenny and Clive, while it was all going on, you know? All the press outside and everything. We talked about coming round to see if you were OK, but then we thought, well, we didn't really know you, and ... and, well, it was all so awkward. We probably should have though, sorry.'

'Oh gosh, please don't be sorry. I'm the one that's sorry, so sorry, for all the commotion. I did see Clive a few times, and I could tell he felt really uncomfortable. I don't blame him, or you. It was a horrible situation.'

Jo smiled.

'Well, good. Anyway, it's over now, and I thought with all

the shenanigans you probably haven't had much time to cook. So here you go. It's just a sausage stew but it generally goes down well when I've got friends round. Oh gosh – you're not vegetarian, are you?'

'I'm not. And it smells delicious. Honestly, this is so kind of you. And Albert clearly thinks so too. He doesn't seem to want to stop eating at the moment.'

I pointed at my dog, who was staring eagerly up at the dish, tail wagging wildly. Jo smiled.

'He's a sweetie. I'm sure there's enough there for him to have some too.'

I smiled back.

'Oh, he'll make sure of that. He has ways of making me do whatever he wants, trust me. But seriously, people are being so, so kind, I can't tell you how much I appreciate it. And again, I'm so sorry you've had to put up with the press outside all this time. They've gone now, for good hopefully.'

Jo smiled again, her kind eyes wrinkling at the corners, and pushed an errant strand of hair back off her face. She was wearing it loose today, and it hung in a heavy grey curtain down her back.

'No problem. And when you're feeling up to it, come round for a drink. I'll get Jenny and Clive round too. It would be nice to get to know you better.'

'I'd love that, thank you. How do I heat this up?'

'About half an hour at 170 should do it. Just make sure it's piping hot. And now I must go, my friend Ally's coming round in ten and I've got scones in the oven. Pop that in the fridge for now. I'll let myself out. Take care, Gemma.'

She patted me on the arm and headed out of the kitchen door and down the hallway. As I opened the fridge with my elbow and carefully manoeuvred the large dish onto the middle shelf, I heard her calling.

'Gemma? Another visitor for you! I've let him in, bye for now!'

A visitor? Clive maybe? I grabbed the towel that hung on a hook next to the sink and wiped my hands. Then I turned as I heard footsteps entering the room. A man was standing there, a tall man with a beard and glasses, his hair covered by a black beanie hat. Albert turned too, paused for a second, then yelped and launched himself at the visitor, yapping frantically, leaping in the air with joy, tail a frenetic blur.

'What ... who ...?' I stammered. I stared at the man.

It couldn't be. Could it?

'Hello, Gemma,' the man said, and I gasped.

Danny. It was Danny. He'd come home.

Chapter 39

In the incident room, the air was thick with nervous tension, the low hum of excited conversation fading to a whisper and then to silence as Helena strode to the front of the room and raised a hand.

'OK, listen up. We now have a suspect, as you all know. The forensic evidence is very clear – the person who was interrupted during the attack on Declan Bailey and ran off, dropping the hammer being used as a weapon, left DNA behind, as we hoped. And that DNA was a match for a profile on the National DNA Database. It's a shock, yes, but our priority now is to find the suspect as soon as possible and see if we can tie that attack to our two unsolved murders here, and quite possibly to the two London killings as well. It looks very likely, given the similarities between the cases, that this perpetrator is indeed the one we've all been looking for, and that the press have been right with their speculation all along too.'

She took a deep breath.

'What I'm saying is that we're now officially on the hunt for a serial killer. And now we have a face and name too. Just not the face or name any of us were expecting, is it?'

Chapter 40

Danny and I sat at the kitchen table, Albert stretched out underneath it, just like old times. Except it wasn't like old times at all, because my husband had just finished telling me exactly how he'd managed to disappear so completely. Eva and I had been right about that, after all. He *had* been hiding in plain sight in Bristol, he *had* planned it all. He hadn't told me *why*, not yet – he said he'd come to that later. But he'd told me *how*. How he'd planned it all for ages, worked out exactly how to do it, and how to do it perfectly, and how Quinn, who knew everything after all, had helped him. Helped him stage his own death. The blood. Cleaning our house with bleach to make it look like he'd barely been there. Making sure I didn't see that he was using a strange, foreign bank card when he paid for things, using the cash he'd stashed away as often as he could. Squirreling money away for his future. Finding out the locations of all the CCTV cameras in Bristol and choosing our new house because it was in a location where he knew there were none. Deleting all my recent photos of him and emails from him from my phone. Pulling out of his new job in Bristol, and instead spending his days at the gym, hiding away. I'd been right about that too, but the plan, all of it, the whole incredible, organized plan which had worked so well, so brilliantly, stunned me. He'd known, too, that the police would suspect me of attacking him. He'd *hoped* they'd suspect me. He'd even confessed, almost as an after-thought, that he'd been repeatedly unfaithful throughout our marriage, 'addicted' to sex with other women, sneaking off for regular hook-ups with people he'd met online, when I thought he was working late or off on one of his solitary bike rides. With each new revelation came an apology, an expression of regret at what he had put me through, but I barely heard his remorseful words, the scale of his deception hitting me with such force that I felt as if I was being physically attacked, my chest so tight I was struggling to catch my breath, waves of nausea washing over me. If it hadn't been my life, if I'd read about it in a newspaper, I would have thought someone had made it up. But it *was* my life, and I felt yet again as if somebody had just thrown a bomb into it and blown it into a million pieces.

'So go on, Danny. Why, for God's sake? You've told me *how* you did it, now tell me *why*. Why did you have to run, to pretend you were dead? What can have been so bad, that you had to do that? That you had to *frame* me, for your murder? Me, your wife?'

My voice was shaking. If, over the past few horrible weeks, I'd ever dared to allow myself to imagine this day, the day when Danny would be home, safe and well, I'd never imagined it like this. Never imagined that the man I loved so much could treat me like this, use me, deliberately put me in such

353

a terrible situation. I'd been suspected of being a *serial killer*, for fuck's sake, and it was all down to him. I stared at him, waiting for him to explain, to tell me *why*, my heart thudding dully in my chest, and I realized with sudden, awful clarity what I had suspected for a while; that I had never known this man at all. This man who I had vowed to spend my life with, for better or for worse. This man who had made the same vows to me. It had been a lie, every single tiny bit of it, and although I had wondered about that in the dark days of the past few weeks, now it was real, and I was reeling. In fact, no, not reeling – reeling was too small a word for what I was feeling. Reeling sounded kind of fun, a gentle, dizzying spin across a dancefloor, maybe. What I was actually feeling was as if my world was spinning wildly, completely out of control, at sickening, breakneck speed, and with no return to normality ever possible. How did you recover from something like this? How would that ever be possible?

'I do love you, you know.'

I jumped. He'd started talking again, my husband, looking at me with those beautiful, chocolate brown eyes, and I tried to drag my attention back to him, away from my own anguish, away from the edge of the abyss I was sinking into, the dark, deep place I knew I would plunge into fully as soon as he left, the place I doubted I would ever be able to return from.

'What?' I laughed, a short, hoarse laugh, and he flinched a little. He'd taken his disguise off, removing the hat and glasses, peeling the beard from his chin. It sat on the table between us like a small, sleeping animal.

'I do. I know you won't believe that, not now. But I do. All

I wanted was a normal life, a family. You, me and a couple of kids, living somewhere lovely like here in Bristol. It just didn't work out like that.'

I snorted.

'Love? You don't know the meaning of the word love, Danny. Nobody who loves someone would treat them the way you've treated me. And you still haven't told me why. WHY, DANNY?'

I shouted the last two words, banging my fists on the table, and he flinched again.

'I'm sorry, so sorry, that you've had to go through all this. I'll never be able to tell you how sorry I am. But I thought it was the only way, you know? To properly disappear. You'll understand, when I tell you. Just give me a minute, please. This isn't easy for me.'

I shook my head slowly, my anger and misery dissipating for a moment as sheer disbelief took over.

'Seriously? Easy for you? You think it's been easy for me? You tried to frame me, Danny. For MURDER. Do you realize how sick that is? Just because, for whatever reason, you wanted to go and start a new life abroad? What the fuck is wrong with you? WHY, DANNY? WHY ANY OF THIS, FOR FUCK'S SAKE?'

I was screaming by then, on my feet, leaning across the table, almost spitting at him. Albert was on his feet too, looking uneasily from me to Danny, tail between his legs. Danny shrank back in his chair, and I stayed there, looking at him for a moment, then groaned and turned away. I walked across the kitchen to the window and stared blankly out of it. I didn't know what else to say, what else to do. He was probably going to tell me he'd fallen in love with someone else, and I suddenly realized I didn't even *care* anymore. I just needed him to go. Out in the hallway, I heard my mobile phone begin to ring. I ignored it.

'Leave, Danny,' I said softly, without turning around. 'Go away. Start your new life. We're done here.'

Chapter 41

'Gemma O'Connor's not answering, guv.'

DC Frankie Stevens waved his desk phone handset at Helena, and she nodded.

'OK, I'll try her again in a bit. In the meantime, I need to get on the road. Devon, you're with me, OK?'

'Sure,' he said grimly. 'No place else I'd rather be right now.'

She flashed him a tight smile. 'We're going to get him you know. We *are*. If it's the last thing I ever do in this bloody job.'

And it might be, she thought. *It might be the last thing I ever do in the job. We've messed this up, I've messed this up. I got this so, so wrong. Wasted so much time looking at it in completely the wrong way, looking at the wrong person. And now I have to put it right. Somehow. I have to.*

She took a deep breath and straightened her shoulders, then turned to the board, where a big red ring had been drawn around one of the photos that had been pinned up there for the past two and half weeks.

'So let's go and do it,' she said. 'Let's go and find our serial killer. Let's find Danny O'Connor.'

Chapter 42

'Go, Danny. Get out of here. I can't even look at you.'
I still had my back to him, trying to fight back the tears.

'Not yet. I *need* to tell you everything, I *need* to get it off my chest. But first, Gemma, I need you to promise me something. I know you owe me nothing, not after this. Not after what I've done to you, what I've put you through. But please, Gemma, if you ever loved me, promise me one last thing? Promise me that when I tell you what I'm about to tell you, that you'll keep it to yourself? That you won't tell anyone, anyone at all? Please, Gemma, can you promise me that? And then I'll tell you, and I'll go. You'll never have to see me again.'

Seriously? He's seriously asking me for a favour, after what he's done? For a moment anger swelled inside me, then just as quickly subsided. Suddenly I felt tired, so very, very tired. I didn't know if I could actually take anymore; what he'd already told me had been more than enough, way, way more. *But fine, whatever. What does it matter, now?*

'Oh, for fuck's sake. I'm assuming you've met someone else, Danny, and do you know what? I don't care. I really, seriously, don't give a flying shit. But go on, if you must. I'll keep your tawdry little secret. Let's just get it over with,' I said, wearily. I turned to look at him, my stomach twisting with misery.

'Promise? Is that a promise, Gemma?'

'Bloody hell. Yes, it's a promise,' I spat the words at him.

'OK. OK. Thank you. Well, here we go.'

He clenched and unclenched his fists once, twice, three times, staring down at his hands. Then he looked back at me.

'I lied to the police, Gemma. I made up a cock and bull story to explain why I needed to disappear. I told them my life was in danger, and yours too, because I'd got myself in trouble with a dodgy client, and they believed every word. But that wasn't true, and I want to tell you what really happened. And it's not that I've met someone else I want to be with, by the way. I wish I had, I wish that's all it was. It's ... well, it's something different. Something ... something awful, Gemma.'

He stopped talking, took a deep breath.

'OK, here we go. So, when I was a kid, my dad ... well, he was a bastard. And I mean a real, nasty bastard. He drank, heavily, and when he was drunk he'd come home and beat up my mum. Beat her up badly, you know, hospital bad. For no reason, other than he liked to be the big man, to keep her at his beck and call. He hit me too, any excuse. He'd batter me black and blue, for things like dropping toast crumbs on the floor at breakfast or bringing mud in from outside on my shoes. There was rarely a day when one of us didn't get punched or slapped. Rarely a day, for years and years.'

For a moment, puzzled, I didn't reply, the unexpectedness

of this change in direction taking me by surprise, and trying to reconcile this description of Donal with the frail pensioner in the armchair I'd met on the one occasion I'd visited the family home. I mean, I hadn't liked the man at all. He'd seemed cold, hard, deeply unpleasant. *But violent, really?*

My scepticism must have shown on my face, because Danny said: 'Oh, he wasn't like that in his final years, obviously. Too old, too ill, thank God. But back then ... he was an animal, Gemma. You can't even imagine.'

Maybe I can, though, I thought. Yes, Donal had been frail when I'd met him. But he had still been very much in control of that household, I remembered suddenly. Bridget still scurrying around, doing his bidding. Still scared of him, even then? Was that why she was how she was? If what Danny was saying was true, it must have been dreadful, for all of them, to live like that. Still not understanding why he was telling me, what his childhood had to do with *any* of this mess, I said quietly: 'I'm sorry. That's awful,' because it was.

Danny didn't respond, his eyes fixed on the table in front of him.

'And he was unfaithful to Mum too, over and over and over again. He'd stay away night after night, shagging other women, and then he'd come home and brag about it, tell her a good lookin' fella like him didn't have to settle for a frumpy little woman like her, he could have anyone he liked. She was there to cook and clean and iron his clothes, nothing much more than that. I can remember maybe three or four times in my whole childhood that they went out together for a dinner or a party. It was toxic, the worst possible atmosphere to grow up in. I spent years being afraid, waiting for the next blow, the next fist in the stomach, the next row.'

'Shit, Danny.'

He was staring into space now, his eyes glazed, as if watching his childhood play out in front of him, and I had a sudden urge to cross the room and take him in my arms, to comfort him, to take some of the pain away. Then I remembered what he'd done to me, and my heart hardened again.

Unfaithful? Over and over again? Like father, like son, I thought bitterly, and I stayed where I was. The sooner it was over, the sooner I could get him out of there.

'It went on for years, Gemma. And you know what the worst thing was? We put up with it, both of us. Me and mum. When Liam was born – and God knows how that happened, but I don't want to think about that – I felt sick for weeks, sick scared that Dad would move onto him next. But he never did. I never knew why, but he never did. Liam was special, in more ways than one, and the fact that my father never laid a hand on him in anger is the one redeeming feature of his whole sick, twisted life. But he carried on, same old same old, with me and Mum, and we carried on putting up with it. And to this day I don't really know why, you know? It was like he had this ... this *power* over us. We never told anyone, we never reported him. We blamed our injuries on accidents, on falls, if anyone ever asked, though God knows why anyone believed us, we'd need to have been falling over every second day to account for the number of bruises we both had all the time. Maybe it was partly because we were ashamed I suppose, ashamed of what our lives were like when all around us everyone else seemed normal, happy. But mostly, we were scared. Scared of him, scared of what he'd do to us if we fought back, if we stood up to him. We let him carry on, and we did nothing. We did absolutely feckin' *nothing*.'

He punched the table, hard, his face flushing with anger, and another wave of sympathy rushed over me. Poor Danny, I thought. And poor Bridget too, still so angry at everyone and everything. What a life she must have lived.

Danny was still talking, engrossed in his story.

'I left as soon as I could, when I was eighteen and went off to university. But even then, even though I was big and strong enough by then to fight back, to defend my mother against him too, I still didn't do it. I couldn't bring myself to. It was as if after a lifetime of it, he had this ... this hold, over both of us. We never fought back, we never told. Well, except Quinn.'

He paused for a moment, rubbing a hand across his face.

'He didn't know all of it, not how constant it was, how bad it was, not back in those days. He knows more now. But he walked in one day, came round unexpectedly, when Dad was laying into Mum, and I'll never forget his face, Gemma. I'll never forget how shocked he was when he saw the blood, saw how viciously Dad was punching her. Dad didn't know he was there, which was probably lucky for him, and I begged him not to tell anyone, told him Dad would kill him *and* us if he did. And so he kept the secret. He's had my back ever since we were kids, that lad. I looked after him too, you know? He probably wouldn't be here today if it wasn't for me, but that's a story for another day. But he'd do anything for me, Quinn. Always would. Still would.'

I know that story, I thought. *And that's why Quinn lied through his teeth to the police about me. You saved his life, and he'd have done anything to protect you.*

The bitterness was back. Why was he telling me all this? Yes, it was awful, horrendous. But all this was in the past. He'd moved on, made a new life for himself in London. What did this have to do with anything now?

'And so he kept the secret too, as I said.' Danny was saying. 'We all kept the secret. I'd got so used to hiding it, as a kid, it became second nature. And when I grew up, and moved over here, there didn't seem any point in telling anyone about it at all, so I never did. Except it was still there, inside, you know? A lot of the time I could forget about it, but it never really goes away, something like that. And I suppose it ... it *festered*. The knowledge that I could have done something to stop him, and I didn't ... as the years passed, I began to hate myself for that. And I mean really, really hate myself. So much so that it started to ... to *consume* me, Gemma. I thought about it all the time, the shame, the guilt ... even if I'd let him do that to me, why had I let him do it to *her*, to my mother? Why didn't I protect her, when I was old enough to fight him back? Was I that much of a coward? I was, and she knew it too. She knew I was a coward, and she hated me for it as well. She still hates me. She's never forgiven me for the way I let her down.'

I thought back to how Bridget had reacted to Danny's disappearance, how disinterested she'd seemed, and then to

363

how she'd been with him on our visit; his pathetic eagerness to please his mother, and the coldness of her response. He was right, she'd never forgiven him, I thought, and my heart, already rent in two, shattered a little bit more for both of them, these two broken people, who needed each other so desperately but, for whatever reason, couldn't find a way to help each other through their living hell.

'I was always told I was the spitting image of my father,' Danny was saying. 'Even you said that, when you met him, remember?'

I gave a small nod, remembering. Donal had indeed been an older, greyer-haired version of Danny.

'But that used to make me feel sick, when people said that. I'd think: "No. NO! I'm nothing like him, I'm nothing like that bastard". And then ... then, Gemma, I started to realize that I was. I *was* like him.'

I stared at him.

'What do you mean?' Danny had never been violent. I couldn't even imagine him hitting a woman, or anyone come to that.

'Not the violence,' he said, as if reading my mind. 'But ... the other stuff. The women, the shagging around. Even from the first time I found myself a girlfriend, I couldn't settle for more than a couple of weeks. Always looking, always on the prowl for the next one. And I knew I'd got that from him, Gemma. I *was* like him, and I hated him for that, so much. But I hated myself more. And then ... well, then I met you, and I thought, finally. *Finally.* I loved you, Gemma, and I knew you loved me, and I thought, this is it, this one's different.

This one, I'm going to marry, and I'm never going to stray, and I won't be like him, not anymore. It's over, and I'm going to *win*.'

He banged a fist on the table again, hard, and something flashed in his eyes, and as if in response I felt a hot spark of anger.

'Except you didn't, did you? You *didn't* win, Danny. Because you carried on, didn't you? You married me, but you *still carried on*. You even joined a dating website when you were married to me, for fuck's sake.'

His eyes met mine, and his shoulders slumped.

'I know,' he whispered. 'I tried. I tried so bloody hard. But it was like a sickness, Gemma. An addiction. Out of my control. I just couldn't do it. It was only now and again, after we got married, I promise, only the very odd time. But I couldn't ... I just couldn't stop. And I'm so, so sorry about that. You'll never know how sorry I am.'

I exhaled heavily, shaking my head. What did any of it matter now?

'Look, why are you telling me all this? What does any of it have to do—?'

He held up a hand.

'Please. I'm nearly there. You'll understand when I ... anyway, as the time passed I got more and more angry. The hatred, for him and for myself, for what he'd made me ... it was like a living thing, Gem. It was eating me alive. All I could think of was why didn't I *do* something, why didn't I *stop* him? I even dreamed about him, dreamed about going back to Ireland and finally doing what I should have done all those years ago,

finally giving him the punishment he deserved. And then ...
and then ...'

He swallowed, his eyes fixed on the table in front of him.

'And then he died. And it was too late.'

There was a long silence. I stood watching him, waiting,
and unexpectedly, I felt a little surge of guilt. My husband
had been in so much pain, so much torment. How had I not
known, how had I not noticed? All of those times, after Donal
died, when Danny would go off on his own, disappear for
hours. It was so much worse than I had thought, grief of a
totally different kind, I suddenly realized. Not grief because
he *loved* his father, grief because he *hated* him. Grief because
he despised the man so much, and wanted revenge, and grief
because he'd lost the chance, forever. If only I'd known, if only
I'd realized back then, maybe I could have helped him, maybe
we could have avoided ...

'And then one day, something weird happened.'

He was talking again.

'Something so feckin' weird, Gemma, that it seemed like
fate, seemed like it was meant to happen. I'd just joined that
dating site, Elite Hook Ups ... I know, I know, and again, I'm
so, so sorry. Anyway, I was flicking through profiles, trying to
work out what to write for mine. And then I saw him.'

He paused again, looked at me, looked away.

'Saw who?'

'I saw a man who looked like Dad. Who looked just like
him, when he was younger, when he was my age, when he
was *hitting* us and *beating* us and *whoring* ...'

His eyes had narrowed, his voice low and angry now.

'... and suddenly, it was as if the sun had finally come out, and I knew what to do. I knew what I had to do, to make it all better. To make it all go away, finally. To heal myself. Except, of course ...'

A small laugh, bitter and hoarse.

'Except, ironically, that's when it all started to go wrong.'

He paused, took a breath, and his eyes were suddenly bright and shiny with tears. A little ripple of unease ran through me.

'What did? What went wrong, Danny?'

He was staring at me, clamping his lips together, looking at me with a sudden intensity, a slight frown on his face.

'Tell me! Danny, please.'

There was a long silence, both of us motionless, him still sitting, back rigid, hands clasped in front of him on the table, me standing, leaning against the hard edge of the kitchen worktop, waiting, a cold creeping sensation sweeping up my spine.

'Danny?' My voice sounded too loud, too shrill.

He swallowed.

'I started to kill them,' he whispered.

Chapter 43

My stomach rolled. *What?*

'You ... what?'

What had he just said? I couldn't have heard that properly, I thought. He couldn't mean ...

He was standing up now too, walking around the table, moving closer to me. He was still talking, talking faster and faster, the words spilling out of him.

'I saw the first one on the app, like I said,' he said, and his voice sounded hoarse. 'I didn't think the cops would work that bit out, you know, about the app. Thought I'd covered my tracks. They're not as stupid as I thought. Anyway, I saw him, and I knew I had to meet him. This guy, his face ... he looked like Dad, Gemma. And like me, of course, in retrospect, but isn't it strange, how that never entered my head, at the time? I just saw Dad. I just saw my father's face. And it was easy, so feckin' easy. I just set up a fake female profile, picture of a beautiful woman, set up a date. Simple as that. It was the night of my stag do, so I went along early, before I was due to meet the others at the pub, you know? And as soon as I saw him, standing there at the spot we'd arranged to meet at in Richmond Park, all unsuspecting like ...'

His eyes were glazed again, and a terrible fear was beginning to grip me.

No, Danny, please, please no.

'There'd been a storm, branches down all over the place, and I just felt this rage, this anger, like nothing I'd ever felt before, and I just bent down and picked up this fallen branch and I just hit him, so hard, and ... I just knew, straight away, that I'd killed him. It was that easy. And I stood there, and looked at him, looked at him for ages, and I just felt this wave of ... of peace, and ... and relief. It was like a release, you know? As if somehow the healing process had begun. I'd never felt like that, like I did in those few minutes, Gemma. It was as if I'd killed him, my father, the monster, the thing, the thing that had caused me so much pain. I know it sounds crazy, but ... do you get it, Gemma? Do you understand?'

He moved a step closer, and I stood there frozen, my eyes wide, fixed on his face. Was this real? Had my husband really just told me he'd killed somebody? My brain didn't seem to be working properly, and a strange numbness was beginning to spread through me, upwards from my toes, my legs rigid and heavy, my stomach contracting. I stared at him, and opened my mouth to say something, but nothing came out.

Richmond Park? One of the London murders being linked to the Bristol cases had happened in Richmond Park, hadn't it? Did that mean? ... please, no ...

'I felt good, for a while.'

369

He was talking again, and his eyes had taken on a slightly wild look now, casting around the room, not looking at me.

'But then a few weeks after we got married, I went for a drink after work, and I just saw this guy, on the other side of the bar, and again, he looked a bit like Dad. He did, Gemma. Like it was my father, just sitting there, and I know, I know, there are a lot of guys around who look a bit like Dad, a bit like me, when you think about it ... dark hair, dark eyebrows. But at the time, well, it was like fate, you know? I thought, here's another one, sent to me. So I went over, and I said, "hey, are you my long-lost brother, look at us!" some bollocks like that, and we got chatting, and then he said he needed to get back home to his girlfriend, so I followed him. He got on the tube, I got on the tube ... he'd left his car at Hounslow West tube station, parked in a nice dark corner, and even when I got there, watching him from the shadows, I wasn't sure if it was going to happen again; I thought I might be able to control it that time, you know, but it was like the rage took me over, Gemma. It took me over. And so I grabbed something that was lying on the ground, I think it was a broken exhaust pipe, something like that, it was just there, and ... well, the same thing again. The relief, the peace.'

'The dead man,' I whispered. My throat was beginning to constrict, and I wondered if soon I might not be able to breathe. *Was this real? Was I really hearing this?*

Danny laughed, then his face grew serious again.

'The dead man,' he said softly.

We looked at each other for a moment, then he took another

step towards me. I could smell a faint odour, a mix of sweat and aftershave, sour and sweet. My mobile phone had started ringing again. Danny glanced towards the door to the hall, but the ringing stopped, the call going to voicemail. He looked back at me.

'And then, nothing. I was OK. I felt better,' he said. 'I thought, that's it. I'm OK, I'm over it, I can finally move on. Everything was good, for ages. I had you, we were planning our future, and everything was going to be OK. And somehow, I'd got away with it, too. Killing them, I mean. I hadn't touched either of them, not with my hands, my body, so I knew there wouldn't be any DNA or anything, and the two murder weapons ... I'd got rid of those, stuck them in my backpack, chucked them away miles from where I'd used them. Even remembered to get rid of the app on the first one's phone, and wiped all his emails so there'd be no evidence of any communication between us. Came in handy, having the job I do. It wasn't hard. I had access to software to hide my own IP address, all that stuff. I won't bore you with it, but I knew they'd never find me. But it didn't last long, the peace. A few months later, it was back again, the anger, the hatred, and I knew I wasn't done, Gemma. But I also knew that my luck couldn't last, that one day soon it would run out. And I didn't want to spend my life in prison, Gem. I couldn't handle it. And so there was only one solution. To run. To disappear, and start a new life, with a new identity, away from it all. Away from what I'd done.'

His words were calm, but there was a crazed look in his eyes now.

'I could have killed myself, that would have been one solution, of course,' he said. 'And I did consider that, briefly. But then I thought, what a waste. I have so much to give, Gemma. I thought, maybe I could go and work with victims of domestic violence somewhere, give something back, redeem myself ... but I thought about you too, you know? I put money aside for you, lots of money, you would have been OK, for a while at least ... I did think about you, you know that, don't you? You know I loved you right? So, anyway, we moved to Bristol, and the plan was all coming together beautifully. My plan, to get away, as I already told you. Except then ...'

I was starting to feel sick, my stomach lurching.

He sighed.

'Well, then there were a couple of little blips. And I'm assuming you've guessed what those blips were, by now, haven't you?'

The tone of his voice had changed suddenly, a manic edge creeping into it, and a shiver ran down my spine. He seemed to be waiting for me to reply, looking at me quizzically, as if he'd just asked me to solve a riddle. His dark eyes looked almost black, and his lips twitched as if he was about to laugh. I nodded, my hands gripping the edge of the worktop behind me, my head beginning to swim. I felt faint. Yes, I'd guessed. Of course I'd guessed.

'The two Bristol murders. The two men who died on The Downs. You killed them, as well,' I said, my voice barely audible. 'You're the serial killer.'

He did laugh then, throwing his head back, then stopped abruptly.

'I suppose I am,' he said. 'Well, that's what they'll call me, isn't it?'

He looked at me questioningly, then carried on talking.

'That fucking app ... it was too easy, finding people who fitted, who had the right look, and when the urge struck again in Bristol ... well, you know. Used the fake female profile, met them early evening, when it was dark. The first one was a keen runner, so I said I was too and suggested we meet up on The Downs for a run and then go on for a drink. Told the second one I lived round the corner and suggested we meet in that side alley. Only took a few minutes each time. Made sure the weapons I used were dumped where they'd never find them. Easy, easy, easy. Somehow, I was able to come home to you and just carry on as normal. It was too easy to stop the police finding me too. I wiped the emails and texts from the guys' phones, and I was able to crash the app site, EHU, remotely too, wipe all their search data, just in case anyone somehow linked the murders to the app. Look, I saw the news, I know that the police suspected you of those too, of all of those murders in fact, and I am sorry about that, Gem, honestly. It wasn't fair to put you through that. I wanted them to think maybe you'd hurt me, but I didn't think ... I'm so sorry. Still, all's well that ends well, isn't it? You're in the clear, and the cops want to charge me but they won't find me. Gemma. I'm way ahead of them. I'm going to get away and start afresh, and I won't have to hurt anyone ever again. I'm done now. You probably don't believe that, not after what I've just told you, but I am. I've finally got my bastard of a father out of my system, and it's all over, and ...'

He smiled, then his brow crinkled.

'There's just one little thing, which I hope won't be a problem. Had a bit of a cock-up, last week. Was having a bad day, the day Quinn met up with you. I was nervous, wondering why you'd called him and what you and he were chatting about, wondering if the cops were getting close to finding me. I'd seen the press, I knew they were linking the London and Bristol murders, and I needed to do something, to calm the nerves and, bad idea in retrospect, I decided to have one more go on the app. Found this guy, yet another Daddy looka-like – there are so many of them, Gem, so many! – and persuaded him to meet me, or my female persona I should say, there and then. But just after I'd hit him, this bloke comes into the alleyway. My own fault, it was far too risky, meeting up at that time in a place like that ... so I ran, but the hammer I'd used slipped out of my hand, and I thought they'd prob-ably twig that was what had been used to attack him, and maybe that they'd be able to link it to me. I'd worn gloves, but I was hot, sweating, and some of it might have dripped, I don't know, maybe not ... but also, I didn't have time to delete the app from his phone, you know, the EHU app, so maybe ...'

He was talking quickly again, a crazed look in his eyes, and I shrank back against the worktop, the wood digging into my back. He was sick, really, really sick, I realized now. Mentally ill, deranged. How could I have lived with a mentally ill man for so long and not known it? How? My head was buzzing, words rushing through it on repeat.

My husband is a serial killer, my husband is a serial killer ...

'Quinn did well, when he met you. Put on a good show, by the sound of it. He's been so good to me, Quinn. He was shocked, of course he was, when I first told him about the men I'd hurt ... killed. Was still killing. I mean, who wouldn't be shocked? He nearly lost his shit, told me he loved me and he'd always had my back but this, this was way beyond what he could help me with. But when I explained why, he got it, eventually, you know? Quinn's a funny one, really. Got some real morals when it comes to adultery, to infidelity. He would have gone bloody mental if he knew I was shagging around. I didn't tell anyone, none of my friends knew about that. The shame again, I suppose. And Quinn would have gone ballistic at me. But this ... even though this was a million times worse, a billion times worse, he knew what had happened to me as a kid, what had happened to my ma, and he got it. It took time, but he finally agreed to help. Help me get away.'

Quinn's reaction when I mentioned Bridget, I thought. That makes sense now too. He knew about everything, he knew why she hated Danny so much.

Danny was still talking.

'He made me promise that when I did go, that I wouldn't hurt anyone else, obviously. When I slipped up, when the Bristol ones happened, he went mad again, nearly pulled out. Two was bad enough, but four ... but he was committed by then, and he was already helping a killer, I told him. Did it really make that much difference, whether it was two bodies or four? So he stayed with me. He was struggling with it by then, really struggling, but he stayed with me. But things had obviously got pretty serious at that point, and after the cock-up in the alley that was when Quinn started sending you messages. I didn't want to scare you, Gemma, I didn't. But we knew I'd screwed up, and we hoped you'd show them to the police ... he just thought if the cops thought that somebody else thought you were the killer, and was threatening you, that might keep their attention on you and give me more time to get away. Except then Quinn fucked up, didn't he? The stress got to him. Used his own phone for that last message instead of the cheap throwaway one he was meant to use. And that brought the cops round to our door, and, well, here I am. Clearly they haven't linked me to that bloke in the alley, not yet anyway. But I might not have much time, Gemma. I need to get out of here.'

He took another step towards me, and reached out a hand, running a finger gently down my cheek, his eyes fixed on mine. I glanced at Albert, and he growled softly, his hackles raised. He took a few steps towards us and I swallowed hard as Danny continued to stroke my cheek, trying not to flinch. I needed him to go, I needed to get to my phone, I thought frantically. I needed help, fast.

Get him out of here, then call the police. Go, Danny. Go. Please.

'So, are we OK, Gemma? I've told you everything now, and it's over, OK? And I promise, I promise, that I'll never do anything like that again, Gem. So we're OK, aren't we? You promised not to say anything, and you won't, will you? You'll keep your promise?'

He moved even closer, his lips brushing my earlobe, his voice lowering to a whisper.

'Quinn's been driving around, waiting for me. I'll call him in a minute, and he'll come and get me, get us both to the airport,' he said. 'It's just the two of you now, who know what really happened these past few months. And I can trust Quinn. He's family. He's decided to come with me for now, and I know that whatever happens in the future, he'll never tell what he knows. He hates it, what I've done. But he's part of it now. He's always had my back and he always will. And you will too, Gem, won't you? You're family too, and we still love each other, don't we? Despite everything? So promise me again. Promise me one more time that you'll say nothing, that you'll forget all about what I've just told you. Please. Promise me. And then I'll go.'

For a moment I stood there, frozen, horrified, incredulous. Yes, I'd promised not to tell anyone his little secret, but that was before, that was when I thought the secret was that he'd met some other woman or something ... something small, something stupid, something inconsequential. Not this. Not this ... this horror story. He expected me to keep quiet about this? How could anyone ...?

Suddenly, unexpectedly, a white-hot flood of rage surged through me, and in one swift moment I raised my hands and pushed him hard in the chest, so hard that, taken by surprise, he staggered backwards, almost falling over.

'NO!' I screamed.

His eyes widened, shock registering on his face.

'What?'

'NO!' I yelled again. 'NO, I WILL NOT KEEP QUIET ABOUT THIS! WHAT THE HELL IS WRONG WITH YOU, DANNY?'

He opened his mouth to speak, taking a step towards me, but I held up a hand.

'Stay away from me, Danny.'

'But ...'

'Stay away from me.'

My mind was racing. How to play this? He must know, he must, that I couldn't keep this quiet. That I wouldn't. But how far would he go to stop me? He'd killed people, he'd just told me that. Would he hurt me? He'd just told me he loved me ... I took a deep breath and made a decision. He was still standing a few feet away, silent, waiting.

'I want you to get out of this house, now,' I said. I was surprised at how steady my voice sounded, how calm. 'And then I'm calling the police. I am, Danny, I'm sorry. When I made that promise, I had no idea ... but I'm going to give you a chance, Danny. For the sake of us, for everything we had, I'll wait before I make the call, give you a head start. You can still get away, OK? What do you need, fifteen, twenty minutes, something like that? So call Quinn, now, get him to come and pick you up and go, OK? And I'll wait for a bit, and then I'll make the call.'

I was lying, obviously. I'd be on that phone the second he was out of the door.

'OK, Danny? That's fair, isn't it?'

No reply. Danny was still motionless, staring at me, his expression unreadable. Then suddenly, Albert growled again, a low menacing sound. Danny turned and looked at him, and the growling grew louder. My husband looked back at me once more and his eyes narrowed. Then he turned, grabbed

Albert by the collar and dragged him to the kitchen door, opening it and pushing the dog into the hallway. Albert's rumbling growl became loud, angry barking as Danny slammed the door shut. He turned back to me, moving closer, closer, his expression calm as the barking became even louder, Albert repeatedly throwing his body against the other side of the door, claws scraping the wood.

'That's better. And now, to answer your question, no Gemma. That's not OK. You made me a promise, and now you're breaking it, just like that? That's not OK, not fair. Not fair at all.'

His voice was gentle, his hand caressing my cheek again.

'Danny, look ...'

Had I played this wrong? I shrank away from him, and he gripped my waist with his other hand, fingers digging painfully into my flesh. I gulped in some air, trying to stay calm. I just needed to get him out, make him go ...

'Sssssh. I trusted you, Gemma. I wouldn't have told you if I hadn't. I trusted you, and you've let me down. So, to use a cliché ...' he said, and then paused, his grip on my waist tightening.

I swallowed hard, and the air in the room suddenly seemed thick, heavy, my breathing laboured. SHIT. Shit, shit, shit. I had misjudged this, hadn't I? Totally misjudged him, completely misjudged how unhinged he was. Could he ... no, he couldn't, could he? He wouldn't. Not me ... so think, Gemma, think ...

'Danny, please, I'm sorry, I'll ...'

He wasn't listening, and there was a darkness to his gaze now, a malevolence. My breath caught in my throat.

'Danny ... please ...'

He shook his head, eyes fixed on mine.

'As I was saying, to use a cliché, I've told you my story, and now I'm going to have to kill you.'

And slowly, very slowly, he moved his hand from my face, and slid it inside his jacket pocket. And he pulled out a knife.

Chapter 44

Helena felt sick, her stomach churning. They had buggered this up so badly, and the thought was almost unbearable. *What a bloody screw-up*, she thought. And yet, the discovery of Danny O'Connor's DNA on the hammer used to half kill Declan Bailey in that London alleyway had suddenly made everything fall into place. She'd been so focused on *Gemma* O'Connor, so certain that the woman was lying to them, and the circumstantial evidence had all fitted so neatly too; the two murders in London, not far from where she'd lived, the two in Bristol, happening shortly after she moved in, even the Declan Bailey attack, happening as it did on the day she happened to be visiting London, and just up the road from where she'd been having her meeting in Victoria. Even the blood in the bedroom of her old apartment, convincing them that she'd attacked and probably killed her husband there too. It had all *fitted*. Except, of course, that it hadn't, had it? Because Danny O'Connor had faked that bedroom attack. And if it was Danny who had carried out the Victoria attack, as they now believed he had, then it stood to reason that he'd also carried out the others. She wasn't a hundred per cent certain of that, right now, but she was ninety per cent of the way there. Why exactly he had felt the need to murder men who looked like him she still hadn't worked out, but there was clearly a lot the man had been hiding from everyone, his wife included, and she was sure that once they found him, they'd get the truth out of him. *If* they found him of course. Because they'd lost him, hadn't they? The man was, very likely, a highly dangerous serial killer, and they'd had him, quite literally within their grasp. And now they'd *bloody lost him*. And that was something they needed to put right, and fast.

'Five minutes, boss.'

'Thanks, Devon. He won't be there, but we have to rule it out just in case.'

She was in the passenger seat, Devon at the wheel, as they drove through the already dark streets of Bristol, heading for the O'Connors' Clifton house. The hunt for Danny had only been going on for a matter of hours, but already she was beginning to despair. They'd managed to keep it from the press so far, but she knew that if they didn't find him soon, maybe by the morning, she'd have to release it, make an appeal to the public for help in finding him. It was that, as well as everything else, that was making her feel sick; the wrath of her superiors, the scathing newspaper stories that would surely appear in the next few days. She could see the headlines already.

BUNGLING POLICE LET SERIAL KILLER GO FREE

IS THIS THE GREATEST COP COCK-UP OF ALL TIME?

FEAR ON THE STREETS OF BRITAIN AS SERIAL
KILLER ESCAPES POLICE

So far, the media blackout had been successful, but it had been the only thing that had. She'd done everything she could in the past few hours, but it all felt like too little, too late. In London, officers had searched Quinn O'Connor's flat, just in case, and were visiting his known hangouts, local bars and snooker halls, trying to find someone who might know where either of the two men were. In Ireland, local gardai were checking both Danny's and Quinn's family homes, as well as the properties of as many friends and relatives as possible, in case the runaway O'Connor cousins had somehow managed to already cross the Irish Sea despite the all-ports alert. Elsewhere, Danny's friends and ex work colleagues were being contacted, and photographs had been circulated to police forces across the UK. Helena herself had called Gemma's number again in the past half an hour, to warn her that her husband was now a wanted man, suspected of multiple murders, but there had still been no reply.

'Probably out, celebrating her freedom,' Devon had remarked. 'I know that's what I'd be doing. Either that or she's asleep. Can't have got much shuteye in that cell. Beds are like wooden planks.'

But not being able to contact the woman had worried Helena, and finally she'd decided they should call round and speak to Gemma in person. She owed her a huge apology too, she thought ruefully, remembering all the occasions when she'd treated Gemma so unkindly, convinced she was lying, convinced she was hiding something. Plus, although the chances of Danny returning to his Bristol home were minimal, it was another box that needed to be ticked in the hunt for him.

'Here we are. Doesn't look like anyone's in though.'

Devon turned the engine off, and for a moment they both sat there, staring at the house, its windows dark. Then Helena reached for her seat belt.

'Come on.'

She was first up the path and rang the doorbell. From inside, there was the sound of scampering feet, and a dog began to bark frantically, but the door didn't open. Helena rang again, keeping her finger on the buzzer for a full twenty seconds, the bell sounding shrill and loud even through the sturdy front door. The barking intensified, but still nobody came. Helena felt a little ripple of unease.

'As I said, out partying, or asleep. Although she'd have heard that racket even if she was dead to the world. Gone away, maybe?' asked Devon.

'Not without her dog.'

The uneasy feeling was growing, a tight little knot forming in Helena's stomach. Something didn't feel right. Gemma had never struck her as the partying kind, especially after all she'd been through recently. *Maybe* she'd gone away for a few days, and arranged for someone to look after her pet, but she hadn't been answering her phone, and that was worrying. She needed to be sure.

'Let's go round the back,' she said.

They made the short journey around the corner, down the narrow lane that skirted the rear of the row of houses. The O'Connors' back gate was unlocked, and they slipped quietly into the courtyard, Devon heading for the back door, rattling the handle.

'Locked,' he said.

Helena was peering in through the kitchen window, hands cupped around her eyes. And then she gasped.

'Oh my god. Oh my GOD!'

'What? What is it?'

She rushed towards him, hands outstretched, grabbing at the door handle, shaking it, thumping at the wood.

'No, no, no!' she screamed. 'Devon, we need to get in there, quick!'

He paused only for a second, staring at her, then put both hands on her shoulders and moved her firmly to one side.

'OK. My shoulder's still killing me from the last time I did this, but I'll give it a go. Stand over there,' he said, then took a few steps backwards, angled his left shoulder towards the door and ran at it, aiming for the lock. There was a sickening thud and, simultaneously, the sound of wood splintering. The door swung open, and Helena rushed past Devon, who was leaning against the doorframe, groaning softly and clutching the top of his arm. Then she stopped abruptly, staring in horror at what was lying on the tiled floor in front of her: the shape she'd seen through the window which had struck her with fear, but which she had desperately hoped would turn out to be something else – a pile of discarded laundry maybe, waiting for its turn in the washing machine; a dropped coat.

It was neither of those things. It was Gemma O'Connor or, probably more accurately, Helena thought, as the nausea rose, the *body* of Gemma O'Connor. Motionless, curled in the foetal position, a dark pool around her crumpled body. And then she saw it. Saw exactly what had happened to this woman, the woman she now knew, with a sense of overwhelming grief and guilt, that she'd totally and utterly let down. She saw, very clearly even in the darkness of the unlit kitchen, that Gemma's throat had been cut.

Chapter 45

'We need to find him. We need to find that *bastard*, and we need to find him *now*.'

Helena was pacing up and down the hospital corridor, her face contorted with anger and frustration, streaks of Gemma O'Connor's blood on her jacket, a dark smear on her cheek. From his seat on one of the hard plastic chairs lined up along the wall, Devon watched her, his own fury growing, but a fury directed only at himself. He'd had Danny O'Connor within his grasp, had sat and drank tea with him, *for Christ's sake*. And he'd let him go. He'd let him go, and so this was his fault. What had happened to Gemma O'Connor was all down to him. He sank his head into his hands, squeezing his eyes shut, trying to obliterate the memory of the slumped body on the kitchen floor, the vivid gash across her throat, the blood ... so much blood ...

And yet, by some miracle, Gemma wasn't dead. She had looked dead, so very, very dead, but when a white-faced Helena had bent to take her pulse, to check for any signs of life, she'd crouched there for several moments before suddenly whipping around and screaming at Devon.

'She's breathing! She's still breathing! Ambulance, quick! Quick!'

As he'd dialled the number with shaking hands, Helena had looked frantically around the room, grabbed a tea-towel from a hook on the wall and pressed it to Gemma's throat. That had been two hours ago. The doctor who'd come out to see them as Gemma was being rushed into theatre had muttered something about her being lucky; her neck had been slashed low down, across the thyroid, but the knife had missed the main veins and arteries.

'Thyroid bleeds like hell, but if you have to have your throat cut, well ... he didn't get the carotids or jugulars, or her wind-pipe. You must have arrived within minutes of it happening. She'd have died if she'd been left to bleed out much longer. We're about to operate, and she's a very ill lady, but we think she'll get through this. Lucky, as I said.'

Lucky? Devon shook his head. Gemma O'Connor was probably the *unluckiest* woman he'd ever met. She'd married a man who had used her, tried to frame her for his own murder. Married a man who might well turn out to be one of Britain's most prolific serial killers, if the fears they now had turned out to be real. And – and they had no proof of this yet, he thought, but who else would have done it? – a man who had, for whatever reason, taken time out from being on the run to call in on his wife and slit her throat.

Please, Gemma, please live, he urged silently. *For yourself, so you can get over this and live the life you deserve. But for us too. We need you. We need you to help us catch him.*

'He said he had a fake passport when you interviewed him, didn't he?'

Devon jumped, and looked up to see that Helena had stopped pacing and was standing in front of him.

'Yes ... yes, he did. I don't know what name it was in or what nationality it was though, or anything ... oh *shit*, boss. I'm so sorry.'

She stood there for a moment, looking down at him, her face blank. Then she shook her head and sat down on the chair next to him.

'I'm sorry too, Devon. Sorry I didn't listen to her; sorry I didn't believe her. We've all screwed up here,' she said quietly.

'And now he's gone. With a fake passport, and a good one, he could be anywhere. I mean, we know he's an IT wizard, he could probably get the very best, couldn't he? Dark web, plenty of places to go there, and he'd know how. And if he wore some sort of disguise, even the all-ports alert wouldn't help us ... he probably went straight to Bristol airport after he attacked her and hopped on a plane. Or maybe a boat, from the docks? If it was a private one ... we've lost him, Devon. His cousin too, most likely. But we're going to find them, OK? We're not giving up. We'll find them, if it's the last thing we ever do.'

There was a sudden fiery determination in her voice, and he smiled briefly, then sighed.

'If we keep our jobs,' he said.

She was silent for a moment.

'Yes, there is that,' she said. Another pause. 'You know what? When all this is over, I'm going to have a baby, Devon. Well, not me. Charlotte. But, same thing really. I'm going to be a mum, a parent. I've been putting it off and putting it off, and ... well, life's short, isn't it? And you never know what's around the corner, what's waiting to bite you on the ass. Sometimes you've just got to jump, haven't you? And hope that bloody safety net appears before you land.'

He looked sideways at her, raised an eyebrow.

'Good for you, boss. OK. You do that and I'll start dating again. See if I can do it properly this time, not mess it up. Deal?'

He offered her a fist, and she smiled and bumped hers against it.

'Deal.'

Then she stood up abruptly, as the doctor who'd spoken to them earlier suddenly appeared in the corridor.

'She's awake,' he said. 'And she says she needs to talk to you, urgently.'

Chapter 46

It was morning. At least, the light outside the small, square window opposite my bed made me think that it was probably morning; I had long since lost all track of time, drifting in and out of sleep, men and woman in white uniforms constantly checking on me, prodding me, asking me questions in low voices. My head was muzzy from the drugs which had been dripping into me all night through a needle in my arm, but the pain which had been so agonizing and terrifying was now reduced to a dull, tight ache. I moved my right hand slowly up the smooth bedspread, cautiously touching my throat, feeling not skin but bandages, tight and soft. The knife, the blade, the pain, the awful, shocking *pain* ... a sudden rush of fear ran through me, and I tried to breathe deeply, tried to remember. I was safe. I was in hospital, and Danny was gone, and I was safe. *Danny* ... the fear rose again. My husband, the serial killer. My physical injuries would, I'd been told, heal – but the rest of it? How did anyone, *could* anyone, recover from that? I'd been married to a monster, and I'd had absolutely no idea. How stupid did you have to be, how dim, to be married to a man who spent his spare time murdering people, and not realize it, any of it? To be married to a man who was so clearly deranged, and not know? I groaned. What was wrong with me?

But none of it was my fault, that's what they'd told me, the two officers, and I had to believe them. The woman, DCI Dickens, had pulled her chair close to my bed, looking stricken, telling me how desperately sorry she was, had even, briefly, held my hand, her touch cool and strangely comforting against my hot, dry skin. DS Clarke had remained standing, shifting from foot to foot, making rapid notes on a pad he pulled from his pocket as I, slowly and hesitantly, through the acuteness of the pain and the haze of the medication, told them everything, everything Danny had told me. Everything he'd done, why he'd done it, and what he planned to do next.

They had remained silent for a long time when I'd finished, staring at each other, horrified expressions on their faces. Then DCI Dickens had turned back to me, gripping my hand again.

'I can't even imagine what he went through as a child. It's horrendous, and no kid should ever have to experience an upbringing like that. But it doesn't change what he's done, Gemma. He's clearly a very sick, and very dangerous man. He's killed four men, tried to kill a fifth, and nearly killed you too. And I promise you, we're going to stop him hurting anyone else. This ends *now*.'

And then they'd gone, telling me that everything would be OK. Would it though, really? How could it be? I'd asked them that, and they'd looked at each other, and then she'd squeezed my hand gently. One day at a time, one *hour* at a time, that was the only way to get through this, she said. Get well first, worry about the rest later. But it would get easier. Hour by hour, day by day. I'd find happiness again, she promised.

'You're strong, Gemma. You're so bloody strong. Look at how much you've gone through already. You've had your throat cut, for goodness' sake, and you're still here, you're still fighting. You can do this, and we're going to make sure you get all the help you need, OK? And we're going to find Danny and make him pay for what he's done to you, and to all those men. We're going to leave here and make an urgent press appeal, and within hours his face is going to be on every TV news bulletin, in every paper, on every news website, not just here but across Europe, across the world. We're *going* to find him, Gemma, OK? And his cousin too. He's going to pay for this as well, they both are.'

She'd told me, to my great relief, that Albert was fine, distressed but unhurt, and had been taken again to the local kennels to be cared for until I was better. She made some phone calls for me then too, breaking the news, and Eva was coming today, and my parents too, I remembered. Tears suddenly sprang to my eyes, and I moved my hand from my throat to wipe them away. My parents ... how would they ever understand all of this, how could I explain ...?

And then another thought struck me, and I gasped. Danny had tried to kill me to stop me telling anyone what I now knew, what he'd done. But I wasn't dead, and I *had* told. And very soon, he'd know that, because the police would make their appeal, the appeal that would see his face being beamed from TV screens and on social media sites around the world, naming him as chief suspect in the UK serial killer case.

Danny would see that, there was no way he wouldn't, and he would *know*. He would know I was still alive, and what I'd done. And what would he do then?

Fear began to sweep over me, and suddenly my breaths were coming fast and shallow, black spots dancing before my eyes. When Danny had pulled out that knife, in our kitchen, it had been so quick, so unexpected, that I hadn't had time to feel real fear before the sharp blade whipped across my throat. I'd felt the blood spurting, oozing, felt the weakness in my body as I sank to the floor, heard Danny's footsteps crossing the room, pausing, moving on again, heard Albert howling in the hallway, heard the front door slamming, closed my eyes as the darkness descended. But fear ... not fear, not really, not then. Now it was there though, in every rasping breath, in the tremor running up my spine, in the pain shooting across my throat, in the sweat running down my forehead into my eyes, blurring my vision.

'Mrs O'Connor? Mrs O'Connor, are you awake? Are you OK?'

I jumped in terror, then took a shuddering breath as I recognized the doctor who'd been treating me. He was peering down at me, a concerned expression on his kind face.

'Fine. I'm fine,' I managed.

'Well, good. Because I have some news for you,' he said.

Chapter 47

Seven months later

'Gemma, are you coming in? We're pouring the bubbly!' Clare's voice rose above the hubbub of chat and laughter coming from the living room. They were all there today – Clare, Tai, Eva and a whole group of other women too, ones I'd met over the previous months at the classes I'd unexpectedly found myself attending, women who were now firm friends, my support group, my Bristol family. Women I could laugh with and cry with in equal measure; there'd been plenty of the latter but, thankfully, enough of the former to keep me sane, to keep me moving forwards, to stop me from looking back too much. I still did, of course, in the dark, silent hours, when the fear would grip me and I'd cling to Albert, shaking, desperate for dawn when the sunlight would drive away the shadows. But I was trying, and I was winning, most of the time.

Out in the hallway, I bent to scoop a small pile of letters from the doormat.

'Be there in a mo. Just checking the post!'

I flicked through the envelopes, most of them clearly greetings cards. I'd had so many in the past week, from friends, former colleagues, even from strangers, all sending me love and wishing me well as I embarked upon this new, unforeseen journey.

As I put the pile down on the hall table, there was a burst of laughter from the living room, and then the pop of a champagne cork followed by a yelp from Albert and a booming 'well done!' I smiled. Dad. My parents were in there too, had come to stay for a few days, instantly hitting it off with my neighbours, Jo, Jenny and Clive, who I now saw almost daily and who were currently buzzing around in the kitchen, laying out neat triangular sandwiches and dainty fairy cakes on platters, food they'd insisted on providing for the party. There were balloons too, tied to the backs of chairs and to door handles, bobbing on their long strings. Blue balloons, to greet the guest of honour.

I turned to stare at him, and he stared back at me, wide awake, alert. I reached out and gently stroked his forehead, then moved my hand slowly to my throat, running my fingers across the livid scar that ran across it, less painful now, less raw, but still raised and ugly, a permanent reminder of the day my life changed forever.

He was still out there somewhere. Danny, and Quinn too. The police kept me updated on a weekly basis, but each time they called, there was less and less to say, less information to give me. At first, police forces across the world had been inundated with sightings, people who believed they'd seen Danny in a restaurant in Marbella, or Quinn working in a supermarket in Manhattan, or both of them hitchhiking at the side of the road at Bondi Beach. But none of the sightings had come to anything, and slowly the reports began to dry up. Helena and Devon – that's what I called them, these days, the formality of DCI and DS long behind us – were in the living room too, taking time out from work to attend the celebration, and I was glad, not just because I'd come to think of them as friends, but because somehow they made me feel safe. They had, after all, saved my life. Saved *two* lives, because if I had died, he would have too.

I looked down at him again, his eyelids fluttering wearily now, the soft white blanket tucked under his chin, a rainbow-striped teddy bear nestling at his feet. I reached for the pram's handle and began to rock it gently. My baby. My son. When the doctor had told me, that day in the hospital, that I was pregnant, the shock had been so immense I'd been unable to speak for a full minute. *Pregnant?* I'd actually *lost* weight in the previous few weeks. And yet it explained so many things; the tiredness I'd been feeling, the frequent waves of nausea, things I'd assumed at the time were simply reactions to the situation I was in, the stress and my grief at Danny's disappearance. I'd conceived, it seemed, just a few weeks before the move to Bristol, back in January. Back in January, when Danny had already killed two men and was planning his escape. The thought of it chilled me. How could he have made love to me then, knowing what he'd done, what he was about to do? Knowing the hell he was about to put me through?

As I lay in hospital, recovering after the father of my new baby had slit my throat, had tried to kill me, I'd considered, briefly, terminating the pregnancy. How could I bring a child into the world when one day I'd have to tell him that he was the offspring of a serial killer, one of the world's most wanted men? But almost immediately, I dismissed the thought. I could already feel my child's presence, his life force. There had been enough killing.

And now he was here, my baby, born just a few days ago, and we were about to celebrate his arrival. The only significant person in his life who wasn't there was Bridget, and although we were now slowly building some sort of relationship by phone, I knew we still had a very long way to go, me and this damaged woman who had suffered so much. It was as if she'd spent so many years keeping the secret about her abusive husband, shutting the world out, that it was just too hard for her to let anyone in, even now. Or maybe especially now, when the world knew she was the mother of a serial killer. She seemed to be dealing with that the same way she'd dealt with everything that had gone before – quietly, and alone. But at least she took my phone calls, asked a few questions about how I was, had even sent a 'new baby' card. We would never be close, I knew that, but I hoped that maybe one day I might be able to visit, let her meet her grandchild, the child I'd now be rearing alone.

We'd manage though, the two of us, wouldn't we? The three of us, I corrected myself, as I heard another excited bark from Albert. For a while, I'd wanted to move from the Clifton house, terrified that Danny would come back, shaking every time I walked into the kitchen, remembering the horror of his words, the knife, the pain. And then, quite suddenly, I'd changed my mind about that too. I loved this house, loved my courtyard, loved my neighbours now too. And Danny had taken so much from me. He wasn't taking this place as well. One day, when I could afford it, I would buy somewhere, but for now this was home, and to my surprise, I could afford to live a comfortable life in it. The money Danny had claimed he'd put away for me never materialized, not that I would have taken it if it had. But far from drying up, as I had feared, work offers had doubled, trebled, after my ordeal, and although I knew that this was due to my newfound notoriety as the wife of an on-the-run serial killer, I was grateful for it. The Lookalike Killer, that's what they'd dubbed Danny. The murderer who'd killed men who looked like him, trying to slay the ghosts that haunted him. At first inundated by requests for interviews, for the inside story, I turned every single one down, and in the past couple of months things had returned to near normality.

'And I'm lucky enough to have a job I can do at home, with you,' I whispered. I turned away from the pram for a moment to check that the front door was double locked, that the chain was secure. I'd heard noises again last night, as I had the previous couple of nights too, scraping, tapping noises that chilled my blood, noises that made me sit bolt upright in bed, rigid, gasping for breath, shaking finger poised over the panic button the police had installed, just in case. But the noises had stopped, or maybe they'd never been there at all, and I'd fallen back into an uneasy sleep, the baby's hungry cries waking me again what seemed like just minutes later.

'Gemma! Come on!'

Jackie Kabler

Clare again.

'Coming! Just settling the baby, one minute, I promise!'

I turned back to the pram. His eyes had opened again, wide dark pools framed by fluttery lashes. Dark hair too, a surprising amount of it, not just wispy peach fuzz but a thick dark mop, soft curls on his forehead. Eyes like Danny's, hair like Danny's. Danny's son. Son of the Lookalike Killer. A baby who looked just like his father, like his grandfather. Like four dead men, his father's victims. I looked into my child's eyes, and suddenly I felt a creeping sensation, like insects running across my skin. I shivered, and turned again to check the door, testing the chain, taking deep breaths, trying to slow my suddenly racing heartbeat. It was fine. We were safe, we were OK. The house was full of people, full of love and laughter. For today, at least, nothing bad could happen here.

I looked at my baby again. He'd fallen asleep, lashes resting delicately on his cheeks. I gripped the pram handle, watching him for a moment, the way the blanket gently rose and fell with each tiny breath. I glanced at the door again, checking one more time. Then I wheeled the pram carefully into the living room and went to join the party.

400

Acknowledgements

My previous book, *Am I Guilty?*, marked a change in genre for me; my first three books were a series of cosy crime novels, but I had increasingly begun to feel that I wanted to try writing something a little darker. It was a huge risk, and I really wasn't sure whether I could it pull it off. The response, however, has been amazing, and I want to begin these acknowledgements by saying a massive thank you to everyone who took a chance on me and my first psychological thriller/suspense/domestic noir/whatever you want to call it novel. I am so grateful not only to my agent and publisher (more on them later) but to all of the book bloggers, reviewers and fellow authors who have supported me through this change in direction, and to everyone who bought and read and wrote such wonderful reviews about the book.

Now here we are with psychological thriller number two. The idea for *The Perfect Couple* came to me rather randomly, when I was sitting in our garden in Gloucestershire one sunny day playing the 'what if' game that so many authors play: what if this happened? What if that happened? What if a woman came home from a business trip one day to find that her husband had simply vanished? And so another book baby was conceived.

As always, writing a novel and getting it to the point where it is ready to be released into the world is by no means a solo effort: so many people help to make it the very best it can be. My husband, friends and family, who know how important writing is to me and give me the time and space to do it. My wonderful agent, Clare Hulton, who is always there if I need a helping hand. The team at HarperCollins and One More Chapter (and oh my goodness, what a summer party that was!) especially my fantastic editor, Kathryn Cheshire (thank you *so* much for your brilliance when it came to editing *The Perfect Couple* – there were moments when I thought I'd never get this book right, and you got me there in the end!); marketing queen, the super-stylish Claire Fenby, always so supportive; my fabulous copy editor Janette Currie; and the very talented Lucy Bennett, who designed the cover.

Thank you yet again to all the members of the wonderful book blogging community, who are always so kind and supportive, shouting loudly about cover reveals and release dates and taking the time to write such considered reviews; none of us could do this without you.

And of course, thank YOU. Without readers, we are nothing. When I wrote the acknowledgements for my very first book back in 2015, I told my agent and publisher that my book deal had made a little girl's dream come true and a big girl very happy. Even now, I sometimes still can't quite believe that I get to sit at home making up stories and that people are willing to pay money for them; it really is a dream come true. Thank you so very much.

Karin
Slaughter's
Killer Reads
Exclusive to
ASDA

EXCLUSIVE ADDITIONAL CONTENT

Dear Readers,

The Perfect Couple starts with a simple idea. What if one evening, you came home and your husband, the love of your life, was nowhere to be found? Initially, you might think he was just running late, and that he'd be home soon. But what if he doesn't return the next day, or the next, or the next? This is the terrifying situation Gemma finds herself in at the start of *The Perfect Couple*.

When Gemma goes to the police, the story kicks into a new gear. Because there's a serial killer on the loose in Bristol, and the victims all look exactly like Gemma's husband, Danny. As secrets are revealed about the marriage, the reader is left questioning everything. Who can we trust? Where will the killer strike next? And above all, what happened to Danny?

This story hooked me in right from the very first page, and the twists and turns kept me gripped until the final shocking revelations. I hope you enjoy it as much as I did.

Karin

READING GROUP QUESTIONS

(Warning: contains spoilers)

1. 'The perfect couple or the perfect lie?' is the subtitle of this story – why do you think we're so intrigued by this notion of people that seem to have it all?

2. This book is half a psychological thriller told from a 1st person POV and half a police procedural. How did this structure affect your reading?

3. What did you think of Gemma? Did your opinion of her change as the story went on? Did you ever doubt her innocence?

4. Do you believe that in a good marriage, there can still be some secrets, or do you believe you should know absolutely everything about the other person?

5. What was your favourite scene in the story, and why?

6. Did you enjoy the final reveal in the epilogue? What do you think the future holds for Gemma?

7. What would you say about the book when pressing it into someone else's hands?

A Q&A
WITH JACKIE KABLER

(Warning: contains spoilers)

Can you tell us about your inspiration for
The Perfect Couple?

The idea came to me during a little brainstorming session. I have
an ever-growing file of half-baked novel ideas and sometimes I
spend an hour or so playing around with some of them to see if
they might actually work. On this occasion I was sitting in our
back garden one sunny day – my husband was at work – and
tossing an idea about a missing partner around in my head.
I thought: "what if my husband came home from work this
evening and I just wasn't here?" Then I thought: "how about if *I*
came home from work one day and *he* wasn't here? And what if
he just didn't come back, and then I began to discover all sorts
of strange things about him, and realised he'd been lying to me
about huge parts of his life? What would I do, how would I react,
how would I cope with those sorts of revelations?" It all started
from there really. (I hasten to add that my lovely husband is
nothing like Danny!)

The theme of how well we can ever truly know
another person is very prevalent in the book. Do
you think we can ever know someone inside out, or
do you think some things will always be a mystery?

I think we like to believe that we know those close to us inside
out, and maybe there are some people who reveal themselves
completely to others, but I think many of us have little secrets
and keep small parts of ourselves hidden. That's not always for
sinister reasons – it might be because we don't want to hurt
someone's feelings. My late father-in-law, for example, let me
carry on buying him a certain brand of chocolate for over a
decade, before finally confessing he'd been pretending to like it
for years, and actually couldn't stand it! Of course, for a crime

writer it's the big deceptions that are the most interesting:
the person with a double life, with two partners and two families
in different parts of the country; the respected professional
who's a pillar of the local community but who turns out to be a
secret sex offender or serial killer. I find human nature endlessly
fascinating, and the secrets people keep is a great source of
material for novels. I very much hope that nobody in my life has
a very dark secret but...who knows?

Who is your favourite character in the story?

It has to be Albert the dog! Well, all of the human characters
are flawed in some way, as we all are, but a dog – well, that's just
pure love and loyalty, isn't it? Albert nearly wasn't in the book at
all though – he was actually a late addition to the story. When
the first draft went to Kathryn Cheshire, my editor, she felt that
Gemma was quite lonely and isolated as a character and that it
might work well to give her either a baby or a dog. I thought a
baby would change the plot too much so I went for the dog. It
sounds like quite a small change but when you add a dog into a
book you basically have to do some rewriting on every single
chapter, because if you introduce a dog and then don't mention
him very often readers will ask: "where's the dog gone?". The
dog has to be walked and fed and be *somewhere* all the time; if
Gemma goes away he has to be looked after by someone else,
and if someone comes to the house he has to react in some way,
and so on and so forth! I'm glad he's there though. I'd love a dog
myself but I'm away from home so much it just isn't possible at
the moment, so I made Albert a miniature schnauzer, the breed
I'd love to have one day. He became my virtual pet while I was
writing the book!

The story is split into two quite different strands – one from Gemma's POV and one from the police's. Did you find one strand easier to write than the other? What did you need to do differently for each?

Both sides had their challenges. Gemma's was written in the first
person, which was something I hadn't actually tried before, and
the police side was written in third person, so I had to be in a
different mindset with each alternate chapter. As some of

the book's reviewers have commented, the police don't come off too well in this story (a little single-minded in their approach to the investigation, to say the least!) and I wanted to show the difficult professional side of their lives while also making them into rounded human beings. I enjoyed giving them personal lives, Devon trying and failing to juggle his job and his love life, and Helena trying to decide if the time was right to have a baby with her wife. I think I did find Gemma's side easier to write though, because it was just a matter of mentally sliding into the bizarre situation she found herself in and asking myself: "how would this feel?" and "what would I do now?" Sometimes I made her do quite the opposite of what I'd do, just for fun. I enjoyed writing in the first person, so much so that my next book is being written entirely like that. I think it really helps you get under a character's skin.

There are so many twists and turns in the story. Do you plot everything before you start writing, or does the story evolve as you write?

I'm definitely a plotter, and I always think of starting a new book as a little bit like doing a jigsaw puzzle, where you start with the corners and the outline and then fill in the middle. I always know how the book is going to start and end, and the big plot points and twists in between. I tend to write myself a vague outline of the entire story first, then outline the first half a dozen or so chapters, and then start writing. Then I outline the next half a dozen and carry on like that. But the story does still evolve as I write too. Extra little twists creep in, often if I think there hasn't been anything terribly exciting happening for a few chapters and it's time something did. The finished book is generally quite different from the original synopsis!

The settings of Bristol and Clifton really come to life. Why did you choose this setting?

It was partly because I really enjoy urban settings for my books, because so much goes on in towns and cities, and also because I know Bristol quite well so I didn't have to do too much research! I'd hate to get something about a location really wrong because I've haven't been there and haven't researched it properly; it's much easier to use places that you know. I used to work in Bristol for ITV West when I was starting out as a TV news reporter, and in that sort of job you get to experience many different aspects of a city, from its most salubrious spots to its darker side. I also live in Gloucestershire so very close to Bristol, and I like to go shopping and eating there now and again. I still have friends I visit there too. Clifton Downs in particular really appealed to me as a setting because it's a beautiful open space with spectacular views during daylight hours but at night, as a big area of unlit parkland, it can feel like an entirely different place. While I did use the city and The Downs as my setting, I did make up some of the street names, and also created a fictional police force, Avon Police, as opposed to the real Avon and Somerset Police. I tend to mix real and fictional settings a little sometimes, just in case someone gets really annoyed with me because I've written about a horrific crime happening in their real-life street!

For readers who enjoyed your story, what 3 other books would you recommend?

My favourite book of the past year or so has to be *Blood Orange* by Harriet Tyce. It's just so dark and totally gripping. I also love the Tuva Moodyson series by Will Dean – the first one is called *Dark Pines* – which has a wonderfully atmospheric setting in a remote town in Sweden. And *The Family Upstairs* by Lisa Jewell was fantastic too.

Can you tell us what you're working on now?

It's another stand-alone psychological thriller called *The Happy Family*. When Beth was 10 years old, her wild, beautiful mother walked out one day and didn't come home again. Thirty years later, she suddenly appears on Beth's doorstep, and at first everything is wonderful. But slowly, things start to fall apart, and as events in Beth's life become darker and more dangerous, she's forced to question everything. The book will be released in June 2021.

THE
LAST WIDOW

**She might be the first victim,
but she won't be the last.**

Three...
A woman is abducted in front of her child.

Two...
A month later, a second is taken in explosive circumstances.

One...
But the web is bigger and darker than anyone could imagine.

The clock is ticking to uncover the truth.

THE
SILENT WIFE

He watches.

A woman runs alone in the woods. She convinces herself she has no reason to be afraid, but she's wrong. A predator is stalking the women of Grant County. He lingers in the shadows, until the time is just right to snatch his victim.

He waits.

A decade later, the case has been closed. The killer is behind bars. But then another young woman is brutally attacked and left for dead, and the MO is identical.

He takes.

Although the original trail has gone cold – memories have faded, witnesses have disappeared – agent Will Trent and forensic pathologist Sara Linton must re-open the cold case. But the clock is ticking, and the killer is determined to find his perfect silent wife....